Praise for the novels of

ANGELA HUNT

"Prolific novelist Hunt knows how to hold a reader's interest, and her latest yarn is no exception...Hunt packs the maximum amount of drama into her story, and the pages turn quickly. The present tense narration lends urgency as the perspective switches among various characters. Readers may decide to take the stairs after finishing this thriller."
—*Publishers Weekly* on *The Elevator*

"Christy Award and Holt Medallion winner Hunt skillfully builds tension and keeps the plot well paced and not overly melodramatic."
—*Library Journal* on *The Elevator*

"Angela Hunt has over three million copies of her award-winning novels in print today, and this poignant tale about breast cancer will only help to make the number rise. Jonah and Jacquelyn are both strong characters, and the medical terminology is well-written without confusing the reader. Both must learn to trust in a God they weren't sure really cared about them anymore, and ultimately find that God's grace will see them through."
—*Romance Junkies* on *A Time to Mend*

"Only a skillful novelist could create such a multilayered, captivating portrait of Mary Magdalene...Hunt's attention to detail in her historical research, combined with her bright imagination, fills in the sketchy biographical facts and creates a fascinating and convincing Magdalene. First-rate biblical fiction."
—*Library Journal* on *Magdalene*

Also by
ANGELA HUNT
A Time to Mend
The Elevator
The Face

ANGELA HUNT

Dreamers

LEGACIES OF THE ANCIENT RIVER

Refreshed version, newly revised by author

Steeple
Hill®

Published by Steeple Hill Books™

STEEPLE HILL BOOKS

Steeple
Hill®

ISBN-13: 978-0-373-78633-6
ISBN-10:   0-373-78633-6

DREAMERS

This is the revised text of the work, which was first published
by Bethany House in 1996.

Copyright © 1996 by Angela Elwell Hunt

Revised text copyright © 2008 by Angela Elwell Hunt

Excerpt from BROTHERS

Copyright © 1997 by Angela Elwell Hunt
Revised text copyright © 2008 by Angela Elwell Hunt

Printed in U.S.A.

CONTENTS

For Gary

But I, being poor, have only my dreams;
I have spread my dreams under your feet;
Tread softly because you tread on my dreams.
—*"He Wishes for the Cloths of Heaven"*
William Butler Yeats

TUYA

And they said one to another, Behold, this dreamer cometh. Come now therefore, and let us slay him, and cast him into some pit, and we will say, Some evil beast hath devoured him: and we shall see what will become of his dreams.

Genesis 37:19–20

Prologue

Dothan

The collision of bones and rock stopped his fall.

He did not immediately lose consciousness, but gasped in the depths of the narrow cistern, his limbs and tongue and vision paralyzed by shock and a wave of unspeakable horror. Murder had gleamed in their eyes. Did they truly hate him so much?

Pinpricks of pain ripped along every nerve of his body, and after a moment of senseless suppression Yosef released the scream clawing in his throat. The sound echoed through the rock-walled cistern and grew into a chorus of agonized cries. From somewhere above him, his brothers heard. And laughed.

Familiar voices, crackling sharply in hostility, came spiraling down from the mouth of the cavern. "Hear that? The dreamer is not hurt badly enough. We should have found a deeper pit."

"The brat isn't so high and mighty now. Yet just last month he had visions of authority and power!"

"They were but the dreams of a seventeen-year-old, for all youths think themselves invincible and immortal. Even you, Dan, were of such a mind when you were his age."

"Dan never had the gall to predict that even our father would bow down to him. Yet our father scrapes before the boy already, he gives Yosef everything—"

"We should kill him, I tell you. If he survives, this tale-bearer will run to our father. He'll take even our birthrights, for he is the pampered favorite—"

"Yehuda is right, our father sides with the would-be king in every argument. Have you noticed how the old man smiles at him? My stomach churns when I think of it. My own son is older, stronger and better-favored, and yet—"

"I despise his pride, as do you." Re'uven's voice quieted the others and echoed in the pit. Listening below, the boy bit his lip in an effort to quiet his involuntary moaning as Re'uven continued: "I, too, have reason to hate him. I should receive the first-born's inheritance, but I know our father will honor this stripling with the largest share of his goods. But we are of the same flesh. I cannot kill him, and neither can you."

"Then we will have someone else do it." Dan's voice brimmed with eagerness. "If you are hesitant, Re'uven, I will hire someone to spill his precious blood over this cursed coat—"

"We will say a lion caught him," Levi interrupted. "Our father will believe it, and we will forever be rid of the troublemaker."

Re'uven's stentorian voice hushed the others. "Would you have our father die of grief? We will not kill him. We shall leave him here, and let him ponder his own fate. Let him who aspires to rise a king pass the night in the depths of the earth."

The brothers mumbled and murmured, but most of them moved away. "I'd still like to spill his guts," Asher grumbled, his voice overriding the fading voices. "Look at him whimpering there! If he rises from this pit, our father will never forgive us for his injuries. But if we cut out his tongue, he will never boast again."

"We'll shed no blood before dinner," Re'uven answered. "Come, Asher, our meal is waiting."

Yosef remained still until he was certain the last of his brothers had gone, then he struggled to focus his blurred vision on the walls around him. Re'uven would not let them kill him. Re'uven was respected; he would be obeyed, but for how long? Murderous intent might bring any of the brothers back during the night with a dagger thirsting for blood.

He had to escape. He pulled his heavy head from the rock and steeled himself to ignore the white-hot pain that shot along his limbs as he fumbled against the stone beneath him. His left arm would not cooperate, and when he glanced down at his side he saw why: above his elbow, where there had once been smooth skin and healthy muscle, a white shard of jagged bone protruded from an oozing red wound.

A hoarse cry escaped his lips as unconsciousness claimed him.

Chapter One

Thebes, Egypt

A high-pitched giggle broke the stillness of the garden. From between the branches of the bush where she hid, Tuya saw her mistress pause in mid-step on the path. "Tuya, I command you to speak," Sagira called, peering around the slender trunk of an acacia tree. "You must make more noise, or how am I to find you?"

Tuya deliberately rustled the ivy on the wall behind her, but the noise was slight and Sagira did not turn toward the sound. Finally Tuya took a deep breath and spoke: "Life, prosperity and health to you, my lady!"

"Aha!" Sagira turned and sprinted toward Tuya's hiding place as the slave girl darted from the bush. "I found you!"

"But you haven't caught me!" Tuya cried, arching away from Sagira's grasping hands.

The two girls ran, laughing, through the garden, until Sagira tripped over a rock at the edge of the pond. Pinwheeling, she struggled to keep her balance, then surrendered to the pull of the earth and fell with a splash into the shallow water.

Tuya's heart leapt into her throat, but after a moment Sagira sat up and howled with a twelve-year-old's unrestrained glee. Tuya laughed, too, then stopped. The lady Kahent might be watching. Would she have Tuya whipped for this mishap? She glanced toward the house. "I am sorry, mistress, truly I am."

Sagira pulled dark ribbons of wet hair from her face and stood in the knee-deep water, then took a deep, happy breath. "It wasn't your fault, Tuya," she said, moving to the edge of the pool. Her thin linen sheath clung to her wet body and accented her budding figure. A trace of mud lay across her delicate face and her dark eyes sparkled with mischief. "Would you like me to pull you in? The water is wonderfully cool."

"No, my lady." Tuya looked toward the house again. "I should not like to muss my dress. Your mother would not approve."

"Then I command you to keep still." The floating lotus plants jostled each other as Sagira climbed out of the pool. "Our little game is not done."

Tuya stood as still as a post, her arms hanging rigid until her mistress dripped in front of her. "There!" Sagira clapped wet hands on the slave's bare shoulders. "I caught you! I win again!"

"Yes, my lady."

"I must win." Sagira grinned wickedly as she flung water from her hands into Tuya's face. "It is only fitting that Pharaoh's niece should win in everything she undertakes."

Tuya said nothing, but smiled as Sagira pirouetted in front of the long reflecting pool. She paused and studied her watery image. "Do you think me beautiful, Tuya?"

Tuya lowered her gaze as she pondered her answer. Should she speak as a friend and tease Sagira about the small gap between her front teeth? Or should she reply as a dutiful servant and assure her mistress that no girl in the two kingdoms could rival her beauty and charm?

Not an easy decision, for Tuya had lately been reminded

of the solid line between friendship and servanthood. She
had been only six years old when presented as a gift for
Sagira's third birthday, and as children they had shared everything. But though she often felt like Sagira's older sister,
when her mistress's red moon had begun to flow, Sagira's
mother, the lady Kahent, had urged her daughter to put aside
her baby name and assume a mantle of dignity. Her new
name, Sagira, or 'little one,' referred to her petite frame.

Tuya had never been called anything but Tuya, for slaves
were not permitted the luxury of adult names, and of late
Sagira's mother had been quick to emphasize the gulf existing
between masters and their slaves. Certain attitudes and actions
were proper while others were not. Twice Tuya had been
whipped for overstepping the bounds of propriety, but Sagira
seemed not to have noticed the newfound care with which
Tuya formulated her answers, attitudes and comments.

Diplomacy won out. "You are beautiful, mistress," Tuya
whispered, lowering her head in an attitude of deference.
"Lucky is the man who will be your husband."

"And you, Tuya? Do you never dream of marriage?" Sagira
cocked her head and gave her slave an engaging smile. "Do
you wonder what it is like to kiss a man? To sleep with him
as my mother sleeps with my father?"

Tuya felt her cheeks burning. "I dare not think of those
things," she said, stealing a quick glance toward the wide
doors that opened into the courtyard. "I am your servant. I will
go where you go, and serve you always."

"Tuya." Sagira's voice rang with reproach, for she had
seen her servant's frightened glance. She took Tuya's hand
and pulled her into the privacy of an arbor. "You can speak
freely now," she said, a slow smile crossing her face. "You
need not fear my mother."

"I don't—"

"Don't pretend with me, Tuya. I know about the whippings. Even though you acted as though nothing had happened, I saw the mark of the lash on your shoulders and asked Tanutamon about them. He said my mother ordered both whippings."

"I am sure I deserved them." Tuya's stomach tightened as her ears strained for sounds of eavesdroppers beyond the trees. Would even this conversation be reported to Lady Kahent?

Sagira's eyes lit with understanding. "You did not deserve it. The first time was because you were wearing my jewels, but you did not tell my mother I asked you to model them for me. And the second time was because we were laughing together—"

"I was too familiar. A slave should not be on such close terms."

"You are my friend, Tuya. We have laughed and cried together since I was a baby. Can we stop being friends now?"

Tuya smiled in a fleeting moment of hope. Sagira seemed earnest, and her mother could not see into the thickly green arbor. Perhaps she could safely open her heart.

"I do not know how to behave anymore," she confessed, lifting her gaze. "Your mother says now that you are grown, I must be your servant, not your friend. She said although you may confide in me, I must not speak what is on my heart, for no one cares what a slave thinks."

Sagira flushed to the roots of her hair. "She did not say such a thing!"

Tuya pressed her lips together and kept silent.

"My mother is the best mistress any slave could have," Sagira said, turning on Tuya with a flash of defensive spirit. She crossed her arms and sat on a low bench in the arbor. "Our slaves have greater freedom than any house I've seen. My father is as rich in graciousness as he is in gold."

Tuya slowly lowered herself to the bench. "You are right, my lady."

Sagira sniffed. "Well, then, you do not need to worry about anything. And I have a surprise for you. When I am married, I shall take you out of this house and give you your freedom. Then you can marry as well, and we shall live next to each other and talk every day as we do now."

Hope rose from Tuya's heart like a startled bird. "You would do that?"

"Truly." Sagira's eyes glowed. "And then you shall tell me all about your husband just as you told me about what to expect with the flowering of my red moon. And when you have a baby—" Sagira looked down and twisted her hands "—you shall tell me if it is truly as terrible as it seems."

"It cannot be too terrible," Tuya softened her voice, realizing that Sagira now spoke out of fear. "I am sure that bearing the child of a man you love must be a great joy. And the priests say that offerings to the goddess Taweret will keep evil away from a woman giving birth."

The two girls sat in silence, pondering the mysterious rites they were just beginning to understand. Overhead, a hawk scrolled the hot updrafts, precise and unconcerned, a part of the sky. Tuya envied his freedom.

"Do you ever think about love, Tuya?" Sagira said, running her hands through her wet hair.

"Love?"

"How and when it begins. My mother says love comes after marriage, but I have heard scandalous things from some of the other servants. They say one of the serving girls fell in love with one of the shepherds. For the love of this shepherd, she openly defied Tanutamon. He sold her that very morning for her rebellion."

"I am sure," Tuya said, a creeping uneasiness rising from the bottom of her heart, "that the captain of your father's slaves acted wisely. Rebellion cannot be tolerated."

Sagira tilted her head and gave Tuya a searching look. "You wouldn't do that, would you? Fall in love with some man and leave me?"

"I don't think love is meant for one like me," Tuya answered slowly. "I love you, mistress. I want to follow wherever you go. I have not left your side in nine years, so I am not likely to leave it now."

"Nor would I have you leave it," Sagira answered, now serious. She reached out and clasped Tuya's hands. "By all the gods, Tuya, my heart goes into shock when I think of marrying and leaving my father's house. Only because I know you will be with me can I think about going at all."

Tuya's heart warmed at the light of dependence in her young mistress's eyes. "There is no need to worry. Your mother and father are in no hurry to find a husband for you. You are no commoner, Sagira. Pharaoh himself must be consulted."

Sagira sighed, then her mocking smile returned. "Then we will marry at the same time, and you will be my friend always." She planted a brief kiss on Tuya's cheek, then dropped Tuya's hands and stood to stretch. "Oh, this wet dress grows cold! Come, find me a dry garment, and bind my hair. We will play the hiding game in my chamber until my mother tells us it is time to eat."

Tuya smiled and hurried to match her mistress's eager step.

The girls' happy voices danced ahead of them into the house. Reclining on a pillow-laden couch in the villa's reception room, Kahent heard the sound. "Our daughter is growing up," she whispered, her dark, liquid voice intended for her husband's ears alone.

Intent on studying the scrolls on his lap, Donkor grunted. "It is time, I believe," Kahent persisted, "to approach

Pharaoh about finding Sagira a husband. Surely the king knows his sister has a daughter of noble blood."

Donkor finally looked up. "Pharaoh knows what?"

Kahent sighed, careful not to let her frustration show. "Our king knows we have a daughter. Now he must be told that she has reached marriageable age. Her red moon has flowed twice now."

"She is too young." Donkor waved his hand carelessly and returned his attention to his scrolls, but Kahent would not be deterred.

She had borne his indifference for years. If he had been more attentive, or she more beautiful, they might have had more than one child. But Donkor cared more for his treasures than for the people who lived in his house. After resigning herself to her husband's cold heart, Kahent had invested her love and life in her daughter.

She stood and leaned against one of the columns in the room, steeling herself for a confrontation. "Sagira is young," she said, not daring to contradict him, "so we have time to find the best man for her." She lifted her chin so the beads in the heavy wig she wore clicked together as they fell against her smooth shoulders. "This endeavor will not require your effort, my husband, only your permission. Grant me your blessing to speak to my brother about our daughter. Your honor demands that I do this."

Donkor's brow furrowed as he looked up from his scroll, and Kahent knew he had only half heard her words. "Pharaoh will see to the girl's marriage when I publish the news of her maturity."

"We must proceed slowly," Kahent said, with a cautionary lift of a manicured finger. "We should find a suitable man before we reveal our intentions, then we may drop the suggestion on Pharaoh's ear. Our daughter's husband must be close to Pharaoh, for the line of kings flows through my veins and Sagira's. If something should happen to Pharaoh or to his sons—" She finished with an expressive shrug.

Donkor gave her a smile of reluctant admiration. "I have seen eyes like yours in the faces of my enemies." He lifted his scroll again. "I would not like to have your determination set against me."

"Why should you?" she asked, glad that he had looked at her with the light of amusement in his eyes. "There is one other thing. I must be rid of the servant girl, Tuya."

The scroll dropped again. "But Sagira would be lost without her. It is impossible to imagine one without the other."

"Have you looked at Tuya lately, my husband?" Kahent found it impossible to keep an edge from her voice. "The slave has become quite attractive. If Tuya follows our daughter into her marital home, the slave will capture the groom's attention."

Donkor scoffed. "Our daughter is lovely. I cannot believe that you, her mother, would belittle her—"

"I do not dispute Sagira's loveliness." Kahent sank onto a gilded settee and reached for one of the figs piled atop a golden platter on a nearby stand. "But I want to give our daughter every possible advantage. Sagira is attractive, but a woman must believe herself beautiful to become so. I fear Sagira will compare herself to Tuya, whom the gods have unfairly blessed."

"So how to you intend to separate the girls?" Donkor's voice had flattened, and Kahent knew she had already lost his attention to the papyrus scroll in his lap.

"I will make an offering to the goddess Bastet," she murmured, bringing the fig to her lips. "She will show me the way."

Chapter Two

The glare of the desert sun blinded Potiphar for a moment. He raised his hand to shade his eyes, and nodded in silent satisfaction as warriors laid bodies before him: twenty-six rebels dead, their blood staining the sand, thirty-three others now in the bonds of defeat. He would present the slaves to his royal master, Pharaoh Amenhotep II, and further prove that he had earned the name Potiphar, captain of the guard, the appointed one of Pharaoh.

He signaled for his men to leave the dead as a warning to any others who might invade Pharaoh's peaceful delta. Let their mongrel bodies be consumed by worms and rats; their immortal souls did not deserve to travel through the afterlife.

"Potiphar!"

The cry from a warrior on a cliff above them wrested his eyes from the dead.

"Horus, the falcon god, salutes you!"

The warrior lifted his hand to the sky where a hawk circled lazily above the blood-soaked sands. Potiphar smiled in reply. "So be it." He turned from the grisly scene and murmured under his breath as he strode toward his waiting chariot. "But it is not Horus's approval I seek."

* * *

He had entered royal service during the latter part of the reign of Tuthmosis III, the pharaoh whose first battle had been to unseat his stepmother from the throne of the Upper and Lower Kingdoms. A common man with an uncommon love for battle, Potiphar joined the king's army for the campaign that culminated at the fortress of Megiddo, Armageddon. Overflowing with youthful enthusiasm, drive and shrewd intuitions, Potiphar discovered that the prospect of war affected him like a fever. In a moment of reckless abandon, he approached the king's generals and suggested that the Egyptian army cross Mount Carmel to surprise the enemy from behind.

Tuthmosis appreciated the subtlety of the strategy. The Asiatics expected the Egyptians to approach in a direct attack from the southern plains, so when the Egyptian cavalry appeared on the northern horizon, the panicked enemy fled into their fortress. Leaving Potiphar to maintain the siege of the stronghold, Tuthmosis raided the lands of neighboring kings and chieftains, then returned to the starving fortress to claim his victory. Pharaoh completed his conquest by harvesting the crops of the land. The Asiatics, who had to eat, bowed before the Egyptian king in submission.

The king's victory at Megiddo secured Potiphar's place in the royal retinue. Under Tuthmosis III, Potiphar led armies that conquered lands from the fifth cataract of the Nile to the Euphrates River. Tuthmosis, like Potiphar, relished the thrill of war. His standing army included hundreds of ferocious Nubian warriors whose ancestors had won battles for previous pharaohs.

Iron-willed and hard as stone, Potiphar thought himself invincible until he was taken prisoner on one expedition with the Nubians. After his capture, he spat in his captors' faces, fully expecting to die. The king of Kadesh, a wily and able adversary, wielded his sword and extracted from Potiphar what many would have considered to be the ultimate sacrifice a man could make for his king.

But after days of blinding white pain, Potiphar did not die. A contingent of Egyptian troops stormed the enemy's camp and rescued their general, bringing the wounded Potiphar back to stand before Tuthmosis. The fading warrior-king, in the fifty-fifth year of his reign, proclaimed before his entire court that Potiphar was a friend of Pharaoh and would henceforth serve as captain of the king's bodyguard. Potiphar was awarded a villa, a staff of slaves and a secure position, but before his body could heal, the great king died.

From his bed of convalescence, Potiphar watched with trepidation as the crown prince assumed the throne. Twenty-year-old Amenhotep II loved the sea and had spent most of his princely preparation at the Egyptian naval base at Pernefer, near Memphis. Potiphar wondered how the new king would feel about joining his father's court at Thebes, but join it he must. The pharaoh of Egypt could not afford to appear weak or indecisive. With the mighty Tuthmosis III dead, the Asiatic city-states and their allies would undoubtedly attempt to throw off the Egyptian yoke. They would put the young new king's military prowess to the test.

In the following months, neither Potiphar nor the far-flung cities found the new king lacking. Excelling in battle, archery and horsemanship, Amenhotep delighted in hand-to-hand combat. With Potiphar at his side, he led his troops into battle, howling in royal rage. Often the mere sight of his ferocious visage convinced dismayed enemy troops to surrender.

Now, in the thirteenth year of his reign, Amenhotep had accomplished his military goals. The far-flung provinces dutifully sent tribute to their king and toiled to keep peace in the land. Military maneuvers now involved only infrequent skirmishes from rebellious territories, and Potiphar rarely rode with the army. He found it difficult to admit, but at forty-four, he had grown tired of the wind in his face and sand in his teeth. But he continued to venture onto the battlefield in the hope that a spectacular victory would bring him the one prize he lacked—the Gold of Praise to encircle his neck.

The Gold of Praise—the most obvious and visible symbol of Pharaoh's favor—was a solid gold chain awarded to the man who had proved himself a friend of Pharaoh. Though Tuthmosis had proclaimed Potiphar his friend, that noble king had died before presenting his wounded general with the Gold of Praise.

Potiphar had earned it. If the gods were just, at some point in this life he would yet wear it around his neck.

Chapter Three

A bitter wind howled around the caravan, and Yosef found
himself wincing with every step across the desert sand. A stout
rope bound his wrists, while the end of the rope connected him
to the saddle of a sour-faced camel belonging to a caravan of
Yishmaelites from Gilead. With each step of the Yishmaelites'
beast, the rope tightened and tugged on Yosef's broken arm.

Every step, every breath, brought exquisite pain. He had
fainted when they first wrenched his arm to tie him with the
other prisoners bound for Egypt; one of the traders tossed a
bucketful of foul water in his face to wake him. Now Yosef
stumbled through the desert in a stupor of agony and grief. In
lucid moments he wondered why his life had taken such a
vicious and unpredictable turn.

His father, the one constant loving figure in his life since his
mother's death, would feel this loss even more keenly than the
grief of losing his beloved Rahel. "At least I have you," his father
had often said, his gnarled hand patting Yosef's as they walked
together. "As long as I have you, Rahel lives on in your eyes."

How could his brothers do this to their father? To him?
Why did they hate him so?

Nothing in his past warranted such treatment. A loving and obedient son to his father, he had been the favored first-born of Yaakov's favorite wife, Rahel. His brothers were less than doting, probably because they were envious of the close relationship he shared with their father. When Rahel died while giving birth to Binyamin, Yaakov pulled Yosef aside and spilled his heart, opening a window through which Yosef glimpsed a love as strong as God and a grief as deep as death. For the first time, Yaakov recited his personal history, explaining to Yosef how each of his other brothers came to be born. Compassion conceived the sons of Lea, duty resulted in the sons of Bilhah, guilt fathered the sons of Zilpah. Only with Rahel, Yaakov told Yosef, were sons given life in love.

Perhaps this knowledge gave birth to his dreams. One night not long after his mother's death, Yosef had dreamed that he and his brothers were binding sheaves of grain. Suddenly Yosef's sheaf jerked itself out of his hands as if it possessed a life of its own. Dancing away from the rope with which he would have tied it, the tall sheaf moved to the center of the cleared field and stood upright. Within minutes, the sheaves of his brothers were similarly animated, but those sheaves circled Yosef's, then prostrated themselves on the ground before the golden sheaf in the center of the circle.

His brothers had not found the dream at all entertaining. "Do you intend to reign over us?" Yehuda sneered when Yosef told them of the strange vision. "Will you actually rule us?" Only Re'uven's diplomatic intervention prevented a fistfight.

The next night Yosef had a similar dream. In this dream he sat on a star while the sun and moon and eleven other stars drew near and bowed to him. When he described the dream the next morning, even his father laughed. "What is this?" Yaakov said, his face darkening to a deep shade of red as he sat before the breakfast fire. "Will your departed mother and I join your brothers and actually bow before you? Surely you think too much of yourself, Yosef, and of these dreams. Forget them, my son, and remember that when pride comes, disgrace follows."

His father's words proved strangely prophetic. Yosef had taken quiet pleasure in those dreams while he dwelled securely in his father's favor. But now, in the harsh light of reality and the bitterness of pain, those mocking fantasies seemed as false as vows made in wine. He had dared to dream that God would honor him as primary inheritor of the blessings and promises of Avraham, but those hopes, too, were surely foolish. Disgrace and despair walked with him across the desert.

From the chatter of the Yishmaelites Yosef knew he was on his way to the "black land," Egypt. He had heard much of the place, for his great-grandfather Avraham had found trouble among its people. Plagued by fear and blessed with a beautiful wife, Avraham lied to the Egyptians and told them that Sarai was his sister, not his wife. Unaware that he desired another man's wife, Pharaoh took Sarai into the royal harem and suffered the plagues of God for his sin. When the truth was revealed, Pharaoh asked Avraham to take his wife, his livestock, all that he had, and leave the country. The king's army had escorted Avraham from the land to ensure that nothing remained behind.

Now Avraham's great-grandson was returning to Egypt as a bloody and broken slave, reeking of camels and filth. Was this God's divine punishment for Avraham's sin? Were the Egyptians now to have their vengeance on one of his descendants?

Despite the pain, Yosef lifted his head in pride as the rope bit into his wrists and pulled him forward. Whatever happened, he would not repeat Avraham's sin. He would not lie. But to preserve his life, neither would he admit to anyone that he was of the house and lineage of the one they had known as Avram.

Chapter Four

Kahent woke before the sun's rising and dressed in her finest garment, a narrow sheath of white linen that fell in intricate pleats from her shoulders to the floor. She selected her favorite beaded necklaces, bracelets and belt, then sat at her table to paint her face. Dipping an exquisitely carved copper applicator into the container for her kohl, she outlined her eyes and dabbed her fingers into a secret compartment inside a carved ivory duck on her dressing table. With a deft movement, she swiped a mixture of ground malachite and animal fat across her eyelids, effectively giving them a golden-green glow. Green, she reflected, was the color of fertility, the root and purpose of the petition she would bring today.

When her face had been properly painted, Kahent's maid lifted her heavy wig from its stand and placed it on her mistress's head. Like all Egyptian noblewomen, Kahent wore her hair clipped short, a necessity when no woman of standing went out in public without her wig. The massive wig was as wide as Kahent's shoulders and several layers thick. A lush fringe of bangs accented the dark lines around her eyes, and the beads that had been woven into the ends of the woolen strands clicked together with a pleasing sound.

Kahent slipped her feet into her papyrus sandals, then lifted a bag of silver from her husband's treasure chest. Offerings of fruit and meat would not be enough for today. She planned on asking the goddess Bastet for a serious boon, and a note-worthy offering would certainly be required.

Her maids stood back and Kahent pointed wordlessly to the one who would accompany her to the temple. The other blinked, probably in relief, and the chosen slave lifted the earthen lamp from its stand and moved toward the outer court-yard where a special bundle waited. Kahent had chosen the goddess Bastet as her patron god, and since cats were sacred to that goddess, more than thirty cats lived within the walls of this household. When they died, Kahent paid handsomely to have the animals mummified and wrapped in linen. A store-room near the temple of the house was stocked with cat-shaped coffins in which the mummified cats rested in their eternal journey.

The sleepy servant lifted one of the papyrus coffins into her arms and laid it across her mistress's open palms. Reverently, Kahent carried the burden through the gate and led the way through the streets of Thebes to the temple dedicated to the goddess Bastet.

After entering the rectangular enclosure surrounding the temple, Kahent left her maid in the outer courtyard and carried the small coffin into Per-Hair, the House of Rejoicing. In front of its towers stood twin statues, two cats carved of green marble. Dark crevices loomed where the eyes should have been, and golden rings hung from the nostrils. A silver pectoral with the sacred eye of Horus decorated the chests of both animals, sig-nifying that Horus himself protected the cat from evil.

Kahent always felt a sudden chill whenever she saw an amulet depicting the wadjet eye. According to the legends of the gods, Seth, a god of evil, tore out the eye of Horus in a struggle for the throne of Egypt. Once in a temple play Donkor forced her to attend, an actor portraying Seth had actually plucked the eye from an unfortunate prisoner. After the bloodletting, Kahent had left her husband's side and fled the theater, knowing full well that the ancient legend would require that the prisoner also be dismembered before the play's end.

No bloody legends were associated with Bastet. She was the daughter of Re, the sun-god, and represented the benign power of the sun to ripen crops.

After kneeling before the two regal statues, Kahent proceeded to the sacred burial grounds and placed the cat coffin in an empty space. She bowed her head to the earth and murmured words of allegiance, then walked slowly back to the Per-Hair and passed through the entryway.

The morning sun had begun to beat on the earth in relentless waves of energy, but cool air filled the House of Rejoicing. Moving through a long, columned hall adorned with wall-carvings of the king and queen, she came to the chamber known as Gem-Bastet—the Finding of Bastet. A long, narrow court stretched ahead of her, crowned by an altar atop a flight of steps. Beyond the altar a causeway ran toward yet another pair of lofty columns. Kahent passed through them into a second court, then into a third, and finally into the smallest sanctuary.

By reading her dress and jewels, the temple priests and priestesses allowed her to pass, correctly intuiting that the offering in the bag at her waist would permit entry into the holiest of holies.

The floor rose at a gentle angle under Kahent's feet as the roof gradually lowered, and soon her steps brought her to the innermost sanctuary. The goddess sat on a platform behind the altar; her priestesses hovered near with towels and basins of water to wash and dress Bastet for the day. A pile of discarded nightclothes lay in a heap on the floor, while another slave stood nearby with a platter of fruit and meat for the goddess's breakfast.

Kahent fell to her knees and bent her head to the floor three times. She was as devout in her practice of religion as Donkor was indifferent in his, yet still the goddess had blessed them. Kahent and her husband and daughter were strong and not afflicted with any of the diseases that struck less wealthy people.

In gratitude and reverence, Kahent remained on the floor. She would wait until after the goddess had breakfasted, then present her petition.

The priestesses adorned the goddess with robes and jewels, then placed the food on the altar. Her attendants waited in silence as the tall statue stared down on the platter, her emerald eyes twinkling in the shafting rays of sunlight from the high clerestory windows. After several moments, at a signal from a shaven-headed priestess, one slave whisked the food away, another clothed the goddess in a fresh collar, and a priest solemnly announced that Bastet was ready to receive visitors and deliver oracles.

Kahent was the only petitioner in the sanctuary. She took a deep breath and clasped her hands to her breast. "Oh, most divine Bastet," she began, rising to her knees before the imposing statue, "behold your servant, who came into being from your goodness! I have a daughter of marriageable age who needs a worthy husband."

Her words echoed in the stillness of the chamber, yet nothing moved. Kahent waited, breathing in the bittersweet aromas of the burning incense, the tiled floor hard under her knees. The few priests who moved in the shadows beyond the goddess paid her no heed.

No answer came to her, nothing at all. She shifted uneasily, not sure how to proceed, then a flat, inflectionless voice cut through the silence. "Bastet will hear you."

A young, thin woman stepped out of the shadows, the pale skin of her shaved head gleaming in the torchlight. "The majesty of Bastet says to you, 'Listen to this my servant Ramla, who will work my magic. Tell her what you will, and she will relay my divine message.'"

Kahent studied the girl. Tall and slender, she wore the simple white robe of a priestess and a golden collar about her neck, a symbol of the goddess's ownership. The girl could have been anywhere from fifteen to thirty, so unlined was her sculpted face. Kahent made a mental note of approval, but as her eyes traveled downward, one sight gave her pause: the girl's right hand was malformed—only three fingers grew where five should have been. How could this be? Most malformed children were thrown to the crocodiles of the Nile.

"Do not let the sight of my servant disturb you." The priestess's eyes hardened, and Kahent knew the girl had seen the revulsion in her glance. "She has been given graces and power to atone for her physical losses. Ramla will serve you well."

With these words, the slender girl bent at the waist and bowed before Kahent.

"So be it," Kahent said, frowning. She paused, then dropped the bag of silver at the girl's feet. "My petition is a matter of the heart. My daughter, who must marry well, has spent nearly every day of her life with a slave who surpasses her in beauty. I want to rid my daughter of this girl, but do not know how to proceed without arousing her to anger or breaking her heart."

Straightening into the ramrod posture of a royal guard, the

priestess closed her eyes and tilted her head as if she were listening to a far-off voice. After a moment her face cracked into
a smile and she nodded drowsily. "Yes, Bastet," she murmured, opening her eyes.

She shared the smile with Kahent. "Love cannot easily be
killed, but it can be distracted." Casually, she tossed the bag
of silver onto the altar, then walked to Kahent's side and took
the lady's arm, lifting her to her feet. "Take me to your home,
lady, and give me a day with your daughter. Bastet has
directed me to make the proper spells and incantations. I can
divine the future, and will not leave your daughter's side until
all be well."

Stunned by the magnanimous gesture, Kahent allowed
Ramla to lead her from the sanctuary.

"You sent for me, mother?" Sagira called, rushing into the
reception room. She was about to complain about the interruption of her playtime, but the sight of the stranger with her
mother left her speechless. The young woman who sat in one
of the gilded chairs wore the shaved head and golden collar
of a priestess from one of the temples.

"Sagira, this is Ramla." Her mother gestured to the visitor
with a graceful hand. "She is a priestess at the temple of Bastet."

Feeling awkward and gauche, Sagira barely managed to nod.

Ramla gave Sagira a warm smile. "I do not live at the
temple all the time—only one month out of four. Tomorrow
I begin my time of absence, and your gracious mother has said
I may spend three months as part of your household."

"We need the blessings of the goddess," Sagira's mother
said, studying Sagira with careful eyes. "Don't you agree,
my daughter?"

"Yes." Sagira managed a crooked smile. For what reason
did they need the special favor of the gods?

"I am especially looking forward to getting to know you," Ramla said, rising from her chair. In that moment Sagira saw the woman's misshapen hand, and knew from her mother's disapproving gasp that she had not managed to disguise her horror.

But Ramla did not seem to care. "Pay no attention to things that can be observed with the eyes," she said, reaching for Sagira's hand with her whole one. "I can teach you how to discern with your heart. The gods have compensated for my missing fingers with other gifts, and I can teach you secrets you have never known. I can read the future for you, child."

"Truly?" Fear fell from Sagira like a discarded cloak, and wonder slipped into its place.

"Yes." Ramla's voice was low and soothing, and her hand slipped up to stroke Sagira's hair. "Kneel before me while I work a spell of divination."

Sagira caught her breath as she fell to her knees. Her mother had often participated in such religious rituals, but until now Sagira had been considered too much a child to have a priestess divine her future. That her mother would now allow such a practice spoke more of Sagira's maturity than the flowering of her red moon…

As Sagira's mother stood to fetch the family's divining bowl, Sagira smoothed her face and tried to copy the look of earnest interest her mother wore. A moment later Lady Kahent returned with the bowl of blackened silver. The bottom of the inner bowl had been engraved with the figure of the jackal-headed Anubis, the opener of roads for the dead.

Ramla accepted the bowl and placed it on a stand, then filled it with water from a pitcher. Murmuring prayers and incantations, she poured a small amount of fine oil into the bowl from a clay vial. As the oil swirled and eddied over the surface of the water, Ramla closed her eyes and lifted her hands.

Hail to you, O Re-Harakhte, Father of the Gods!
Hail to you, O ye seven Hathors,
Who are adorned with strings of red thread!
Hail to you, Anubis, Lord of heaven and earth!
Cause Bastet to appear before me,
Like an ox after grass,
Like a mother after her children,
Send her to me so I may ask the future of Sagira, born
     of Donkor and Kahent!

The sweet incense in the room seemed overpowering,
and a cold lump grew in Sagira's stomach as she studied the
priestess. Beads of perspiration appeared at the woman's
temple; her features twisted into a maddening grimace.
Tendrils of apprehension wound through Sagira's body as
the priestess opened her black eyes and seemed to stare
straight through flesh. Strange words flew from the seer's
mouth, and her gaze darted to the bowl where oil swirled on
the waters.

"I see, Sagira, that you are surrounded by people who love
you," Ramla said in an awed, husky whisper. A slight smile
twisted one corner of her face. "You are much loved. You will
marry a man of great importance according to your parents'
wishes, and Pharaoh will pronounce his blessing on the union."

"Children?" Lady Kahent called from a corner of the room.
"Will she have children?"

Pearls of perspiration shone on the young woman's forehead.
"You will be remembered through all time," the priestess droned,
her eyes as dark as a cavern. "As long as men walk on the earth,
they will speak of you. Your memory will be immortal—"

Sagira couldn't believe what she was hearing. "Me?"

Ramla trembled, then her hands flew to the sides of the
bowl as she steadied herself. "Not your name," she whispered

hoarsely. "Your…role. You will leave an imprint on the sands of time that cannot be erased."

At these words, the seer's eyes rolled up into her head and she slumped to the floor, her limbs thrashing in a seizure. Sagira scrambled backward and shrieked, but Kahent flew to Ramla's side and held the woman's flailing arms. "For you she has borne this," she said, looking at her daughter with something like awe in her eyes. "You will be remembered, daughter, longer than Pharaoh, for more years than those who built the ancient pyramids."

Sagira placed her hand over her mouth and tried to stop crying. The body of the priestess stilled, but the young woman did not move. Kahent left Ramla on the floor and reached for her daughter.

"My little one," she crooned, enfolding Sagira in an embrace. "How often did I dream that you would bring glory to this house! And now I find that your glory will eclipse that of all other women!"

"She didn't say that," Sagira mumbled, her mind whirling with confusion. "She said I would be remembered. And not my name, but my role." She raised her head to look at her mother. "What can that mean?"

Kahent pressed her lips together and helped Sagira rise from the floor. She said nothing as she led her daughter to the couch, then she motioned for Sagira to sit beside her.

"It can only mean one thing," she whispered, a smile dimpling her cheek. "And you must never speak of this to anyone, for to do so would be treason."

Sagira felt a shiver pass down her spine. "Treason?"

"Yes." Kahent pressed her finger to her lips as she thoughtfully weighed her words. "As you know, daughter, the royal blood of the two kingdoms passes down from woman to woman. Amenhotep, my brother, is Pharaoh because he married the heiress Merit-Amon, the daughter of Tuthmosis."

"But you are also a daughter of Tuthmosis," Sagira pointed out.

"My mother was a lesser wife."

"So what does this have to do with me?"

"I am also a daughter of Tuthmosis," Kahent answered, her voice a thin whisper in the room. "If the gods will that Pharaoh's house, all his sons and daughters, should be destroyed, I will be the heiress. And when I die, you will be the heiress. Whomever you marry will be Pharaoh, and your sons and daughters will continue the dynasty."

As the words swirled around Sagira, she clutched the arm of her chair, stunned by the revelation. "Your role," Kahent whispered, the breath from her lips stirring the hair at Sagira's ear, "is obvious. You will be the mother of pharaohs. The mother of a new dynasty, the greatest in all Egypt. You and your children will leave an imprint on the sands of time that cannot be erased."

Kahent's head fell on her daughter's shoulder in a bout of joyous weeping, but Sagira sat still, thinking. She had been relieved enough to hear that she would marry well. This prophecy of immortal influence was too much to comprehend.

Tuya noticed a difference in her mistress almost immediately. In the days following Sagira's introduction to the strange priestess of Bastet, she seemed withdrawn and tense, but she would not give an explanation for her altered mood. In the mornings as Tuya arranged her mistress's toilet, Sagira was snappish and irritable, quick to complain about Tuya's heavy hand or chattering tongue. The long hours of play in the courtyard disappeared as Sagira spent time alone with Ramla. Once when Tuya casually asked what Ramla and Sagira talked about, her young mistress turned on her and said that if Tuya didn't mind her manners she'd have Tanutamon administer yet another whipping.

Two weeks after Ramla had come to live in the household, Tuya made her way to the kitchen. Taharka, the chief butler, had always been a friend and used to give both girls sweet treats from his lunch box whenever they managed to sneak into his workroom. On this day he was tasting a new wine especially selected for a party Donkor intended to give for several noble guests, and he had little time to spare for a lonely slave girl abandoned by her mistress.

"Taharka, can I speak with you?"

"Not now, my pretty one," Taharka said, frowning as he looked at her sad face. "The master has invited guests to eat, drink and be merry through the night. Spiced wine and beer, the wine jars and even the alabaster vases have to be made ready."

"Can I help?"

Taharka smiled as though out of pity for her. "You are bored, aren't you?"

"I'd love to help. Surely there is something I can do."

"All right. You can see to the perfumed cones. The animal fat must be set out into the sun to liquefy, then mixed with the precious oils of perfume. When they are mixed, bring them into the coolness of the house and pour the liquid into the molds."

"I can do that," Tuya replied, moving toward the large copper pots of animal fat. The cones of perfumed fat were a treat enjoyed only by the nobility, for perfume was precious. As each guest arrived, a perfumed cone would be placed on his head. As the afternoon and party wore on, the cones would melt and run down the heavy wigs and sweltering skin of the overheated guests.

Tuya lifted one of the pots and staggered toward the doorway, but halted when Taharka let out an earsplitting scream. She dropped the pot, startled, and whirled to see him standing at a table, his hand purpling before her eyes. A scorpion scuttled across the table.

"I am bit!" the butler screamed, his eyes wide in fright and pain. "Oh, daughter of Seth, why am I bit tonight?"

Obeying a primitive instinct, Tuya scooped up a handful of ashes from the firepit, mixed them with animal fat, and placed the mixture over the rapidly swelling spot on Taharka's hand. Stunned by the pain, the butler leaned against the wall, still holding his wounded hand out in front of him.

As if in response to his call, Ramla and Sagira appeared in the doorway.

"What happened to Taharka?" Sagira snapped, her eyes drilling into Tuya as if she were somehow to blame.

Tuya lowered her gaze. "A scorpion."

Ramla stepped into the room and dramatically lifted her hands. "I am a priestess of Bastet, and have come to lay bare the poison that is in the limbs of Taharka, Donkor's servant. As Bastet lives, so shall live Taharka!"

Taharka clenched his jaw against the pain as Ramla swayed in front of him. "You, poison, shall not take your stand in his forehead; Hekayit, Lady of the Forehead, is against you! You shall not take your stand in his eyes; Horus Mekhenty-irty, Lord of the Eyes, is against you! You shall not take your stand in his ears; Geb, Lord of the Ear, is against you!"

Tuya watched Sagira's face as Ramla continued the roll call of the various gods. Her mistress's eyes shone toward the interloper with devotion and admiration.

"You shall not take your stand in his nose; Khenem-tchau of Hesret, Lady of the Nose, is against you! You shall not take your stand in his lips; Anubis, Lord of the Lips, is against you! You shall not take your stand in his tongue; Sefekh-aahui,

Lady of the Tongue, is against you! You shall not take your stand in his neck; Wadjety, Lady of the Neck, is against you!"

Taharka groaned as Ramla called out for the gods of the arm, back, side, liver, lung, spleen, intestines, ribs and flesh to stand against the scorpion bite. A crowd of servants gathered as the priestess continued to chant, calling on the gods of the buttocks, perineum, thighs, knee, shins, soles and toenails.

Finally, as sweat dripped from her brows, Ramla raised her voice in a terrible shriek. "You, poison, shall not take your stand anywhere in him! You shall not find refreshment there! Go down to the ground! I have incanted against you, I have spat on you, I have drunk you! As Horus lives, so does Taharka. Go down to the ground! I know you, I know your name! Come from the right hand, poison, come from the left hand! Come in saliva, come in vomit, come in urine! Come hither at my utterance according as I say! Grant a path to Taharka! As the sun shall rise and as the Nile shall flow, so shall Taharka be better than he was!"

She ended in a hoarse shout and flung her arms toward the heavens. As if on cue, Taharka leaned sideways and vomited onto the packed earthen floor. Tuya lifted the poultice she had used to cover the scorpion bite. The wound was still red and slightly swollen, but seemed less violent than it had before.

The assembled crowd cheered Ramla, and Sagira slipped her arm around the priestess's waist and helped the exhausted woman from the room. Two slaves from the kitchen helped Taharka to his feet, and after a moment Tuya found herself in the workroom with only a handful of servants while guests were arriving at the entryway.

"Hurry," she commanded, gesturing toward the pots of animal fat and the trays of fruit. "The party begins, and our master will not care that Taharka has met with a scorpion. This food must be ready, so help me!"

Knowing that Tanutamon's lash awaited anyone who displeased Donkor, the slaves did as she commanded.

Kahent sighed in satisfaction as her slave poured a pitcher of cool water over her tired back. She lay on a slab of polished granite in the bathroom of the house and her maid had just massaged the worries of a hectic week into oblivion.

Not that her worries were major ones. In the three weeks since the priestess Ramla had come to dwell with them, Sagira had spent less and less time with Tuya. It would not be difficult now to manufacture an excuse to remove the girl from Sagira's quarters. And when Sagira had been weaned from her dependence on the slave, the serious search for a husband could begin.

"Excuse the interruption, my lady." Another of the maids appeared in the doorway. "Your daughter and Ramla wait to see you."

"I'll see them at once," Kahent said, sitting up. Her handmaid threw a light gown over Kahent's upraised arms. She stood and shimmied into it, then went with open arms to embrace her daughter.

"Sagira, what brings you to me in the middle of the day?" she asked, resting her hands on her daughter's shoulders as she kissed the girl's cheeks. Behind Sagira, Ramla stood in practiced detachment, her arms crossed, her gaze fixed on Kahent's face.

"I've been thinking." Sagira's lower lip edged forward in a pout. "If I am truly to be the mother of kings, perhaps it is best if I am not attended by such a familiar slave. Tuya knows too much about me to be properly respectful. Ramla has suggested that I send her away."

Kahent blinked in honest surprise. She had not dared to dream that Ramla's influence would work so quickly. "You would be rid of Tuya?"

Sagira crossed her arms. "She's jealous and spiteful and I don't trust her. For months she's been looking at me with a strange gleam in her eye. I don't like it. She frightens me."

"Perhaps one of the dark gods has invaded her heart," Ramla suggested in a cool voice.

"Exactly!" Sagira slammed a clenched fist into her palm. "That's what I'm afraid of, Mother. You gave her to me, but now I'd like to be rid of her."

Kahent gave her daughter an innocent smile. "Perhaps she could work with the butler. Taharka seems to think much of her."

"No!" Sagira snapped. "I will not have her anywhere near. I want her out of the house as soon as possible. She does not understand my destiny. She sees herself as my equal, and that she can never be."

Joy flooded Kahent's heart. "As you say, Sagira," she said, placing her hands on her daughter's shoulders again. "And because she is yours, whatever silver comes from her sale shall go to you."

"I shall give it all to Ramla as an offering for the goddess." Sagira turned to the priestess. "Without her I would never have learned of my future."

Ramla leaned forward in a gentle bow. "Thank the goddess we discovered it."

Kahent closed her eyes in relief. "Bastet be praised."

The sun bark of the god Re had moved only a short distance across the sky when Ramla came alone into the women's room of the villa. Surprised by the visit, Kahent put aside the scroll she had been reading and waited for the priestess to speak.

"Your daughter is resting," Ramla announced, gazing at Kahent with dark eyes that seemed to probe the recesses of her soul. "And your petition has been heard."

"I trust it has." Kahent straightened on the couch where she had been reclining. "I owe you a great debt."

"Your daughter's offering will suffice," Ramla answered. "That, and the opportunity to watch the future unfold. I did not fabricate or elaborate on my vision, Lady Kahent. Sagira will leave a mark on the world." When she hesitated, Kahent toyed with the fabric of her dress, dimly aware that she was fidgeting. What was she supposed to do now? Did the priestess expect special favors in return for good news?

"Please sit." Kahent gestured to an empty chair. Ramla moved to the chair and sat down without breaking the straight line of her back.

"You and Sagira have become friends," Kahent said, casting about for some avenue of conversation. "I am sorry you must leave soon. I fear Sagira will be lost without your company or Tuya's."

"She will never be lost," the priestess answered. "We have already made arrangements. I will serve my month for the goddess, then live with your daughter for three months." Her pale lips curved into a mirthless smile. "I have become your daughter's spiritual counselor. She has decided that we shall remain together."

Kahent forced a laugh. "You want to remain with Sagira? But she is a child while you are a mature woman. Surely there are others who will value your unique gifts."

A dark brow shot up, creating a startlingly oblique line across the young woman's face. "May I speak frankly?"

"Please do."

The corner of the priestess's mouth dipped slightly. "I am old enough, lady, to know where favor and fortune lie. A woman cannot find them within the temples of Egypt's gods." She shrugged. "But I know Sagira's future, and I know she will need a friend. You asked me to pull her away from the slave girl, but your daughter is weak, she cannot stand alone. She needs love and a companion. She has found both in me."

"I am grateful, of course," Kahent answered, her stomach tightening at the thought of having the strange priestess in her home for nine months of the year. "But you know Sagira will be married soon."

"I will go to the house of her husband," Ramla answered, tilting her head. "You should be grateful for my help, Lady Kahent. Without my special gift, you would never have known of the gods' plan for Sagira's future." Her lips curved in a half smile. "But you will not want Pharaoh to know of these things."

"Of course not," Kahent snapped. She could feel sweat beading under her heavy wig. It was treason even to think of taking the throne from the one who ruled as the incarnate god. If Pharaoh heard that those in Donkor's house were grooming themselves to become the next rulers of Egypt—

"Do not fear, lady," Ramla said, a sweet ripple in her voice. "As long as I am your daughter's spiritual counselor, I will say nothing of her destiny. With the patience of the gods I will wait for her sun to rise."

Kahent recognized the implied threat in the words. "Then I," she answered, "will wait with you."

She pressed her finger to her lips as the priestess rose and left the room.

Taharka rolled a heavy barrel into his workroom, his short, graying hair gleaming silver in the slanting rays of the open window. He saw Tuya and frowned. "Why, my pretty one, are you alone so often these days?"

Tuya kicked a shard of broken pottery out of her way. "Sagira is busy," she muttered, not looking up. "She's with Ramla. She talks to that priestess for hours, and she's made it clear I am not supposed to overhear their conversations."

"A passing fancy, nothing more," Taharka promised, standing the barrel upright. "Don't you remember the time you and Sagira swore you would eat nothing but pigeon? You drove me crazy with your quirks and Lady Kahent nearly went out of her mind with worry for Sagira's health."

Tuya laughed. "I had forgotten. But this is different, Taharka. Sagira's changed somehow. She's not playing a game. In fact I've never seen her so serious. Sometimes I think she went to sleep and a stranger woke up in her body."

"Tuya!" A hoarse voice bellowed through the kitchen, and Tuya wiped her hands across her skirt as the master of the slaves stalked into the room. As broad as he was tall, Tanutamon was a man to be feared, especially when ill winds blew through Donkor's household. He never called for Tuya unless the lady Kahent had commanded that she be whipped.

Despite the chilly dew forming on her skin, Tuya stepped forward to meet him. She dipped her head toward him in submission. "What is it, master?"

Tanutamon gestured toward the door. "Come with me."

What had she done? Tuya threw a questioning glance toward Taharka, but he waved her through the doorway with a hurried gesture that said *go, and don't ask questions!*

Tuya followed the master of the slaves through the winding halls until they reached the gatekeeper's lodge at the entrance to the villa. The gatekeeper rose from his stool as Tanutamon approached, then backed away.

Tuya held her breath, dreading whatever was to follow. There was no whipping post in the lodge, so what new punishment was this?

In answer, Tanutamon pulled a length of chain and four shackles from a corner of the gatehouse. "Your hands," he said, his voice strangely flat.

Bracing herself for an assault, Tuya lifted her trembling

arms. Had Lady Kahent heard about the cup of wine she accidentally spilled in Taharka's workroom? Had Sagira complained about Tuya's sad countenance?

Tanutamon's rough hands caught hers. With a deft gesture, he snapped the shackles on her wrists, then secured them by running a length of chain through the loops.

"Am I to be whipped?" Tuya whispered, afraid to lift her voice. "What has the mistress said, Tanutamon?"

The giant did not answer, but knelt to clasp the other pair of shackles around her legs. The cold metal chilled her skin and pressured the fragile bones in her ankles as he threaded chain through the loops.

"Tanutamon," she asked again, dismayed at the sound of tears in her voice. "If I have done nothing wrong, what is this? And if I have done something, tell me what it is so I may avoid trouble in the future."

"You have done nothing," the master of the slaves answered gruffly. "Your mistress wishes to sell you. It is her right and her request."

"Lady Kahent?"

"The young Lady Sagira."

For a moment the words did not register in Tuya's mind. She had been a part of Donkor's family since her childhood. She and Sagira had bounced on Lady Kahent's knee, eaten their meals together, splashed in the same pool, shared gossip and dreams. It should have been easier to stop the yearly inundation of the Nile than to separate her from this family! Yet heavy shackles bound her wrists and ankles, and even now Tanutamon was adjusting the length of chain so he could lead her through the gate.

"Where are you taking me?" she cried, the world blurring as tears distorted her vision. "What happens when a slave is sold? I'm sorry, Tanutamon, but I know nothing of these things."

"You must trust me," Tanutamon said, not looking at her. "You are a good girl, Tuya, and if I were the master, I would not allow this thing. But I will do as I am told, as will you. You should be grateful that you have been pampered for so long. I will do what I can for you. I have friends…in high places."

She wanted to ask other questions, but terror rose like a lump in her throat and blocked her speech. Hanging her head, she shuffled forward as the gatekeeper opened the gate and Tanutamon led her away from the marvelous house of Donkor, kinsman of the king.

Chapter Five

Tuya shook like a frightened child as Tanutamon led her through the dusty streets of Thebes. She felt nothing but the chains that bound her and heard nothing but her own frantic gulps of air and the pounding of her heart. When she awkwardly lifted her hands to steady her throbbing head, she realized her cheeks were wet with tears.

How could Sagira have sent her away? The answer was obvious—for some reason, Ramla had poisoned Sagira against her beloved friend. But how could Sagira have allowed herself to be misled? Tuya had always given Sagira the affection she craved, while Ramla was about as warm as a corpse. But Ramla was fascinating and foreign, and Tuya had always sought to be helpful rather than interesting…

Her tears quickened as a wave of sorrow swept over her. Perhaps Ramla had nothing to do with Sagira's change of heart. Sagira was ready for marriage; hadn't she said so? Perhaps she thought of Tuya as a playmate, not a noble lady's handmaid. The slave had outgrown her usefulness, and was being consigned to the trash heap like a discarded toy.

Tuya stumbled through the streets, grappling with her

thoughts, and nearly ran into Tanutamon when he stopped outside a tall brick wall. A narrow gated entry guarded whatever grand house lay inside, and Tuya wiped her nose with the back of her hand. When a fresh wave of grief threatened to engulf her, she bit her lip to substitute one pain for another.

"Tanutamon of Donkor's house wishes to see Kratas, the keeper of Pharaoh's slaves," Tanutamon announced. Pharaoh's slaves! Tuya struggled to breathe as bands of apprehension tightened around her chest.

"Tanutamon—" she whispered, but the burly man cut her off with a sharp glance. He waited until the gatekeeper stepped away, then he turned and flashed into sudden fury.

"Keep quiet!" He blazed down at her. "Slaves should be seen and not heard, or haven't you learned that yet? You were spoiled in Donkor's house, and it is possible your beauty will enable you to be pampered here as well. But if you speak or protest or cry, you'll be sold in a common auction to the highest bidder—do you want that?"

Scared speechless, Tuya shook her head.

"Then say nothing and do nothing until you are told to speak and do."

"Tanutamon may enter." After the gatekeeper unlocked the gate, Tuya followed her master into a long corridor painted with scenes from daily life in the king's house. She recognized the sharp, clear features of Amenhotep II and his royal consort, Queen Merit-Amon, whose pictures also adorned a wall in Donkor's house.

A tall, regally dressed black man appeared from a doorway in the corridor. "Welcome, my friend Tanutamon." Tuya lifted her eyes to look at the stranger. He was not Egyptian, but bore the features of the people from the southern reaches of the Nile. A small paunch hung over the waistband of his kilt, and deep lines creased his dark face.

"It is good to see you, Kratas," Tanutamon said, bowing. "May you remain in the favor of Amon-Re, king of the gods, of Ptah, of Thoth, and of all the gods and goddesses who are in Thebes."

"The same to you, my friend," Kratas answered. "And how may I help you today?"

Tanutamon pivoted slightly and pointed at Tuya. "My younger mistress has outgrown her childhood maid and wishes to sell her." He rolled his eyes, effectively sending the disloyal message that he disagreed with his mistress's judgment. "Because I am obedient, I thought to take her to the marketplace, but surely such a young woman should be offered first to his majesty Pharaoh. Surely there is room in his harem for a young beauty?"

Kratas's eyes swept over Tuya's slender figure. "She is… unspoiled?"

"She has been carefully guarded. She is of age, at least fifteen years, and has excellent manners. Donkor, as you know, is a man of breeding and noble reputation. I can assure you that any slave from his house will bring honor to the house of Pharaoh."

Kratas stepped toward Tuya and ran his hand over her arm. She blushed, uncomfortable with his familiarity.

Kratas's mouth tipped into a faint smile. "Pharaoh likes the shy ones. Not for him a brazen prostitute."

"So you will buy her?"

"For one hundred deben weight of silver, with an extra ten for you," Kratas said, snapping his fingers toward a boy who waited in the shadows of a broad pillar.

Tanutamon smiled with warm spontaneity. "It is agreed. You are most generous, Kratas."

The boy ran to his master, a gilded chest in his hands, and Kratas withdrew a handful of silver coins. "I am not being overly generous," he said, emptying a handful of silver into Tanutamon's broad palm. "I am sure such a girl is worth much more."

Kratas paused outside the women's room where he kept recent additions to Pharaoh's slaves. The new girl sat with crossed arms while other women sponged her body and washed her hair.

Tanutamon was right to bring the girl to Pharaoh's house. She possessed a sweet shyness that was refreshingly different from the practiced, pouty beauties of Pharaoh's harem. Perhaps, in time, she would harden and grow into a stupid, bovine woman, but Kratas was certain Pharaoh would find this youthful flower to his liking. If not for the knife that had made him a eunuch, Kratas would have bought her himself.

He leaned against the wall and rubbed his chin. The new girl was taller than most, and held herself like a lady. She had not shaved her head as did so many wig-loving slaves of rich women, but kept her long hair, which framed her face and elongated her neck. Her facial features were elegant, her nose slender and the nostrils delicate. When she looked up, her eyes shone like a stream of gold in the fading light; they were deep, watchful eyes that missed little.

A chuckle of satisfaction escaped him. In one week, if the girl proved willing, he could turn her into a queen to rival Merit-Amon, or even the king's favorite wife, Teo. With the right garments, a proper wig, cosmetics and jewels…

Kratas clapped for his servant and frowned when the boy did not appear. Most slaves were a defeated, worthless lot. He'd give his right arm to purchase one that was dependable and trustworthy, but he could more easily count the waves of the Nile than find such a creature.

Chapter Six

Outside the throne room of Amenhotep II, Potiphar paced and cleared his throat. His men, Pharaoh's bodyguards, had already taken their positions beside the throne dais. Usually he stood in front of them, facing all who dared approach the king, but in the night Potiphar had received word that Pharaoh insisted on formally greeting him after the battle in the desert.

He shifted uneasily. The enemy had been defeated, but not without cost to Egypt's armies. At least a score of Egyptian warriors had perished, and three had been captured by the rebels. Potiphar wasn't sure if this formal audience had been arranged for public praise or punishment.

Behind Potiphar, a corps waited, their arms laden with an assortment of swords, helmets, spears and cunningly worked arrows. These represented the spoils of war Potiphar gathered after the skirmish, but they were a paltry symbol of the battle's true success. Rebels had dared to rise and challenge Pharaoh's authority, and the king had again proven himself to be every bit as cunning and fierce as his father. The rebellious outer settlements should not rise again in this king's lifetime.

"Potiphar, captain of the guard, Pharaoh calls for you!"

As two slaves pulled open the great double doors, Potiphar inhaled a deep breath and moved into the long, sunlit throne room. Brilliant murals depicting the king's military exploits had been painted on the walls of the room, and in front of these paintings, to Potiphar's left and right, the king's courtiers and members of the royal family witnessed the day's business. In a far corner, a group of musicians played softly on harps and lyres. The green tile floor, gleaming like the Nile itself, stretched before Potiphar in a seemingly endless vista. Conscious of hundreds of eyes on him, he walked toward the throne.

With military discipline, Potiphar kept his gaze focused on the king and his favorite wives though he jerked his chin in a brief acknowledgment of his guards, who stood alert around the royal family. To the right of the king's throne stood his eldest son and heir, seven-year-old Webensennu, and behind the eldest son stood the younger, four-year-old Abayomi. The queen, seated to the left of the king, was surrounded by a group of fashionably dressed ladies of the royal harem. Her majesty's pet dwarf waddled in front of her chair, scowling at Potiphar as if he took too long to traverse the royal throne room.

After Potiphar bowed his head toward the queen, the dark eyes under the gold tiara and weighty wig blinked slowly in response. To keep from glancing in fear to Pharaoh, Potiphar forced himself to read the bold engraving on the queen's gilded chair: Mother of Upper and Lower Egypt, Follower of Horus, Guide of the Ruler, Favorite Lady.

Finally Potiphar allowed himself to look on the person and face of his sovereign and only god. Amenhotep had dressed in complete royal regalia for this meeting, a sign that could portend evil or good. On his head Pharaoh wore the red and white double crown signifying the union between Upper and Lower Egypt. At the front of the headdress gleamed a golden model of the cobra goddess Wadjet, who could deal out instant death by spitting flames at any enemy who dared threaten the king. A long white robe disguised the king's wiry, athletic body, and the wide pectoral at his breast covered the battle scars he had won while fighting with Potiphar against the Asiatic city-states. Over everything, beating against Pharaoh's heart, hung the heavy necklace known as the Gold of Praise. Pharaoh wore it because he was King. A select few men wore it because they had earned Pharaoh's admiration.

Potiphar allowed his eyes to dart toward the battle paintings to remind Pharaoh that they had been through much together. *I remember, my king. Do you?*

Amenhotep's dark gaze met and held Potiphar's as he extended the crook and flail. "Come forward, Potiphar," Pharaoh called, the tip of his false beard wagging like the finger of a scolding tutor.

Potiphar's feet obeyed.

"I am the embodiment of the god Horus," Amenhotep continued, speaking slowly for the scribes who transcribed every word. "I am Golden Horus, the king of Upper and Lower Egypt. I am the son of the sun-god Re. I am your father, Potiphar, and I wish to honor you this day."

Potiphar closed his eyes, afraid he gazed too hungrily on the heavy chain of gold around Pharaoh's neck. By the king's favor he had a house and cattle and sheep and goats and slaves. He had more than he knew how to manage, but the Gold of Praise had always eluded him.

"What can I give you, my son Potiphar, that you do not already have? I have long pondered this question. I and my fellow gods have already blessed you with life and health."

"It is enough, O Pharaoh," Potiphar answered. He fell to his knees and pressed his forehead to the ground. "It is enough that you, a god, have consented to rule over us. I am honored beyond any man because you allow me to serve as the captain of your guard."

"And yet I think it is not enough," the king answered.

Potiphar rose from the floor, in grave danger of losing his self-control as he stared at his king. The royal hand was fingering the Gold of Praise…

"My wife, mother of all Egypt, has given me the answer," Pharaoh said, his paint-lengthened eyes narrowing in some secret amusement. "What you need, noble Potiphar, is a woman's touch to steady the lion's heart that roars in your breast. You need a wife."

Potiphar stared at Amenhotep in the paralysis of astonishment. Gold and favor he had expected, but a wife? He had no interest in women, no need for one, and his independent spirit rebelled at the thought of an equal to share his house and wealth.

"I—I have not thought of taking a wife," Potiphar stammered, finding his tongue. An idea leapt into his mind and he ran with it, pouring forth golden words to soothe Pharaoh's prideful ear. "A wife, my king, might impede my service to you. You are a god, you can divide your limitless time and power between your duties and your pleasures, but I am a man of restricted capacities. I would rather surrender my life than one iota of my devotion to you."

"Well spoken," Pharaoh said, nodding. He raised the ancient crook, the symbol of the shepherd's staff by which Pharaoh guided his people. "But you will not deny me this gift, Potiphar. I will give you a woman, and you may marry her or not, as you please. As the sun-god embarked this morning, the keeper of the royal harem reported that an exquisite maiden has been brought to the palace for my pleasure. I give her to you, noble Potiphar, as a token of my divine approval."

"A thousand thanks, my king," Potiphar said, not daring to protest again. "I will honor and cherish this beneficent tribute."

"I know you will." Pharaoh placed the crook across his chest. "Go now, and walk in the favor of Amon-Re and your king."

The return of the crook to the king's chest meant the interview was over. The musicians played louder as Potiphar stood and walked backward from the throne room. He would have to find the harem girl and take her to his house straightaway, or some wagging tongue would tell the king that his favor had not been readily appreciated. Though Potiphar felt secure in Pharaoh's favor, never was it wise to assume anything in the royal court.

Since only emasculated slaves and the king might enter the harem's chambers, Kratas escorted Potiphar's prize from the royal apartments to the wide room where foreign slaves were sorted and evaluated. Despite his disinterest, Potiphar smiled in appreciation at the sight of the slender girl walking by the eunuch's side. Tall and willowy, her skin was the color of burnished honey and surely as sweet. She wore a simple linen sheath that accented her regal posture, and her face, when she finally lifted it, was as elegantly chiseled as the goddesses in the finest temples.

"I must thank you as well as Pharaoh," Potiphar told Kratas, his eyes sweeping over the girl. "She will be a beautiful addition to my household."

The eunuch bowed. "Is your house fully staffed, my lord Potiphar? We have just purchased several slaves from traveling Midianites. The Asiatics will not do for Pharaoh—he wants only Nubian slaves."

"I don't know, Kratas." Relieved for an excuse to turn from the fear-widened eyes of the girl, Potiphar glanced around the room. Several bearded men, uncouth and raveled in appearance, sat or lay on the floor in a molten mess of humanity.

They looked at him with burned-out eyes, soured with bitterness. Most wore defeat like a banner, but one youth caught his eye. Though stained with dust and fatigue, the teenager's face seemed lighted from within. Some god had chiseled indomitable pride into that flushed face, along with intelligence and hard-bitten strength. This lad, if harnessed correctly, would pull more than his share of the workload.

"That one." Potiphar pointed to the boy. "How much?"

Kratas frowned. "You don't want him. His arm has been broken, and his body burns with fever from the devils of the desert. He'll die before two suns have set."

"I don't think he is ready to die," Potiphar countered. "How much?"

The eunuch scratched his chin and eyed Potiphar thoughtfully. "Fifty deben weight of silver."

"You have just said he is worthless. Ten."

"I paid forty for him. Do you want your king to suffer a loss?"

"Within two days the crocodiles will have him. Take twenty, and be content."

Kratas frowned again, then he nodded. "So be it, Lord Potiphar. But I do you this favor only because our divine pharaoh holds you in high esteem."

"So it would appear," Potiphar answered, pulling his purse from his kilt.

Through a haze of exhaustion and pain, Yosef saw the exchange of silver and realized that he had been sold to the loud man who had come for the pretty girl. The king's man accepted the money, then one of the guards yanked Yosef upright. Colors exploded in his brain as the rope chewed on his splintered arm. The long journey had not afforded his body a chance to heal, and fever coursed through his veins like the quick, hot touch of the devil.

The girl's wrists were bound as well, then a broad-shouldered slave took the ropes and led Yosef and the girl out of the chamber. They followed the loud man as he walked through the palace courtyard and along the streets of Thebes. People babbled in an unfamiliar tongue as they walked, and though Yosef had managed to pick up a few words on the journey southward, his thoughts drifted into a fuzzy haze in which nothing made sense. He was exhausted, and every step taxed the small store of energy he possessed. His body cried out for rest, water and peace.

He walked, dimly aware of the hot sun, whining wind and the rushing Nile at his right, then the sound of the river retreated into the gray fog around him. He slumped to the ground, surrendering to the cloud of pain that had threatened him since Dothan.

He thought he slept for a long time, perhaps days. When he opened his eyes again, he was lying on a narrow bed in a darkened chamber. A rushlight burned in a corner of the room, and in the flickering light he could see walls covered with a patina of dirt. The air felt as if it had been breathed too many times, and he gasped for breath. He had passed his life in tents and open fields; the confining atmosphere of the small space was almost unbearable.

At the sound of his gasp, a dark shape on the floor stirred. Yosef blinked in surprise when a blanket lifted and a pale face peered out at him. A spirit? He stared in astonishment as the pale face spoke, but Yosef could not understand the words.

"Have I died?" he whispered, struggling to sit up. For a moment he dared hope that he was at home in his father's tents and the memories of the past few days were only a lingering nightmare. But then the creature murmured something and pressed a hand to his chest, gently forcing him back onto the bed. He realized then that his guardian was no ghost, but a flesh-and-blood creation. Slowly, the memory of his last conscious day returned. The girl beside him was the slave who had journeyed with him to this place.

"You are—?" he asked in Hebrew, pointing to her.

The girl lifted her brows, then the light of understanding lit her dark eyes. "Tuya," she whispered, resting her delicate hand on her chest. She pointed to him. "Paneah."

"No." He shook his head as an inexplicable surge of anger rose within his breast. Had his brothers stolen even his name? "I am Yosef."

"Yosef?" She shook her head and pointed toward the doorway. "Potiphar." Her hand fell on his head. "Paneah."

Yosef sighed and let his head fall back to the bed's curious headrest. Anger and denial were of no use. He had a new name. A new position—because of his brothers' treachery he who had been the favored son was now a slave.

What had God done with his dreams of power and authority? Who would bow to him in this foreign place—cattle?

As the girl settled beside him, Yosef closed his eyes in frustrated grief. At least a measure of his strength had returned. His arm no longer throbbed, and the fever-fog that had clouded his thoughts had lifted. He lay still, helpless in his ignorance and weakness, lost in the lonely silence of the night.

He would never see his father again. Nor his brothers, nor the two bright-eyed daughters of the camel-trader he had teased with promises of marriage. Grief blossomed in his chest, crushing his lungs, stealing the air he needed to breathe. Like a drowning man he gasped aloud, trying to lift his head, reaching out for the family he would never see again—

The girl caught his hands, then stroked his brow and murmured gentle sounds. As if she sensed his thoughts, she began to hum, and the room warmed to the odd melody.

Someone had tended him—probably this slave. Yosef lifted his head to look at the fine shape of her mouth and the slender column of her throat. A blush colored her cheeks when her dark gaze caught his, but she didn't look away. A half-hearted smile tugged at his lips and she returned it, her face shimmering like sunbeams on the surface of the ribbon of river that ruled this land.

Perhaps, Yosef thought, steeling his heart against grief and despair, God had shown mercy by bringing him to a girl who could be a well of understanding and hope in this heathen wilderness.

After her arrival at Potiphar's house, Tuya was spared from her new master's attention because the sick slave needed a nurse and no one else in the household seemed willing or able to care for him. And during the days that she nursed Paneah, Tuya discovered that although Potiphar owned a vast villa with many rooms and many servants, the poorly organized estate barely functioned. Because he spent most of his time on military expeditions or in the presence of Pharaoh, Potiphar had neither the time nor the inclination to oversee his own property.

But Tuya's first concern was for her patient. On the day the master placed him into her care, the young man from Canaan was flushed with fever beneath the stubble of his beard. Under the dirty bandage around his arm, Tuya found an oozing wound from which bare bone protruded. While the young man was unconscious, she sent for a surgeon to set the bone and pour wine over the broken skin. After manipulating the bone and wrapping the arm in clean bandages, the surgeon assured her he had done all he could do. Now the young man's fate rested in the hands of the gods.

Tuya sat by the side of her fellow slave and worried. She had tended to this young man's physical body, but what if the gods wanted appeasement before he would be healed? She knew she could never make an offering to Bastet. Though that goddess had been the favorite in Donkor's house, Ramla's cool betrayal had hardened Tuya's heart against the cat goddess. Finally she begged one of the kitchen slaves for a stone statue of Montu, the war god and guardian of the arm.

The statue depicted a man with a hawk's head surrounded by the golden disk of the sun. Tuya took the statuette to the sickroom, where she placed it in a shaft of sunlight and began a healing chant: "As for the arm of Paneah, it is the arm of Montu, on whose head were placed the three hundred and seventy-seven Divine Cobras. They spew forth flame to make you quit the arm of Paneah, like that of Montu. If you do not quit the temple of Paneah, I will burn your soul, I will consume your corpse! I will be deaf to any desire of yours. If some other god is with you, I will overturn your dwelling place; I will shadow your tomb, so you will not be allowed to receive incense, so you will not be allowed to receive water with the beneficent spirits, and so you will not be allowed to associate with the Followers of Horus.

"If you will not hear my words, I will cut off the head of a cow taken from the forecourt of Hathor! I will cut off the head of a sacred hippopotamus in the forecourt of Set! I will cause Sebek to sit enshrouded in the skin of a crocodile, and I will cause Anubis to sit enshrouded in the skin of a dog! Then indeed shall you come forth from the temple of Paneah!"

Every morning Tuya threatened the statue of Montu with her fierce refrain, and every morning the young man on the bed seemed stronger. He ate gruel from her bowl before the first week had ended, sipping the broth from the wooden spoon without speaking, his dark eyes flickering with a reserve Tuya couldn't understand. Why didn't he seem more grateful? He was a slave, as she was, and slaves were not often blessed with the tender care he had been allowed to receive. He could have been sent immediately to work in the fields; few masters would care if a slave costing only twenty deben weight of silver dropped dead over a furrow.

As he slept, Tuya studied the stranger. Though his illness had left him wafer-thin, finely defined muscles slid beneath his skin's golden tan. A head taller than most Egyptians, his dark hair flowed in gentle waves to his shoulders and was perfectly matched by the beard that had filled in the clean purity of his profile. His hands, with long, sensitive fingers, were well-kept, and Tuya noticed the lack of calluses on his palms. Perhaps she was wrong in assuming that he had been born to slavery.

After a few days he began to speak and gesture with his good arm. In the weeks that followed, he proved to be a willing pupil as Tuya schooled him in the basics of the Egyptian tongue. He had a sharp and clear mind; rarely did she have to explain anything more than once.

"Who is that you pray to?" he asked one morning when she had finished bowing to the statue in the sunlight.

Tuya rose and reverently put the statue away. Montu had met all her requests; he deserved to be handled with respect. "Only the king has access to the gods. Only he can pray. I was chanting before Montu, an ancient war god. He has healed your arm."

Horror flashed in the young man's eyes. "Please don't think such a thing! It is an abomination for my people to bow before any stone object. We worship the invisible god, the one and only creator of heaven and earth."

Tuya sank to a papyrus mat on the floor. Only one god! Despite his quick intellect, this youth was utterly unsophisticated. She tilted her head and looked at him. "Does your god have a name?"

"The god of Avraham, Yitzhak and my father Yaakov spoke

to my forefathers as El Shaddai," he answered, lifting his chin. "He is God Almighty, the unseen god."

Tuya shook her head. "Amon is the invisible god," she explained in the voice she would have used to teach an ignorant child. "He is Amon-Re, king of the gods, the chief god of our king's empire. He is the creator, the one who rose from chaos and created maat, the principle that guides our actions. He created all things that move in the waters and on the dry land, then he took a form like ours, becoming the first pharaoh. After a long life, he ascended to the heavens and left the other gods in charge of the earth." She couldn't resist smiling. "There are many gods, Paneah. Our land grows gods as freely as it grows grain."

The young man gave her a quick, denying glance. "My god is not Amon-Re. And my name is not Paneah. It is Yosef."

Tuya lowered her voice. "Our master gave you a new name in the hope that you would survive. The name is a gift, for Paneah means 'he lives.' This Yosef is foreign to our ears, and the master will not like it."

The young man did not answer, but regarded her silently for a moment. Then a shy smile tweaked the corner of his mouth. "If my master will not call me Yosef, then you must. I give my true name to you and you alone, for you are the only one in this land who has shown kindness to me."

His eyes touched her with warmth, and Tuya struggled with the inner confusion his smile always elicited. "All right, Yosef," she said finally, managing the foreign pronunciation as best she could. "But I will not speak that name in front of the master. I will do nothing to offend him, for a slave who offends will be sold."

His heavy eyelids closed. Outside the small chamber, darkness approached with the silken slowness of a languid tide. Shadows lengthened in the room, and Tuya shifted uncomfortably as she looked out at the fading light. Sunset had been her favorite time of day in Donkor's house, the time when she and Sagira relaxed and settled down to sleep. Now darkness brought nothing but phantoms of the past.

She swallowed hard, over a throat that ached with sorrow.

"Was it so terrible?" Yosef asked, his voice quiet and low in the darkening room.

Tuya started; she had assumed he slept. "What?"

"Whatever it is that fills your face with sadness."

His gaze held her tight, and Tuya had an odd feeling that he had forgotten himself and cared only for her. No one had ever made her feel that way before. She shivered, recalling her overwhelming feeling of helplessness, her fear of facing Pharaoh as a concubine, her still uncertain future. "Why does the past matter?" she finally answered, whispering in the gloom. "You have faced terrible things, too. Your hands tell a story, Yosef, and they say you were not born a slave."

His nod was barely perceptible. "I was betrayed and abandoned by my brothers," he said, his voice somber and flat. "I once dreamed of greatness, and now I am a slave on an invalid's bed." In his eyes Tuya caught a glimpse of some internal struggle, but he did not weep or grow angry. "All I have seen teaches me to trust El Shaddai for all I have not seen."

Bitter tears stung her eyes. "I was abandoned by one who called herself my sister," she whispered, tearing her gaze from his face. She stared into the darkness, reliving those terrible hours. "During the one night I spent in Pharaoh's house I dreamed that I stood on a round disk while the sun-god threw his arms around me. In that moment I felt protected, safe and loved."

She looked up at Yosef again. "I don't believe in dreams, because we slaves always wake up to a new fear. There is no escape, because a slave cannot know what lies ahead."

"God knows," Yosef answered, his hand reaching for hers. Stung by the unexpected gesture, Tuya withdrew her arm, then relented and placed her fingers in his strong grip. She did not want to become attached to this youth, for Potiphar might sell him once his health had been restored.

But for now, she felt blessed to have a friend.

Chapter Seven

Tuya had entered Potiphar's household at the beginning of the inundation, the four winter months of the year. Within two weeks the fever had left Yosef's body, but since he could not work in the house or the fields with a broken arm, Tuya began to teach him the written language of the Egyptians. She had learned the seven hundred signs of the hieroglyphic language along with Sagira, and though her rendering of the pictorial elements would never be as perfect or as elegant as those of a professional scribe, Yosef had no trouble understanding the meaning of her scratchings.

As the Nile receded and the fertile silt-laden land reappeared, his mind became occupied with learning. Tuya found that Potiphar did not care what his slaves did; his concerns centered on Pharaoh, the prison and his guards. So each morning after bringing Yosef his breakfast of bread and parched corn, she spread before him several shards of broken pottery and a basket filled with flakes of limestone. A papyrus reed made a fine pen, and Yosef often detained her, asking questions as he practiced his writing and honed his understanding. His brain was like a sponge, always absorbing, always demanding more. In a few months he would master what the royal scribes took years to learn.

"What is the sign for 'captive'?" Yosef asked one day, looking up from the shards he had covered with scrawlings.

Tuya peered over his shoulder. "It is the sign of a kneeling man that you have drawn, but the hands extend behind him and are bound," she said. "The sign can also mean 'enemy' or 'rebel.'"

Yosef chewed on the end of his pen. "What is the sign for 'Pharaoh'? And how may I show it with other signs?"

"You wouldn't dare." Tuya took a step back. "Pharaoh's name is sacred. To write it is almost a sacrilege. If it is absolutely necessary to write his name, you must enclose it in a circle, the sign of the sun."

Yosef turned back to his writing, and Tuya hurried out the door with the breakfast tray. Distracted by her thoughts, she nearly stepped into a pile of dung in the courtyard. She gritted her teeth, annoyed that someone had left the cattle pen open. She'd have to speak to the stockyard boys.

Donkor's prosperous household and Potiphar's estate were like a tree and its reflection on the Nile, Tuya decided. The former thrived in prosperity, the latter, being insubstantial, only appeared to flourish. Though Potiphar's large estate was well-situated, his slaves were a disjointed mass of workers, a hive without a queen. After a week of trying to function in total disorganization, Tuya called the servants together, announced that she had come from a nobleman's house, and assigned her fellow slaves to various stations. She gave orders to the kitchen slaves every morning, saw to it that the bathrooms, cattle yards and stables were cleaned out, and ordered that the waters of the pool be changed and stocked with fish. Anyone who did not obey would be brought before the master, who might choose to beat them or sell them...

Used to the lazy life of fat cats, the slaves obeyed, but they grumbled as they worked.

Tuya could not believe that Pharaoh's captain lived in such a disorderly house. Despite his lionlike reputation, the slaves did not fear or respect him, for he did not respect his home or his lands. Discipline did not exist in the household, for as long as Potiphar had an edible meal and a bed to lie on, he made no demands. He held no parties, commemorated no feasts or festivals. The captain of the guard found his amusements elsewhere and spent most of his time in the palace.

Tuya took her problems to Yosef, and discovered that although he had never lived in an Egyptian house, he had strong opinions as to how people should be handled. He had a gift for administration and his diplomatic suggestions about how to handle the recalcitrant slaves helped Tuya establish the changes she wanted to make.

When Yosef was strong enough to move about, Tuya took him on a tour of the villa. Potiphar's house resembled every other Theban nobleman's except for two things: it contained the jail for Pharaoh's prisoners, and it held little charm. Surrounded by a high, crumbling wall of mud-dried brick, the house stood in the center of an extensive plot of valuable riverfront land. A towered gateway led into the estate, and the prison warden's lodge rose immediately at the visitor's left hand. The prison, a collection of stone buildings, lay off to the east, far away from the main house. Tuya assured Yosef they would have no responsibility for the prison. Potiphar kept a slovenly house, but his guards ran a secure dungeon. Their lives depended on it.

To the right of the entry, a small path lined with drooping trees led to the family temple. "When I first came here, the dilapidated look of this place revealed that our master is not a religious man," Tuya whispered to Yosef. "No incense burned in the censers, no offerings had been spread, and the gods themselves were covered in dust. No wonder they have not blessed Potiphar's household! I cleaned the statues and appointed one of the slave children to bring food, water and incense each morning and night."

Yosef said nothing as she led him from the temple. The narrow dirt path in front of them pointed a curving finger toward the west, leading to a flight of steps and a pair of peeling columns. Beyond them was an inner courtyard and a doorway framed in stone. The lintel had been carved with Potiphar's name and position, but the paint had weathered out of the fading letters. A vestibule stood at the end of the porch and led to the north loggia, a reception room that had been poorly furnished and barely decorated. The west loggia, used by most families as a sitting room in winter, stood totally unfurnished and smelled of dust, as did the guest rooms.

The master's bedroom was as primitive as a battlefield tent, and the bathroom offered neither a slab for bathing nor a basin for washing the hands. Throughout the house, sprained doors hung open and walls shed their coats of fading paint. The stables, servants' quarters, kitchen and stockyard were located on the southern and eastern sides of the house so the prevailing wind would carry away the odors of dung fires, cooking food, horse sweat and the slaves' sour beer, but the servants of Potiphar had allowed sewage, garbage and manure to accumulate for so long that the sirocco winds accumulated in a single blast could not have diffused the stench.

Tuya noticed that Yosef perked up when she led him to the stockyard. Potiphar's horses were in fine fettle, for the master loved to ride and often engaged in chariot racing, but the few cattle in the pen were scrawny and blotched with skin diseases. Yosef paid special attention to the cattle, probing their skins with deft fingers and examining their eyes and noses with great care. "I know how to cure this condition," he said, catching up to Tuya as she strode through the stockyard. "With the right grains and a poultice or two, these cattle can be made well."

"That would please our master."

From the stockyard, an open, roofless corridor led to the well, and beyond the wall surrounding the well lay the master's formal gardens. Tuya showed Yosef the small door that led to the gardens. The pool, which had been stagnant and laden with green scum, now glimmered in the sun while lotus plants dotted its surface. Yosef gave the area an admiring smile. "This is beautiful."

"The blue lotus is my favorite," Tuya said, unwillingly remembering the lotus blossoms of Sagira's pool.

"Not just the flowers," Yosef answered. "Everything. You have done well."

"Not I alone," Tuya answered, taking his uninjured arm as she led him back to the servants' quarters. A thin sheen of perspiration shone on Yosef's forehead, and she knew the brief walk had tired him. "Without your encouragement, I would never have had the nerve to speak to the other servants."

If any of the older slaves bore resentment toward Tuya, they did not dare show it after Potiphar praised her administration. He called her into his presence one evening as he sat at dinner in the central hall. From the high windows near the ceiling, the rays of sunset tinged the room with gold.

"You were presented to me on account of your beauty," Potiphar said after she knelt at his feet. "But now I find that you are more than ornamental."

Bent into submission, Tuya felt her stomach tighten. Donkor had never summoned her into his presence, and the few occasions she had faced Kahent had ended in punishment or rebuke. What did Potiphar have in mind?

"Rise, girl, and speak freely," her master mumbled through a mouthful of food.

Slowly, Tuya stood, lifting her head at the last moment. Potiphar sat before her, his hands busy with his food, his eyes bright and alert as an eagle's. She gathered her courage. "What would you have me say?"

He swallowed. "How does a harem girl know so much about running a house?"

"If it please you, my lord, I was not reared for the harem. Before entering Pharaoh's house, I was companion to Sagira, daughter of Donkor, a kinsman of the king."

Potiphar bit into the pigeon the cook had prepared according to Tuya's direction. "Does Donkor know you live now with me?"

Tuya shook her head. "I have no way of knowing, my lord. I was sold when his daughter no longer wanted—had need of—a companion."

Potiphar lifted his goblet and took a deep drink, then sighed and smacked his lips. "Well, Tuya, I have no harem and no need of a concubine. But I like what you have done, so you may continue to oversee the house."

Relief washed over her, but Tuya did not leave. In three months, Potiphar had spoken to her only once, and if all went well in his house he might never speak to her again. If she wanted to speak to him of Yosef, she'd have to do it now. For despite her intentions to remain aloof from the young man's dancing eyes, she could not bear the thought of waking one day to find him gone.

"If it please you, my lord—"

The master lifted a brow. "You have a question?"

"A suggestion. If you want your estate to truly prosper, you would do well to heed the advice of Paneah, the injured slave you bought from Pharaoh's court. His arm is now mended, and he has cured your cattle of a mange that would have spread through the herd. He is a capable overseer. Let me supervise the kitchens, but place everything else in Paneah's hands. By Pharaoh's life, I swear he will not fail you."

"By all the gods, I knew he was bright." Potiphar grinned. "Bring him to me at once."

Tuya hurried away, her heart as light as her step. Yosef would turn the estate into the pride and treasure of Thebes. And soon he would be as important to Potiphar as he had become to her.

Potiphar

And it came to pass from the time that he had made him overseer in his house, and over all that he had, that the LORD blessed the Egyptian's house for Yosef's sake; and the blessing of the LORD was upon all that he had in the house, and in the field.

Genesis 39:5

Chapter Eight

A year passed. The waters of the Nile altered from the thick silk of the inundation to the green of verdigris shining on copper. Potiphar's slaves tilled the soil of his lands during the proyet, the months of the land's emergence, and harvested during shemu, the four months of drought. Far to the south, monsoon winds swept inland from the great ocean and dumped torrential rains on the highlands of the continent, feeding the tributary known as the Blue Nile. Through steep mountain gorges, tracts of marshland, and fetid jungles, the swollen river roiled northward and merged with the White Nile. Beyond the point of their convergence lay six cataracts; the northernmost cataract, a craggy gorge through which the floodwaters tumbled in an angry rush, marked the southern boundary of Egypt.

Unaware of the natural forces at work, at the summer solstice the priests made their offerings to Egypt's gods and waited for the annual arrival of the bounteous flood. Pharaoh prayed to the god Hapi, begging him to pour the holy waters into the river known since ancient times as Hep-ur, or "sweet water." According to legend and Egyptian belief, Hapi sat on a mountain and poured the Nile on the land from two bottomless pitchers. One pitcher brought forth the sweet bright green river of harvest time, from the other flowed the gray, silt-laden waters of the inundation, needed to flood and fertilize the thirsty Egyptian fields. Pharaoh and the priests did not doubt that the gray waters would come, but they begged the god to dispense his gift with mercy and wisdom. Too much water and villages would be swept away; too little and Egypt would starve.

When Sirius, the dogstar, arrived in the vast and immeasurable canopy of the night sky, the priests announced that the waters were near. As they had predicted, the flood rushed northward a few days later. Over the centuries, natural levees had built up along the Nile, and on the Night of the Cutting of the Dam, the people of Thebes mounted these natural walls along the riverfront and waited for Pharaoh's signal. Once the dam was "cut," or broken, the precious waters flooded a series of man-made channels and carried their nourishment to the fields.

Scowling at the noise of celebration, Potiphar climbed one of the towers built into the walls of his villa. To the west he could see the silver water and a shimmering skyline where earthen dams at the border of his property bristled with life as the sun dropped behind the horizon. Already glowing orbs of torchlight moved through the darkness.

A twinge of nostalgia struck him. In every year until this one, he had been at Pharaoh's side for this ceremony. He would have been on the royal barge this year, too, but a royal courtier called Narmer had convinced Pharaoh that Potiphar needed time to rest.

The high squeal of the priests' trumpets rent the air. Though he couldn't see clearly in the darkness, Potiphar knew that long boats of bundled papyrus reeds were breaking through the banks to allow the river to spill into the land. He smiled.

Aside from Narmer's tiresome presence, he had no reason to complain. The gods had been good to him in the past year. Under Paneah's direction, his cattle had begun to produce and his fields to grow. His slaves, a motley crew who had once managed his house in spite of themselves, had become a disciplined corps, each content to labor in his or her assigned task.

While Paneah oversaw the stockyard, fields and business of running the estate, the girl, Tuya, had become a valuable housekeeper. Under her direction Potiphar's new cupbearer had become almost as skilled as Taharka, the esteemed slave who had been purchased to grow, ferment and offer Pharaoh's own wines. Potiphar wasn't sure what sort of magic Tuya had worked, but he now slept on perfumed linen sheets and wore pressed and pleated kilts.

Even Pharaoh had noticed a change. "How polished and well-fed you look, Potiphar," he had remarked only a few days before. "Age certainly seems to agree with you."

"I only reflect your bounty, divine Pharaoh," Potiphar had replied, bowing. "The light of your favor has caused the Nile to bring forth a good crop. Your people will not hunger this year."

Paneah had worked wonders in the fields outside the walls of Potiphar's villa. What had been a sprawling field of haphazard planting was now a neat arrangement of small squares, each divided by mud walls the height of a man's hand. Between the squares a runnel conveyed water from a shaduf at the river's edge. Each square could be watered separately by blocking the runnel with a mud wall, thus insuring that thirsty crops received plenty of water while the drier crops were not overwhelmed.

After the floodwaters had receded in the spring, Paneah urged the serfs to walk slowly and drop seed in neat rows across Potiphar's muddy fields. Teams of long-horned African cows followed the slaves, their hooves burying the seed deep inside the life-giving earth. To ensure that the seed lay snug beneath the silty soil, Paneah had the stockmen drive a herd through the fields. Potiphar had been home long enough to watch the merry affair. A scampering young boy lured the stubborn goats through the fields with a handful of grain while the adult herdsmen chased the beasts with whips of twisted rope.

With a steadfast and sure hand, Paneah directed Potiphar's slaves through each stage of agriculture: plowing, sowing, treading in the seed, reaping, treading out the grain, winnowing, loading on donkeys and depositing the harvest in granaries. The result was a crop that filled Potiphar's coffers to overflowing. In the past he had relied on his wages as an officer in Pharaoh's army to supply his haphazard household, but after a year of Paneah's leadership, he was pleasantly surprised to realize that his household might be able to support itself. He might even become rich.

Quiet laughter interrupted his musings. Someone walked through the garden below, and Potiphar's hand automatically crept toward the dagger sheathed at his side. Rubbing his tongue against the back of his teeth, he peered through the shadows of the trees, but saw only Paneah and Tuya walking along the edge of the lotus pool.

Potiphar released his dagger. His training as a warrior kept him too much on edge. Perhaps Paneah had been right to suggest that Potiphar learn to relax in his own home. What better place could there be? The house that used to remind him of his own inefficiency had become a place of refuge, an oasis away from the quicksand of Pharaoh's court. Paneah had made the villa efficient; Tuya had filled it with the sweet sounds of singing.

He took a deep breath, forcing himself to relax his rigid posture.

"You did not!" Tuya's voice was a teasing caress in the warmth of the night. "You would not do such a thing!"

Surrendering to the human urge to eavesdrop, Potiphar stepped back into the shadows on the wall.

"I did," Paneah said, facing the young girl at his side. Her face, lit by the moon, tilted toward his. From his hiding place Potiphar could see love shining from Tuya's eyes like a star streaming in the night.

The nearness of that lovely face seemed to steal Paneah's breath for a moment, then he caught the girl's hands and held them close to his breast. "I did," he repeated, looking at her as if he could drink her in. "I did ask the shepherds to name a lamb for you. So when I go out to the fields, I will think of you instead of—"

He looked away for a moment, and Potiphar noticed the way her body curved toward him. "The old dreams again?" she whispered.

"The old memories," he said, turning his dark eyes to her glowing countenance. "My brothers. I think of them every time I walk under the sun, every time I see a herd of sheep or cattle. I pray that God will rid my heart of my sorrowful bitterness—"

Tuya's fingertips flew to his lips. "Speak not of it anymore. Anger is a poison that destroys the soul. It will destroy our happiness, too, Yosef, if you dwell on these things."

"I would not destroy your happiness for the throne of Egypt," the young man answered, his words running together in a velvet sound. As he bent to brush his lips over the girl's forehead, Potiphar felt the gall of envy burn the back of his throat. How could two slaves without power, position or possessions find happiness while he, Pharaoh's Potiphar, wandered on the wall of his villa with nothing to fill his lonely heart? It was natural that a handsome youth and a beautiful girl should find each other, for they were young and the appetites of love are fierce in youth...

But he had always been more stirred by bloodlust than lust alone.

Potiphar stood motionless until the couple parted to walk to their separate chambers, then the master clasped his hands behind his back and took the stairs down to his empty room.

Anticipation of nights in the garden with Yosef dulled the cutting edge of Tuya's loneliness. The young man had stepped into the void left by Sagira and more than filled the empty spaces in her life. He was handsome enough to set even the oldest kitchen slave's tongue to wagging when he appeared in the doorway, but Yosef's attraction for Tuya went far beyond his physical appearance. In him she found a depth of understanding and insight sorely lacking in the slaves around her. Her people were simple, cheerful and quick to learn, but most of the Nile's children were practical and unimaginative. Not given to deep speculation or thought, they were unwilling to evolve or express the abstract ideas Yosef delighted in debating.

Yosef differed from the typical Egyptian in other ways, too. While the average resident of Thebes was highly superstitious and quick to placate any god he might have offended, Yosef often spoke with deep and abiding respect of El Shaddai, the god to whom he prayed every morning. And yet his devotion could not have been based on blind faith, for though most Egyptians accepted everything the priests said without question, Yosef wanted to know the reasons behind every law or precedent Tuya mentioned.

He seemed to take a particular pleasure in bantering with Tuya about the pantheon of Egyptian gods. "You say Pharaoh is one of the gods," he teased one afternoon, "and yet they say

Pharaoh has a headache today. How can a god suffer pain? And when Pharaoh's life is done, how can a god die?"

"He is both God and man," Tuya explained, trying not to lose her patience. "When a pharaoh dies, the divine spirit is removed and placed within the heir. The chosen heir becomes God and Pharaoh, and the dead and buried god becomes king of the dead, ruler of the underworld. He becomes the great and terrible judge to whom the dead must answer for their deeds on earth."

"I would rather serve a god who cannot die," Yosef answered, laughter in his eyes. "A god who is the same yesterday, today and forever."

Tuya waved him away. "You are a dreamer."

She was about to add that dreams were foolish and risky, but the light in his eyes dimmed. "Yes, I am," he replied, and his expression filled with such pain she had resolved never to speak of dreams again.

She knew he had come from a large family in the land of Canaan. From his speech she had gleaned that he was a Hebrew, but in the last year he had taken great pains to become fluent in the Egyptian language. With his quick ear and agile tongue, every trace of his Canaanite accent had been erased. He now shaved his beard in the Egyptian fashion and wore his hair covered by a cloth of ribbed black silk. He wore the traditional white linen kilt of a slave, ornamented with an enameled collar and bronze armbands. Nothing of the Hebrews remained but his memories, and Yosef clung to them with the tenacity of a terrier. Occasionally his eyes darkened and he spoke bitterly of his brothers, but he would not dwell on the subject or speak further when Tuya pressed him.

Like the Egyptians, Yosef was gentle, devoted to his friends and his god and easily pleased. He had the confidence of a lion, a quiet air of authority and even seated he looked taller than any man in the house. She could feel the power of his presence from across a crowded room, and her heart thudded like a drum whenever he happened to pass. Without stopping to analyze her feelings, Tuya allowed her attraction for him to blossom into love. What she couldn't understand was why he seemed to resist caring for her in the same way.

His eyes had caressed her in the garden, and she knew by the way he smiled at her that he felt something for her. She could tell from his admiring gaze that he appreciated her skill at managing the household fully as much as he esteemed her beauty. Interest had radiated from the dark depths of his eyes from the first day she began to nurse him, and their friendship had deepened on a number of levels. But whenever the conversation turned to personal topics, or whenever Tuya felt Yosef was close to opening his heart, an invisible wall rose between them and he withdrew as surely as if he had moved across the garden.

Tonight Yosef was intent on the scroll in his lap. The air of the garden vibrated softly with the insect hum of the trees, and Tuya sat on the tiled walkway and trailed her fingers over the still waters of the reflecting pool. The lotus blossoms on the water moved gently in the quiet of the night shadows, a romantic picture, but Yosef's thoughts were far away.

"The language is fascinating," Yosef murmured, running his hand over the papyrus spread between his knees. "Such beauty in these hieroglyphics! You are a good teacher, Tuya, and I a poor student. If I could only learn to write this well."

"You will have no more time for learning in this house," Tuya said, glancing over her shoulder. "Those who go to scribes' schools labor from dawn until dusk for a dozen or more years. Their signs must be perfect, and the teaching priests believe a boy's ears are on his back." She smiled when Yosef looked up with an inquisitive glance. "They are great lovers of the whip," she explained, leaning toward him. "But you, Yosef, know nothing of this. Potiphar does not beat his servants."

"Only because Potiphar does not care for his household," Yosef answered, returning his attention to the scroll. "I am certain he would not hesitate to use his whip on his soldiers."

Tuya jerked upright when leather slapped against the cool stone of the patio. Potiphar stepped out of the shadows and stood before them, his eyes gleaming like lighted coals. What had he heard? She and Yosef might feel the whip yet.

"Greetings, master," she blurted out, extending her arms toward him as she touched her forehead to the floor. She closed her eyes and hoped Yosef would have the good sense to follow her example.

"Good evening," Potiphar replied. Tuya blinked in surprise. He spoke in a composed voice, like a man out for a casual walk in his garden. Had he heard nothing of their conversation?

"You may rise," the master called, and Tuya lifted her head, half expecting to feel the sting of his hand across her cheek.

But Potiphar stood before them with his hands joined loosely at his waist. Their master's weather-beaten face was calm, but something flickered in his dark eyes.

"Paneah—" he began, looking at Yosef.

"Yes, master?"

"Why does Tuya call you by a strange name?"

Yosef hesitated only for the flash of an instant. "It is not because I dislike the name you gave me. I have come to appreciate the name Paneah. The life in which I was known by another is far behind me."

Potiphar lifted a brow. "And yet this girl calls you by the other name." In one disobedient glance Tuya allowed her eyes to leave her master's face and dart toward Yosef.

A wry smile curled on Yosef's lips. "She is my bridge. She brought me from the old life safely into the new. If she had not nursed me—"

"It was you, master, who rescued him from the slave

market," Tuya added, eager to return the conversation to a more proper vein. "Paneah owes his life to you."

Potiphar nodded, but Yosef interrupted. "No. My life is owed to God."

Tuya cringed. Apparently Yosef had not been enslaved long enough to learn proper humility.

Potiphar did not take offense. "They say we owe everything to the gods," he said, offhandedly waving in the direction of the river. He returned his hands to his waist and squinted in amusement. "Which god do you credit for your health and intelligence, Paneah? Which god gave you those good looks? Hathor? Amon? Osiris, perhaps?"

"The Egyptians do not know El Shaddai," Yosef answered, giving the master a look of prideful superiority. "He is the god above all others, the Almighty God who sees and knows all."

A spasm of panic shot across Tuya's belly. Hadn't Yosef learned that a man was only as great as his gods? With one mention of his almighty deity Yosef had claimed to be greater than everyone in Egypt, even Pharaoh himself.

Potiphar nodded as if considering Yosef's reply, and a smile played briefly on his lips. "Believe in whatever you like, Paneah, for you have done well. Though I am sure your success has less to do with divine blessing than with your sharp intellect."

"I appreciate your kindness, but I must disagree," Yosef answered, bowing his head. "I have found that faith is a higher faculty than reason. Though, of course, faith is only as strong as the object in which it is placed."

Potiphar pushed his bottom lip forward. "You know I do not worship any gods. Are you saying I am weak?"

Tuya felt the blood drain from her head. What had Yosef done?

Ever the diplomat, Yosef smiled. "Each man must test his

own faith, and his own gods. You, Master Potiphar, must find strength great enough to sustain you through life. Where you will find this strength, I cannot say."

The moon, sailing across a cloud-laden sky, cast a sudden beam across Potiphar's face. His granite eyes locked on Yosef, but after a moment, he lifted his head and folded his arms. "You are clever," he said, the corner of his mouth lifting in a grudging smile. "For surely you know that I have the strength I need, Paneah, right here." His clenched fist knocked on his chest. "And because I appreciate cleverness, one day I shall reward you. Perhaps I shall reward the affection you have developed for this girl."

When the master's bony finger pointed to Tuya, she felt her frantic smile jell into an expression of shock. She had tried to hide her feelings for Yosef, for with one word Potiphar could send her away forever.

"Who can say?" Potiphar folded his arms again. "If you both serve me well, in time I will allow you to take her as your wife. If you teach my household to run itself, in six years or so I may even grant your manumission." An understanding, cocky grin spread across his features. "The collar of slavery does not suit you, Paneah. 'Twould be shameful for you to wear it too long."

With that astounding promise, Potiphar turned and disappeared into the house.

Tuya turned to Yosef in stunned surprise. "Freedom!" she whispered, hardly daring to hope. "And marriage!"

Speechless, Yosef nodded.

Yosef clasped his hands behind him as he walked down the narrow corridor to the room he shared with the other male slaves. Potiphar's offer of emancipation and marriage had taken him completely by surprise, and his emotions were still spinning like a broken twig caught in the Nile flood. After six more years of service he would be twenty-four, a young man still, and capable of building an estate of his own. Was this the avenue by which his dream would be fulfilled?

He stopped in the darkness and closed his eyes, double-checking his memory. In his dream, the sun and moon and stars had bowed before him—could they not represent the merchants of Thebes? He could be a wealthy man before he reached thirty years of age.

Perhaps. He gave himself a stern mental shake and moved on toward his room. He did not want to second-guess the god who had blessed everything he touched and everyone who touched him. Tuya, without whose guidance he could never have begun to understand the Egyptian way of thinking, had blossomed under his attention. Devoted, dependable and sympathetic, she had worked hard to ensure his success with the other slaves. Her rich, fawnlike beauty warmed his heart every time he looked her way. He could marry her without hesitation if not for—

The past. She did not know the hidden part of him, the history he concealed beneath industrious activity and casual conversation. She thought him an ordinary son from a large family, a foreigner with only fragile connections to the past. Yet he was the favored son of Yaakov, the firstborn of Rahel, the son who had stood to inherit the major portion of Yaakov's flocks and treasures and goods. Though he was younger than most of his brothers, his would have been the blessing and birthright of the eldest son, for Yaakov had loved his beautiful mother most.

As the snores of the other slaves punctuated the darkness of the room, Yosef lay down on his papyrus mat and settled his thoughts about him. He had not told Tuya the entire story of his past because the act of submerging himself into memory hurt too much. During his illness he had scarcely felt the pain of his shattered arm because his few coherent thoughts centered on his father's grief and his brothers' betrayal. Had his unfaithful brothers told their father that insane story about Yosef's fatal struggle with a wild beast? Had not one of them listened to the convicting voice of the spirit of God and confessed the truth?

Another, darker fear hovered at the edge of his mind: did they intend to kill or kidnap his mother's other son in the same way? His brother, Binyamin, was yet a boy, but with Yosef gone, Yaakov would cling to Rahel's remaining son like a shadow. Binyamin had undoubtedly been forced into Yosef's place as the favored son, and that gentle boy would never suspect that the older brothers he admired were capable of murder and betrayal...

A sudden rise of panic threatened to choke Yosef where he lay. He had nursed his wounds for too long. He should escape and join a caravan heading north; he should return to his father and expose his brothers for the misbegotten malefactors that they were—

Trust me. The voice fell on Yosef's consciousness even as he realized that the stillness of the room had not broken. The snorers slept on, undisturbed. Yosef shivered with a cold that did not come from the air. He was not alone.

As I called Avraham from Ur, I have called you to this place. Forget the former things, do not dwell on the past. I am making a new path for you! Now it springs up before you, do you not perceive it?

Yosef sat up and blinked at the shadows as the hair on his forearms lifted. Abu, the goatherd, and Bebu, the chief baker, tossed and turned as they did every night.

Yosef's heart thumped against his rib cage. If he had not heard the voice of a man, then God spoke to him—but why?

"Will you speak again?" he whispered.

No answer came in the night; he heard nothing but the scattered breathing of his fellow slaves. After a long moment, Yosef lay down again and made an effort to calm his pounding heart. Eventually he withdrew into a thin and dreamless sleep.

Tuya readied her brightest smile the next morning, but the smile died on her lips as Yosef approached the well. Hollows lay beneath his eyes, dark, bluish-gray circles. He looked as if he hadn't slept at all.

"Are you ill?" she whispered, hurrying to his side.

He gave her a polite smile that did not reach his eyes. "I am fine."

"You wear the face of a man who has been troubled by dreams."

"Would that I had been. I slept little last night."

Tuya felt the thin, cold blade of foreboding slice into her heart. Yosef had been fine before their meeting with the master and he had gone to bed immediately afterward. Apart from Potiphar's suggestion of freedom and marriage, what could have kept him awake all night? Since no slave would refuse liberty, Yosef's distress could only have come from the idea of marrying her.

"Did our master's promise...upset you?" she croaked, barely able to force the words past her unwilling lips.

His face emptied of expression. "I can't talk now. Let us begin our work, Tuya."

The sudden heaviness in Tuya's chest felt like a millstone. She dropped her water buckets and sat on a bench. "Can't we talk now?"

"No." His voice was as gentle as his words were disturbing. "I am not ready to talk about the future." A host of emotions struggled beneath the surface of his handsome face. "Some things cannot be shared before they ripen into clear thoughts."

"Even with one who loves you?" Tuya whispered, lifting her eyes to his.

Right or wrong, she'd said it. No slave dared to love another, for a life of slavery was too transitory and fleeting, but she'd just admitted her love to Yosef. Her feelings had grown in the past year; they now ran far deeper than affection and stronger than the pleasure of their stolen embraces.

"Tuya—" he began, his voice thick.

"I love you, Yosef." She slipped from the bench to fall at his feet. "I would follow you to the end of Egypt if the master were to sell you. If Anubis opened the road of the underworld for you, I would follow into death's darkness and find you in the gardens of paradise—"

"Tuya!" Yosef knelt beside her, gripping her arms in his strong hands. All shadows of restraint fled from his face as his eyes blazed. "Such fierce longing can bring only sorrow and pain."

"So you have loved," she whispered, wilting in his grasp like a thirsty lotus blossom. "At last the gods have put a figure on the barrier that stands between us. Who is she, Yosef? A Canaanite girl?"

"No." He stood and regarded her with sadness in his eyes. "Not a girl—my father loved me with the love you speak of. And now he thinks me dead while I, who would have been his heir, am enslaved in a heathen land."

Her feminine perception instantly understood. Yosef's heart had not been wounded by lost love, but by the grief of separation.

"Beloved," Tuya whispered, rising. "Don't you think we all understand what you're feeling? Every slave has a story like yours, for we lost our families when we lost our freedom. I have never known a mother or father, but I have grown accustomed to my place. And you, Yosef, remember how our master trusts you! He could not be more proud if you were his son. He believes you are blessed by the gods."

"Potiphar believes in no one but himself," Yosef answered, folding his arms. "But last night when I considered running away, God spoke to my heart…and I know I am to remain in Egypt. Perhaps my father could accept my death more easily than he could accept me—" Yosef swept his hand over his body to indicate the bronze collar at his neck and the linen skirt of a slave "—like this."

A lump formed in Tuya's throat at the thought of Yosef leaving, but she clutched at the hope that Yosef's god approved of their love.

"Surely your god is wise," she answered, leaning close. "Surely he can be trusted. You have trusted him thus far—"

"I have had no choice." Yosef looked past her toward the great blue bowl of sky. "He is the nameless longing, the voice who called Avraham out of Ur. He set a dream in my heart, and called me away from the bosom of my father. Now he bids me trust him."

"Trust him, then," Tuya said, wrapping her arms around his narrow waist. Not caring who might see, she placed her cheek against the smooth skin of Yosef's chest and heard the proud beating of his heart. "Trust your god, Yosef. As Potiphar trusts in your common sense and I trust in the strong arm of Montu, trust in your god and all will be well."

Chapter Nine

Potiphar bristled as Narmer entered his bedchamber and extended a scroll bearing a seal from the king's scribe. "Why does Pharaoh send a message instead of calling for me?" Potiphar asked, sliding his weary legs from beneath a linen sheet. "Even at this late hour I have often been summoned to the royal presence."

The young courtier regarded Potiphar with a look of unutterable boredom, but no amount of studied nonchalance could conceal the jealousy in his eyes or the disdain in his posture. Yet the man never failed to shine in Pharaoh's presence.

Narmer lifted a shoulder in a shrug. "The king thought it best to send his wishes with me," he said, underscoring his position in Pharaoh's confidence. "Perhaps you should not keep him waiting."

Scowling, Potiphar broke the seal on the scroll and read the message penned there:

In life, prosperity, health, and in favor of Amon-Re, king of the gods, and of the Ka of King Amenhotep II. Greetings, Potiphar, most trusted guard of Pharaoh. The empire enlarged by my father, Tuthmosis III, may his name be ever praised, has experienced turmoil in the eastern nomes along the river known as Euphrates. I am ready to vent my displeasure on these rebel chieftains, and await your presence for this venture. Come at once, and do not delay. Narmer waits to bring you to me.

The scroll had been sealed with Pharaoh's official scarab, and Potiphar knew he could not waste a moment of the king's patience. "I will make ready at once," he murmured, not looking up. "You will wait outside in my reception rooms. I will send a girl to wash your feet."

Narmer held up a defensive hand. "I would not stop to wash my feet while the king waits."

"Nevertheless, you shall, for I am not ready," Potiphar answered, standing. With shameless efficiency he propelled Narmer toward the doorway. When he saw Tuya walking in the corridor, he clapped his hands. "Tuya! Take this messenger to the central hall and wash his hands and feet."

"I am not, Lord Potiphar, a mere messenger," Narmer said, fury lurking beneath his smile.

"Today you are," Potiphar answered with an easy grin. "Our divine pharaoh will not mind if you are a moment out of his presence. And I will have you back at the palace before your youthful face can sprout its next pimple."

Narmer flushed and clenched his fists, but he followed Tuya.

Potiphar stalked back into his chamber, indignation seething beneath his breastbone. The trouble lay in his spending too much time at home. Of late his villa had become a refuge from the pitfalls of the palace, but while Potiphar was away, a new cat had come to toy with the royal favor. The smell of ambition rose from Narmer like a cheap perfume, and Amenhotep was wily enough to goad his old friend and fellow soldier with a fresh and competitive face.

This Narmer would not act high and mighty for long. *I may be an old cat,* Potiphar thought, stepping into a fresh kilt and fastening a belt at his waist, *but I have learned tricks from the wisest souls in this world and the one beyond.*

Abruptly, he bellowed for Paneah.

The dim haze of sleep still filled Yosef's head when he entered Potiphar's chamber and stooped to help his master dress.

"I must go away," Potiphar said as Yosef strapped on his sandals, "and I am leaving the household in your care. I cannot say how long this whim of Pharaoh's will last, for something has aroused the bloodlust in him. We are traveling to the eastern dominions and back, a journey of some months."

The sleep haze vanished like fog before the sun. "Through the lands of Canaan?" Yosef asked, not looking up. Did he dare suggest that he accompany Potiphar? The army might cross the lands of Yaakov, might even encounter the family. Yosef could return to his father in the company of the foremost military general of the world's greatest king. He could repay his brothers' treachery with righteous vengeance; in one bold move reveal that ten of Yaakov's sons were fiends and one, thought dead, alive and strong.

"Of course we'll pass through Canaan," Potiphar snapped, fumbling with the leopard-skin belt that held his dagger. "The Mitanni tribes are causing trouble, probably feuding with the Hittites."

Yosef finished fastening the sandals and reached up to hook the enclosure of the dagger belt. "You might have use for a servant on the journey."

The master's brows knitted in a frown. "I have ten thousand soldiers at my bidding, Paneah," he said, his voice surprisingly gentle. "What I need—what I have never had till now—is a home waiting when I return. I place you in charge of everything you find here. Speak with my full authority and act as my steward."

Narmer stalked into the room as Potiphar finished speaking. With a superior smirk, he lifted a jeweled hand and pointed to Yosef. "Dare you leave your house in the care of a slave? You will have nothing when we return, for even this boy will run away." He snickered. "Can Potiphar's renowned wisdom be fading?"

"My gift of discernment is still strong," Potiphar answered, not bothering to look at the younger man as he made a last-minute check of his person. "I would trust Paneah with my life."

He turned to Yosef and lowered his voice, his eagle eye staring down his nose. "I trust you, Paneah, with all I have. Do not prove my intuition wrong."

Yosef straightened. "I will not, my lord."

Potiphar nodded, then scowled out the doorway.

Rebellious would-be kings from the northeastern provinces of Carchemish and Tegarama had amassed a sizable force, but their troops proved no match for the swift battalions of Pharaoh's golden warriors. The well-organized Egyptian army, comprised of both infantry and chariot troops, flew across the desert like a whirlwind, churning up sand and wind and debris. The chariots, each manned by two soldiers and two horses, were made of the lightest wood available and designed so wounded horses could be unstrapped and the chariot hauled by prisoners of war if necessary. Behind the chariots came the infantry—foot soldiers carrying spears, shields and battle-axs to wipe the field clean of enemy troops that might have survived the first onslaught.

Potiphar rode next to Amenhotep's own chariot. The king's

charioteer, a grizzled veteran of several foreign wars, held the horses steady as the king bellowed and sent arrows in a whistling cloud toward the enemy. Potiphar preferred the battle-ax to the bow. His weapon, a curved golden blade resting in a silver-shafted handle, had been blessed by Pharaoh and had never failed to leave a battle without tasting blood.

The ground around them bristled with enemy arrows, but Amenhotep's courage did not fail. Delighting in the combat, he sent his arrows flying into waves of approaching rebels. A descending arrow glanced off the king's forehead, and blood from the wound transformed his features into a glistening mask that did more to discourage his foes than the overwhelming Egyptian weaponry. Whether from fear or intimidation, the enemy fell back, and Potiphar smiled in grim relief. This battle would not last long.

When at last the rebels threw down their weapons, scores of men lay motionless on the ground, the life gone out of them like an extinguished light. Potiphar drove his weary horses to Pharaoh's chariot and bowed. "A good victory, my king," he said, taking pains to keep his voice strong and pleasant. "Are we ready to turn for home?"

"By all the gods, no!" Amenhotep roared, his eyes still shining with the thrill of combat. "I will follow in my father's footsteps and subdue these troublesome kings again. We will march from this place to the river Euphrates, and there I will raise a stela of victory to record my accomplishments and military successes. We will return to the Nile with a host of captive kings to sacrifice to Egypt's gods, and the tale will go forth from this place. None of these will rise up against Egypt again!"

Potiphar forced a smile. "I will tell the men," he said, gathering the reins of his chariot. "Rest well, my king. May the morrow bring yet another victory."

Chapter Ten

Slanting sunlight shimmered off the glowing green foliage of the trees; the day was far too pretty to waste. From the gate of Potiphar's villa, Tuya called to Yosef. "Will you never finish? The festival is beginning!"

"The cattle and sheep don't know today is a feast day," Yosef grumbled, striding out of the stockyard. He left his box of papyrus scrolls with the gatekeeper and paused to give the man instructions. No one worked during the Feast of Opet, but Yosef seemed determined that neither Potiphar's fields nor his livestock would feel neglect during the holiday.

Yosef stepped out of the gatehouse and gave Tuya a smile as bright as the sun. "Your escort awaits you, my lady."

A deep sense of happiness flooded Tuya's soul as she took Yosef's arm. With Potiphar away, she could almost imagine that she and Yosef were lord and lady of the house. For nearly a full year Yosef had handled the estate with a firm hand, monitoring the servants who ran the fields and the stockyard and managing to keep Pharaoh's tax collectors at bay while he stockpiled Potiphar's crops and treasures. When and if the master returned from his military foray, he would find himself a vastly wealthy man.

Tuya took a deep breath of the dry air and enjoyed the warmth of the sun on her face. The rising sun had swallowed up the wind, and the dazzling blur of the sun-god's boat stood proud and fixed in the white-blue sky. Heat covered the city like a blanket, but Tuya felt deliciously cool in the exquisite white linen sheath she had sewn for herself. As fine as any lady's gown, the loose garment fastened at the shoulders with delicate tassels. A pair of red leather slippers adorned her feet, and she felt especially pampered because yellow scented saffron oil perfumed her arms and neck. The precious scent had been a gift from Yosef, and she had protested its extravagance when he slipped the vial into her hand.

"Potiphar's name will be praised when people see that even his slaves conduct themselves like royalty," Yosef murmured, giving her a heart-stopping smile. "And when they see you, my beautiful Tuya, Potiphar's reputation will ascend to the heavens."

So she had relented, hoping that the sweet scent would draw Yosef to her in the way a flower attracts a bee. Like any man who loves work, he found it difficult to relax, but Tuya took his hand and led him through the streets, explaining the meaning of the festival ceremonies and the altars and stelae that had been set up to commemorate the occasion.

"The festival begins when the shrine of the god Amon is carried from the dark chamber of his temple at Karnak into the sunlight," Tuya whispered, pulling Yosef through a jostling crowd of merrymakers who vied for a spot along the riverbank.

"Why does the god wish to leave his temple?"

"Well—" Tuya blushed "—he goes each year to visit his harem at the temple of Southern Opet."

Yosef laughed, his eyes twinkling with mischief. "And what pleasure can a harem give a god of stone?"

"Quiet!" Tuya glanced around, afraid someone would overhear his blasphemy. "Who knows what the gods do? Men cannot see into the underworld. We cannot divine things of the spirit."

"Perhaps we can," Yosef answered, but Tuya wasn't in the mood for one of his debates. Craning her neck, she pointed toward the river. "Here they come! Closer, Yosef, stand here. You've never seen anything like this!"

He didn't answer, but rested his hands on her hips as they swayed in the throng along the riverbank. They heard the anticipatory roar of the crowd, then the whine of the priests' horns and the pounding of the drum. Finally the god's cedarwood barge came into view. On the flat platform a host of bald priests in long white robes stood guard over an object swathed in white linen and supported by a gleaming altar. Many in the crowd fell to their knees as the barge passed, and petitions to the great god Amon filled the air.

"Merciful Amon, hear my cry!"

"Restore unto me the money I have lost!"

"Amon, hear the plea of a childless woman!"

"Amon-Re, grant our king safety and return him to the land!"

The barge did not travel under its own power, but teams of horses on both sides of the river's banks pulled it forward. The pious pilgrims closest to the banks scattered as the animals approached, but a few of the most fervent dashed beneath the ropes as if they meant to swim out and personally present their petitions to the god. The appearance of leather-skinned crocodiles in the water kept even the most religious celebrants on shore, however, and within a few moments the god's barge had passed.

"Now the real excitement comes," Tuya promised, smiling at Yosef. Behind the sacred god came the gold-plated barge of Pharaoh, commanded in the king's absence by Queen Merit-

Amon. On this barge the queen and the high priest of Amon made continual offerings of food and incense to the god, while on the riverbank opposite them paraded a great host that included befeathered Nubian drummers, a band of lute players, scantily clad acrobats, blind harpists and Egypt's finest wrestlers. A company of soldiers in the gilded chariots of Pharaoh's guard followed, their standards lowered to indicate that their captain was away.

"Potiphar's men," Tuya said, pride stirring in her breast as she watched the guard. "They are probably anxious for his return."

Yosef's hands tightened about her waist. "Are you?"

"No," she answered, then turned to face him. "I mean, yes. He is a good master, but it has been so nice—"

"You don't have to explain," Yosef answered, smiling. "I, too, have found myself imagining what it would be like if the house, the horses, the fields, the servants—" his gaze focused on her lips "—were mine."

The crowd around them surged and moved to follow the procession, but Yosef and Tuya stood as if rooted to the riverbank. "You could pretend until the master returns," Tuya whispered. Gathering her slippery courage, she entwined her arms about his neck. "No one here will know, Yosef, that you are not the master and I am not...your wife."

She knew he wanted her. They had worked and laughed and worried together for nearly two years, and their souls were as close as two could be without joining their bodies in the mystical union the gods had ordained for husbands and wives. She had labored to bring Yosef back from the edge of the underworld, and he had rescued her from unendurable loneliness and erased the sting of Sagira's rejection. Why shouldn't they enjoy each other? No one would care if two slaves did not wait for marriage; no one would bother two sub-citizens who found delight in each other...

"Ah, Tuya," he whispered, gazing at her with something deeper than mere masculine interest.

Her heart shuddered expectantly. The crowd continued to jostle them and a passing company of merchants argued over the price of some trinket. "Come." Yosef pulled her away. "This is not the place for us."

A trembling thrill raced through her as Yosef linked her fingers with his and took her away from the crowd of revelers.

Yes. No. Yes. No. With every step Yosef's heart turned from one conviction to the other. Why shouldn't he take this girl who loved him? Over the months he had come to trust Tuya, and in the security of her steadfast devotion he had finally found the courage to confide the secrets of his past, his hopes, even his strange dreams. Surely the feeling between them was as strong as that which had existed between his father and Rahel! And Potiphar had practically promised to grant them permission to marry. It was not a question of if, but of when. So why not now, when the bloom of youth still graced them and the fragrance of love filled the air?

He had become a man of Egypt—he dressed like an Egyptian, spoke like an Egyptian, wrote the language of the Egyptians. The Egyptians would see nothing wrong with his taking Tuya into his arms and mingling his flesh with her own. Egypt had a dozen gods and rituals dedicated to the celebration of fertility, and the act he was considering would be a ritual of worship in the eyes of the pagan priests. The other slaves did not curb their passions. Sometimes, when darkness obscured faces, some of the men in the slaves' quarters baited Yosef with doubts about his masculinity because he hadn't already surrendered to Tuya's considerable charm.

His body yearned to possess her. His heart slammed into his ribs every time he thought about pressing his lips to hers, and the sight of her shadow slipping over a wall was enough to send a wave of warmth along his pulses. He was nineteen years old, strong in limb and desire, and alone in a place where kings and slaves thoughtlessly devoted themselves to the pursuit of pleasure. Tuya was willing, he knew. Only her great love for him had preserved her patience.

The crowd buzzed around him, but his ears centered on the sound of the quiet puff of her eager footsteps in the dust. She had no doubts about his reason for seeking a private place— she was certain the time had come.

Had it? Yes. No. Perhaps.

Unbidden, Yaakov's voice and image came to him on a wave of memory. His father spoke slowly, still staring at the mound of rocks where they had just buried Rahel. "For seven years I worked and waited for your mother without taking her into my tent. The years passed like hours, so great was my love for her." Yaakov let out a short laugh touched with embarrassment. "Though her beauty drove me to kiss her the first time I saw her, I did not sleep with your mother until her father gave her to me in marriage. Remember this, my son—a patient man is better than a warrior. A man who controls his desires is stronger than one who rules a city."

Yosef stopped in the middle of the street, knowing what his decision must be. "Oh, Tuya," he whispered, turning to her. He caught his hands in her hair as shafts of restless energy coursed through his veins. What words could make her understand?

"Yosef," she murmured, ignoring the passersby as she lifted her lips and flowed toward him.

"What are ye waitin' for?" an aged crone called from the side of the street. Startled, Yosef looked up to see a toothless hag regarding him with bright eyes. "Kiss her, boy, and get on with it!"

Yosef flushed as a rush of warmth washed over him. He yanked Tuya forward, desperate to be free of the crowd.

* * *

The fierce sunlight cast deep shadows on the street, and Tuya willingly followed Yosef into the shadows of an acacia grove. Away from the teeming multitude along the river, the world seemed now to consist only of two. How fitting that he should lead her here, for trees were the confidantes of lovers…

"Tuya," Yosef said again, and she turned to face him, offering her heart and her embrace.

"We cannot do this." His hands tightened on her arms, but Tuya did not feel the pressure, so startled was she by the dart that had pierced her heart.

She shivered in the chill shock. "You do not want me?"

"This is wrong. You belong to Potiphar, and he has placed his trust in me. To do this would be a sin against God and a crime against my master."

"Potiphar will not know! He is far away, perhaps dead."

"God will know. I will know, and you will know that I have committed this wrong."

Tuya stared at him, her mind reeling with his denial of their mutual desire. "Is it wrong to share love? You cannot tell me you do not want me."

"I do want you," he whispered in an aching, husky voice she scarcely recognized. "God knows how much. But I cannot sin against him. We will have to wait."

Her heart sank with swift disappointment. "For how long, Yosef? Until tomorrow? Next year? When will this god of yours approve?" She narrowed her eyes. "Perhaps you are waiting for some Canaanite girl to enter the household."

"No," he whispered, dropping his hands from her arms. Without the warmth of his touch, she felt alone and vulnerable. "I love you with all my heart and soul," he said, his eyes raking her face. "But here—" he tapped the space of flesh over his heart "—I know we need to wait."

She choked at the sight of his hand on the place where she had so often pressed her ear to hear the reassuring beat of his pulse. In that instant, her capacity for understanding reached its limit and her emotions veered from frustration to fury. "You have mocked me with your talk of love!" she snapped, turning away.

His strong arm caught her and pulled her back. "I honor you too much to mock you. I honor you too much to commit this wrong. We will do what is right, and when our master returns, he will see that his faith in us was well-served."

Tuya turned her face from his as she struggled to gather her thoughts. He did not truly love her. The trees, the gray and blue-green shadows of the grove reminded her of the garden where once, during another lifetime, she had offered her love to Sagira. That love, too, had been spurned.

"I have often thought," she whispered, watching a slender finger of light that probed the foliage, "that I was not meant to find love. Love is not for slaves."

"How can you say that?" Yosef lifted her chin with his fingers. A wounded look lay behind his dark eyes. "Love has found you, it has found us. But we will have to wait, and trust our master."

She closed her eyes. "Our master will not know what we do today."

"He might. If you have a child, Tuya—what would we do then?"

She took a deep breath, then exhaled slowly. The priestesses had potions and charms for women to use, but Yosef would not want to hear of those things.

"Trust the master," Tuya echoed. She lifted her hand and gently ran her fingertips over the lovely face she could never deserve to call her own. "Perhaps you are right, Yosef. We must honor the master. We must not lose our heads." She gathered her composure and gave him a brittle smile even though she longed to throw herself on the ground and weep in frustration. "We will wait for Potiphar, my Yosef."

She had taken three steps toward the street when his words made her pause. "I love you, Tuya," he called, his voice heavy with longing.

She was certain he spoke only out of kindness, but she could not be angry with him. Her wounded pride would heal, but not without the balm of friendship from the only person she dared trust.

"I love you, Yosef," she answered, glancing over her shoulder. She held out her hand and breathed a sigh of relief when he took it and led her from the acacia grove.

Chapter Eleven

Potiphar bit back an oath when he learned that Narmer, the king's obsequious courtier, had been named a standard bearer and placed in charge of two hundred fifty men. In addition to the elite guards Potiphar commanded, other troops were organized into various corps. At the head of one of those corps, Narmer now strutted like an ostrich.

Amenhotep II and his troops had been in the east for fourteen months. During their trek through the numerous buffer-states, Pharaoh's warriors either put down rebellions or his courtiers visited the camps of kings to confirm existing peace treaties. For his help in subduing the warlike Hittites, the king of the Mitanni tribe, a plump polyp of a warrior, demanded and received assurance that one of his daughters would wed the next pharaoh of Egypt. Tribes from many kingdoms sent tributes to Pharaoh, and those who did not were engaged in battle and forcibly vanquished. Kings were captured and defeated men pressed into service as Pharaoh's army covered the land like a swarm of locusts.

At last Pharaoh stood on the banks of the Euphrates where his father and grandfather had erected stelae to commemorate their victories. Amenhotep raised his own pillar to record his meritorious accomplishments. After the proper sacrifices, chants and prayers, the king ordered his army to return to Egypt.

The captive kings were bound and marched overland in front of the advancing army. When Pharaoh boarded the royal barge at the naval port of Peru-nefer, his warriors hung the captive chiefs upside down on the prow of Pharaoh's boat to be displayed before the throngs of adoring, triumphant Egyptians. Potiphar knew the chiefs would eventually die at Pharaoh's own hand as he beheaded them in a religious ceremony.

The army was finally on its way home. The late afternoon sun streaked the water crimson as Potiphar stood at the stern of the king's boat. "Sweet breath of the Nile, lead me southward," he whispered, absently staring at the line of boats following Pharaoh's. Their oars flashed like the wings of dragonflies, churning up the river with furious motion. Along the side of the ship, living water sang the king's praises; along the riverside, Pharaoh's adoring people wept and fainted from unexpected joy. Their god, the divine pharaoh, had returned.

Potiphar concentrated on the rhythmic beat of the drums giving the rowers their stroke. He was too old to enjoy the adulation of the crowd; he had cut too many throats to relish blood sport. Foolish young men and idle kings were better suited for war. If this god-king had at last had his fill of it, perhaps the kingdom could rest in peace.

The blue-green ripples of water glistened as the barge cut through the summer Nile. Thinking of home, Potiphar clasped his hands behind his back and wondered if Paneah would prove worthy of the trust his master had placed in him.

At his first glimpse of the walls of his villa, Potiphar thought he'd come to the wrong estate. The tall, crumbling walls had been repaired and painted; sweet flowers grew outside the entrance gate. The gatekeeper, an older slave Potiphar had never seen, bowed and was about to discreetly ring a bell when Potiphar stopped him. "Please," he said, his scarred hand falling on the other's tanned one. "I would like to enter my house alone."

The man nodded stiffly, his heavy cheeks falling in worried folds over his slave's collar, and Potiphar moved past the gate onto the curving path. A new wall had been erected to separate the prison from the villa, and Potiphar noted with satisfaction that neither the sights, smells nor sounds of the prison would now intrude on the house. The guard at the prison gate saluted sharply at Potiphar's approach, but Potiphar only nodded and turned his back on the somber structure. Paneah would not have wasted his efforts there. The prison undoubtedly remained as it had always been, a bitter, foul place for bitter, foul prisoners.

The house rose from the sunbaked ground like an oasis, its little temple gleaming like new silver in the savage sunlight. The crumbling statues of Anubis and Osiris had been removed, and nothing remained inside the chamber but a clean altar and a bowl of burning incense. Potiphar found that the spareness of the place pleased him. He had never pledged allegiance to any personal deity, so why should he play the hypocrite and pretend at piety in his own home?

Potiphar left the temple and continued toward the house. The sand beneath his sandals had been sprinkled with water to control the dust, and for the first time in his memory, he could not smell the stockyard. Through an opening in a wall ahead he could see women carrying baskets of grain, and beyond them, three tall, cone-shaped granaries to hold stores of grain and wheat. There had been but one granary when he left.

"I feel like a stranger visiting the house of a prince," he said, then he laughed at the absurdity of his words. Briskly climbing the steps to the house, he saw that the doorway had been repainted, and his name outlined on the lintel in bold, black letters. A servant prostrated himself at Potiphar's approach, so the master stepped over the slave's body and waved the man away.

He swept through the north loggia and into his reception room, then stepped back, amazed at the sight that greeted him. This central hall, the heart of every nobleman's residence, had been a hollow, vacant symbol of Potiphar's empty, single-purpose life. Now the room glowed with vitality. The bare ceiling had been painted the soft blue of a morning sky and accented with gold wherever the ceiling joined its supporting pillars. The high windows in the softly painted walls stood open so air stirred in a sweet morning breeze. The four matching pillars had been covered in red paint bold enough to satisfy even Pharaoh's elaborate tastes. Against one wall someone had built a low brick dais on which Potiphar would sit, and next to the dais a brazier glowed with burning charcoal to chase away the morning chill. On the other side of the room, a carved limestone slab waited for the dusty hands and feet of Potiphar's guests. A pitcher of pure white marble stood ready to splash away the irritating desert sand.

Handsome panels of red and yellow moldings gleamed from above the doorways, and niches had been carved into the opposite walls to balance the openings in the room. At the northern end of the hall, a staircase led up to the roof. Peering through the opening, Potiphar could see that a light shelter had been built to provide shade from the sun.

When a pair of sandaled feet appeared on the staircase, Potiphar stepped behind a pillar and waited. A tall, imposing man came into view, a scroll in his hand and a frown on his face.

Potiphar stepped forward and pursed his lips. "Do I know you?"

The frown eased into a smile, then the man lowered himself to the floor. "Master! Welcome home. I am Paneah, your servant."

"Can it be you?" Potiphar stooped and tapped the young man's shoulder. "Lift your head, so I may see you better. I did not realize the desert sun had blinded me so completely."

"There is nothing wrong with your eyes," Paneah answered, lifting his face.

Potiphar crossed his arms and stared at the stranger before him. By all the gods, how a year had changed him! The awkwardness of adolescence had completely vanished from the lad's limbs, leaving him slim but powerfully built. He had always been agreeable, but the man before him had been favored with a striking face, a broad pair of shoulders and an easy, open manner. His eyes snapped with intelligence, his smile glimmered with goodwill—unusual in a slave.

"I can only hope I have not changed as drastically," Potiphar answered, finally finding his tongue. "I come home to find my house a different place, and my youthful steward a man."

"You honored me by placing me in charge of your household," Paneah said, standing. "I hope you have found everything to your liking."

Potiphar raised a hand toward the ceiling, then let his arm fall to his side. "I can find nothing to dislike, Paneah, unless you have spent all your energy on this room and no others."

"Never fear, master, all your affairs are in order," Paneah said, laughing. "If you would like a tour of the villa—"

"Of course, lead and show me what you have done." Potiphar thrust his hands behind his back. "I only hope you have not depleted my treasure room so completely I will have to sell you to feed my sheep."

"Your treasures are intact and increased," Paneah answered, leading the way from the reception room. "The cattle produced well this year. Every cow brought forth a calf. The sheep, too, were fertile, and the harvest of your lands has been so bountiful that I purchased additional slaves to bring in the harvest. I have trained them all in other jobs, too, so you will have no fear of waste during the winter months—"

"I do not fear anything, Paneah." Potiphar clapped the slave's back as he fell into step beside the young man. "With you in charge of my house, I shall not worry about anything but Pharaoh."

One week after his return, Potiphar joined the other royal troops at the palace for Pharaoh's awards ceremony. Feasting and rituals would take place throughout the day, beginning with the sacrifice of the enemy kings at dawn and concluding with the transportation of Pharaoh's gods along the Nile at sunset.

After the bloody sacrifice at the temple, Pharaoh's nobles, warriors and courtiers moved to the throne room in Pharaoh's palace. The gigantic hall was as crowded as Potiphar had ever seen it, and he gripped the handle of the dagger in his belt as the crowd churned and surged behind the guards at the open doors. One by one, the royal scribes read off the names of those who had been with the king on his military expedition, and those men, great and small, came forward to acknowledge Pharaoh's gratitude. Foot soldiers who had done well in combat received tiny golden flies for "stinging" the enemy; to others Pharaoh presented golden daggers, carved and painted shields and handsomely carved bronze arrowheads. To the archers, Pharaoh gave painted leather forearm protectors, and to captains like Narmer the king awarded permission to kiss his royal foot, not just the ground at his feet.

The crowd around Potiphar buzzed when the royal scribe looked his way. Every standard bearer, petty officer and foot soldier had been rewarded, only the captain of the king's elite guards waited to receive his prize. For the first time since the presentations had begun, Pharaoh stood from his throne.

"Potiphar! Your king and god summons you!"

Potiphar stepped from the line of guards at the king's right hand and prostrated himself before Amenhotep. He had lain in this position before, hoping for the golden chain that hung around the king's neck, but this time he had certainly earned the prize. The Gold of Praise was an exalted honor few men could wear, and Potiphar had served not only this pharaoh, but Pharaoh's divine father...

"Potiphar, how can a king reward his most trusted servant?"

"The warmth of your favor is enough, my king," Potiphar called, lifting his head just enough for his words to be heard.

"It is not enough. I must do something more for you, my friend, and have thought many days on this matter. Horus himself has shown me what I can do. Rise, Potiphar, and accept the gratitude and devotion of your king."

Potiphar pressed hard on the floor, feeling his age as he pushed himself upright, then bent his head in submission as he walked toward the king's throne. The king could thank him properly by retiring from war. Another eastern expedition would likely mean the end of his faithful captain.

"I have thought, faithful friend, about what you do not have," Pharaoh said, his voice low.

Surprised at the king's conversational tone, Potiphar lifted his eyes to meet Amenhotep's.

"And I am prepared this day to give you what you lack. You have received every honor Egypt can give, and every right a pharaoh can bestow. You kiss the royal foot, even the leg, you travel by my side and stand beside my throne. A hundred golden flies decorate the animal skins you wear for a mantle, and yet you do not possess one reward I can give."

Potiphar's disobedient eyes slipped to the Gold of Praise about Pharaoh's neck.

"Once I gave you a beautiful woman. Now I will give you a noble one. Donkor, my kinsman, has a daughter of fourteen years. She was born in the royal line of pharaohs, and today she will become your wife."

The saving grace of long habit prodded Potiphar to crumple at Pharaoh's feet in the proper pose of overwhelmed gratitude. Reflexively, he murmured his thanks, but his brain roiled with the king's words. A wife! Pharaoh did not know, he could not know! Potiphar was a forty-six-year-old soldier, not the sort of man to be a husband, and yet Pharaoh wanted to give him a young royal wife who would demand to be petted, teased and spoiled...

An audible hush fell on the droning gossips who had sprung to life at Pharaoh's words, and the soft swish of fabric reached Potiphar's ears. "Rise, Potiphar, and meet your bride," Pharaoh called, and the warrior's arms trembled as he pushed himself up and turned to face the child who would share his house...and his future.

Clothed in a diaphanous sheath of reddish-gold, a young goddess stood before him. She wore a pleated dress bordered with rich fringe, and the gauzy fabric of the garment allowed him to see the handsome shape of plump legs, a solid stomach, strong arms. Distracted, he looked up and into the wide eyes that peered from beneath a heavy wig. "I am Sagira, my lord," a treble voice whispered. "Daughter of Donkor, and kinsman to the king."

At first he thought the wreath of lotus blossoms circling her head put forth an unusually heady scent, then he realized that the lady also carried a bouquet. She had come to the palace dressed for a wedding.

Pharaoh must have guessed at Potiphar's discomfiture, for

an abrupt burst of laughter escaped him. "My old friend," he said, smiling with as much warmth as he dared before a jealous court. "Did you think you could escape matrimony forever? Your duty lies in raising sons as brave and devoted as you are. Take this girl as your wife, here and now, and do not fail your king."

Potiphar bowed deeply. "I would not fail you," he answered, his stomach tightening as the crowd broke into pleased applause.

In his younger days, he'd have seen such a trap coming long before it snared him.

Sagira felt a blush burn her cheek. Despite his posture of gratitude, in her new husband's eyes she could read his displeasure about this marriage. He should have been overjoyed, for many fathers had sought to have her for their sons. But, unwilling to marry Sagira without Pharaoh's permission, her anxious parents had waited for the king's return from the east. In a private meeting arranged by one of the royal courtiers, Donkor and Kahent approached Pharaoh and mentioned their desire to find a suitable husband for their noble daughter. Flushed from the thrill of his military campaign, Pharaoh had been eager to honor his captain and declared that the resolute and courageous Potiphar would prove an admirable husband for Sagira. He needed to honor the grizzled veteran of a hundred wars, and his royal niece needed a husband. What could be a better match?

Potiphar, Kahent had later confided to Sagira, was strong-willed enough to serve as Pharaoh should Ramla's prophecy be fulfilled in his lifetime. If he proved to be less than a good husband, he was old enough to die and give Sagira many more years in which she could marry again.

Sagira knew her fate could have been worse. Despite his age,

Potiphar was known as a fair and dutiful man, and his house-hold had prospered in the year of his absence. She had asked her father to drive his chariot past Potiphar's villa, and she found it was one of the most handsome in Thebes. As the villa's mistress, she would bring grace and elegance to the place. In time the old goat would be grateful for Pharaoh's favor.

Lifting her eyes from her promised husband, she pivoted gracefully and walked down the aisle extending from the throne of all Egypt. Promptly on cue, the priests from the temple of Bastet, her patron goddess, brought forward the marriage canopy that had been woven from river rushes. Sagira met her father under the canopy, then turned and waited for her groom.

A heavy silence settled on the chamber. Potiphar stood without moving, his mouth gaping like a fish that has been taken from the safety of the river. For a desperate moment Sagira thought he would refuse the king's gift.

Pharaoh's voice filled the strangely thickened air. "Potiphar," he called, a thin note of warning in his voice, "surely you will want to thank the man who has served you in this venture. As I searched for a way to honor you, Narmer came from Donkor and put your bride's name into my thoughts."

Sagira saw Potiphar jerk his heard toward the spot where the courtier stood like a cocky rooster preening his feathers. Dressed in fine linen and animal skins, Narmer stepped forward and fell to his knees before Pharaoh.

"And what should I give you, faithful Narmer?" Pharaoh asked, glancing down. "You who have provided so many answers to my questions?"

"Nothing could ever replace your affection in my heart," Narmer said, his eyes humbly fastened to the floor. "But if I could wear the Gold of Praise about my neck, I would forever be reminded that Pharaoh holds me in esteem."

Amenhotep smiled and laid aside the crook and flail. "So be it," he cried, lifting the heavy chain from his neck. "Narmer will wear his king's favor on his shoulders. He has received the divine praise of Pharaoh and had a part in bringing Potiphar his noble bride!"

A decidedly ugly look settled on Potiphar's features as he turned from the strutting courtier to face the bridal canopy. Sagira shivered and vowed to remember that expression. Potiphar was a warrior, and would undoubtedly be violent if pressed. For the sake of her survival, she would be careful never to rouse her husband's anger.

The wedding was but another celebration on the program of Pharaoh's grand festival, and Potiphar was irritated by his role in it. In time he might have considered taking an older, quiet woman to be his wife, for he had occasionally longed for a companion to share his home, but he did not care to have a youthful bride thrust on him. The daughter of Donkor was lovely, in the dark fashion of most Egyptian girls, but she lacked Tuya's devoted smile and the long-limbed gracefulness of women he had observed in the northeastern provinces. At fourteen, she was still much a child, but her face was composed when she turned to face him.

He should have studied his bride-to-be as the priests began the incantations of the ceremony, but he couldn't help being distracted by her entourage. Behind the girl stood a bald priestess in a spotless robe, a sour-faced, somber creature who regarded Potiphar with distrust in her eyes. Donkor stood at his daughter's right hand, a royal relative whose enormous belly advertised his prosperity far better than words. Behind this trio Narmer paced confidently, his hands behind his back, a smile on his lips and the Gold of Praise glittering about his neck.

Why hadn't he simply asked for it? Instead of prattling

about Pharaoh's favor and indulging in false humility, why didn't he tell the king what was owed? Then he'd have the Gold of Praise and a young fool like Narmer would have this girl.

But the gods worked in mysterious ways, and Egypt's divine pharaoh was the most unpredictable of them. On any other day, if a man dared to ask for the chain about Pharaoh's neck, he'd be crocodile meat before sunset. Narmer was a fool, but Potiphar could not deny his boldness.

The high priest of Bastet, a bald, sallow-faced man, gestured for Potiphar to extend his hands and feet. Potiphar obeyed, as did Sagira, and with fresh water from the Nile the priest washed the limbs of bride and groom to symbolize the purity of their union. After the washing, a servant offered up a corn loaf, and Potiphar fumbled with memories of the few weddings he had attended. He was supposed to feed his bride, a visible pledge of support, but his hands felt clumsy and oversized as he broke the corn loaf and placed a crumb of its crust between the red lips of the girl beside him.

The priest uttered another incantation as the priestess behind Sagira waved a stalk of sweet-smelling incense. Another servant handed Potiphar a jug of wine. He would gladly have drunk the wine in a mad guzzle—better to be rip-roaring drunk than endure this humiliation—but the eyes of Pharaoh focused on him.

Potiphar placed the jug on the ground according to the tradition, then drew his sword and smashed the jug with a single blow. With that action, the wedding was finished.

The crowd responded with cries of praise and approval, and Potiphar lifted his bride's hand and presented her to the people. Sagira, daughter of Donkor, kinsman to the king, had officially become Potiphar's wife.

Chapter Twelve

"He has taken a wife?" Tuya asked.

Speechless with surprise, Yosef could only stare at the messenger, who nodded and wiped perspiration from his forehead with the edge of his tunic. "This very hour. The master and his bride are feasting at Pharaoh's palace, soon they will return. You must make everything ready."

A nervous fluttering rose in Yosef's stomach as he turned to Tuya. "I don't know what to do," he whispered. "How do the Egyptians marry? In my time here, I've never seen anything to tell me—"

"How we marry is not important," Tuya teased, sweeping the messenger's dusty footprints from the floor with a palm frond. "What matters now is how they spend their wedding night. And that, Yosef, is the same in any culture."

"Fresh linens on the bed, fresh water in the basin and pitcher," Tuya called as she moved toward the master's chamber. "Hot coals in the brazier. Flowers in the basin, and a garland of blossoms for the room, I think."

"But how can our master be married?" Yosef took three sprinting steps and caught Tuya's arm, turning her toward him. "Surely he will not marry unless he is in love, but he has said nothing of it—"

"Yosef, are you truly so simple?" Her fingers lightly dusted his brow and pulled a stray strand of hair from his eyes. "Sometimes I think you are not the wise and capable Paneah, but a simple shepherd boy from the desert. Our master may not love this woman now, but he will. The divine pharaoh has arranged the marriage, and so it will be."

"But does no one ever protest Pharaoh's wishes? My father was forced to marry a woman he did not choose, but he protested and insisted on marrying my mother as well. If he had been allowed to marry the one he loved from the beginning, much strife could have been avoided."

"Who are we to question the will of a god?" Tuya quipped, tapping him on the cheek. Yosef clung to her for a moment, relishing the feel of her in his arms, then she laughed and pulled away. "Let me go, or our new mistress will be screaming for us to be whipped before she even knows our names. I must tend to the bridal chamber, and you must see to the rest of the house. Warn the butler and the baker, have Mert-sekert bring a supply of linen, for the lady will want to see what we can offer her wardrobe. There is no time to waste."

Sighing, Yosef let her go.

Darkness had settled its black cloak over the villa by the time Potiphar and his wife arrived. Tuya watched from behind an arbor in the courtyard as the master helped a female figure out of the chariot and into the house. Impossible to tell what the woman looked like, for her wig was like that of any noble lady, and her size obscured by the wine-colored robe that proclaimed her a virgin bride.

Tuya heard Yosef's confident greeting in the entryway and knew he was welcoming their new mistress. Potiphar answered in a low murmur and escorted his bride into the house. After a moment Yosef slipped out of the entry and into the courtyard.

"Did you see her?" Tuya hissed from behind the arbor. "Did you get a good look? What's she like? Is she very beautiful?"

"Wait," Yosef murmured, walking calmly over the pathway. He barred the gate and snuffed the single burning torch, effectively plunging the courtyard into darkness.

After a moment, Tuya's eyes adjusted to the dim light of the moon. When Yosef's back was turned, she crept from behind the arbor and needled her fingers into his ribs. "Is she beautiful?"

"God spare me from a curious woman!" he yelped as she ducked under his arm to confront him.

"Tell me everything." She pulled Yosef into the privacy of the shadows. A bench waited in the arbor and she tugged him toward it, twining her fingers with his. "So—is she beautiful?"

"She is…fair. Very young."

"Younger than me?"

"Probably. But I am not skilled at guessing a woman's age."

"You are too diplomatic. Is she plump or thin?"

"Shorter than you, and therefore she seems—thicker. But lovely, with dark eyes and hair."

"How could you tell anything under that wig?"

"Her eyebrows." Yosef turned and brushed his lips across Tuya's forehead. "Her brows were black as night."

"Don't speak of other women when you're doing that," Tuya breathed, squeezing his hand as his breath warmed her ear.

"What other women? I saw only Potiphar and you, out here hiding behind the bushes."

"I wasn't hiding, I was waiting. I had a thought to share with you."

He draped an arm about her shoulders. "Only a thought?"

She pulled back to give him her brightest smile. "One thought."

"Well…what is it?"

She hesitated, then lightened her tone. "Do you remember when our master suggested that we might be married if we served him well?"

He picked up her free hand and pressed it to his cheek. "He mentioned six years. We have five remaining."

"Doesn't that seem like a long time?"

An inexplicable, lazy smile swept over his face. "My father worked seven years for Lea, and another seven years for Rahel. He told me the fourteen years flew by like days, so great was his love for my mother."

"Has your time here flown by, Yosef?"

He cradled her hand in his as his eyes grew thoughtful. "In the beginning, no. I wondered what God meant by bringing me here. Then I wouldn't allow myself to love you for fear that I'd be taken away again. But now—" his smile warmed her "—now the days fly and I wait and pray and hope that God will be merciful."

"I offer petitions to Montu." Tuya lifted her chin and strengthened her voice so he would know she was serious. "I think our master's marriage may be a great boon for us. If Potiphar, who never thought to marry, finds joy with his bride, perhaps he will wish the same joy for us. He likes us, don't you think? There is no reason we could not marry and serve him five more years before he grants our freedom."

The grooves beside his mouth deepened into a full smile. "You truly believe our master will discover the happiness we've found?"

"In time, certainly," Tuya went on, studying his face. "Don't you think it could happen? If we offer sacrifices to the gods—"

"My god delights in obedience, not sacrifice." Yosef's hands closed about her wrists. "My beautiful girl, there is so much I don't understand. I cannot speak for God, or assume to understand why he moves as he does. I don't know why he called me out of my father's tents. I don't know what he has planned for my tomorrows. And I don't know why he has rooted your image in my heart."

She was about to say that reasons didn't matter, but his finger fell across her lips.

"I do know that the touch of your satin skin is enough to drive me to distraction," he whispered, his voice husky. "But my father taught me that a righteous man does not touch a woman until she becomes his bride. So until our master allows us to join in marriage, your Paneah should keep a careful distance from the lips you offer so willingly."

To challenge his resolve she lifted her face to meet his, but Yosef only smiled and stood, still holding her hands. "Goodnight," he whispered, squeezing her hands before he dropped them into her lap.

Could he not see that he was driving her insane? "Yosef—"

Only an echo came through the night shadows. "Goodnight, my love."

Chapter Thirteen

Sunlight had burnished the warm morning air when Tuya walked to the series of storage and workrooms that served as the kitchen. Her new mistress would probably sleep late, but would then welcome a bath and a bowl of fruit to break her fast. Tuya had seen no slaves accompanying her mistress, so if the lady did not own a personal maid, Tuya was prepared to offer her services.

Abu, the goatherd, stood in the doorway, stuffing grapes into his mouth. "Have you met the new bride?" she asked.

The man shook his head and muttered around a mouthful of fruit. "Our master left early this morning to attend to his duties at the palace. Paneah is in the house now, trying to find a suitable chamber for the lady's companion."

"A companion?" Tuya frowned. "Will her maid sleep in the house?"

"She's not brought a maid, but a priestess," Abu answered, rolling his eyes. "The lady decreed this morning that Potiphar's temple is to be dedicated to Bastet." Abu glanced around as if the goddess might hear him, then lowered his voice. "They're bringing a horde of cat mummies this afternoon. The lady says they're to be kept in the temple, and no one's to argue about it."

A sense of foreboding descended over Tuya with a shiver, but she thanked Abu and carried a bowl of fruit to the house. Hundreds of priestesses served the nobles of Thebes, and thousands of people claimed Bastet as their patron goddess. Surely Abu's words meant nothing.

She climbed the steps to the outer porch and met Yosef. "Is our lady awake already?" she said, sharing the smile she reserved for him alone.

He returned the smile, and for a moment she thought he would have kissed her in greeting, but too many others milled about. "She is awake," he said simply, checking a sheet of parchment in his hand. "And she has a list of needs and wants I am to see to at once. Our master is out for the day, but we are to make our lady happy."

"I'll see what I can do," Tuya offered, moving past him into the central hall. The room was empty, spacious and quiet in its grandeur, but noises came from the master's chamber at the end of the hall. The women's sitting room stood empty, as usual, but would now have to be furnished. Tuya made a mental note of mentioning this to Yosef—suitable furnishings could be found immediately, of course, but if the lady wanted spectacular she would have to give the carpenters and artisans time to work.

A wailing sound came from the master's chamber, and Tuya paused on the threshold, uncertain how to proceed. Peering around the edge of the doorway, she saw a short-cropped head swathed in sheets, a huddled mass in the center of Potiphar's bed.

The shrouded figure silenced its weeping as dark eyes fastened on Tuya. The slave carefully lowered the bowl of fruit to the floor, then prostrated herself. "I am here to serve you, mistress," she said, hoping the lady hadn't seen her spying glance.

The sheets rustled, a bare foot smacked the floor. Footsteps padded over the tile until ten pampered and painted toes moved into Tuya's range of vision.

"Rise, slave, and let me have a look at you," a young voice commanded.

Steeling herself for confrontation, Tuya stood, lifting her head at the last moment. The bride gasped before she did, but Tuya had heard a warning in Abu's words.

"Good morning, Lady Sagira," Tuya said, her heart skipping a beat. It would be easy to turn and walk away, leaving Sagira as alone and frightened as Tuya had once been. But the girl had stared out from beneath the bedsheets like a frightened animal looking out from the brush.

Tuya gave her mistress a polite and practiced smile, then folded her hands and lowered her head, waiting to see how this joke of the gods would play out.

She stepped back, stung, when Sagira rushed forward and embraced her.

Sagira did not know whether to laugh or cry at the sight of Tuya. Part of her wanted to flee in embarrassment, but another part yearned to embrace her childhood friend. Finally she did both. She hugged Tuya for the sake of their former friendship, then retreated back under the bedcovers. She did not have to act the part of a regal bride and noble lady before Tuya.

"Mistress, what's wrong?" Tuya asked, stepping to the edge of the bed. She bent and lifted a corner of the sheet. "You can come out. No one will hurt you."

"Oh, Tuya, it was awful!" Sagira blushed, the horror of the memory sweeping over her again. "Never in my life have I imagined that marriage would be like the night I've just passed."

Tuya lifted a brow. "Did your mother not prepare you?"

"I was prepared for a night of love." Sagira wiped her damp nose with the back of her hand. "I was prepared for anything and everything except—"

Tuya gazed at her in bewilderment. "Except?"

"Nothing!" Sagira cried, fresh tears stinging her eyes. "Potiphar lay down and fell asleep. I sat beside him, waiting, until I knew he would not wake, then I paced this chamber all night, trying to decide what I should do."

Tuya sat on the edge of the bed, a look of confusion on her face, and Sagira threw herself into the older girl's arms as she had a thousand times when they were younger. It felt good to fall into Tuya's comforting lap. The slave had always been unflappable. Whenever Sagira did wrong as a child, Tuya took the blame or made everything all right. And now the gods had returned Tuya, and Tuya knew Potiphar. She would know how to correct Sagira's problems.

"Our master Potiphar did not plan on being married yesterday," Tuya was saying, so Sagira sniffed and tried to concentrate on the girl's words. "He has just returned from the military expedition. He is older, and he was tired. He probably wanted to rest."

"He doesn't think I'm pretty," Sagira said, lifting a corner of Tuya's skirt to wipe her nose. "I read that much in his eyes as we were married. I don't know what kind of woman he likes, but I'm not his—"

Abruptly, she shrank back and glared at Tuya. "Are you his concubine?"

"No, no." Tuya flushed scarlet. "Never. The master has kept me busy with work of the house. He has never invited me to his bed."

"Do you swear this by the goddess Bastet?"

"By whatever god you like, my lady. You can ask the other servants. Our master sleeps alone."

Sagira sighed, then lay down and propped her head on her hand. "He has never had a wife?"

"No."

"Or a concubine?"

"None I know of."

"He is not—" Sagira raised a brow.

Tuya blushed. "He is not like that."

Sagira idly ran her finger over the linen sheets. "Tired or not, if he is a man, he can be stirred to action. Ramla has told me what I must do. The prophecy demands that I bear a son."

Tuya stiffened at the mention of Ramla's name. "The prophecy, my lady?"

Sagira pressed her lips together. She had said too much, especially in the house of the captain of Pharaoh's bodyguard. Even a hint that Pharaoh's lineage might not be established for eternity would be tantamount to treason.

"Nothing." She waved the matter away. "I want a child. Doesn't every woman?"

Ramla's sharp voice interrupted the reunion. "I thought we had rid ourselves of this slave."

"Ramla, don't scold," Sagira said, sitting up. She smiled at the priestess. "Tuya assures me that my husband was tired last night. I am not to blame for his diffidence."

The priestess crossed her arms. "I am not surprised."

"He went to sleep," Sagira said, standing and taking the sheet with her. "But he will not sleep tonight. Prepare my bath, Tuya, and spread the fruit on a mat for me. I'm hungry."

Tuya reached for one of the papyrus mats rolled in a corner of the room. "You should eat first."

Sagira glanced at the gleaming grapes, pomegranates and dates. Tuya must have taken pains to gather the ripest, most delicious-looking fruit...

She reached for a bunch of grapes, but Ramla stepped

forward and slapped her hand. "I cannot believe you would listen to the suggestion of a slave," she snapped, fire in her eyes. "You are the mistress here. You are no longer a child. Such softness was allowable in a girl, but you are now a woman of means. You do not confide in slaves, you do not obey them, you do not heed their wishes. Do you understand?"

Sagira shrank back as if the goddess herself had chastised her. Ramla had often been coyly disapproving, but never had she let loose with an outburst like this. "Tuya is an old friend and means me no harm—"

"Tuya is a slave who once thought herself your equal. Have you forgotten the words I taught you? The instruction of King Amen-em-Hat warns those who will rule that they should be on their guard against subordinates—'Trust not a brother, know not a friend, make not for yourself intimates, for in these things is no satisfaction.' Remember the prophecy, Sagira! Live like a queen, discipline your heart!"

Sagira grimaced at Ramla's words, but Tuya turned to face the priestess. "I mean no harm to my mistress," she said, her voice firmer than Sagira had ever heard it. "I would not harm her or my master Potiphar for the world."

Ramla lifted her hands to the sky in an eloquent gesture. "Bastet, preserve us! Must I endure a pair of fools?"

Torn between the longing for the past and her hopes for the future, Sagira buried her head in her hands. "Where is the master of the slaves in this house?" She spat the words between her clenched fingers. "I would speak to him at once!"

"There is only one master below Potiphar," Tuya answered, her voice distant. "Paneah is the steward."

"Bring him to me at once!" Sagira muttered, not lifting her eyes. "No! Send him. You need not return."

She waited until Tuya's footsteps faded before lifting her gaze to meet Ramla's.

"Sometimes, my Sagira, you behave like a simple-minded child," the priestess said, crossing to an elegant chair in the corner of the room. She seated herself and inclined her head like a queen granting favors. "Tuya is a great beauty, can you not see it?"

"She is a slave," Sagira whispered. "I am a lady."

"Your mother sent Tuya away because she knew the slave's beauty would overpower yours." Ramla's dark eyes glowed with cunning. "She thought you would never win a husband if you stood in your maid's shadow. And yet today you embraced your enemy, completely blind to the fact that your husband will never look at you with desire or give you the child you need as long as she remains here."

"Potiphar has not touched her—"

"Would she tell you if he had? But even if she speaks the truth, how do you know he does not dream of her?" Ramla released a delicate, three-noted giggle, as out of character as her misshapen hand was out of place. "A wise woman never allows competition to exist in the same room."

The oily tone in Ramla's voice, so different from Tuya's soft responses, brought bile to the back of Sagira's throat. "Then why," she whispered, fighting an impulse to gag, "do you stay with me?"

The priestess tented the fingers of her good hand against the deformed digits of the other. "I have seen the future, and it fascinates me," she whispered. "You, Sagira, will be immortalized in this world as well as in the eternal one. Men will speak of you for as long as the Nile flows." Her eyes narrowed. "I hope to follow in your shadow."

Yosef found the two women eating fruit in Potiphar's bedchamber. The bride, who looked more child than woman in the dazzling light of early afternoon, regarded him with a frankly admiring glance. The other woman, a tall, slender creature with the shaven head of priestess, did not lift her eyes to acknowledge him.

"I am Paneah," he said, bowing to the stranger. "I assume you are our mistress's priestess. A chamber not far from this one has been reserved for you."

"I will need it only three months out of four," the woman answered, nodding slightly to acknowledge his comment. "When I am away, I must attend to my duties at the temple."

Yosef turned to his mistress. She paused with her hand in the fruit bowl, watching him. "I met you this morning," she said, turning so that a bare leg peeked from beneath the sheet she had wrapped around herself.

"Yes, mistress. You gave me a list of your desires, and we are hurrying to find the things you need."

"There is another thing I need," the girl said, plucking a grape from the bunch in her hand. She regarded the grape for a moment, then popped it into her mouth and gave the priestess a one-sided smile. "There is a slave here who does not please me. I want you to sell her immediately."

Yosef felt his smile stiffen. His staff had been trained to be quick, efficient and subtle. How could any of them have displeased this girl? "Perhaps, my lady, there has been a misunderstanding."

"No misunderstanding," the mistress answered. "The slave called Tuya is offensive to me. My priestess has suggested that the gods might be pleased if she were surrendered as an offering to the temple of Bastet. See to it at once, Paneah."

Yosef blinked. "Tuya, offensive?"

"Yes."

"But, my lady, Tuya is capable and strong. She is one of the master's favorites."

"It matters not." The lady Sagira cast him a bright smile.

"I want her gone by day's end, or you will find yourself sleeping in the slave market tonight."

Unthinking discipline took over his limbs as Yosef nodded and withdrew. His feet carried him from the lady's chamber into the courtyard. Once he was safely away from his mistress's eyes, he held his head and rocked back and forth, trying to regain his sense of balance.

What had happened? He had worked hard, he had found love. He had hoped God would have mercy, but his soul had just been torn asunder again. Like any slave, Tuya knew she could be sold at any time, but she had fallen in love, she was clinging to the master's promise. This separation would kill her…especially since Yosef would have to enforce it.

For the second time in his life, someone dear to his heart would suffer the deepest throes of grief on his account.

Staggering with the realization, Yosef made his way to the workroom where he fell on his knees and begged God for an answer.

Mercifully, the answer came with Potiphar's arrival. The master entered the courtyard just as Yosef called Tuya out from the kitchen, about to break the terrible news. Potiphar took one look at the stricken look on Yosef's face and asked what troubled him.

"My mistress, your wife," Yosef said, taking pains to keep his voice under control, "has ordered me to take Tuya to the temple of Bastet before the sun sets today."

"By all the gods, why?" Potiphar's voice snapped through the courtyard like a whip. "What has the girl done?"

"Nothing, my lord." Tuya turned horror-filled eyes on Yosef. "On my honor, I did nothing."

"I asked our mistress, and she admits Tuya has done nothing wrong," Yosef told Potiphar. "Apparently the lady's priestess thought Tuya would make a favorable offering to the gods. I was ordered to take Tuya or surrender myself to be sold at the slave market." He lifted his chin. "And although it would pain me to leave you, sir, I would endure such a fate if necessary."

Potiphar snatched a quick breath, then sent a dark look toward the house. "You shall do no such thing." For a moment he glared at the walls as if he could see the lady within, then he softened his glance and laid a hand on Yosef's shoulder. "You are like a son to me, Paneah, and I would sooner lose a wife than you. Trust me—neither you nor Tuya will be forced out of this household as long as you continue to serve me as you have in the past."

With his hand on the dagger in his belt, Potiphar climbed the steps to his house and went to confront his wife.

Though Ramla hovered near when Potiphar entered the women's reception room, Sagira thought the iron-willed priestess cowered slightly before the warrior's fierce gaze.

"What are you thinking, girl?" he roared, the muscles of his face tightening into a mask of rage. "I leave you for the space of a few hours and find that you have already begun to destroy my household!"

Sagira thrust her chin upward. "The slave Tuya is no stranger to me. I have known her for years, and know she is not a suitable ladies' maid."

"Then find another girl to be your maid," Potiphar snapped, planting his feet as though he intended to fight. "I have twenty slave girls in this house. Surely one of them can paint your face. If not one of them, let this one do it!"

He indicated Ramla with a disdainful flip of his hand, and Sagira saw the priestess's bosom heave in indignation.

"Ramla is my counselor," Sagira answered, smoothly arranging her skirt. "She will not do a slave's work."

"Tuya and Paneah have been in my household over two years," Potiphar answered, his voice steadier. "You will not dismiss them on a mere whim."

Sagira saw the seriousness in his eyes and decided not to argue the matter. Instead, she folded her hands and gave him an obedient smile. "As you say, my lord and husband."

"And now you will dismiss this one from the room—" Potiphar jerked his chin toward Ramla "—for I wish to have a private word with you."

For an instant Sagira considered arguing that Ramla should stay, but perhaps it was time she learned to live with the man she had married. She needed a son, but would never have one if she made this man her enemy.

"Leave us, Ramla," she said, hoping her voice was sufficiently regal to impress her husband.

Ramla gave Potiphar a killing look as she moved out of the room. As her footsteps faded, Sagira threw Potiphar her brightest smile, but apparently the old dogfish wasn't hungry.

Potiphar lowered himself into a chair across from her. "I am glad to talk alone with you." Obviously uncomfortable, he took a long, slow swallow, his Adam's apple sliding up and down the wall of his throat as if it were made of words he could not bring forth.

Perhaps he needed help. "What would you like to tell me?" she asked, crossing her legs so her posture was less formal. "I am pleased to be your wife, Potiphar. I have heard many stories of your bravery."

He shrugged at her words, then drew the back of his hand across his brow. "I am a man of war," he finally said, resting his hands on his knees. "I do not know how to be a husband. Pharaoh's favor was a complete surprise, and I must apologize that you were not better received."

"I was well received by all but one." Leaning forward, she looked up into his strained face. For the sake of the prophecy, she would win this man's heart. "You, Potiphar, did not properly welcome your bride last night."

A shudder shook him. He rose from his chair and turned to face the wall. "I will honor you as my wife," he said, thrusting his hands behind his back. "But I have no desire to embrace you. You are a child, and yet a stranger to me."

"Surely you want children. Every man wants children." She stood and moved toward him until their shadows mingled on the wall. Even at this slight contact, Potiphar flinched.

"I never thought to have children. I am content to serve my king."

She dropped her cool hand on his arm. "Every man needs an heir." His muscles were firm under her palm, his waist trim, his legs sturdy beneath his linen kilt. Though three times her age, Potiphar was still a striking figure, a husband of whom she could be proud.

His skin seemed to contract beneath her touch, but he did not move away. "I thought I would leave my estate to Paneah," he said, his throat working. "He has managed it so well—"

"You should not leave your estate to a slave when you could have a son of your own." Carefully, tenderly, she lifted his hand and placed hers under it. His eyes widened at her boldness, then he tilted his head and examined her as he might have studied an intricate painting in the temple.

"You are…exceptional."

"I am your wife, Potiphar, and I could love you if you'd let me," she murmured, her voice a silken whisper in the quiet of the chamber.

She stepped closer and ran her free hand over the bronzed skin of his chest, feeling rippled scars beneath her fingers. Three, no, four rough welts lay under her hand; how many times had he been injured? She felt the whisper of his quickened breath on her cheek. Surely he would step into her arms—

She pressed her lips to his shoulder, awaiting his shuddering sigh of surrender, but Potiphar abruptly moved away. "I am sorry, my lady," he said, his face and neck flooding crimson. "But duty calls me to the palace. If you need anything, call Paneah. I may be gone a few days."

Before she could open her mouth to protest, Potiphar whirled and left her alone.

The next morning, Tuya tiptoed through the corridor outside the master's chamber, hoping that Potiphar and Sagira had found happiness in each other's arms. But a clattering crash from the chamber drew her upright, then she heard Sagira's scream: "I don't care what his duties are! He can't leave me like this!"

Tuya peered around the corner. Ramla sat on the edge of Sagira's bed, her arms folded and a dark look on her face. Both women frowned to see Tuya in the doorway, and the slave's pulse quickened when she sensed the hostility in the room. These women, she told herself, had tried to send her away. Perhaps she should not have come into the house.

But she'd already been spotted. She stepped into the doorway and bowed her head. "Is there anything you need, Lady Sagira?"

"Have you forgotten how to make a proper bow before your mistress?" Ramla barked.

Tuya dropped to the floor and pressed her forehead to the cool tile. "Mistress," she repeated, "is there anything you need?"

"No," Sagira snapped, her voice a sharp stiletto in the quiet. "Wait—I will need a maid. Send Paneah to me so I can describe the sort of maid I want."

Tuya nodded and rose to leave.

"Has your mistress dismissed you?" The priestess's iron voice drizzled disapproval.

Tuya dropped to the floor again.

"Now you may leave," Sagira said, her tone flat. "But send Paneah at once. Do not keep me waiting."

Chapter Fourteen

Potiphar stayed away for a full ten-day week, then sent a message instructing Paneah to prepare a comfortable, separate chamber for Sagira and her maid. The instruction was not unusual, for most noble ladies lived in separate quarters from their husbands, but without being told the entire household knew that Potiphar had been less than enchanted with his new bride.

In her new chambers, Sagira fumed with frustration and embarrassment.

Again and again, Potiphar came home and left again, treating Sagira with the polite interest he might have displayed toward an esteemed visitor. Often he brought her a trinket, a piece of jewelry, or the latest court gossip which he shared over a breakfast tray, but he never returned to the house until night had fallen and Sagira had retreated to her room. On rising, she often heard his easy laughter in the stockyard as he checked the horses with Paneah, and occasionally she heard him tease Tuya in an almost paternal manner. Yet for her, his wife, he had nothing but insignificant conversation and the most casual of greetings.

Sagira's temper rose to a flash point each time she thought of her husband's disinterest, then she remembered the prophecy. She had to win his affection. Her father had been a coolly indifferent figure in her life, and it galled her to think her husband might prove to be as distant. But one way or another, she would bear a son. She had not studied the love lyrics of the ancient poets for nothing.

"Rehearse for me the song I will sing to Potiphar," Sagira called to Ramla one afternoon as the women sat by the reflecting pool in Potiphar's garden. Two servants had loaded a stand at Sagira's right with fruit, flowers and wine; a harpist and fan bearer stirred the warm air in an effort to make their mistress's afternoon a little more pleasant. The sight of the lotus-filled pool stirred Sagira with memories of playful days gone by, and for a moment she wished that Tuya, not Ramla, sat with her at the water's edge. But Tuya kept a careful distance from both Sagira and Ramla.

Ramla opened a papyrus scroll and ran her finger along the colorful images as she read:

My god, my brother, my husband—
How sweet it is to go down to the lotus pond and do as
    you desire—
To plunge into the waters, and bathe before you—
To let you see my beauty in my tunic of sheerest royal
    linen,
All wet and clinging and perfumed with balsam!
I see my husband coming—
My heart is in joy, and my arms are opened wide to
    embrace him;
And my heart rejoices within me without ceasing—
Come to me, O my lord!
When I embrace you and your arms enlace me,
Ah, then I am drunk without beer!

O would that I were the ring on your finger,
So you would cherish me as something that adds beauty
     to your life!

"Stop," Sagira commanded, emotion clotting her voice.
Her husband did not cherish her, for she did not possess
beauty enough to add to his life. Why should he long for a wife
when he could feast his eyes on Tuya, whose beauty put all
others to shame? Even the handsome Paneah possessed more
beauty than Sagira did. No amount of perfume, cosmetics or
fine clothing could disguise the fact that she was the plainest
thing in Potiphar's household. No wonder he despised her.

"You are pitiful." Ramla's icy voice intruded on Sagira's
thoughts. "Sitting in a gilded chair while you feel sorry for
yourself."

Sagira turned away. "I do not need you to help me feel worse."

"I won't flatter you now," Ramla said, rising. She moved
toward Sagira like an approaching vulture. "Years ago, your
childish ego could not bear the truth. Your mother and I assured
you of your beauty, your intelligence, your wit. That time is
finished, Sagira, and yet you still yearn for childish coddling."

"I do not!" Sagira blazed up at the priestess. "I am a wife,
mistress of this house—"

"You are nothing here. The slave Paneah runs this house, for
Potiphar does not trust you. Tuya pleases your husband more
than you do, for I have heard them laughing together in the
courtyard, and Paneah has become the son of Potiphar's heart.
You are good for nothing, Sagira, and yet you sit here, loving
your wounds. A born whiner, all you ask for is a little neglect—"

"You're wrong! I am going to do something about Potiphar!"

"Prove it."

Ramla tossed the challenge casually, then sank gracefully
back into her chair. Sagira looked away and bit her thumb-

nail. How could she do anything with a man as strong-willed as the captain of Pharaoh's guards? Ramla was right, Potiphar didn't trust her to even dispose of a troublesome slave. But if he saw her administrative and social talents on a small scale, perhaps he'd appreciate her. Then he'd spend time with her, just as he visited with Paneah whenever he came home.

She sat up and clapped her hands, then smiled when her handmaid came running. "Send the household scribe to me at once, and have a messenger ready to take a message to Potiphar at the palace," she said, tossing her head so the weight of her wig fell back over her shoulders. "And send Paneah to me. Tell him to drop everything he is doing, for Potiphar is going to host a party."

Ramla laughed when the girl had gone. "Do you truly think a party is going to win your husband's heart?"

"It's something I do well," Sagira answered, bounding out of her chair with the first burst of energy she'd felt in weeks.

She wasn't sure how Paneah managed to convince him, but Potiphar agreed to host a party, the first he had ever given. All of the greatest nobles in Thebes received invitations to the villa, and not one of them declined the opportunity to visit Potiphar's fabled estate.

The celebration fell on a quiet day after an entire week of wind, and Sagira rejoiced to see the house look its best. Fresh flowers adorned each room, the braziers burned with incense, the perfumed cones of fat sat in orderly rows on a tray by the front porch. After making certain the house stood ready to receive its guests, she retreated to her chamber to make herself as beautiful as possible.

She had ordered new jewelry, for Potiphar's treasure chests contained nothing worth wearing, so now the finest creations the jewelers of Thebes could provide adorned her neck, wrists,

fingers and ears. Cunningly wrought in gold, silver and elec-
trum, the ornaments dazzled her handmaid and even impressed Ramla as Sagira pirouetted in her dressing room.

"Be still and let us adorn your face as well," Ramla said,
pressing Sagira onto a stool before her dressing stand. The
maid stood ready with kohl and ground red ochre to color
Sagira's lips.

Ramla studied Sagira's face for a moment, then motioned
for the maid to begin. "You will be so beguiling that Potiphar
will forget his insane notions of not needing a wife."

"He thinks me a child," Sagira said, pouting so the maid
could freely apply the lip color. "Tonight he will see a grown
woman in his house."

"He will see only you." Ramla picked up the perfumed
cone that would adorn the top of Sagira's wig. She sniffed at
the cone and nodded in approval. "With perfumed and oiled
skin, you will win him," she said, smiling. "Tonight you will
have all the weapons of a woman at your disposal."

Sagira studied her sparkling reflection in her bronze mirror,
then closed her eyes. The image that had looked back at her
was mature, sophisticated and as magnificently adorned as
Pharaoh's queen. Surely Potiphar would be impressed. If he
was not, by night's end, at least he would be drunk.

She nodded at the priestess. "Tonight, the old warrior will
surrender to me."

Yosef crinkled his nose as he and Tuya stood apart from
the merrymakers in a doorway off the central reception room.
Before them, in various stages of revelry, the most illustrious
nobles of Pharaoh's court were eating, drinking and singing.
The guests had been drinking since their arrival at noon, and
the sickly sweet odors of beer and perfume mingled in the
hall. To counter the sour odors of sweat and beer, Tuya had

placed garlands and fragrant flowers throughout the house, and to Yosef had fallen the task of securing enough jars and cups, bowls and vases of gold, silver and alabaster to lend an air of opulent gaiety.

"Potiphar's house was lovely," Tuya whispered, leaning toward Yosef's ear. "Tonight I find it gaudy. I prefer the ordinary arrangement of things."

Yosef nodded in wordless agreement as he surveyed the scene. Though he had long ceased to be surprised by the ostentatious Egyptians, his senses were overwhelmed by the abundance of fleshly pleasures in the room. An orchestra of thinly clad maidens played double-reed pipes, lutes, lyres and harps, while a dancing girl clad only in a bronze belt beat out rhythms on a rectangular tambourine as she whirled in front of the drunken guests.

The mood of the gathering had been formal and decorous when Potiphar and Sagira first greeted their guests, but the party had gathered momentum as the wine and beer flowed. Now it surged with raucous life in the tinkly rhythms of the slave girls. Those who chose to dance had progressed from slow, dignified posturings to wild gyrations. One dancer, a dark slave brought by one of the nobles, culminated her dance in a series of leaps, somersaults, back flips and hand springs. The delighted partygoers applauded with heavy hands and loud cries for more.

An army of serving maids circulated among Potiphar's guests, plying the drunken nobles with food of every description. Servants wended their way through the crowd, refilling silver cups with pitchers of flavored beer and wine, while other slaves supplied disheveled guests with fresh floral garlands or paused to tidy up kilts that had slipped out of their proper positions.

Yosef thought he could almost measure the disintegration of the party by the speed with which the cones of perfumed fat had begun to drip down the persons of the formerly dignified guests. Only two participants at the party had kept their composure—neither Sagira nor Ramla had partaken of more than one cup of wine. Ramla sat apart from the company, her dark eyes surveying the group as if she measured and weighed their hearts, and Sagira contented herself with wandering through the crowd and overseeing the needs of her guests. But as the sun set and darkness came on, Sagira surprised the entire gathering by standing on a stool and clapping for attention.

"Hear me, oh guests of Potiphar, the appointed guard of Pharaoh!" she called, her voice ringing over the gathering. A silence, thick as wool, wrapped itself around the revelers. Secure in the limelight, Sagira lifted her hands and turned toward her husband, who leaned heavily on the arm of his chair.

"My husband!" she cried, clapping her hands over her head. "I have composed a poem for you!"

"Let's hear it!" came the cry.

"A poem for Potiphar!" another voice called.

"Tell us!"

"Speak!"

Swaying like a palm tree in the desert, Sagira let the long cloak she had worn all night fall from her shoulders. She stood before the crowd in a sheer golden sheath as transparent as a clear sky. Yosef felt a blush burn his cheek. Embarrassed, he averted his eyes from Sagira's slender figure and studied his master.

"Hurriedly scampers my heart," Sagira recited, swaying in the pulsing rhythm of the room,

When I recall my love of you—
It does not allow me to go about like other mortals—
It seems to have been uprooted from its place.

It doesn't even let me put on my tunic or even take my
    fan—
I am not able to paint my eyes or anoint myself with
    perfume.
'Don't linger thus! Get back to yourself!' I say when I
    think of you.
'Don't cause me silly pain, O my heart!'
Just sit cool and he'll come to you, and everyone will see!
Let not people say of me, 'There's a girl fallen hope-
    lessly in love!'
Stand firm when you think of him, O my heart! Don't
    bound about so!

Wild applause met the finish of her poem, and Sagira stepped down from the stool and prostrated herself at Potiphar's feet, her hands on his ankles. Yosef could not hear if she said anything to the master, but amid the wild hooting Potiphar stood, lifted Sagira to her feet and covered her lips with his in a rough kiss that set the crowd to cheering. Sagira blushed and pulled away, suddenly modest and coy, and in response the master swept his bride into his arms as the guests raised their cups and cheered his prowess. In the rhythm of the drunken throng's escalating roar, Potiphar winked and lurched from the dais where he had been sitting while Sagira tightened her arms about his neck. While the others laughed and lifted their cups, the party's unsteady host and hostess departed the hall for the privacy of the master's chamber.

Yosef and Tuya exchanged glances. It had taken a party and two hin of wine to accomplish it, but Sagira had finally won her husband.

Sagira

*And Yosef was a goodly person, and well favoured.
And it came to pass after these things, that his
master's wife cast her eyes upon Yosef; and she said,
Lie with me.*

Genesis 39:6b–7

Chapter Fifteen

Shadows wreathed Potiphar's chamber as the sun rose, and Sagira moved away from the bed where her husband snored off the effects of the party. Grabbing up her gown, she retrieved her wig and sandals from the floor and slipped wordlessly through the corridor until she came to her own room. Ramla was still asleep, a thin covering thrown over her.

Sagira tossed her expensive wig toward its stand and sank onto her bed, biting her knuckles. She wanted to scream, to beat someone, to cry and lament and tear her clothing. Life wasn't fair! She had entered this marriage fully expecting a normal, happy union, but last night's reality had hit her like a cold slap in the face. Potiphar should never have married her, but her parents, Pharaoh and Narmer had not given him a choice in the matter. The entire world had conspired against the bride and groom to play an ironic joke, a terrible trick.

When Ramla stirred, Sagira dropped her hand from her mouth and sat upright, gathering what little dignity she had left. Last night she had behaved like a prostitute, flaunting herself before a drunken crowd and gyrating to silly, useless poetry to please a man who could never be a husband to her. Did everyone know the truth? How many nobles would mock her name this morning over their breakfasts? How would the gossips magnify her forward behavior? What would Pharaoh say when he heard? What would her mother think?

"Bastet have mercy," she murmured, dropping her head into her hands.

Ramla sat up in the gloom. "Are you happy now, little one? Shall I begin counting the days until your son is born?"

Drained of will and thought, Sagira shook her head.

"Well, perhaps I will wait," Ramla murmured. "And if a child does not come from this occasion, there will be other times when Potiphar will call for you. Now that the wall between you has been breached—"

"There will be no son," Sagira answered dully. "No daughter, no child. The mighty Potiphar has left his manhood behind on some battlefield."

Ramla's face went pale. "You lie."

"I do not." Sagira clenched her jaw. "I may be young, but I am not a fool."

"Pharaoh would never—"

"Pharaoh does not know," Sagira answered, shaking her head. "How could he? If this were the morning after our wedding, I would demand that the marriage be set aside. But how can I explain to Pharaoh that I did not discover this truth until now? Too many months have passed, Ramla. I would die of embarrassment if I had to expose the truth before Pharaoh's court and—"

"You cannot have the marriage set aside," Ramla interrupted, settling her elbows on her bent knees and steepling her fingers. "You will lose Potiphar's property if you do." Her eyes narrowed in speculation. "You must say nothing of this to anyone. Keep Potiphar's reputation intact. Be kind and respectful to him—he was so drunk he will probably recall nothing of last night. He will think you went to your chamber as usual."

"But what of my son?" Sagira cried. "The prophecy! How am I to have a child with Potiphar? The gods have made a mistake, I was not meant to marry him—"

"Hush for now," Ramla soothed her. "The gods cannot be wrong. There is a way out of this, there has to be." The priestess swung her thin legs out of her narrow cot and drew near, then placed her cool hands on Sagira's hot shoulders. "Sleep now, my lady, and let me consider this. I will consult the goddess about what we should do."

Relaxing in the older woman's authoritative tone, Sagira allowed herself to be pressed back onto her bed. Ramla dropped a linen cover over her, and Sagira closed her eyes to block out the haunting knowledge she'd gleaned in the last few hours. How many others knew of Potiphar's war injuries? Did Paneah know? Had he told Tuya? Last night she had felt their eyes on her as she swayed before her husband in the ritual of seduction—were they laughing at her now?

She turned onto her side and thumbed tears of anger and frustration from her eyes as Ramla began a sacred chant.

For three days Sagira moved throughout the household in a false and brittle dignity. Underneath her artificial smile seethed an anger and indignation unlike anything she had ever felt, but no one seemed to sense it.

When she could no longer endure the sickening sensation of her life plunging downward, Sagira decided to confront her husband.

Potiphar came home after dark, as usual, probably hoping that she had already gone to sleep. She waited until the rushlight burned steadily in his room before creeping to his door. She was about to enter when she heard Potiphar speak, so she flattened herself against the wall and coiled into the shadows.

Paneah answered, his voice like steel wrapped in silk, and for a moment she forgot her resolve and concentrated on the sound. Now there was a man! How handsome the slave was, and how youthful! But he didn't like her, and she had made no attempts to win his approval since the awful day she'd tried to send Tuya away.

She lingered until Paneah finished his report and left Potiphar's chamber. He walked out with his gaze fastened to a papyrus scroll, and did not look back. Relieved, Sagira pushed the door aside and boldly entered to stand before her husband.

"Sagira! Is something wrong?" he asked, obviously startled by her appearance. He had removed his sword and his wig; she could see ginger-colored freckles on his bald skull. "Do not worry, my husband," she said, her gaze darting to the bed where he would soon take his rest. "I do not intend to stay. I came only to say that you have wronged me. You should have told me the truth long before this."

His face flamed crimson, but he did not deny the unspoken problem between them. "I tried to tell you I did not intend to marry," he said, fumbling with the clasp of a leopard-skin mantle across his shoulders. "But who can deny the divine pharaoh?"

"Still, you should have been honest with me. For months I thought you did not take me into your arms because—" She paused and took a deep breath. It hurt to speak the truth, but since she was urging him to be honest, she should be just as forthright. "I thought you did not love me because I am not beautiful."

The warrior's stone face cracked into humanity. "Ah, Sagira, I never meant to hurt you. I thought you would be relieved that I did not call you into my chambers. Why should a young girl yearn for a scarred battle horse like me?"

Without his wig, he looked like a day-old hatchling, bald, wobbly and uncertain. Sagira could almost feel sorry for him, but he had wronged her too deeply.

He shook his head. "I did not think my indifference would hurt you. You seemed content with your friend, and I—"

"You did not want the court to know the extent of your scars," she whispered, looking at the floor. "Does anyone know?"

He hesitated. "Tuthmosis knew, and would probably have forced me to leave the army, but he died before doing anything about it. Amenhotep has no idea…and I am not going to tell him."

He delivered the last remark with a commander's conviction, yet Sagira sensed that it was also a plea. "Fear not, Potiphar," she said, giving him a small smile. "I will not reveal your secret. To do so would tell the world that Pharaoh made a mistake."

"A god cannot make mistakes," Potiphar said, a note of fond indulgence in his voice. "How often I have reminded myself of that truth." He turned and motioned toward a chair. "Won't you sit down, my dear? Perhaps we should talk of other things. I find that this conversation has left me feeling quite…relieved."

Sagira took the seat he offered while Potiphar squatted on the edge of his low bed. "Do not think you are not beautiful," he said, looking at her with something that might have been sympathy in his eyes. "You are a true daughter of the Nile, a composite of all that is good in our people. I've seen your cleverness and your zest for living. I must confess…bringing you into my house has made me feel old."

Sagira studied her husband carefully. She had never imagined that he thought about anything but Pharaoh and his warriors. Had she truly affected him?

"Beauty counts for little at the end of a man's life," Potiphar continued. "Faithfulness is what I have come to treasure most.

The faithfulness of Pharaoh, of the men in my command, of my able Paneah, who has brought blessings on my humble house. I don't ask you to shine as a beauty, Sagira. I only ask that you be faithful to a husband who will do you no wrong. And someday—" he gestured toward the outer hall "—this will all be yours."

"Faithful," she whispered the word. "I can be faithful."

"I believe you." He rested his elbows on his knees and chuckled softly. "When a man has more yesterdays than tomorrows, he learns the value of forthrightness. I will always speak truly to you, Sagira, and ask that you speak plainly to me. Let there be no more secrets between us."

"Agreed," Sagira said, rising. She walked toward her husband and pressed her palm to the battlefield of wrinkles on his cheek. "No more secrets," she echoed, then she kissed his forehead and left him alone to his sleep.

"What did he say?" Ramla demanded when Sagira reentered her chamber. "Was he angry? Did he deny the truth?"

"He denied nothing." Sagira slipped her heavy wig from her head, placed it on its stand, then sighed and reclined on her couch. "He was glad to be honest with me. He said if I am faithful to him, he will treat me well. And someday I will inherit all he possesses."

"When he dies," Ramla whispered, her eyes wide. A sudden smile broke her usually stern countenance. "So that is how the gods will work. When Potiphar dies, Sagira, you will remarry. Then you will bear a son to head the next dynasty!"

"No," Sagira answered, studying her nails. "I will have a son of my own choosing. I am tired of waiting for the gods to work their will. I will travel the road of my own life."

The priestess blanched. "You speak blasphemy. Bastet will not listen to you."

"Bastet may do whatever she likes," Sagira answered, her voice tight with mutiny. "If Bastet does not approve, I'll send my offerings to Hathor or Horus or the temple of Amon-Re. One of them will hear my petition. You have said, Ramla, that the prophecy cannot be changed. So any god can come to my aid, and one of them will."

Ramla stiffened and took on a defensive air, but Sagira ignored her disapproving frown. In time she would change her opinion, for Sagira could easily cast off the priestess of Bastet in favor of a representative from one of the other temples.

"Perhaps, with the proper offerings, Bastet can be persuaded to assist you," Ramla finally murmured. "But how will you choose a son? You cannot plant seed into your own womb—"

"I will have a son whose beauty makes up for my lack." Sagira swung her legs onto the floor, then stood and paced in the room. "I will bear a son whose presence will slap Potiphar in the face, just payment for the grief I have endured on his account. My son will be well-suited to wear the double crown of Egypt—he will possess my cunning and his father's gifts of administration and knowledge. The royal blood of the Two Kingdoms will flow through his veins. I have promised Potiphar to be faithful, and I will be—faithful to the prophecy, to myself."

Ramla moved to block Sagira's path. "Who?"

Sagira lifted her chin. "I will present Potiphar with the son of Paneah the slave, and he will not deny my son's legitimacy."

"He will have you put away for adultery!" Ramla hissed, clenching her fists. "The captain of the king's guard will not accept a child he knows is not his—"

"He will," Sagira answered. "All who attended our party think Potiphar the embodiment of virility. His pride will not allow him to disown the son I will place into his hands. He is firmly in my power, for I know his secret." Her mouth curved in a mirthless smile. "A slave's child will become Potiphar's heir and Egypt's king. The ever-faithful and capable Paneah will sire my son."

Ramla felt her way through Potiphar's garden, easing through a darkness so complete it felt like liquid. She experienced a similar feeling each time she invoked the powers that gave her the ability to see into the future. The first time she had attempted it, fear of the unknown knotted and writhed in her stomach, but that terrible sensation faded as the heavens opened and revealed their secrets.

Those secrets bound the priestess to Sagira even now. She had known for years that Lady Kahent would call at the temple of Bastet, and the first time her eyes fell on Sagira she had known she would find her destiny in the swarthy little girl.

If not for that certainty, Ramla would have left Potiphar's house long ago. Sagira was spoiled, headstrong and prone to be foolish, but Ramla could not deny what she had seen. The girl would make an impression on the sands of time, and Ramla wanted to be a part of it. She wanted to be…significant.

As a baby, she had been deposited on the steps of Bastet's temple, a nameless, malformed creature whose mewing elicited pity from the hearts of the priests. With bitter pride as her strength, she had grown wise in the ways of the priesthood. One dark night, much like this one, she had opened her soul to the powers of the gods.

Those powers had led her to Sagira, and her unwavering faith in the vision of the future would force her to stay.

Sagira sailed through the next few days like a waterfowl on the Nile—calm on the surface, but paddling furiously beneath. The seduction of Potiphar's steward must be carefully planned, for several obstacles lay in her path. First and foremost, the entire household knew of the deep love between Paneah and Tuya. Perfectly attuned to one another, the two slaves could read glances and upraised brows without speaking a word. Such a bond would not be easy to break.

Sagira's second problem involved Paneah's inscrutable detachment. He had learned far better than Tuya how to maintain a respectful gap between master and slave, and he kept a careful distance between himself and his mistress. Winning his confidence would not be easy. Sagira knew that if she stepped toward him with anything akin to interest in her eyes, the young man would turn and leave without hesitation.

Other complications begged to be considered—the when and how and where of the conception, as well as what should be done about Potiphar when her belly began to swell. Perhaps he could be pacified with a story about how a god assumed human form and visited her to beget the worthy and wounded Potiphar a son. After all, thousands of Egyptians believed a variation of that tale every time a son of Pharaoh was born. Without such a visitation from the gods, Pharaoh would not be a son of his father god, Osiris.

Sagira smiled in contemplation of her success. Her son's birth would punish those who had hurt her most, and the child would be a destroyer of Egypt's enemies throughout his life. He would be the greatest pharaoh the world had ever seen, and as his mother, she would live forever in the memories of men. *For as long as the world exists, men will speak of you...*

Such had the prophecy promised.

In order to win Paneah's participation, Sagira set out to understand him. Without calling him to her side, she studied the slave as he served meals; she peered down at him from the roof as he moved through the stockyard, the granaries and the slaves' workrooms. Once she realized that he rendezvoused with Tuya every night in the garden, Sagira secreted herself among the bushes to spy on the lovers sitting at the edge of the pool.

On her first night amid the acacias, she thought them as boring as old people who had been married for years. Tuya inquired about Paneah's day in the fields; Paneah asked about the bakers and butler and supplies of oil. Soon they exhausted the topics of ordinary conversation, however, and fell silent. The sky was black and icy with a wash of brilliant stars, a perfect night for lovers. When Paneah ran his hand over Tuya's glossy hair, Sagira leaned forward, her hands pressing on the moist black earth and her knees sliding over the slippery carpet of fallen leaves.

"I don't know what I'd do without you, Tuya." Paneah's voice gentled as he spoke to the girl by his side, and Tuya's oval face glowed as she sighed and called her lover Yosef.

Yosef? Sagira frowned. The name was not Egyptian, but it fell from Tuya's lips as if she had spoken it a thousand times. It must have been his name before Potiphar's house, or perhaps it sprang from his boyhood. Yosef. The word had an Asiatic sound, perhaps it was a name from one of the Canaanite tribes.

Sagira made a mental note to ask Ramla to investigate, and turned her ear to listen more closely. The black earth had to be staining her linen dress, but she didn't care.

"I like the cornflowers and nightshade along the garden wall," Paneah was saying, his head inclining toward Tuya's. "But the lotuses...the fragrance is so sweet, especially when the flowers have been around your throat."

When he ducked to sniff the flesh of her neck, Tuya laughed and gently pushed him away. "The blue lotuses are my favorite, but I shall not wear a lotus garland ever again if you cannot control yourself," she said, teasing him with her eyes. "I shall wear plain ivy. It has no fragrance at all."

Tuya rose to her knees, then moved behind Paneah and rubbed his shoulders. "Ah, you have found the spot," he murmured, his head tipping back to rest against her. He closed his eyes and sighed. "I could spend the entire night right here, but only if you'll promise to continue until morning."

"And how can I do that?" Tuya leaned forward. "When the sun rises, my work begins, and I must have sleep."

"As must I," Paneah murmured. His hand rose and clasped hers. "We must say goodnight, my love. Until tomorrow."

"Until tomorrow," Tuya answered, lowering herself until she sat facing him. Their foreheads met for a long moment of communion, then Paneah lifted his head and pressed his lips to the girl's forehead.

From behind the bush, Sagira held her breath, imagining his lips on hers.

"Four more years," Tuya murmured when they parted.

"They'll fly like hours," Paneah answered, then Tuya stood and moved away, releasing his hand only when his arm would reach no farther. Sagira waited until Paneah left the garden, too, then she emerged from her hiding place and brushed the soil from her knees and hands.

Four years? What did they mean? She frowned, then set her feet toward Potiphar's chamber where a thin stream of lamplight still glowed beneath his doorway. He would know what Tuya meant. And, being in her power, he would tell her.

Sagira fidgeted uncomfortably in the garden's heat. The fan Tuya moved back and forth did nothing but displace hot air, and the water in Sagira's goblet was blood warm, impossible to enjoy.

Ramla approached, back from her month at the temple, and Sagira sat up, eager to hear news from other parts of the city. "Welcome, my lady," Ramla said, as cool as ever in her spotless white gown and golden collar. "Bastet has smiled on you."

"I'm glad to hear it," Sagira remarked, giving the woman a half smile. "Sit down, Ramla, and tell me everything you've heard this month. What's the latest gossip of Thebes?"

"Dismiss these slaves," Ramla ordered, tossing the back of her hand toward Tuya. "I find them distracting."

Sagira nodded toward Tuya and the girl who stood ready at the pitcher, and both slaves hurried into the house, eager to be out of the hot sun. When they had gone, Ramla frowned and shook out the linen veil she used to protect the tender skin of her shaved head. "By the wisdom of Bastet, why do you sit here when you could be inside? The sun has obviously baked your brains."

"I like the garden," Sagira said, smiling at the memory of spying on Paneah. In the last few days she had given Tuya work to keep the girl busy into the night. Paneah had wandered in the garden alone, waiting, unaware that Sagira watched his every move. "Tell me." She leaned toward the priestess. "What have you learned about the name Yosef?"

Ramla sighed, but a satisfied smile curled on her lips. "It is a Hebrew name meaning 'add to me.'"

Sagira tilted her head, marveling. "Our Paneah is a Hebrew?"

"The Hebrews," Ramla went on, lifting a brow, "have a history with the ancient pharaohs. The father of the Hebrews, Avram, came to dwell in Egypt years ago. He traveled with a beautiful woman he called his sister. She, of course, was taken into Pharaoh's harem, so Avram's god closed up the wombs of Pharaoh's wives. Several of them bore dead babies, and others lost the fruit of their womb before their time had come. Pharaoh's priests divined the truth—Sarai was not Avram's sister, but his wife."

"How terrible," Sagira said, relishing every word of the tale.

"When the priests of Amon-Re revealed the plague's cause to Pharaoh, he called Avram and expelled him, his wife and all his possessions from Egypt's borders. A sizable military force escorted them from the land of the Two Kingdoms. In the temple scrolls it is written that Pharaoh prayed he would never again see a Hebrew in the dominions of Egypt."

"Yet we have one in our house," Sagira whispered, staring at the reflecting pool.

Ramla leaned forward. "Do you not think this a bad omen? You want to have a child with this Hebrew, and his god has the power to kill babies in the womb—"

"My Hebrew has but one god, and I have a plethora of them," Sagira said, turning to the other woman. "Are many not more powerful than one?"

Ramla threw her a questioning glance, but Sagira only smiled and tucked her leg under her skirt. She had Bastet, Amon-Re and all the gods of Egypt to do battle for her. Above all, she had time to consider her challenge and study the object of her desire.

Chapter Sixteen

With pleased surprise Yosef noticed that the crop of his fourth year in Potiphar's house was more than triple the amount harvested in his first year. The healthy cattle lowing in the stockyard pressed for larger quarters, and Potiphar's horses won so many chariot races that the noblemen of Thebes clamored for the foals of the estate's stallions. Potiphar now paid more taxes than any man in Thebes, and this fact finally earned him the coveted Gold of Praise.

His master wore the face of a happy man, and Yosef thought the household a contented one. Tuya seemed satisfied to wait out the remaining years until they should be freed and wed, and Sagira seemed to have settled into her role as pampered mistress of the sprawling estate. Ramla kept to her mistress's side or to herself in the small temple at the villa. Though the priestess regarded Yosef with wary eyes, she stayed clear of his approach and did not bother him.

Though deprived of precious freedom, the slaves of Potiphar's household were a great deal more prosperous than the poor of Pharaoh's kingdom. Well fed, clothed and housed by their affluent master, they did not have to work past sundown or labor to pay taxes to the divine pharaoh. Now even Potiphar's most disgruntled slave admitted that Paneah was a gift from the gods. The young man was a compassionate but firm taskmaster who listened to their grievances and requests.

Most of the slaves even bore a grudging respect for Potiphar's wife. Though headstrong and spoiled, Sagira had brought the household into the circle of nobility. The once dull and dusty villa now regularly rang with the cultured voices of visiting nobles and their wives. Potiphar's slaves felt themselves superior to the poor and quite the equivalent of the merchants who lined the dusty streets of Thebes.

One afternoon Yosef had just finished settling a squabble between the cook and the baker when Tuya came with word that Lady Sagira wanted to see him in the garden. "I'll go at once," Yosef said, giving Tuya a conspiratorial wink. "She probably wants me to decorate for another of her parties."

"Shouldn't she ask me to do that?" Tuya asked. "What would you know about a lady's party?"

Yosef waved her away. "I was joking. I'm sure it's nothing important."

He found his mistress alone in the garden. Her back was to him as he approached, her thick wig heavy with golden beads that sparkled amid the darkness of her hair like stars in a midnight sky.

"Mistress? You sent for me?"

Her eyes were strangely veiled when she turned to look at him, but the smile on her face was warm, the smile between two equals, not slave and owner. "Thank you for coming, Paneah," she said, her voice as golden as the sun overhead. He was about to prostrate himself, but she noticed and motioned for him to remain on his feet. "Please, don't bow. When we are alone, you need not observe foolish formalities."

Yosef nodded. "How may I serve you?"

Her smile deepened. "I wonder if you could give me a few suggestions about this garden. I have come to love this place, and want to expand it beyond its present borders."

"Did you want to expand it for some special occasion?"

"For every day." She tilted her head as she looked up at him. The deft makeup around her eyes gave her the sleepy-eyed look of an elegant kitten. "I want to have it beautiful always, so I can enjoy its charm whenever I want."

She stepped forward on the tiled pathway and gestured for him to follow. "I love the serenity of a garden, don't you?"

Yosef's mouth went dry. Masters did not often ask their slaves for personal opinions. Even Potiphar, who trusted Yosef to run nearly every detail of his life, did not trouble himself to ask for Yosef's personal preferences. "I like the garden," he said, feeling tongue-tied and dull. The mistress would think him a total imbecile.

But Sagira only walked farther down the path. "I like all flowers, but the lotus blossom is my favorite." She turned to smile at him. "The fragrance is perfect—not too sweet, not too woodsy. Don't you think so?"

Stunned by yet another personal question, Yosef could only nod in agreement.

"So what do you think?" she asked, moving again along the walkway. "What plants can we add to bring more beauty to this place?"

She was two steps beyond him before he found the words. "Mandrakes, irises, narcissuses and poppies for the ground. Blue water lilies and white lotuses for the pond," he said, grateful she had finally asked a question that did not require a personal reply. He hurried to keep pace with her. "And we can bring in additional white lotus plants. They grow well in water."

"And they bloom at night," Sagira whispered, almost to herself.

"The blossoms remain open almost until midday," he said, hurrying to defend the plants Tuya loved. "It is only the heat of the sun they cannot stand."

"Don't worry, Paneah, I shall not want them at midday. I like the garden at night, and think I shall walk here often. And of course, I shall want all of the flowers to myself." She gave him a guilty smile. "Tell the servants not to touch them, will you please? Those I don't wear I shall offer to the goddess in the little temple."

"As you wish," Yosef answered.

Sagira stopped to reach for a lotus blossom growing near the edge of the pool, then smiled helplessly when her short arms couldn't reach the flower. Taking the hint, he splashed into the water to retrieve the blossom, then bowed and presented it to her.

"Thank you." A blush colored her cheek as she inhaled the sweet scent. Yosef waited with his hands folded while her eyes closed in pleasure. "You must share this," she murmured, not moving the blossom from her face. "Bend down, Paneah, and let the lotus entice you."

He paused, uncertain how to proceed, and her dark eyes flew open. "Don't you like the scent of lotus blossoms?"

"I like it very much."

"Then breathe in this one," she whispered, closing her eyes again. "It is sweeter than most, for it is offered by your mistress."

Yosef bent at the waist. Feeling like an adolescent boy, he lowered his head toward the flower only inches from her lips. He scarcely dared to breathe lest he offend her with his nearness.

The lids rose from her black velvet eyes. "Isn't it wonderful?" she asked, her gaze holding him.

"Yes, mistress," he whispered.

With the unpredictability of a butterfly, her hand rose to tap the bridge of his nose. Shocked into stillness, Yosef did not move as her fingertips trailed across the wings of his nostrils, then dropped to caress his lips.

"You are as beautiful as the lotus, my Paneah," she said, a sultry tone in her voice. "A most striking and unique Egyptian."

An alarm bell rang in his mind as she emphasized the latter word. Why was she toying with him? Did she suspect that he was not of Egypt?

She did not seem to notice that his breathing had quickened. She turned without further comment and tucked the lotus blossom into the neckline of her dress.

"See to the flowers, will you, Paneah?" she asked, moving toward the house. "Have them installed as soon as possible. I do love the garden."

Yosef sighed in relief when her small figure disappeared beyond the gate.

"I couldn't believe it," Yosef said, glancing over his shoulder as he spoke with Tuya in the garden. "She made me uncomfortable."

Tuya struggled to smother a smile, for Yosef was as jumpy as a kitten. "What did she do, exactly?"

He lowered his voice. "She asked me to smell a lotus blossom. And then she touched my face."

For an instant, a white-hot dart of jealousy pierced Tuya's heart, but she smiled and tried to ignore the pain. Yosef loved her steadfastly. And Sagira had a husband.

"You are making too much of this," Tuya said, placing a comforting hand on his arm. "Think, Yosef, of all our mistress has endured! I know her like no one else, and though she is spoiled and headstrong, I fear Sagira is lonely." She turned her gaze to the moon's reflection in the shallow pool. "I think she has grown tired of her priestess. She has spurned me and is too proud to call me back, but Sagira cannot live alone. She needs company, the fellowship of friends, and our master is not home often enough to give her the society she needs."

"She has parties every week," Yosef pointed out. "Surely you can't want her to have more guests and feasts—"

"No, I have all the work I need," Tuya answered, softening her voice. "And Sagira does love parties, but what happens when the last guest is gone? She is left alone. She needs a friend, Yosef, and you are close to Potiphar. Perhaps she hopes to win her husband's attention through you. She's turning to you—"

"I'd rather she turned to one of her maids."

"Maids and mistresses cannot be friends. Such things are not done."

"Potiphar and I are friends."

"Potiphar is an unusual master," Tuya answered. "And while he treats you as a confidant, does he invite you to eat with him? Does he take you with him to Pharaoh's court? No. You are his slave, and you will be kept in your place."

She knew these things instinctively, but Yosef had not been born a slave. His had been a privileged life, and moments like these revealed his upbringing.

Tuya ran her hand over his back and began to knead the tense muscles. "Please, Yosef, be kind to Sagira," she whispered. "Then Potiphar will reward you for being a friend to his lonely wife. Perhaps our time of waiting will be shortened."

Yosef groaned and tipped his head back as his muscles relaxed. "For you, Tuya, I will be her friend," he finally said, giving her a sidelong glance.

She nudged him gently with her shoulder. "You are wonderful."

Something rustled in the nearby bushes, but when she turned to investigate, the garden shimmered still and quiet in the moonlight. "Did you hear something?"

"Only the pounding of my heart," Yosef murmured, smiling.

* * *

Sagira ran her finger over the rim of the bowl she had placed on the altar at the villa's temple. Ramla had been gone for a full month, fulfilling her religious duties, and Sagira was anxious to speak with her. The priestess should have returned two days ago, but perhaps she had been delayed—

A commotion at the gate distracted Sagira's attention, and she lifted her head and peered through the temple's doorway. A tall, veiled woman was greeting the gatekeeper, and Sagira recognized the disfigured hand on her traveling veil. Good! She turned back to the altar, determined that the priestess should not know how eagerly she had been awaited.

Sandaled footsteps slapped on the pavement, then Ramla prostrated herself before the statue of Bastet. Sagira pressed her lips together and allowed the priestess a moment of silence, then nudged the woman with the edge of her sandal.

Ramla sat up and regarded her friend. "How are things in Potiphar's house?" she asked, lifting an eyebrow. "What have you done in my absence?"

"Nothing," Sagira said, sinking to the floor. "I nearly lost my self-control once, but then I realized that I need the gods to help me through this. If Paneah's Hebrew god is truly powerful, I dare not proceed without Bastet's protection."

"So you still plan to conceive a child with this Hebrew?"

"So you still disapprove?" Sagira turned her eyes to the stone idol. "Bastet has answered my petitions thus far. She must approve of me."

Ramla slipped the dusty veil from her shoulders. "Bastet sometimes allows her children to do things they ought not to do. Many hard lessons of life are learned this way." She paused, her dark eyes fixed on the floor. "As a priestess, I would advise you to wait until Potiphar's death. Then you can remarry and bear a legitimate son. But as a woman—"

"Yes?"

"As a woman, who would not desire Paneah?" Ramla's lean shoulder lifted in an elegant shrug. "My own heart has been stirred by the beauty of his countenance. He is truly a man among men."

"Keep your heart focused on the goddess," Sagira answered, bracing herself on the altar as she rose from her knees. "Paneah is mine. But if you're still willing to help, I need you."

The priestess's mouth curved in a dry smile. "What can I do?"

"Divine the future for me. I know the goddess will allow women to conceive only on certain days, and I would know the proper day for my son's conception. And I would know Paneah's future, to be certain he is the best one for my plan." She fixed the priestess in a determined gaze. "Consult the goddess, work your magic, and you will be handsomely rewarded."

Ramla's thin chest heaved as if she were weighing the cost, then she nodded. "I will do it," she said, rising. "But not for a reward. I do this to ensure your success, my Sagira. If Paneah's future proves your plan, you will have my enduring support. But if the gods reveal a dark future, will you promise to give up this foolish notion?"

"Yes." Sagira nodded, eager to promise anything that would put her plan into motion. "Call on your powers, Ramla, and do it quickly!"

An hour later, Sagira helped Ramla to her bed. The priestess had worked her magic, uttered her predictions and collapsed onto the floor in another of her strange seizures. Such pain was a dire price to pay for knowledge of the future, but Sagira would have been willing to sacrifice even Ramla's life for the final news.

The prophecy was both thrilling and disappointing. Well into her trance, Sagira had moaned and trembled and proclaimed that Paneah would be elevated to a position of power, and every knee in Egypt would bow at his approach. Exhilarated, Sagira had pressed for more news. "So when shall I confront him?" she urged, ready to shake the answers from the wide-eyed priestess. "When?"

"The eighteenth day of the second month of the third year," Ramla muttered. "The first day of the Feast of Opet."

"So long?" Sagira cried. "Three years from now?"

As Ramla collected her strength, Sagira paced through her chamber and chewed on her henna-tinted nails. "I cannot wait three years. I am ready to have a child now!"

"Perfection cannot be rushed," Ramla murmured. "The gods know what they are doing. Besides, you will need time to prepare for this assignation."

"I've already begun preparation," Sagira replied.

"Then slow your pace," Ramla warned. "You will need three years to bind him to your side. And three years to rid his heart of the slave girl's memory."

"Tuya?" Sagira stopped pacing as her throat tightened. "How can I get rid of her? I can't sell her. Potiphar won't allow it."

Ramla pressed a hand over her eyes. "There are other ways. Paneah's love for Tuya is rooted in his heart. His love for you must spring from the flesh, and fleshly love is easily enticed. You must separate them, keep him from her arms so he will be mad with longing for a tender embrace. Then, in time, you will feed him with your kisses and command your will to be done." She lowered her hand, her eyes narrowing as she looked at Sagira. "Together we can do this. You work with the man. Leave the slave girl to me."

Even in her exhaustion, Ramla's eyes glowed with malevolence.

"You truly hate Tuya, don't you?" Sagira asked. "Why?"

"Why does a cat hate a dog? Some beings are natural enemies." Without further discussion, Ramla turned her back on Sagira and walked away.

Two days later, Yosef told Tuya that the mistress wanted her to accompany Ramla to Bubastis, the home of Bastet's main temple. An important center of trade and commerce, Bubastis lay far north in the Egyptian delta. At Sagira's request, Potiphar authorized an escort of ten warriors to safely guide his wife's patron priestess.

Tuya had no time for goodbyes, for she had to gather Ramla's possessions and load donkeys with their bundles of provisions. The ten guards, outfitted with bows and quivers filled with shining bronze arrows, stamped impatiently in the courtyard as Tuya flew throughout the house, leaving instructions to those who would fill the vacancy she would leave. She had no opportunity for a private goodbye with Yosef, for Sagira kept him by her side, reminding him of the arrangements he had promised to make for her new garden.

Take care, and may God go with you, Yosef's smile seemed to say as he caught Tuya's eye in the courtyard. She gave him a timid, fleeting smile, then took her place beside a donkey in the midst of Potiphar's men. Tall and dispassionate, Ramla mounted another donkey and nodded to the guards. Sagira called a noisy goodbye from the porch; Potiphar lifted his hand in farewell.

I won't look back. Tuya kept her eyes fixed on the scrawny tail of the donkey ahead as a nameless fear swept through her soul. *The days will fly like minutes, the years will fly like days. I will be back soon. This means nothing.*

As they passed out of the villa, she balled her hands into fists, fighting back tears that swelled in her chest.

Chapter Seventeen

With a triumphant smile, Sagira watched them go. When no sign of the caravan remained on the horizon, she turned and placed a hand on Paneah's arm. "Bring a pitcher of water and honey to my chamber," she said, taking pains to keep her eagerness from her voice. "This heat—and this day—have drained me."

Paneah bowed, then turned toward the kitchen. Sagira gave Potiphar a bright smile, but his thoughts had already drifted toward his guards, for he gave her an absent wave and stalked away toward the ivy-covered wall that disguised the prison. Sagira shuddered, watching him go toward that awful place. She did not like to remember that condemned criminals lurked in dank cells only yards away from her lovely home, but the captain of Pharaoh's bodyguard was also the overseer of Pharaoh's jail. The king certainly didn't want criminals near his palace.

She ran up the porch steps and hurried through the central hall of the house. Her chambers had been cleaned and aired that morning, and fresh linen curtains billowed about her bed. Sagira touched a burning coal to a coil of sweet incense. She would not win Paneah in a day, but she would teach him not to jump at her touch. With gentle persuasion, any wild rabbit could be taught to eat from the hand.

She checked her face in her bronze mirror, adjusted the angle of her wig, and lay on her bed, artfully spreading her garments so a modest length of her leg peeped through the slit in her gown. She moistened her lips with her tongue, peered at her fingernails, and froze like a nervous bride at the sound of footsteps in the hall.

A discreet servant's cough signaled Paneah's arrival outside her door. *Now it begins.*

"Come in," she called, her voice a mournful wail. The door opened and Paneah's handsome face peered in on her. She forced herself to bite her lip until her chin quivered; she looked as woebegone as her pounding heart would permit.

"Mistress, is something wrong?" He lingered in the doorway, the cup and pitcher on a tray in his hand.

She squinted and pretended to wipe tears from her cheeks. "It is nothing, Paneah, that you would understand. Sometimes I think no one understands."

He paused. From eavesdropping on his conversations with Tuya, she knew him so well she could almost hear two voices arguing in his head. Part of him wanted to leave the tray and run; another part wanted to obey the sweet urgings toward friendship Tuya had given him in the garden.

"When I think no one understands," he answered slowly, "I remember that God does. God is good, a stronghold in the day of trouble, and he is a friend to those who trust in him."

He gave her a safe and impersonal answer, but a man lived beneath that cool exterior. Sagira lifted wide eyes to meet his. "No god cares for me. Put down the tray, Paneah. You may go. But if you do, I will have no one." She lifted her voice in a plaintive wail and turned her face to the wall. "Ramla has left and Tuya has gone and Potiphar is busy with his prison! My mother will not see me because—well, you do not want to listen. Even the servants here care nothing for me."

"You are wrong, mistress," he answered, his voice careful and quiet. "You are held in great—affection—by all who serve you. The master is busy, but he will be back, and Ramla and Tuya will return soon—"

"Each day here feels like a year," she whispered, covering her face with her hands. "Every month an eternity. And I am alone, without a friend in the world—"

Crying came easily, for her heightened emotions had left her fragile. She burst into tears and curled into a ball on the bed. Beneath the sound of her sobs she heard Paneah step toward the door as if to call for help, then he moved to her side.

"Please, mistress," he said. "Do not cry."

She did not stop weeping, but extended her hand in entreaty. For a moment she feared he would retreat, but he must not have been able to resist the impulse to help another. Her senses fluttered when his hand touched hers, and for a moment she nearly forgot her careful plan.

This hand would one day rule Egypt. This man would give her a child.

Like a drowning woman, she pulled him to her side, unwilling to let him go.

"Paneah," she wept, genuine tears flowing freely as she sat up and slipped under the warmth of his arm. "Can you know how it feels to be utterly forsaken?"

His eyes filled with words, yet he did not speak. His tense arm felt as heavy as lead, but he patted her in wordless sympathy. She was breathless, overcome by the thought of his power and strength, but she did not move until many moments had passed.

At last her tears stopped and his hand ceased its gentle

patting of her arm. The tingling effects of his touch had spread through her like wildfire, but she forced herself to be calm and think clearly. This Paneah was still skittish, and very much in love with someone else.

"Oh—" she forced a laugh as she wiped her eyes "—I suppose you think me a silly, homesick girl."

"No, mistress." He lifted his arm from her shoulders and lowered his gaze to the floor. "I know what it is to be abandoned."

"Perhaps you shall tell me your story sometime." She tapped his leg with easy familiarity. "We have much in common, you and I."

She smiled at him when he stood. "Thank you, Paneah," she said, looking into his dark eyes. "I feel—so safe with you."

"I am glad to serve you," he replied, and as he left her chamber Sagira gave her mirror an exultant smile. "Ah, Ramla, if only you could have seen. The wild rabbit is tamed!"

During the two months of Tuya's absence, Sagira called Paneah to her side as often as she could without seeming to grant him undue favor. Keeping the conversation light, she inquired about the fields, the cattle and horses, and the servants. One morning she linked her arm through his and announced that she had decided to become his shadow.

Honest alarm filled the young man's eyes. "But, mistress! It isn't proper that you should walk in some of the places where I must go."

"Paneah," she chided, facing him. She glanced right and left to be sure they were alone, then gave him a shy smile. "I know Potiphar has promised to give you freedom and his permission to marry our lovely Tuya. If you are going to leave us in a few years, shouldn't I know how this household is run? After all, it is a woman's proper place to oversee the house, and I have been spoiled by your competence. But since you will be leaving—" she pinched his muscled arm "—don't you think I should know what you do?"

For this he had no answer. Sagira smiled. "You must wait here while I change into something more appropriate for the fields. Then you shall lead the way, Paneah, and show me how and why Potiphar's house has become the wealthiest in all of Thebes."

Before he had time to protest, she hurried into her chamber where she had already set aside a short tunic that showed her arms and legs to their best advantage. She tossed aside the heavy noblewoman's wig and donned a light hairpiece similar to the short, swinging style the slave girls wore. With quick, deft movements she pulled off her heavy bracelets and earrings, then pinched her cheeks and thrust her feet into leather sandals. She felt like a girl, simple and light-headed, and she knew from the look in Paneah's eyes when she joined him that he approved the change.

"You know," she said, leading the way from the house, "I've never had a brother. How I wanted one! Someone like you who would teach me things..."

"I will be happy to teach you, mistress," Paneah answered, his long stride easily catching hers. He gave her an open smile. "Anyone who wants to learn deserves a willing and faithful teacher."

While Ramla served in Bastet's glorious temple through the months of Thoth and Paopi, Tuya spent her days pacing in the priestess's spare living quarters. Why had Ramla needed a handmaid? Over one hundred slaves served at this temple, all of them eager to fulfill the commands of the priests and priestesses. Perhaps Ramla had brought a maid to give herself prestige, but she had never seemed the type to care what other people thought of her. Whatever the woman's reasons, Tuya counted the days, anxious for her time of service to be at an end.

One night not long after they had completed their second month at the temple, Ramla entered the chamber and sat in her chair, staring moodily at the setting sun's rays on the wall. Tuya ministered as silently as she could, unwilling to disturb Ramla's pensive mood. She had just picked up the priestess's nightdress when Ramla's voice broke the silence. "We will leave tomorrow. You will be happy to return to Thebes, won't you?"

Tuya flinched at the sharp sound, then took a deep breath and forced her pounding heart to remain steady. "Everyone loves to go home."

"Slaves have no home." Ramla paused and ran a long fingernail along the arm of the chair. "Neither do priests and priestesses."

Tuya let the observation pass without comment. She would not allow the poison in Ramla's soul to infect her happiness.

She placed Ramla's nightdress on the bed, but the priestess would not be ignored. "I have often thought it ironic that we crossed paths at Potiphar's house. I did not expect to ever see you again, and when Potiphar refused to send you to the temple, I divined that the will of the gods had brought us together."

Tuya listened with a vague sense of unreality. She had instinctively known that this woman hated her, but how could Ramla believe Tuya's presence was an act of the gods?

Something in the woman's manner gave Tuya the courage to speak bluntly. "Why do you despise me?"

The priestess leaned back and propped her head on her hand, her mouth curving in a one-sided smile. "I am glad you say what is on your mind. I'll be honest, too." She gazed at Tuya with chilling intentness for a long moment, then tented her fingers and centered herself in the chair. "In the beginning, I was jealous of the friendship you shared with Sagira. You were taken from your parents as a child, as was I, but you were placed into a loving family. You had a friend."

Her black eyes widened as she stared over the tips of her fingers. "I was taken to the temple, the place I would have sent you if Potiphar had allowed it. The priests shaved my head and circumcised my female parts to persuade me to remain consecrated to Bastet."

Tuya felt her heart shudder. Every feeling of antipathy she had borne toward Ramla melted into pitiful concern. "I'm sorry," she whispered, scarcely daring to look at the woman who had suffered so much.

"I should have known you would come into my life again," Ramla said, an odd smirk crossing her face. "What a jest the gods have played on their resentful priestess! But I, too, have a sense of humor. Tell me, Tuya, do you want to know the future?"

Tuya shook her head and turned to Ramla's box of possessions. "Some things are better left unseen."

"Some things are better foreseen," Ramla contradicted. She dropped her hands and stood in a single, fluid motion. "Tell me the future, Tuya. Do you think we will find Potiphar's household as we left it?"

Struggling to mask her rising fear, Tuya painted on a warm smile. "The flood has come, so the land will be muddy and gray. But our Paneah will be preparing for the planting—"

The priestess snickered. "Our Paneah? Do not think of him as yours, my dear, for he is a slave belonging to your master and mistress."

"Of course. I did not mean to imply—"

"I'm not implying anything." Ramla moved back to her chair. "I know the future. I know the present. I know that Paneah will give Sagira a son. It is her sworn ambition. Even now your mistress works to win your love's heart. Why do you think you were sent away?"

The lid of Ramla's trunk fell from Tuya's hand as her limbs and feelings went numb.

Unrelenting, the priestess continued: "You know Sagira and her determination. She is a woman of strategy and cunning. She will lure the handsome Paneah into her arms before he can think to resist."

Tuya's breath came in short, painful gasps. "Paneah will not—"

"Paneah will do whatever he is commanded to do," Ramla went on, her eyes gleaming as she studied the effect of her words. "He will give Sagira what she wants, or he will die. If he wants to be rewarded, he will perform his duties—enthusiastically."

A sudden vise pressed on Tuya's stomach. Overcome by nausea, she bent and ran from the room.

Chapter Eighteen

Yosef surveyed the items spread over the wide mat. "Have you remembered everything, Sagira?"

He and his mistress were outside the city, in the center of the Theban Hills. He had spent the greater part of two months showing his lady how the household functioned, and she, in turn, had promised to show him the wonders of the land he had never really seen.

Sagira had ordered the kitchen slaves to load the chariot with special provisions for this outing, and Yosef had been impressed with her preparation. They had left the villa shortly before sunrise, while the rest of the household still slumbered.

"I brought everything," she said, struggling with the last basket.

Yosef sprang to assist her. "Let me get that." The basket seemed enormous in her frail arms, and her eyes lit with gratitude when he carried it to the papyrus mat she had spread on the sand.

"Now that everything is unpacked," she said, placing her hands on her hips, "look around you, Paneah! This is Egypt's glory! Some have called this place the Temple of the World."

Yosef lifted his gaze to the open horizon. A huge semicircle of sheer cliffs rose straight from the floor of the Nile Valley and dominated the west bank of the Theban Hills. Forming an extraordinary foil for the elaborate temples across the yawning chasm, the long prominence of cliffs shimmered as if dancing to a rhythm only audible to desert creatures.

"Look there!" Sagira called, holding her light wig with one hand as she pointed in the opposite direction. To the east, the silvery Nile lay below a black bank of the fertile soil Yosef had come to love. The yellow-green of new crop growth glowed under ochre cliffs as red as Sagira's lips. The entire spectrum of colors brushed up against a blue sky that dazzled Yosef's eyes.

"I told you it was beautiful!" Sagira called.

Yosef nodded, too moved for words.

Far below, in the canyon beneath the cliffs, a whirlwind swayed with the grace of a Hittite dancing girl. He and Re'uven had once seen such a whirlwind, and Re'uven had made a jest about one of Dan's wives, a woman who danced in the same way. The funny-sad memory made Yosef smile and blink back unexpected tears.

The wind ruffled his hair, brushed his clean-shaven cheeks and billowed his kilt about his knees. He had not felt the strength of such a wind since he traveled the open land with his brothers...and his father.

Would his family know him if they saw him with this face, in this kilt? He would go to them if he could, offer his forgiveness...but were they ready to accept it?

"Isn't it— Why, Paneah, what's wrong?" Sagira gazed at him with concern in her eyes and clasped his arm when he turned away. "I am your friend. You can tell me your deepest sorrow." She placed a gentle hand on his cheek. "As you care for me, let me care for you."

The soothing sound of her voice, combined with the pain of memory, broke the dam of resistance in him. Embarrassed at his weakness, he lowered his head into his hands, then allowed her to lead him to the mat where he crumpled into a formless heap and released the bitter tears he had never been able to shed.

He did not know how long he cried, but he felt doubly the fool when he lifted his head from her lap. A man did not cry in front of a woman, and a slave certainly did not weep in his mistress's arms.

"I am sorry." He straightened and hoped she would forget the incident. "I have behaved...improperly."

"Nonsense." Sagira slipped her hand around his upper arm. "You were upset."

"What I did was not appropriate."

"There is no one here but you and me, and we shall judge what is appropriate." Sagira smiled, her eyes bright. "I cried on your shoulder once, remember? I have only returned your kindness." She leaned into him. "What upset you, my Paneah? The sight of the tombs? We do not fear death, you know. We are only afraid of being caught unprepared for it."

He shook his head. "The whirlwind reminded me of my brothers. I try not to think about my family, for the memory is painful, but a moment ago I would have leapt into that chariot and driven northward to find them if you—"

He meant to say that he belonged to Sagira and couldn't very well steal her chariot and leave her stranded, but she seemed to find a deeper meaning in his words, for she pressed her lips to his shoulder. He clenched his fist, resisting the urge to pull away. To do so would offend her, and she had been kind. After all, in his weakness, he had reached for her.

She pressed her warm cheek to his upper arm. "You would not leave me, would you?"

"No, mistress," he answered, shifting uncomfortably. He propped his elbows on his knees and gripped his hands.

"A moment ago you called me Sagira," she said, looking up at him. "I would have you call me that whenever we are alone. In fact—" she lifted her arm in an imperial gesture "—I command it."

"As you wish…Sagira." He couldn't resist smiling at her playfulness. Perhaps he had misread her. She could be quite charming, and he couldn't deny a quiet pride in his position. Of all the slaves, he alone had managed to befriend her.

"You are quick to please me," she murmured, her eyes watering in the wind.

"I am your slave."

"You are my friend."

He inclined his head, remembering the fellowship they had shared over the past two months. "If friendship is possible between a slave and mistress, I suppose we are."

"Of course it is possible." She pouted prettily. "Friends want to make each other happy, don't they?"

"Yes."

"And a slave aims to make his mistress happy, doesn't he?"

"Yes."

"Then it is no contradiction in the matter." She slid across the mat until she sat facing him, then her arms fell lightly across his shoulders. "Kiss me, Paneah. The kiss of friendship."

When he frowned, not at all pleased with this turn of the conversation, she threw back her head and laughed. "If you could see your face," she said, locking her hands behind his neck. "By the eye of Horus, Paneah, what do you think I intend? I am a married woman!"

He forced a smile. "I don't know what to think."

"Have you never heard of the kiss of friendship? Potiphar kisses Pharaoh's leg every time he stands before him, and only truly important people are allowed to kiss the royal leg. But when I offer you a chance to kiss my lips because you are a special friend, you gaze at me as though I had sprouted the horns of Thoth!"

He chuckled, and did not protest when she placed her hands on his face and brought her lips close to his. "See, a kiss is not torture," she said, smiling against his mouth.

Though he felt ridiculous, he managed a reply. "No."

She pulled away, still smiling, then leaned forward and deliberately gave him a childish peck. Yosef bore the kiss with good humor, then gripped his hands, eager to begin the journey back to the villa. His spoiled mistress could be a trifle dangerous when she did not get her way. If only she would finish this little game so they could begin the journey home…

She rose to her knees and pulled his head back, studying him as if he were a life-size doll. "I am glad you do not wear a wig, Paneah," she said, splaying her fingers through his hair. "Your hair is black as a raven's wing, and as lovely as you are."

"Mistress—" he tried to pull away "—the sun dips toward the west. This heat will tire you unless we leave soon."

"In a moment." She took a deep breath and lowered her gaze fully into his. "Kiss me as a man kisses the woman he loves." A small smile curled her lips. "Lie with me here, under the sun."

"No." The word sprang from him before he had time to think. He struggled to rise, but she had planted herself firmly in his lap.

"Come now," she said, still playful. "We are friends, are we not? Don't you desire to please me?"

"I cannot take my master's wife."

"He will never know."

"I will know."

"You don't know what you're missing." When her warm lips smothered his mouth, he stood in a panic, but he could not throw her off. She clung to him like a burr to a cat.

"Sagira!" he cried, pressing against her shoulders with as much force as he dared.

She released him and raised the back of her hand to wipe her lips, then gave him a steady look. "Do not be so alarmed, Paneah. That was only a little test. I can tell Potiphar you passed with flying colors."

Struggling to catch his breath, Yosef eyed her with suspicion. "A test?"

"To discover the strength and resolve of your virtue. I shall tell my husband that you are as unexcitable as a eunuch."

She turned and sashayed toward the chariot with the confidence of a departing queen. To regain his composure, Yosef crossed his arms and turned to face the open canyon. He was accustomed to Sagira's biting wit and flashing temper, but her last remark was a slap at his manhood. She had implied that he was not a man at all, but if he had accepted her proposition, she might have slapped him and had him thrown to the Nile crocodiles.

He shook his head and sighed. His mistress could be hot and cold, loving and sharp, caring and diffident. Compared to Tuya, Sagira was a bundle of sharp angles and rough edges, but for some reason God had placed her at the center of his life.

Amon-Re's blood-red sun had nearly disappeared beyond the western horizon when Ramla's entourage returned to Potiphar's house. Tuya was disappointed when the crowd of welcoming servants did not include Yosef. Where was he? He should have been in the house attending his master at this hour, but Potiphar stood on the porch alone, his hand lifted in greeting.

Sagira, Tuya noticed, was absent as well. As much as she tried to force Ramla's cruel prediction from her thoughts, Tuya could not forget the mental image of Sagira with her arm around Yosef's waist.

But Yosef was no weakling. He would not do what Ramla predicted. He would not even listen to such a suggestion.

The donkeys had been put away and the guards sent home by the time a single chariot churned the dust outside the gatehouse. Tuya ran to the porch, straining to see who had arrived in the gathering darkness.

Sagira's laughter broke the silence of the night. "Paneah, let Enos put our little picnic away," she called, her voice ringing like a bell. "You must be tired after our long day."

The man in the slave's kilt hesitated, then followed Sagira up the path toward the porch. Tuya blinked in bewilderment when Sagira slowed her step and the man—could it be Paneah?—caught up and walked alongside his mistress, like an equal.

Tuya stood on the porch like a helpless rabbit caught in a panther's hypnotic glare. When the mistress and her companion entered the circle of torchlight, Sagira gaped in surprise. "Tuya! You have finally returned! I hope you had a pleasant journey. I should find Ramla, but we've had an exhausting day among the hills."

She swept through the porch on her way to her chamber, but Yosef paused on a step. "Welcome home," he said, giving Tuya a dusty smile, but she could not return it. Red ochre stained his lips and the side of his face.

Gulping back a sob, Tuya turned and sprinted toward the women's quarters.

She wept for an hour, then hiccupped until one of the maids tossed a sandal at her from across the room. "Go outside if you cannot be quiet."

Tuya wrapped a thin shawl about her shoulders and slipped into the night. How could she sleep after what she had witnessed? She might never be able to sleep again. Each time she closed her eyes she saw Yosef locked in Sagira's embrace.

Ramla could foretell the future, and soon a child would be born. Yosef had rejected Tuya's love, claiming that he owed obedience to his god and to his father, and yet he had given himself to Sagira as eagerly as a bridegroom...

From force of long habit, her feet carried her to the garden. At the edge of the reflecting pool, she gazed downward and wondered if it were possible to drown in knee-deep water. She hiccupped again, then wiped her nose on the back of her hand. "Oh, Yosef," she wailed. "Why did you do it?"

"Do what?" He stepped from the shadows of the trees, his eyes as troubled as hers. Seeing that he suffered, too, she could not bring herself to repeat Ramla's accusations. If Yosef had become Sagira's lover, surely he would be with the mistress instead of pacing in the garden. He would not be here...unless his conscience troubled him.

Tuya gave him a wobbly smile. "Did you miss me?"

"Very much," he said, stepping closer. She thought he would draw her into his arms, but he merely lifted her hands and held them on his own. He kept his gaze lowered—was he afraid to look at her?

Somehow she found her voice. "Did you spend much time with Sagira?"

"Yes," he answered, finally meeting her gaze. "Because you told me to. She now thinks of me as a friend."

"Then why—" Tuya tried to keep her voice light "—why was your face stained with ochre when you returned tonight? Have you taken to painting your lips?"

She couldn't tell if he blushed in the moonlight. "She kissed me," he said simply. "A kiss of affection."

"She kissed you," Tuya repeated, lowering her hands. Suspicion rose again and snarled, blocking the voice of reason. "When was the last time a mistress kissed her slave?" she asked, wincing at the edge of desperation in her voice.

"How am I to know?" Yosef folded his arms in a pose of weary dignity. "She kissed me in affection—and you told me to be her friend."

"Her friend, not her lover," Tuya whispered. When defiance lit his eyes, she pressed on. "She kissed you, Yosef, so tell me the truth. Did she not long for more?"

Her question brought a hard frown to his face. "Do you not trust me?"

"Can you not answer my question?"

"Yes, she wanted more! But so did you, remember?" His words cut through the night, lacerating her. Tuya backed away and pressed her hand to her mouth.

Yosef growled and knocked a fist against his forehead. "If I would not lie with you, why do you think I would lie with a woman I do not love?" He turned toward the pool, placed his hands on his hips, and breathed deeply.

"Do you, Yosef? Do you love me?"

After a long moment, he lowered his arms and looked at her. "You know how I feel about you," he finally whispered, his voice husky. "Sometimes I wish God had not gifted me with a form pleasing to women. I walk in the marketplace and hear them call greetings, I walk in the threshing rooms and feel their eyes on my back, I sit behind my master at dinner and catch my mistress's smiles…"

He walked to a tree and leaned against it, crossing his arms as he faced her. "The same beauty that bound Rahel to Yaakov now enslaves me. You should understand, Tuya, for God has also gifted you with beauty."

"I understand some things," she said, moving toward him. "I understand that you long to be free, Yosef, and that you dream of greatness. You are proud, you are ambitious, you dream of the future and aspire to succeed in every effort you undertake. You are a fire-eater. You will do anything to keep faith in your dreams. I wonder if you will do anything to be free—"

He did not answer, but slouched before her, bleary-eyed and weary.

"There is no advantage in loving me," she whispered, avoiding his gaze. "Yet there is much to be gained in pleasing a mistress. I love you, Yosef, and I know about your dreams. And I'll not stand in the way of their fulfillment. I can't."

Before her heart could change her mind, she turned on her heel and left the garden.

The pleasant sounds of people at dinner drifted through the house as Tuya approached the main hall the next afternoon. Sagira, Potiphar and Ramla sat on chairs placed in a circle for conversation and ate from bowls that had been placed on stands near them. Between Potiphar and his wife, Yosef lingered like an obedient shadow, ready to do their bidding.

He caught Tuya's eye as she approached, and for the first time in her memory his face did not light with excitement when she entered the room. His smile seemed strained, his eyes wary. She glanced at him with no more apparent interest than she would have given a wall painting, then prostrated herself on the floor before Potiphar's feet.

"What's this?" He looked down at her over the deep crescents of flesh beneath his eyes. "I did not send for you, Tuya."

"If it please my master," she said, lifting her head. "I have a request."

"Should a slave beg for favors?" Sagira interrupted, but Potiphar smiled and leaned forward in his chair.

"Speak, Tuya. I will listen."

Tuya swallowed hard, knowing she had stepped onto a path from which there could be no return. "Some time ago I displeased my mistress and she wanted to send me away," she said. "You, kind master, would not allow me to go. But if my lady still finds me displeasing, I am willing to leave." She steeled herself to continue. "I have no place here."

"What's this?" Potiphar turned to his wife. "Have you quarreled with this girl?"

"How could I, my lord?" Sagira lifted her shoulder in an elegant shrug. "She has been with Ramla for two months. This request, I assure you, is a surprise to me."

"The captain of Pharaoh's guard would do well to consider her petition," Ramla said, speaking in the low voice she reserved for dreaded things. "An unhappy slave can incite rebellion and mutiny among the others. Even you, Potiphar, may have trouble on your hands if she is forced to remain here."

Potiphar thought a moment, then slapped his knee. "She was a gift from Pharaoh. One does not cast off a presentation from the divine hand." He glanced toward Sagira, another of his favors from Pharaoh, and lifted her fingers to his lips. "Not that I would want to rid myself of any of our king's gifts."

"Still, Tuya is an old friend, and I don't want her to be unhappy," Sagira said, resting her hand on Potiphar's arm. "Perhaps you might approach the king or one of his counselors about the situation. I am sure you can find a solution, my husband."

Potiphar gave her an approving glance. "I shall try, little wife," he promised, rising. He kissed her hand again in farewell, then turned toward Tuya and lowered his voice. "I would hate to see you go, but if you are sure you cannot be happy here—"

"I am certain," she said, bowing before him again. She did not allow her gaze to drift toward Yosef's face.

Yosef fought against the maddening tedium of the after-dinner ritual. Potiphar left the house, Tuya slipped away, and Yosef attended Ramla and Sagira until they finished a lengthy, rambling conversation and moved to the women's quarters. When they had gone, he clapped to summon slaves to clear the chamber, then he hurried from the hall.

He found Tuya in the room where the lowliest of all slaves worked to grind corn into flour. On her hands and knees, she was bent over a slab with a heavy grindstone in her hand. The toothless old hag who usually ground the corn sat on the floor, watching with wide, amused eyes.

"What are you doing in here?" he demanded, pulling the grindstone out of Tuya's grip. "This is not your work!"

"I thought I may as well learn how to do everything," she said, not looking at him. "If a family can afford only one slave, they will purchase a woman for grinding, so I thought I should learn—"

"You're not going anywhere." He pulled her from the room, oblivious to the old woman's curious stare. In the corridor, he stood Tuya against the wall and leaned over her, his arms blocking her escape. "What foolish, womanish, jealous notion entered your head today?" he asked, taking pains to keep his voice level. "You have harmed your reputation with Potiphar. I may be able to dissuade him from approaching Pharaoh, but now the master and mistress both know you are not happy. The damage is done."

"I will leave even if I have to run away," Tuya answered, her eyes large and fierce with pain. "I cannot stay here, Yosef. I love you too much. I cannot bear to watch Sagira trap you—"

"I will not be trapped," he said, pressing against the walls with all his strength. What would it take to make her believe him? "Sagira may be infatuated—" he lowered his voice "—but I am only her friend. My heart belongs to you, Tuya, and she knows it. Soon she will grow tired of me."

"She won't stop until she wins. She has the power to command you."

"Some things cannot be commanded."

Tuya released a bitter laugh, then looked into his eyes. "Then consider this—she hates me and she has the power to take my life. If I stay and you refuse her, she will hurt me somehow. She's already hurt me—"

"So you would exchange this house for some place where I cannot protect you? What if you are sold to a cruel master? What if you find yourself commanded by a man who would ask more of you than Sagira asks of me? You are not thinking, Tuya! You may find yourself in a nest of vipers—"

"I don't know where I will go," she whimpered, sliding down against the wall. "I only know the gods have not smiled on us. Montu's strong arm has not been able to save you from Sagira, and your god is silent—"

He knelt in front of her and reached for her hands, his heart breaking at the sight of tears on her cheeks. "You must trust in the true god," he said, gentling his voice. "Please, Tuya, stay with me. Our time of waiting is nearly over, then we shall be married and have a house of our own. I have handled Potiphar for years, so I can handle Sagira."

"You think too highly of your own abilities, Yosef. You cannot hold Sagira off and cling to me. Such dreams are impossible. She will never allow them."

"Faith is believing in the impossible. Why can't you put aside your fear and trust me? You have no faith in me, no, not even in yourself, or you would see that you are as precious to me as life. Please, dearest, let me tell Potiphar that you have changed your mind about leaving."

"No." She pulled herself free from his grasp, then stood and stumbled as she moved away. "I love you too much, Yosef, and I know Sagira. Whether she wins or loses, you will suffer. Because I can't bear the torture of watching, I can't stay."

Chapter Nineteen

"My husband."

Potiphar was about to oversee the changing of the guard at his prison, when Sagira's voice interrupted his thoughts. He turned, surprised that she would venture into the courtyard in the heat of the day. "Do you need me?"

She gave him a regal nod. "At your leisure, I would have a word with you."

The girl had become a woman of substance and discretion, and Potiphar's spirits lifted at the sight of her petite form. "Gentlemen." He flashed a killer smile toward his guards. "A lady needs me."

While they laughed and watched him go, Sagira gestured toward the garden path. He fell into step beside her, and she linked her arm through his as they walked. "I've been giving this matter of our unhappy slave a great deal of thought," she said, tilting her dark eyes toward him. "Pharaoh has an eye for beauty, and I'm sure there are none to equal Tuya in the royal harem."

Potiphar lifted a brow, following her thought. "She was destined for the harem when Pharaoh presented her to me. If he didn't want her then, how do we know he will want her now?"

"She was a child then," Sagira answered. "Now she has matured. Pharaoh will be honored to have such a beauty, don't you think?"

Potiphar considered her suggestion…and its risks. "I still can't imagine why she wants to leave. I thought she and Paneah wanted to marry. I had promised them freedom in two more years—"

"Childish infatuations vanish like dew under the sun's hot breath," Sagira said. "Now Tuya and Paneah argue whenever they catch sight of one another. I believe she wishes to leave us because she cannot bear to be around Paneah."

"I suppose I can understand," Potiphar said, nodding. "And I am a reasonable man. So be it. I will take Tuya with me when I go to the palace tomorrow." He patted Sagira's hand. "I have to see to the prison. Is there anything else you need from me?"

"You have given me everything I need," she said, giving him a demure smile. "Thank you, Potiphar."

Early morning shadows moved through Sagira's chamber like stalking gray cats, but Tuya refused to cower when she entered the room. Her mistress had sent for her before daybreak, and Tuya obeyed, knowing that this summons might be her last from the poisonous Sagira…as this morning might hold her last glimpse of Yosef.

Sagira announced her intention right after Tuya entered. "You are going back to Pharaoh," she said, glancing at Ramla. "We will make certain he is pleased with you."

"We will personally oversee your toilet," Ramla added, regarding Tuya with a critical eye.

Tuya stood stock-still as Ramla muttered incantations and anointed her skin with perfumed oil. Sagira chose a fitted garment of white linen from her wardrobe, and two handmaids sewed Tuya into it while Ramla lowered the straps until the dress displayed a generous amount of flesh.

Sagira motioned for Tuya to sit, then picked up strands of her dark hair and began to braid them into thin ribbons. As her nimble fingers flew, Tuya's eyes filled with bitter tears of memory. When they were children, Sagira had often braided Tuya's hair in this same way.

While Sagira twined pearls and beads into Tuya's hair, another slave lined the girl's eyes with kohl and colored her lids with shadows the green color of the Nile. An hour later, Sagira stood back and admired her handiwork. "Perfect." She flashed a white smile at Ramla. "Take her to Potiphar. He waits in the courtyard."

Like a sheep led to the butcher, Tuya followed Ramla in tiny, mincing steps, all she could manage in the tight dress. She concentrated on walking, for every room of the house held memories of Yosef, vivid images that closed around her and filled her with a longing to turn back. When concentration could not block her recollections, she recited an ancient spell of forgetting. She did not want to see Yosef or think about him, but the image of his haunted, pleading face still rose before her eyes.

The sun had fully risen by the time she reached the courtyard; the walls of the villa seemed to shudder before her swimming eyes. Potiphar gave her an admiring glance, then motioned for her to climb onto the litter that would carry her to Pharaoh's palace.

The litter bearers held the conveyance steady as she perched on the edge and swung her legs up. One more moment and she would be away. In another hour she could forget Potiphar's house had ever existed. The man she had loved here must not have cared for her too deeply, for he had not come to say goodbye…

A voice from the porch made her cringe in sudden guilt. "Potiphar!"

Yosef's voice.

She did not turn around.

"Paneah?" Potiphar shaded his eyes as he looked toward the house.

Yosef's light, quick footsteps crunched the gravel. "I wanted to be sure, master, that you will not reconsider this action. Tuya is a valuable slave—"

Potiphar held up his hand, then turned toward Tuya. "Do you want to remain, my dear?" he asked, his voice oddly gentle.

Tuya kept her eyes fixed on the gate and braced her arms against the litter. "I am ready to leave."

Potiphar waved in farewell. "She wants to go."

"One moment, sir," Yosef called, and then he stood beside her, love and pain struggling in his eyes. "Believe in me," he whispered. "I need you to have faith. When I am free and a great man, I will find you. I will rescue you from slavery."

She dared not steal one last look at him. "You were a great man when I first met you."

When Yosef did not answer, Potiphar shouted a command and the litter bearers stepped forward.

After arriving at the palace, Potiphar left Tuya with Kratas, the eunuch in charge of the harem, then hastened to see that his guards were in place. Pharaoh's daily ritual, much like the routine of the temples' stone gods, had already begun. The divine king had been roused by priests singing a hymn of praise, then the priests had performed his morning toilet, perfuming his skin with oil and decking him with royal robes and Egypt's red and white double crown. The great king now sat at breakfast, and would soon be brought into the throne room to transact business and receive offerings.

Potiphar paced in the hallway. In that revealing dress and full makeup, Tuya looked like a different woman, and Potiphar had been more than a little surprised by his wife's generosity. His child bride had matured in the past year. The last traces of girlishness, uncertainty and puppy fat had evaporated from her body; she had become a woman of distinction. Since they had reached an understanding, she no longer wasted her energy on silly songs and suggestive dances. She behaved as a modest and mature woman should, and seemed to know nearly as much as Paneah about running the estate.

The sounds of music warned him that Pharaoh's entourage was about to enter the throne room. Potiphar straightened, adjusted the waistband of his kilt and patted the heavy Gold of Praise about his neck. Any other man would have whispered a prayer to his patron god at the thought of what he was about to do, but Potiphar only hoped he would find Pharaoh in a forgiving and generous mood.

"A gift for me?" The royal voice rumbled through the hall as the king's pet lion opened his mouth in a noisy yawn, and several of the queen's handmaids twittered. Despite the distraction, the queen, the court and even Pharaoh's sons leaned forward to see what gift Pharaoh's captain could have brought.

Potiphar straightened his shoulders. "Yes, divine Pharaoh. Several years ago you gave me a beautiful child, who has blossomed into a flower of surpassing loveliness. She has remained untouched and sheltered in my house, and today I offer her to you. You have given me a house, a bride and the Gold of Praise. Since you have been so generous to me, I would honor you today with a gift worthy of a king's notice."

Pharaoh frowned for a moment, and the knuckles that

grasped the crook and flail whitened as he considered his captain's comment. "I am like a man who loans silver to another," he finally said, leaning forward. "Today you bring me the principal amount, plus interest."

Potiphar bowed his head. "In a manner of speaking."

"Well, then." Pharaoh relaxed and cast a sidelong smile to Narmer, who remained as close to Pharaoh as a thorn to a rose. "I suppose, Potiphar, I will be pleased according to how much interest the principal has earned."

"Bring forth the gift from Potiphar, Captain of the Guard!" Narmer called, his eyes dancing with mischievous delight. Potiphar clasped his hands behind his back and bowed as the tall doors at the back of the throne room swung open.

Audible gasps filled the throne room as Tuya inched forward. She walked alone through the cavern created by the opening of the doors, and her white linen dress seemed to glow with an unearthly light. Her braided hair flowed onto her shoulders in a soft tide while her graceful neck curved upward like the sacred ibis taking wing. Her face was as pale as parchment, but her black eyes glowed with inner fire.

Potiphar glanced at the king's courtier. Narmer would love to see Potiphar fail in winning the king's approval, but he was not the only man who wore the Gold of Pharaoh's Praise.

Now Narmer gaped like the fool he was, and even Pharaoh seemed stunned by the sight of Tuya in her glory. Amenhotep's second son, nine-year-old Abayomi, broke the unusual silence. "Father," his treble voice rang through the chamber, "I want her!"

After glancing at his queen, Pharaoh nodded. The king extended his hand to Potiphar and released his eyes to feast on Tuya. "I shall accept your gift in my son's name," he said, his voice tinged with regret. "You have more than doubled my gift, and today you may kiss my hand. This girl shall become the bride of Pharaoh's second son, a royal princess in the land that has given her birth."

The crowd of court observers buzzed as Potiphar bent to press his lips against the jeweled hand.

In the weeks following Tuya's departure, Sagira was careful not to push or press Paneah. The date for which she lived still lay months in the future, and she wanted the slave to come to her willingly, not out of fear or obedience. She watched his moods carefully, taking pains to cheer him when he seemed lonely or praise him when he grew quiet. Most of all, she kept him busy, knowing he would have neither the time nor the energy to mourn Tuya's loss if ambitious projects and plans occupied his thoughts.

With Potiphar's blessing, she called Paneah into the women's reception hall and described her plans to enlarge the villa and rebuild the walls. It would be a difficult project, she declared, but Paneah could undoubtedly master the various aspects of planning and building. When all was finished, Potiphar would own a house second only to Pharaoh's palace in elegance. And Paneah would be in charge of every detail, from what crops were planted to what sheets were spread on the beds.

She called him to a table and spread a papyrus roll in front of him. "I must have a special room," she said. "See this drawing? I want my furniture to be gilded with the purest gold, and lotus blossoms engraved around the legs and armrests of the chairs. I want a bed of gold, with a canopy of gossamer hangings, and lamps in every corner of the room."

He chuckled at her words, but kept his gaze glued to the parchment.

"Do I want too much?" She tilted her head toward him. "I want the world, Paneah. I want everything life has to offer, and something tells me you want these things, too."

"I want to fulfill my destiny." He turned a page of the plans. "If that means remaining a slave, then I am pleased to serve you."

"You won't remain a slave," she said, daring to speak the truth. "I have asked Ramla to divine the future, and she sees great things for you."

Though he tried to hide it, a flicker of interest gleamed in his eye. She smiled. She had always known he possessed ambition.

"It will take some work," he said, tapping a manicured finger on the scroll. "But I have met an architect in the city who has done work on Pharaoh's tomb. If he could spare a crew—"

"Do whatever is necessary." She beamed in an overflow of expectation. "Go wherever you have to go. No chains shall bind you, no purse restrain you. You are Potiphar's steward, and he has complete faith in you." She lowered her voice to a more intimate tone. "The master designer of Potiphar's house will soon be known as the greatest man in Thebes. After that, Paneah, who knows what the future will bring?"

He laughed, and the sound of his sincere humor caught her off guard. "Have I said something funny?"

His smile melted the sudden frostiness of her heart. "It's just that—well, I have dreamed of greatness. And if this is how I gain it—"

"Be not afraid of greatness," she whispered, leaning toward him. She placed her hand on his and smiled when he did not pull away. "Do your best, Paneah, as I know you will. And then you may reach for the stars, and Pharaoh himself will not be able to stop you."

As the young boy stood on tiptoe to place the ceremonial crust of bread between her lips, Tuya felt as though she moved in a dream. In a moment this child, a royal prince, would be her husband. Hard to believe, but that reality was easier to face than the realization that she had walked away from the only love she had ever known.

Abayomi smashed the ceremonial jug of wine with a sword he could barely swing, and spectators broke into perfunctory shouts of approval. No one cared, really, who the boy-prince married. Tuya knew she ought to be grateful. After only two weeks in Pharaoh's household she had exchanged her slavery for royalty; she would be comfortable and protected as long as her husband favored her. If next month Abayomi decided that he no longer cared for her, she would be no worse off than she had been a month ago.

In Potiphar's house, passion had burned while reason slumbered.

In Pharaoh's palace, reason wrapped her in comfort while she buried her passion.

The boy looked at her with a singularly sweet smile and offered his hand. Tuya adjusted the expression of her face and stepped out from beneath the bridal canopy with her husband, a boy eleven years her junior.

Sagira had just approved Paneah's plans for a new stable when Potiphar passed through the main hall looking more frustrated than usual. "What is wrong, my lord?" she called, glancing up from the scroll over which Paneah hovered.

"The royal wedding," he said, shaking his head. "It is finished, but Pharaoh was particularly concerned that nothing spoil it. He has heard rumors of a conspiracy to take his life, and his paranoia has reached the point of foolishness."

"A wedding?" Sagira murmured, making notes about the marble flooring to be installed in her bedchamber. "Did the king take another wife?"

"Not the king. Pharaoh's son married Tuya today."

A sudden shock rippled through her system. "Our Tuya married the crown prince?"

Potiphar sank into a chair. "Not the heir—the king's second son asked for her. And when a slave is beautiful and the queen is jealous, a young prince may command even his father."

Sagira turned to gauge Paneah's reaction to the news. He did not lift his gaze from the scroll, but his face had paled beneath its tan. His eyes, which had blazed with interest as he told her of his plans for the villa, had filled with the dullness of despair.

She looked away, torn by conflicting emotions. Yosef still fancied himself in love with Tuya, but he would never have her now. And while Tuya may have married into the royal family, she would be nothing but a nursemaid to her husband for years to come.

She forced a smile. "Our Tuya has married a baby."

"Don't be concerned," Potiphar said, resting his head on his hand. "Boys grow into men."

The days without Tuya melted into weeks, the weeks into months, the months into seasons. Two full years passed in Potiphar's house, and the estate that had been one of the most prosperous in Thebes now eclipsed all but the king's. Potiphar's nearest neighbors, afraid of appearing shabby next to his affluence, sold their lands to Paneah at bargain prices and moved away from the burgeoning estate. Potiphar's cattle outgrew the stockyard until Paneah built new pens; Potiphar's fields outproduced others' three- and four-fold.

Potiphar was not shy about sharing the secret of his success. "I leave everything to Paneah," he often boasted. "I take care of Pharaoh, and Paneah takes care of me."

Extravagant offers poured in from every quarter of Egypt,

but Potiphar refused to sell his slave. When it became clear that no amount of silver or gold could wrest Paneah from Potiphar's house, stewards from other noble estates came to consult with him, usually bearing gifts of silver, linen or expensive oils and perfumes. They came expecting miracles; they left with practical advice that did increase the productivity of their homes and fields. But no estate came close to matching the success and bounty of Potiphar's enterprises.

Sagira watched in silent approval as the praise of nobles and stewards buoyed Paneah's pride. Like soothing oil on his wounded heart, their flattering words restored the sureness to his step, the confidence to his eyes. He commanded the other slaves with authority, treated visiting nobles with a dignified deference and communicated more in a cocky tilt of his brow than Potiphar did in a hundred gruff words.

At twenty-four, Yosef had become tall, lean and muscular from his labors. Though Sagira felt herself largely responsible for his success, she stood a little in awe of the man he had become. Though she still planned to use him to father her son, now and then she wondered if he was using her. Like everyone else, she had fallen under his charming spell. In the afternoons when he dismounted from his chariot, she had to look away lest she cry out and tell the world she adored him.

She had never intended to love him, but in choosing to make herself pleasing to him, he had become unbearably precious to her. When he was away, her mind curled around thoughts of seeing him again. Her passion was a flower that flourished in the secret places of her heart, and she often confessed to Ramla that she had become caught in a web of her own weaving. Though her plan to seduce Paneah had been conceived in ambition and revenge, couldn't love erase the anger that had first propelled her toward him?

She spent her days dreaming. Potiphar was fifty-one years

old and would not live much longer so her son, sired by Paneah, would also be fathered by him. She would, she assured Ramla, marry the love of her heart as soon as Potiphar rested in his tomb. Paneah would be rich beyond measure, the most powerful noble in Thebes, and when the gods placed the royal throne into her hands, Paneah would be Pharaoh and their son the next king. Two prophecies, his and hers, would be fulfilled.

Sometimes Sagira thought her gnawing hunger would force her to command Paneah into her chamber. But the date had been foreordained by the goddess, and Sagira would not risk divine anger by disobeying. So she waited, feeding her love-starved heart with fantasies and the rich expectation of the moment that would come.

On the delicious occasions when she found herself alone with Paneah, she baited him as she always had, lightly running her fingers over his muscled back or raking her fingers through his hair. He did not shy away from her touch now, but seemed to welcome her massaging hands as he studied evolving plans for the house and she coaxed the tenseness from his neck. Occasionally she planted kisses on his ear, loving the blush that rose from his neck, and more than once she needled him by saying that if he grew any more handsome she'd command him to lie with her.

He shook his head and laughed at her jests, saying, "No more tests, Sagira." She answered with a smile, pretending she had meant nothing even though her arms ached to hold him. Though Ramla still worshipped Bastet, Paneah was Sagira's god in slave's form, joy and torment in flesh. In conversation, whenever Paneah happened to say "we must do this" or "we ought to do that," a thrill shivered through her senses because he had mingled himself with her in a simple word.

So she counted the months and weeks of the final year, looking forward to the day of the Nile's full fertility. On that night she would command Paneah to come to her bed—and on that night she would not jest.

The eighteenth day of the second month finally arrived, the first day of the Feast of Opet. The festival began as priests carried the god Amon from the dark shrine in his temple to visit his harem at the temple of Southern Opet, and Sagira could hear the blast of the priests' trumpets from her bed-chamber. Soon the city's inhabitants would pour into the streets of Thebes to gawk at the gilded shrine as the god traveled down the Nile.

The house of Potiphar would empty as well. Sagira had sent a note to Paneah the night before, asking him to remain behind, but insisting that he grant liberty to all the slaves so no one might be left out on this happy occasion. Potiphar, of course, would remain by Pharaoh's side until the festival ended.

Ramla arose from her bed and murmured incantations as she helped Sagira bathe, then she scented the room with incense while Sagira massaged perfumed oil into her skin. A new wig waited on a wooden stand, a simple, short creation that made Sagira appear as carefree and innocent as a young girl. She had ordered a special dress for this day, a simple garment of the uncluttered design Paneah seemed to prefer.

Wiping the excess oil from her hands, Sagira padded across the room and ran her hand over the sheer fabric. It was as soft as a kitten's ear, and about as subtle as the parade of Opet. When she stood before Paneah in this revealing tunic, he would recognize her intentions.

Only a fool would not.

She slipped the tunic over her head and twisted to study the effect. The transparent garment clung to her like a second skin.

"Careful," Ramla cautioned from the bathroom as she emptied the washbasin. "He is not yet won."

Like a protective mother, the priestess entered the room and slipped Sagira's red cloak over the sheer tunic. The crimson color heightened the hue in Sagira's cheeks and matched her dainty leather slippers.

All was in readiness. Quiet reigned in the area beyond her chamber, no one stirred in the hall or the courtyard beyond.

"I am ready, you may leave me," Sagira finally said, eyeing herself in the new full-length bronze mirror recently installed in her bedchamber. She glanced around the room. Fresh curtains hung about her bed, incense burned on the brazier and lotus petals had been sprinkled on the floor.

"All is ready," Ramla echoed, as intent as a soldier. She bowed toward Sagira, then turned and vanished like a shadow at noonday.

Chapter Twenty

Alone at last, Sagira paced in her chamber, every nerve strung to a high pitch. She had waited so long for this moment! So many nights she had lain awake imagining how it would be. On discovering her here, Paneah, her Paneah, would realize she had taken great pains to ensure their privacy. For him she had designed Thebes's most beautiful bedchamber, for him she wore the most exquisite garment imaginable, for him she had perfumed her skin and softened her heart. She had incanted the proper petitions, given the proper offerings. Not one detail had been overlooked or neglected. They could take their fill of love until late in the evening when the servants would return. If they were discreet, Paneah might remain with her until nearly sunrise…

When she noticed she was walking on tiptoe, she forced herself to take a deep breath. A strange knocking sound filled her chamber and she froze in horror, then chuckled when she realized she was hearing the terrified pounding of her own heart. Far away the wind stirred the trees along the garden path; a horse whinnied and another responded, then all was quiet and still.

Now. Deftly, reverently, she lifted the bell that would summon Paneah and rang it with hope in her heart. The sound pealed through the corridor and echoed in the empty halls, and for a moment she feared he had not receive her message. What if he had gone out to enjoy the festival with the others?

But footsteps sounded on the marble in the great hall, and she turned from the doorway, afraid to face him. After a moment woven of eternity she heard the creaking of the cedar door that led into her chamber. "You rang, mistress?"

Every nerve leapt and shuddered at the timbre of his voice. "Yes, Paneah, I did," she said, turning toward him. "And it's Sagira, now, remember? We are quite alone."

He wore his best linen kilt, a pleated garment of her own design, and the narrow waistline accented his trim waist and his broad shoulders. Handsome leather sandals adorned his feet, and a single golden band lay on his upper arm. His hair hung lush and lovely about his memorable face as he awaited her request. How like a god he was! How appropriate that he had dressed in his best for this day.

He hesitated at the threshold of her chamber. "Do you want me to drive you to the river for the festivities?"

"I don't want to be in a crowd today," she said, smiling at him through tilted eyes. "I want to enjoy this place that we have built—you and I." She opened her arms, but he did not stir from the doorway. She rolled her eyes, amused at his reticence. "Come here, Paneah, don't loiter like a child at the door."

"You know more about childhood than I," he said, stepping into the room. "I'm older than you by far."

"I'm nineteen." She tipped her head back to look up at him. "Old enough to know what I want."

"I think you've always known." He came forward and planted himself on the floor in front of her. "And you have yet to tell me what you want. Do you have plans for another room? Another garden? Perhaps a pool that will put Pharaoh's to shame?"

"We are not working today." She drew in her cheeks until her lips formed a rosette, then blew him a kiss. "I'm in the mood for poetry, Paneah. Read to me from the scroll you'll find on my bed."

He gave her a faintly reproachful glance, then crossed to the bed. He lifted the scroll and began to unroll it, but Sagira draped herself across the bed and propped her head on her hand. "Sit while you read," she ordered. "I am not comfortable with you standing over me like a vulture."

He sighed and sat on the edge of her bed, facing the wall. "Is there anything sweeter than this hour?" he read, the sound of music in his voice. Sagira turned onto her back and folded her arms, hoping the words came from his heart and not just his lips.

For I am with you, and you lift up my heart—
For is there not embracing and fondling when you visit
    me and we give ourselves up to delights?
If you wish to caress my thigh,
then I will offer you my lips also—they won't thrust you
    away!
Will you leave because you are hungry?
I can satisfy your hunger!
Will you leave because you need something to wear?
I have a chestful of fine linen!
Glorious is the day of our embracings;
I treasure it a hundred thousand millions!

"Thank you," she whispered, her voice breaking.
Paneah turned. "What is wrong?"
"Ah, my Paneah—" she stared at the ceiling "—I don't expect you to understand."

"Have I not understood your hurts in the past?"

"You have been the only one who understood—but you cannot understand this."

"Perhaps I can." His voice gentled as he offered a smile. "We will not know until you explain the sound of tears in your voice."

Had any plan ever gone so well? Surely the gods were smiling. "Paneah," she said, letting her gaze mingle with his, "my heart breaks because I am a young woman who will never bear a son."

He turned as if afraid to broach this personal topic, but she pushed herself up and placed her hand on his back. He could not escape her now.

"Potiphar is more feeble than you know," she went on, hurrying so he could not question her. "I am young and yearn to suckle a baby." She spoke the honest truth now, and felt reckless with power. Why not be honest with him? The star of ambition burned bright in his character and the prophecy; perhaps he would seize her dream as his.

"Mistress—Sagira—"

"The royal blood of the pharaohs flows through my veins," she said, slipping off the bed, "and the child I could have will someday be pharaoh of Egypt." She crossed to Paneah and knelt at his feet, then placed her hands on his knees. "If the gods decide to destroy Amenhotep's house, I will be the heiress, the embodiment of Horus, the Lady of Heaven. My husband will be Pharaoh, and our child will be the greatest ruler in the world."

His eyes held a teasing light; he did not understand the significance of the truth she had just revealed. "Potiphar would not accept the double crown, Sagira," he said, gently gripping her hands. "Has Ramla filled your head with these silly visions?"

She clung to him. "The gods themselves have spoken. I will have a child, Paneah, sired by the man I love."

"Potiphar will be pleased."

"Not Potiphar." His eyes were as unreadable as water; she yearned to look into his soul and see what thoughts stirred there. An indulgent smile rested on his lips, and his hands kept her at a distance even though she leaned toward him, drawn by his masculine power. "Not Potiphar," she repeated, swaying as he held her. "My son will spring from the loins of the man who has stolen my heart from its rightful owner."

The meaning of her words took hold. His gaze traveled up and down her as his face flooded with color, then he tried to rise. "Mistress, you do not know what you are saying."

"I know exactly what I'm saying," she said, rising before he could escape. She sat in his lap and wound her arms about his neck. "Today, Paneah, you and I will share everything we should have been sharing for the many months we have known each other. Have you not noticed that I adore you? I admire the curve of your mouth, I appreciate the gentleness in your eye, I idolize the graceful strength of your hands."

"This is not right," he said, struggling in her grasp. "I cannot—"

"Have you never had dreams of greatness, Paneah?" She lowered her head and murmured into his ear. "In divining your future, Ramla has foretold that one day every knee in Egypt will bow to you." As if she had struck a chord, his resistance eased.

Sagira exulted at this first sign of victory. "Have you dared to dream as high as Pharaoh's throne?" she continued, feeling his heart pound beneath her palm. "The way to your destiny lies in my arms. How sweet this path is, my love! How gentle the gods are with us! Imagine it, my god in flesh, kings and queens from the world over will bow before your throne. As the divine son of Osiris, even the sun and moon will bow before you!"

Sagira smiled in triumph when he gasped. Pride had paved the way to his heart, and ambition would propel him into her arms. He had never considered the possibilities she might lay before him. She had already made him the most respected man in Thebes, slave or free, but she had much more to offer.

In one deft movement, she stood and slid her fingers to the catch of the concealing robe on her shoulders. The heavy garment slipped to the floor like a pool of blood at Paneah's feet, and she stood before him as exposed and vulnerable as a newborn baby. He gasped and closed his eyes, confusion and torment warring on his lovely face.

Playing the game with purpose, she ran a finger over his chest, then hooked it beneath his kilt's waistband. She could feel the warmth of his nearness as he shifted in an effort to escape. "Why should you pretend to resist me now?" she said, running her lips over the smooth skin of his cheek. "I am your mistress, my love, and I command you to kiss me."

His pace of his breathing increased, but whether from passion or pride she could not tell.

"Sagira," he whispered, his voice hoarse, but this was not the time for talking.

"Lie with me, Paneah." Her hand tightened around the fabric of his kilt. "Give me a son. The day is ours alone, and the night as well."

Desire, primitive and potent, poured through her veins, the fires within her shooting upward and outward as she pressed him toward her bed.

"No!" Yosef lunged forward, unceremoniously dumping his mistress onto the floor. He moved to the wall and pressed his hands to his head, struggling to regain his perspective. His senses throbbed with the feel and scent and textures of her, but what she was suggesting, no, demanding, was wrong. He was man enough to admit that his common sense skittered into the shadows every time she touched him in that tantalizing way, and she had no business wearing that dress before anyone but her husband.

For an instant he had believed her, had almost followed her into the lunatic fantasy of ambition that extended to the throne of Egypt. When she mentioned the sun and moon bowing before him, he had wondered if God had sent her as the fulfillment of his old dream.

But this devilish swirling heat inside his veins could not be part of God's plan. She was another man's wife, and something dark shadowed her moves and motives. Even though her touch could make him forget who and what he was—

She had not given up, but rose from the floor like a determined tigress, eyeing him with a look of scorching intent. "I can fulfill your dreams. You cannot escape me, Paneah, the house is empty. I know some silly shred of honor makes you regard your duty to Potiphar, but he has never been a husband to me. He cannot be. He was wounded in a battle long ago—"

He put out a hand to ward her off. "Don't."

She shivered and kept coming, as if his prohibition had excited her. He slid along the wall, moving toward the doorway, yet still she came, slowly, seductively, because she knew he was watching. "I hate to assume the man's role and pursue you," she said, her voice low and promising, "but there can be no other way, my dear love. Lie with me, Paneah, and be the real master of the mistress."

He wanted to look away, but she might pounce. "I won't do this thing, Sagira," he said, injecting a note of authority into his voice. "It would be a sin against God and against Potiphar. You cannot command me—I would suffer a whipping first."

"I wouldn't mar this golden skin with a whip," she said,

reaching for him. The touch of her hand burned his flesh, and he gasped as she grappled with the fabric of his kilt.

"Sagira—"

"Don't struggle, beloved."

"God, help me!"

She laughed and Yosef pulled away, but she clung to his garment with all her strength. A ripping sound rent the air, fresh air slammed against bare skin, and then he was out of her chamber. Reaching the corridor, he turned to run for his room, then he realized she'd go there first, seeking him. She would hunt him down until she found him, for he had never seen such determination in the eyes of any living person. She would look for him everywhere, searching the garden and even the kitchen, but she was too fastidious to accost him in the stockyard.

Without thinking further, Yosef turned and sprinted for the cattle pens.

"Paneah!" Sagira called, mimicking the singsong way mothers call their young children. She held up his kilt in case he happened to be watching. "I have something that belongs to you! Come out, come out, wherever you are!"

She moved through the bedchambers and the great hall, but no sign of him could she see. He was being coy, merely playing a game. Men liked to be the hunters, not the hunted, and perhaps she had surprised him with her sudden declaration. But the day was yet early, and if she let him find her…

She walked through the kitchens, idly running her hand over the bowls and pottery, hoping he would step out of the shadows and claim her. She walked more briskly through the servants' quarters, wondering if he had found the courage to replace his kilt, but he did not appear. He was not in the garden, on the porch or in her women's quarters.

He had run away.

She fell onto her couch, exhausted and humiliated. With each passing hour of the water clock she waited, anxious that he appear, and several times she rang her bell to summon him.

He did not answer.

Angry beyond words, furious at her vulnerability before a slave, she tore her dress and ripped handfuls of hair from her wig. She threw cushions, broke vases and upset the furniture in her bedchamber. At one point, she tore Yosef's kilt, then watered it with tears in a wave of regret.

She would have no child. No throne. No love. The prophecy, this day, her expectations, were part of an elaborate jest Ramla had anticipated and arranged.

By the time the first servants returned to the villa, Sagira was weak from weeping. A slave girl found her lying across her mussed bed, her eyes red-rimmed and swollen. "My lady!" the girl exclaimed, stepping over broken pottery as she hurried to Sagira's side. "Who has done this?"

Sagira lifted her head from the mattress and gazed toward the empty doorway. "Paneah."

"Where is your mistress?" Potiphar tossed the reins of his chariot to the boy in the stockyard. "I came as quickly as I could."

The wide-eyed boy pointed to the house, and Potiphar took the steps of the porch in three long strides. A host of silent slaves, white-faced and somber, stood outside Sagira's bedchamber. He pushed the door open and found Ramla crouched in a corner of the room and Sagira lying on her back, her arms folded across her chest in the pose of the dead.

Potiphar glanced at the destruction in the room. "What happened here?"

"Ask her," Ramla said, nodding toward his wife.

The still form moved. "Potiphar?"

He strode forward and sat on the bed, lifting Sagira into his arms. "What happened, little one? Why did you remain here without a guard?"

"I thought Paneah would take care of me," she murmured, her voice as heavy as a sleepy child's.

"I have given her a potion to calm her nerves," Ramla explained. "She was hysterical when I arrived."

Potiphar brushed damp strands of dark hair from Sagira's eyes. A faint bruise marred her cheek, and he traced it with his finger. "How did this happen, wife?"

She groaned softly at his touch. "Paneah."

"Where is he?"

"He—he threw me down. He came into my room and—" She lifted an arm and pointed to a dress thrown over a chair. Even from where he sat, Potiphar could see that it was ripped and torn.

Potiphar smoothed her brow. "Surely you are mistaken. Paneah would give his life to protect you—"

"Paneah attacked me." Her eyes opened and blazed with fury. "See this?" Reaching forward, she pulled a man's kilt from under a linen sheet on the floor. "I threw a vase at him and he ran. But he forgot his kilt. Don't you recognize it?"

Potiphar looked at the garment and recognized the fine pleated kilt Sagira had recently ordered for Paneah.

"Whatever he says, don't believe it." Her eyes narrowed. "He is a Hebrew, and the Hebrews lie, husband. On their account Egypt has suffered before. And this Hebrew, this slave you bought, came in to make sport of me. As I raised my voice and screamed, he left his garment and fled—"

Potiphar patted her shoulder as she broke into honest weeping. "Break into teams of two," he instructed one of the slaves who stood by the door. "Summon my guards for help.

Search the grounds, the fields, the riverbank. No one sleeps tonight until Paneah is found."

"There's no need to search, master," a voice called. "The man is here." The assembled slaves parted as Paneah appeared, a ragged strip of linen tied around his waist.

Like an awakening giant, rage rose within Potiphar as he stood to face his trusted steward. "Should I repeat what my wife has told me?" he asked, his face burning.

Paneah did not answer, but lowered his gaze. Potiphar felt Sagira's eyes boring into his back; outside the chamber, more than a dozen slaves waited to see how justice would be meted out to the greatest man in Potiphar's house.

Potiphar pointed to the garment in Sagira's hand. "Paneah, is that your kilt?"

Paneah lifted his head and met Potiphar's eye. "Yes."

"Did you come in here to sleep with my wife?"

Paneah glanced at the woman on the bed, then locked his gaze on Potiphar's. "No, master, I did not."

"Did you—" Potiphar pointed toward the torn dress "—do that?"

"No."

"Then who did?"

Paneah pressed his lips together as if he waited for someone to confess, then he closed his eyes.

"I suppose there is no one else who could have done this," Potiphar said. "You were the only one here. If you will not speak in your defense, I can only assume you are guilty."

Sagira wailed afresh, the sound grating on Potiphar's nerves. Something came up behind Paneah's eyes; he was defending someone or something, but Potiphar had neither the time nor the patience for games. Too many eyes were watching, too many tongues would carry the tale from this chamber.

He stood and looked at his steward. "You have never lied

to me," he said, an unchecked emotion clotting his throat. "You have been like a son. So instead of ordering your execution, I order you to prison. Go from this house, Paneah, and do not return again."

The proud head bowed before the sentence, and Potiphar watched the servant he had trusted as a friend turn and walk away between two guards.

Yet as Sagira whimpered behind him, he wondered if he would not be better served by ridding himself of his faithful wife and keeping his unfaithful servant.

Yosef

And Yosef's master [Potiphar] took him, and put him into the prison, a place where the king's prisoners were bound: and he was there in the prison.

Genesis 39:20

Chapter Twenty-One

With a show of fierce protectiveness, Ramla urged Potiphar to leave Sagira's chamber. The whispering crowd of servants and guards dispersed, and the priestess closed the door. Turning to Sagira, her malformed hand stroked her chin in a thoughtful gesture. "Was he not all you thought he would be?"

Sagira scowled. "Have you no respect? I was attacked, injured so badly that I cannot rise from my bed—"

"Tell the truth, Sagira. Your handsome Hebrew would not have you, would he? The little cobra was delightful in form, but decidedly deadly in an embrace."

Sagira lifted her chin, seeing no reason to deny the truth. Ramla knew her far too well. "He had the gall to deny me," she whispered, humiliation assaulting her anew. "On the appointed day, after years of preparation, he who swore undying obedience and love refused me!" Tears stung her eyes. "He was ready, Ramla, he belonged to me, but then he cried out to his god and ran as if I had sprouted horns!"

"His god?" Ramla lifted a brow. "The Hebrew god who sees and knows all?"

"What does it matter which god he called? In that moment

I realized that my precious, priceless love meant nothing to him. I loved him truly, Ramla, I did! He awakened feelings I never knew existed, yet in one instant he spurned not only my body, but my heart and soul."

She shuddered and lowered her voice. "And my love, as limitless as the Nile, has turned into an abhorrence I shall carry to my grave. I hoped Potiphar would slay him before me so I might steal the kisses I crave from his dying body, and yet my husband ordered him to the prison." She released a dreary laugh. "And so I lie on my bed while my much loved and hated Paneah rots in a prison cell only a few steps from my chamber. My nerves are on edge. I cannot sleep. I will lie here and listen for his cry in the night. I tremble to think that he might escape and try to kill me in the darkness. For I know any feelings he ever had for me have become a hate as strong as mine. The love that might have blessed us both has become an enmity that will destroy one or the other of us."

"Or both of you," Ramla said, her eyes as hard as the goddess's stone gaze.

Sagira sat up and crossed her arms, ready for the fight she'd been anticipating. "Enough about Paneah, I want to talk now about you, Ramla. You and your divining bowl have lied to me. You said this night was ordained for my child's conception, yet there will be no child. You said I would live forever in the memories of men. You said Paneah would walk before all Egypt and every knee would bow at his approach."

Her eyes locked on Ramla's. "You lied, Ramla, now I see it clearly. A foreign slave cannot become King! I don't know how you convinced me to believe you. You have never spoken a true word. You use your powers to prey on wealthy women. I demand to know why you have manipulated my life!"

"You are pitiful." Ramla stalked toward Sagira, her mouth drawn into a disapproving knot. "I have always spoken the truth to you. What I read in the future will come to pass. And as for missing the chosen night, the fault is completely yours. You have had more opportunities than any woman in Egypt, and yet you fail the goddess on every occasion."

"I did not fail!" Sagira said, violence bubbling in her blood. "I did everything in my power! Paneah failed me! He failed the appointed time! But regardless of your prophecy, I shall yet be remembered, I can still have a child! I will find another man, Ramla, a man of strength and glory, a man in whose frame dwells the brightness of the sun and the beauty of the lotus. I will find such a man, and I will prove I am capable of bearing the first in a new line of pharaohs."

Ramla lifted her head in a stiff gesture. "I told you not to attempt this liaison with a slave, but you would not listen. I waited as you set your plan into motion, and now you have failed. The goddess does not give second chances." Her face emptied of color as she moved closer. "I am leaving. I had hoped to follow you to glory and power. I will not follow you into failure and self-pity."

"You are leaving me? I am casting you out!"

Ramla turned to leave. "Good."

"Wait!" Sagira cried. Ramla turned, one brow raised, and Sagira lowered her voice to a childlike whisper. "If you go, who will I have?"

A corner of the priestess's mouth rose in a half smile. "You have the finest house in Egypt, a gaggle of slaves to wait on you hand and foot, and a husband who spoils you more than you deserve. Take pleasure in that—if you can."

Yosef smiled in grim irony as he approached the tall wall dividing Potiphar's house from Pharaoh's prison. He had never given the prison much more than a disdainful glance, but Potiphar had just decreed that he would spend the rest of his life amid the squalid, sun-bleached stone buildings behind the wall Yosef had heightened and thickened. He knew he ought to be grateful, for Potiphar could have ordered his execution, but his nerves tensed when he thought of the situation that had brought him to this place. Sagira, the woman he had believed his friend, had lifted the veil of pretense and revealed herself as an indulged, lustful, bloodless creature. Far worse than Sagira's defection was the knowledge that Potiphar no longer trusted him.

The guards wasted no time securing their prisoner, for night had swooped over the walls and no guard wanted to tarry in Pharaoh's prison after dark. The chief jailer assigned Yosef to one of the deep, ancient pits he had chosen to hide rather than improve.

As the star-filled sky wheeled about its axis, the Hebrew who dreamed sat with his back against the warm stone and swallowed against an unfamiliar constriction in his throat.

Yosef awoke with memories of the previous day edging his teeth. Because he had chosen honor over ambition, he had become a prisoner for life. What had God done to him now?

He sat up and examined the pit into which he'd been lowered. Somber stone walls twice his height rose from four sides of the rectangular cell while thin streams of light poured through cracks in the thatched covering overhead. He pressed on the orange-tinted walls, testing the strength of possible handholds, and felt the dry mud crumble beneath his fingertips.

The cell held nothing but two leather buckets, one filled with cloudy water and the other intended to serve as a toilet. Last night he had been given a kilt of rough hemp that scratched at his skin. From studying the prison accounts, Yosef knew he would receive one daily meal, a bit of rough bread and greens, which would be lowered in a basket each morning. He would be allowed no visitors, no companions, no comrades, for henceforth he would be regarded as a non-person, the lowliest of all prisoners.

He leaned against a wall and crossed his arms. He did not deserve to be in prison; he had done nothing wrong. Surely God would rescue him.

For several days he waited for news of Sagira's confession, but apparently that hard-hearted woman would not recant her story. The second week he expected Potiphar to appear and announce that he had experienced a change of heart and needed Paneah to resume control of the foundering household.

But Potiphar did not come. As Yosef paced in his cell, straining to hear sounds of normal life from Potiphar's household, days melted into one another, periods of suffocating heat followed by cool darkness that chilled his bones and brought fever to his body.

Yosef lay on the sand in his cell and shivered like a dog even in the heat of the day. His mind wandered in the twilight world of illness and conjured up the faces of people God had taken from his life: Tuya, his father, his mother, eleven brothers.

He had been in a pit once before. This darkness was like that one, this pain akin to the other, these prayers like the petitions he had lifted to heaven after his brothers had turned against him. How could his brothers and his mistress profess to love him in one hour and devise to take his life in the next? What harm had he done? What quality in his personality compelled them to despise him?

After a string of days, the fever broke, but unanswered questions haunted Yosef's sleep and his waking hours. He had only done what he ought to do. He had overseen his brothers' activities because he was a capable manager; he had told his father about their mistakes because correction would benefit the entire family. He had managed Potiphar's affairs because he wanted Potiphar to succeed; he had humored Sagira because she was his mistress and could not be scorned.

Why, then, had his brothers risen against him? Why had Sagira betrayed him after calling him her best and only friend? Why had Potiphar ignored years of faithful service and chosen to believe a lie?

At home he had been the favored son. In Potiphar's house he had been the trusted steward, the de facto ruler of the mightiest estate in Thebes. Now he sat in a prison cell, alone but for the occasional sag-bellied rat that tumbled into the pit while searching for scraps of food.

Why, God? He lifted his face to the sliver of heaven he could see through the thatched cover over the mouth of his cell. *Was I blinded by my dreams of power and authority? But you sent me those dreams; I have sought only your will for my life.*

Sagira offered to fulfill his dreams and Yosef chose to honor God, the one who had left him to rot in a pit. Where was he in this hour? Why didn't he answer? Yosef's pit lay only a few paces from the chamber where he once lived as master of Potiphar's house, yet a world of distance separated those two places.

No one will hear my cries, God, unless you listen. Sagira will not come, nor Potiphar, nor Tuya, nor my father, nor my brothers. All I have is you, and yet you are silent…

His thoughts rambled in an incoherent jumble. Two years before, he recalled, Tuya had seen Sagira's intentions and warned him, but he had not listened. Many years before that, his father had admonished him against boasting and he had not listened. Pride blinded him to his brothers' intentions, just as it led him to deny Sagira's lust-laced infatuation.

You knew how she felt, an inner voice chided him. *Tuya warned you, Sagira herself demonstrated her feelings. But you found secret satisfaction in her attentions. You avoided her presence, yet took pleasure each time she demanded that you appear. You pulled away from her touch, yet you hurried to her chambers each time she called you to work on another of her projects. She made you the greatest steward in Thebes, and you allowed her to do it. You were proud of being her pet.*

Pride. The word stung like the bite of a scorpion, for pride was the seismic fault of his life. He had craved the rich possessions of Egypt, furnishing Potiphar's house with every treasure that struck his fancy. He had looked on Sagira and wondered "what if?" He had listened to the vain flattery of visiting nobles.

Yosef huddled over the ashes of his dreams and bowed his head to his knees. He had been proud to wear his many-colored coat before his brothers, flaunting his position as the most-beloved son among twelve. He had been proud of Potiphar's trust in him, placing his position even before Tuya's unselfish love. He had been proud of Sagira's inappropriate interest and confident of his ability to keep the tigress at bay. Pride had enticed him into her den; only prayer got him out.

And haughty eyes and a proud heart were loathsome to the Almighty God.

The endless monotony of confinement forced him to look at himself, and for the first time he saw Potiphar's Paneah through eyes blessed with humility. God had gifted him with Rahel's beauty, Yaakov's keen intellect, his brothers' strength and the Hebrews' divine covenant of blessing. But Yosef had accepted these qualities as his own, not recognizing that the gifts of God had been channeled to him through others.

"Would that I had been born ugly, dull and weak," he murmured. "Then I would not have cause to lift up my heart against God."

Still bent into a position of submission, he extended his hands and curled the palms toward heaven in supplication. "Speak to me, God, as you have spoken before," he whispered, his face resting on the ground. "Speak to me though I have not spoken to you in many months. Do not forget me as I have forgotten you."

An hour passed. Yosef's eyes felt sandy and his bones ached. Grief throbbed in his soul. God had not spoken. Perhaps God would not forgive. Certainly the dreams would never be fulfilled, for he would remain in this pit forever, a victim of his own pride and foolishness.

He wanted to die, to lie under the desiccating orb the Egyptians called Re until nothing remained but a hollow shell of the promise he used to be.

Woe unto those who go down to Egypt.

He had not heard the voice in years, but he recognized it instantly. His eyes flew open as the hairs on his arms lifted.

Woe unto those who go down to Egypt and do not look to the Holy One of Yisrael. When pride comes, then comes dishonor, but with the humble is wisdom. Return to him from whom you have defected, O son of Yisrael, and like a hovering bird the Lord of hosts will protect you. He will protect and deliver you; He will pass over and rescue you.

El Shaddai had not forsaken him. Yosef covered his face with his hands. Tears of relief came in a rush so strong they shook his body.

"Potiphar!"

Khamat, warden of Potiphar's prison, waved from the gate. Reluctantly, Potiphar slowed his step. Since Paneah's imprisonment he had avoided the jail, not wanting to remember his steward's disloyalty. The memory of Paneah's stricken face still troubled his sleep.

"What is it?" He turned to face Khamat. "I have business inside the house." Indeed he did, for problems had erupted like troublesome weeds ever since Paneah's departure.

"Surely you would like to visit the prison, master. It has been nearly a month since your last inspection and I wondered—"

"I trust you, Khamat. Things cannot have changed so much."

He turned to leave, but the warden's next words made him halt in mid-step. "If the steward troubles you, you do not have to look at him. He remains in his cell, far from the others."

Potiphar set his jaw and bit down an urge to slap the man for making such a presumptuous remark. But everyone knew he felt guilty about Paneah. The entire household still buzzed with gossip about the steward's arrest, and the once-unified team of slaves had divided into quarreling factions. Most of the men thought Paneah guilty, for they understood the urges of a virile youth and had often remarked on the friendship between the steward and his mistress.

Potiphar had noticed the situation, too. He had encouraged the relationship because he knew Sagira was lonely, but he believed his wife regarded Paneah with a feeling akin to the paternal affection he felt toward the young man.

The female slaves, including Sagira's handmaids, took Paneah's part in the debate. He was too beautiful, they insisted, to take by force what any woman on the estate, including the mistress, would have willingly given him. Sagira, the rumors said, had yearned for the steward like a child longs for a dangerous toy, pursuing him with an odd mixture of contempt and desire.

But the rumors would not change Paneah's fate. A noblewoman's word was sufficient to convict a slave of anything. Even if Potiphar had found cause to doubt his wife, the tear-stained kilt in her hand had sealed the slave's sentence.

What was he thinking? Potiphar clenched his teeth as he considered Paneah's blunder for the thousandth time. *Sagira is charming, she is lovely in her way, she has a way of making a man feel important—*

But Paneah should have known better than to fall into her trap. And now Potiphar must support his wife, for to do otherwise would be tantamount to admitting that he had driven her to seek pleasure in the arms of a slave.

Khamat discreetly cleared his throat, bringing Potiphar back to reality. "The prison, my lord?"

"The steward does not disturb me," Potiphar answered, tossing the words over his shoulder. "He is no longer my property, but the king's prisoner. If anyone must worry about him, let it be Amenhotep."

Chapter Twenty-Two

"Take your turn, my wife."

When eleven-year-old Prince Abayomi shifted impatiently on his chair, Tuya forced her attention back to the game board. Her small hound figurines stood in imminent danger of being devoured by her husband's ivory jackals, so she rolled the painted wands on the wooden board. "Three squares, my husband," she said, moving one hound out of the pack and around the circular path. "In a moment my hound will be chasing you."

The royal mouth frowned, but the boy picked up the wands and rattled them enthusiastically. The young prince had inherited his father's long and straight limbs, but his mother's pale beauty had softened the dark eyes that glared from Pharaoh's visage. Abayomi's quick smile was set in the midst of a durably boyish face that either twinkled with mischievousness or glowed in the mystic contemplation of a daydreamer. Like his elder brother, his head had been shaved but for a princely lock of long hair growing from his right temple.

That lock quivered like a snake as he rattled the wands. "By the powers of Osiris and Amon-Re, I command double sixes!" he cried, throwing the wooden sticks. One of the carved wands skittered across the board and landed in Tuya's lap. Amused, she tossed it back. "A five," she said. "You may catch one or two of my hounds, but I shall escape you yet."

Abayomi frowned and fingered his game pieces, trying to decide how best to move his jackals, and Tuya smiled at him with tolerant affection. The all-consuming grief that had covered her like a mantle in the first year of her marriage had eased somewhat. Though a weight of sadness lay on her thin face, few things now touched the secret pool of sorrow within her.

For two years the boy-prince had been her husband. Shortly after their marriage Tuya realized Abayomi had asked for her because he considered her a pretty possession, a beautiful companion to sit by his side, listen to his dreams and play his board games. He was yet too simple and immature to realize that dashed dreams and disillusionment had left her heart a shell, but he was kind and good-natured. He might have sensed her sorrow, for he took great pains to make her smile. At first his frantic efforts to please left her bewildered; in time the mere sight of him gaping up at her was enough to make her laugh. He fancied himself a good husband, often bringing gifts: a golden necklace, a kitten, a bowl of candied dates.

As the wife of a royal son, Tuya had her own apartment in the palace, a bevy of handmaids to do her bidding, the use of a chariot whenever she wished and a wardrobe box filled with the most lovely garments she could have ever imagined. Her husband filled his days with training and games, and called for her in the early evening. She dined with him in his chamber, nodding at his stories, laughing at his jokes and smiling at his compliments. Often they played a board game after dinner or Abayomi would entertain her with a demonstration of his skills in sword fighting or archery. Every once in a great while, when especially tired or weary, he would invite her to remain with him throughout the night.

Because he was yet a child, Tuya realized that these invitations to join him in the royal bed were pleas for companionship. She often thought no life was as lonely as the one to which a royal prince was born, for though tutors, warriors, servants and counselors surrounded him, Abayomi had no true friends or confidants. His secrets were too exalted to be shared with common, less divine folk, and his dreams too sacred to be entrusted to anyone but a wife.

And so, in a vague imitation of his father and his elder brother, Abayomi wrapped his arms about his wife's neck and emptied his soul of its burdens, secrets and joys. And Tuya, her heart stirred with compassion and maternal tenderness, stroked the young prince's brow and resolved that though she might never be truly happy, she would always be grateful. The strong arm of Montu had not been able to restore her to Yosef, but it had kept her from Pharaoh's harem.

"Aha!" Abayomi's cry jolted her from her thoughts. "My jackals have killed all but one of your hounds, wife."

"Yes, my lord," she replied, scanning the game board. "As always, you have won the game. My single hound cannot escape a pack of jackals."

"Shall we play again?" Already he was resetting the game pieces into their positions.

"I am tired, my husband."

"Please, Tuya? If you will play, I will tell you the news of the court."

She shook her head. "I have no interest in people who do not concern me."

"But this is news you will want to hear. It concerns Potiphar—the man who brought you to my father."

"I see the captain of the guard every day in your father's audience chamber. He cares nothing for me, nor I for him."

"But this news—" Abayomi leaned forward and glanced

left and right as if telling a great secret "—concerns the man's wife. Lady Sagira has accused Potiphar's steward, the chief slave in the house, of attacking her."

"She lies!" The words slipped from Tuya's mouth without conscious thought.

Abayomi shook his head. "The lady presented evidence. The slave's garment was in her hand, yet the man was foolish enough to step forward and contradict her."

In a rush of bitter remembrance, Tuya saw Yosef's confident smile. *I can handle Sagira even as I have handled Potiphar all these years...*

He hadn't been able to handle either of them.

"Is it possible," she whispered, "that the steward spoke the truth?"

Abayomi leaned back in his chair. "They say he came forward with only a scrap of a feed bag to cover himself. Apparently his guilt compelled him to run from his crime, but he could not go naked into the streets, for they were crowded with people celebrating the festival of Opet. Potiphar heard the evidence and sentenced the slave on the spot."

Tuya's hand rose to her throat. Ramla's prediction had come true, after all. Sagira had seduced her handsome slave. Perhaps even now her womb stirred with Yosef's child. And after accomplishing her victory, she had thrown Yosef out of the house and accused him of an act for which the penalty was death.

Tuya's hands and feet felt as cold as the tomb. "The slave is—dead?"

Abayomi propped his gangly brown legs on a footstool. "Potiphar sentenced him to prison. Apparently he maintained great affection for this steward, and did not wish to see him die."

A mingling of relief and dread rushed over Tuya. Yosef's unseen god had spared his life, for any other husband would have killed an accused slave on the spot. But prison! She lowered her gaze and shuddered as she recalled Potiphar's jail. The place had lain behind the wall of the house, a desolate strip of red stone buildings and reed-covered pits from which she had often heard the agonized screams of Pharaoh's prisoners...

"My husband," she said, feeling limp with weariness, "the night waxes old and I am tired." *I want to weep. I want to close my eyes and cry for the noble Yosef I once knew, the man who would not betray his god or his father, the one who loved purely and honestly...*

But that man had vanished forever, replaced by a cheapened Paneah who would spend the rest of his life in prison. She would mourn for Yosef; she would water her bed with tears for what might have been. *Please, Montu, please let my husband dismiss me...*

Abayomi leaned forward. "One more game, Tuya, please. One more, and then we shall sleep."

Obediently, Tuya gathered the painted wands.

Potiphar's garden was dense with trees and leaves and blue shadows, and Tuya moved through it as if she had wings. Floods of cornflowers lined the tiled walkway, a blurred and heady bunching of color from potted and earth-sown plants. She felt happy and relaxed, for she had escaped the walls of the palace for an hour of rendezvous with Yosef.

Lowering herself to the ground under an acacia tree, she gazed up through the sun-shot leaves and waited. The turquoise sky brimmed with gold radiance, but nothing could match the beauty of the man she loved.

"Tuya."

He stood before her, awash in the sun's golden light, his eyes snapping with joy. With sure steps he crossed the garden and knelt at her side, his hand lifting her chin, his arm encircling her. Tremors of rapture caught in her throat as he whis-

pered her name; she closed her eyes and gasped in an attempt
to still the wild pounding of her heart. She trembled in his
arms, fire racing along every sinew of her body, and then his
lips touched the moist hollow of her throat.

"Yosef." She reached for him, but her hand closed on
empty air.

Stunned, she opened her eyes. She sat alone in a leafless
garden where a hot, whining wind hooted her name. Somewhere far away, a woman laughed in derision.

She woke herself with weeping and shuddered in the darkness, terrified by the persistence of her dreams.

With careful deliberation, Khamat let the rope slide
through his fingers and into the pit. He'd placed an extra slice
of brown bread and a shat cake into the steward's bucket. The
prisoner had not eaten in seven days, and death would soon
claim him if his appetite could not be tempted and awakened.

"If it please you, my lord, hear me." Startled by the strong
voice, Khamat leaned forward to peer into the pit, wondering
if he had approached the wrong cell.

The Hebrew slave was emaciated, but alive. He sat on the
ground with his legs crossed and his arms resting on his knees.
Through the glistening skin Khamat could count the man's
ribs. "Speak."

The bearded face lifted and dark eyes flitted over
Khamat's face. "If it please you—" The slave paused as if
gathering his courage. "Would you ask the captain of Pharaoh's bodyguard to grant me an audience? I would like to
speak to my master Potiphar."

"Potiphar says you are no longer his concern," Khamat
answered. The slave's mouth was slack with submission, but
his eyes glittered with resolve. Khamat had heard that this
Paneah possessed a keen intelligence, and cunning and des-

peration were a dangerous brew. If this humble pose was not sincere, those eyes might flash with murder and rebellion when the jailer turned his back...

"If he will not see me, perhaps you will relay my message," the slave called. "I would speak to Potiphar not as his favored steward, but as the king's prisoner, one worthy of death. I will not ask for pardon. Even though I am innocent of the charge for which I am imprisoned, I am guilty of a grave error—most grave."

Without rising at all, the prisoner's voice took on a subtle urgency. Khamat leaned forward to hear better.

"I would ask Potiphar," Paneah continued, "not for release or pardon, but for a duty. I served in his house, and would like permission to work in his prison. Let me wait on these who have sinned against Pharaoh so I may learn...humility."

Khamat gaped into the pit. Serve the prisoners? No man wanted to serve prisoners! This place held only those who were beneath idiots, beneath slaves, even beneath prisoners of war. No, this request could not be sincere; the man had to have a hidden motive. Perhaps the cramped conditions of the pit had worked on his nerves. Perhaps he looked for an opportunity to escape...or to return to the house to take vengeance on the lady Sagira.

"If you were to do what you propose," Khamat hedged, testing the waters, "you would not be transferred from this pit. After your work, when you had cleaned the cells of the others, you would find yourself back here again."

"It matters not where you confine me," the prisoner called, shrugging. "Do with me as you will."

"I would watch you like a hawk watches the rabbit, with a whip and sword in my hand. The gates and doors would be locked. There will be no opportunity for escape."

Paneah lifted a dark brow. "Was it not I who ordered that

the wall be made higher?" He smiled as if he had been reminded of something, then lifted his hands. "Use your whip,
warden, even your sword, if you see a single sign of pride or
rebellion cross my face."

Khamat paused. He had never thought to employ one of
the prisoners as a servant, but the idea was delightful. Potiphar
usually assigned the prison's cleaning detail to members of
his guard whose misdeeds warranted disciplinary action;
when there were no rebels Khamat himself had to empty slop
buckets, bandage festering wounds and carry the dead from
the cells in which they breathed their last. Why not use a
slave to do a slave's work? The idea was logical. If the man
disobeyed, no one would mourn him.

"I will speak to the captain," Khamat promised.

Two days later, pressed by his warden, Potiphar stood at
the lip of Yosef's cell and barked out a greeting. Dazed by the
familiar sound, Yosef scrambled to his feet. "Master?"

"I am your master no more," Potiphar said, his face lined
with a scowl that did not quite reach his eyes. "Speak, slave,
for my patience is limited."

"Thank you for coming," Yosef called up, wiping his hands
on his kilt. Now that his master stood before him, the eloquent
words he had prepared slipped from his mind like water
through his fingers.

"This is not a social meeting," Potiphar called. Behind him,
Khamat peered over the captain's shoulder, and Yosef knew the
warden must have had difficulty convincing Potiphar to come.

"Master Potiphar," Yosef answered, finding his tongue. "I
would ask your permission to serve your warden."

"Indeed." Potiphar's dark eyes raked Yosef's face. "My
warden says you have admitted your guilt in this crime."

"Guilt, no," Yosef answered, slowly feeling his way. The

urge to reveal Sagira's role in the situation gnawed at his heart, but Yosef knew that temptation sprang from pride. His task was to align his own soul with God's purposes, no one else's.

"I admit—" he fixed his gaze to Potiphar's "—that the voice of ambition encouraged me to lift my head above my station. I listened to those who praised my efforts in your household, and took those voices too seriously. I was nothing but a slave, a reflection of God's wisdom, the instrument of his will. A slave has no right to claim honor and praise as I did. My god has pronounced his judgment on me, and he has brought me to admit the error of my ways. My faults are mine alone. My successes have sprung from the hand of God."

"Your pious babbling means nothing to me, Paneah. You know I judge men by common sense and loyalty. If you will not admit your guilt, why have you called for me?"

"Idleness chafes at my soul, master. Let me restore my soul to humility by serving the warden of this prison. In this way I can serve you still."

He had hoped that his words would move Potiphar's heart, but the master's granite face remained as expressionless as it had been on the night of Yosef's disgrace. "Do what you will with him," he said finally, jerking his gaze toward Khamat. "I care not what this one does."

And so Paneah, virtual master of the mightiest house in Thebes, became the only slave of Khamat, chief jailer of the king's prison. Each morning Khamat lowered a rope into the Hebrew's cell and Paneah climbed forth to do his bidding. The unruly warriors from Potiphar's guard were excused from emptying buckets of waste from the prison cells, for Paneah cleaned them. He also carried fresh water and food from the prison gate to each individual cell.

Pharaoh's prison contained two different types of cells:

dungeonlike pits to confine the lowest criminals, and stone buildings to house noblemen's servants and Egyptian citizens. Paneah served the inmates of both. When he had finished with his prison duties, he worked in Khamat's stone lodge, scrubbing floors, grinding corn or cleaning the stall that held the jailer's donkey. On slow afternoons when the sky glared hot and blue, Khamat ordered the slave to stand behind him and fan away pesky flies as the jailer napped in the sun. When the sun-god's Boat-of-Millions-of-Years finally finished its journey across the sky, Khamat escorted the Hebrew back to his cell and pulled up the rope.

The other prisoners, accustomed to giving Khamat a measure of surly respect, took pleasure in belittling the new personality that had entered their small world. This bearded and bedraggled scarecrow, obviously a slave and apparently deserving of his fate, accepted the bitterness they spewed on him without comment. When he knelt to slide baskets of food beneath the iron bars, the prisoners in the walled cells spat on him and cursed him for the food's poor quality and limited supply. Even the criminals in the pits scorned him, routinely calling him vulgar names and deriding his manhood because he had been reduced to serving them.

"Surely you are the son of a scared rabbit!" one man called as Paneah pulled up his bucket. "Why else would you haul filth for the men who imprison you? What sort of woman gave birth to you?"

"One who wears bells on her skirt and sells her favors," the man in the next pit called. He made an obscene gesture in Paneah's direction. "I enjoyed her company the week before I came to this place."

No matter how crude or lewd the comments, Khamat noticed that Paneah did not respond in word or deed. He moved through a hailstorm of indignities and insults as though his thoughts were focused on another world, one in which men did not surrender to the vilest inclinations of their natures. While he worked, the slave neither glanced toward nor made reference to the barred door leading to Potiphar's house...and freedom.

Paneah never offered his opinions unless asked, but once Khamat asked for them, he discovered the slave possessed the organizational skill of a military officer and the wit of a royal courtier. Strength and honor supported the skills that were wasted on menial labor, but Paneah did not once hint that his situation should be reevaluated or improved. Khamat could find no trace of ambition or ulterior motive in the slave's conversation; nor did the man's words ever contain less than total truth.

In time, Khamat neglected to carry his sword while Paneah worked, then he put aside his whip. The slave's silent endurance won the respect of the other prisoners; the ribald taunting eventually ceased. Within a year, Khamat stopped supervising Paneah altogether; within two years, he made it a common practice to leave the long rope dangling in Paneah's cell. "Why should I get up early every morning to drop a rope to you?" he asked his servant. "You would tell me if you were planning to escape, wouldn't you?"

Paneah looked up from the sandy floor and regarded the chief jailer with a wistful smile. "God has a purpose for me here," he said, rubbing his hand over the crumbling stone walls as if he felt some affection for the place. "I will not leave until he opens the door for me."

After his brief exchange with Paneah in the pit, Potiphar did not venture into the prison again. The slave's words rankled in his brain, urging him to do something, but Potiphar had no idea what he should do. Paneah had talked of his god, but Potiphar had no use for gods, visible or invisible.

Peace and Paneah had departed from Potiphar's home on the same night. The house that had once brought Potiphar pleasure became a hellish place. Sagira, her charm and cultivated good looks destroyed by an overindulgence in food and wine, flirted brazenly with every man who crossed the threshold. More than once Potiphar had seen sheepish-looking suitors, slaves and noblemen departing from her bedchamber in the dark of night.

He regarded such things with indifference, silently wishing that Pharaoh had ordered him to lose an arm rather than receive a bride. Ramla, the iron-willed priestess whom Potiphar had endured for Sagira's sake, had not returned to the villa. Alone and forsaken, Sagira whined incessantly, returning handmaid after handmaid to the slave market, unable to find a single girl capable of serving as her companion.

Potiphar possessed all he had ever wanted: a fine house, treasure in his coffers, a sterling reputation as a warrior and friend of Pharaoh. The Gold of Praise hung about his neck, prompting all who met him to kneel in reverent respect for one who had been admired and honored by the king.

But his house, which had once been a haven of rest, hummed with tension and distrust. After Paneah's departure, Sagira refused to have anything to do with running the household. Potiphar extracted stern but capable taskmasters from his army and set them over his household, but the estate limped along, barely making a profit, the backs of its slaves bruised and broken by the whip.

No longer was singing heard in his house. The only laughter was drunken and coarse, and usually spilled from Sagira's bedchamber in the darkest hours of the night.

Potiphar retreated to the palace, preferring to spend his time with the king. But Pharaoh had tired of military conquests and spent his days overseeing the craftsmen who were building his tomb in the Valley of the Kings. Thoughts of eternity pressed on the royal mind, and Amenhotep's concern did not lie with his armies, but with the stonecutters and artisans who were fashioning the tools and treasures he would take with him into the next world.

And yet Pharaoh was forty-two; the captain of his guard, fifty-three. Potiphar knew he was closer to eternity than the king, but he was not eager to prepare for it. How could the future hold anything for a man who had no faith in it?

Chapter Twenty-Three

Two years later, in the grand central hall of Pharaoh's palace at Thebes, the entire royal family gathered to celebrate the gifts bestowed by a group of visiting foreigners. Tuya sat on a chair beside Abayomi, her hand resting protectively on the gentle swell of her belly. The priestess of Montu had declared that she would bear a son, and Tuya was careful that the proper offerings be offered every day to ensure her child's safety. She had lost one love because she neglected to placate the gods with proper sacrifices. She would not lose another.

Abayomi, caught up in the music, clapped and occasionally glanced in her direction. She smiled in approval, and he turned again to the musicians, his confidence bolstered. At thirteen, her husband was still much a boy. He had matured enough to earn her respect and father a son, though one had little to do with the other.

She had come to respect her young husband because the prince was a student of life. Anxious to understand the world around him, his insights into natural, divine and human law were curiously creative. He often struggled to communicate his fanciful ideas to others, but Tuya, who had been mother, sister and wife for four years, gave voice to his insights and feelings.

Neither his elder brother, the crown prince Webensennu, nor his father the king understood Abayomi, for their thoughts centered around military ideas of right and might, but Tuya was quietly glad that Abayomi would rather ponder the way of an ibis in the air than plunder an Asiatic village. Instead of swords and shields, her husband's chamber was crowded with scrolls, art and animals, living and mummified. His name meant 'he brings joy,' and after the grief of her former life, Tuya had to admit her husband-child had brought a measure of sunlight to her dark heart. She still dreamed of Yosef, but not as often as she once had.

Pharaoh and Queen Merit-Amon sat across from a dark-robed quartet of Syrian dignitaries, and Tuya found herself studying the strangers' faces. They wore short, pointed beards, heavy robes and no jewelry. For a moment she thought she gazed into a transforming mirror, for they were opposites of the clean-shaven, bejeweled, lightly clothed Egyptians. Awed by the ostentation of Pharaoh's palace, the visitors spoke little and looked much, their dark eyes darting up, down, right and left. Of course they were impressed. Tuya had learned enough to know no palace in the world could rival the beauty and opulence of Pharaoh's court. Thebes was the center of the world, and the center of Thebes was this room. From it Pharaoh's divine glory shone like radiant sunlight.

The crown prince sat at Pharaoh's right hand with two of his wives. Three years older than Abayomi, Webensennu behaved as though he were Pharaoh already, nodding with grave dignity at a pair of wrestlers who competed for his attention while acrobatic dancers in sheer veils whirled before the royal chairs. Though he still wore the prince's single lock of hair on his right temple, Webensennu gripped an ivory-handled flywhisk as though it were the flail or the crook, the symbols of Pharaoh's office.

The Master of the Banquet clapped his hands; the dancers stopped, the wrestlers prostrated themselves before Pharaoh. Without warning, a bevy of male slaves spun into the room, each bearing a bowl of roasted meat or honey-glazed fruits. The delicious aromas of goose, duck, teal and pigeon rose from the steaming bowls, and Tuya thanked the gods that the nausea of early pregnancy had passed. She now had the appetite of a field slave at harvest time, and she intended to enjoy this meal to the fullest.

Pharaoh's family, his noble guests and the visiting Syrians plucked food from the bowls while a group of women musicians danced to their playing of the harp, lute and flute. As a white-robed priestess of Amon-Re strummed the sacred sistrum, Tuya leaned forward to inquire if her husband found the meal pleasing.

The words never left her lips. A sudden shriek interrupted the musicians and the women scattered as one of the king's food-tasters knocked a bowl to the floor and staggered forward, his hands clutching at his throat. As the crowd gasped in horror, the terrified slave tottered toward his god and king, then collapsed as blood ran from his nose and mouth.

In an instant, Abayomi's arm encircled her waist. "To your chamber," he said, pulling her from her chair as his eyes swept the room. "Wait there. You will be safe, I swear it."

Alone in her chamber, Tuya knelt before the stone statue of Montu and numbly gazed at the figure. What power would such a statue have against one who wanted to poison her husband or her soon-coming son? Montu's strong arm had done nothing to aid Yosef, and only blind luck had saved

Pharaoh's life tonight. If the poison that struck the innocent slave had worked more slowly, Pharaoh would be well on his way to the underworld. Yet thousands of priests throughout Egypt offered daily sacrifices to protect their king, the divine one.

Which of the gods of Egypt could help her? She despised Bastet, Sagira's goddess, and Montu had failed her in the past. Amon-Re was Pharaoh's divine father, but though she would not admit it aloud, she felt nothing but contempt for a god who would allow death to come so close to the anointed king.

Yosef had spoken of and prayed to El Shaddai, the invisible god in whom the world lived and moved and breathed, and yet Yosef now passed his days in Pharaoh's prison. Yet there had been no announcement of a child born to Potiphar's wife, so perhaps Yosef had managed to escape the trap Sagira laid for him. Perhaps prison had proved to be a place of refuge for Yosef, a way out of Sagira's reach. Tuya did not know whether this god could be trusted, but she had believed in his existence from the first time she heard Yosef speak of the Almighty One. He was real, for Yosef would not lie, and El Shaddai had manifested his power by saving Yosef's life. Because this god was so different from the gods of Egypt, omnipresent and yet invisible, perhaps he worked in unexpected ways.

She turned from the statue of Montu and stared instead at the painted images of Pharaoh on the chamber walls. Distracted, she closed her eyes. "If you are there, Almighty One," she whispered, "hear the words of Tuya, friend to your servant Yosef. Protect my unborn child, and protect your servant Yosef. If you do not do these things—"

She paused. Most Egyptians threatened the gods with the desecration of their temples or the withholding of offerings if petitions were not answered, but would threats offend an all-powerful god? And how did one punish a god who had no temple and no priests?

"Please do these things," she whispered. "Please hear me, Almighty One. For today I have petitioned only you."

Potiphar strode into Pharaoh's chamber in the quiet of the afternoon, a time when the king usually rested or enjoyed the entertainment provided by his dancing girls. Today, though, Amenhotep sat pensive and quiet in his chair.

Potiphar cleared his throat, hoping the sound would spare him the agony of bending his arthritic knees to the floor. Fortunately, Pharaoh heard and gestured in Potiphar's direction.

The captain of the guard strode into the royal presence. "O Pharaoh, live forever! I have important news, my king. We have investigated and determined that the shame of yesterday's attempt on your life was made with the help of either the palace butler or the chief baker. The surgeons were unable to tell if the poison was ingested as drink or food, so we have arrested both men. They await your divine judgment."

"I will give it—later," Pharaoh said, inclining his head on his palm. His thoughts seemed far away.

Potiphar shifted uncomfortably. "Is there anything else, mighty Pharaoh?"

The king's gaze shifted to Potiphar's face. "Have you thought much about my reign, my captain? You knew my father well—how would you compare my leadership to his?"

Potiphar hesitated, wavering between truth and diplomacy. "You are much the same, and yet different," he said, his hand tightening around the hilt of his sword. "Your father, Tuthmosis, was a warrior and you have the same fierce heart. Your father fought until he died. But you, my king, have thought much of other things."

"The other world," Pharaoh murmured, his gaze drifting

again. "Do you know, Potiphar, that I can boast that no man has gone hungry during my reign? The Nile has brought forth her abundance every year. Therefore I know the gods are pleased with me. No priest has dared to think of bringing death to my door."

Aghast that the king would speak of the age-old rite by which a pharaoh gave his life for his country, Potiphar blinked in silence. In past dynasties, whenever the Nile did not flood sufficiently, famine smote the land so harshly that the people cried out in grief. Because Pharaoh was the giver of fertility and the preserver of all, he was also the Divine Son who might be put to death to ensure the fertility of the land. In the ancient pyramid texts the sages wrote that if the people had not eaten bread, or "the eye of Horus," both the people and the gods should demand the king's death so the fields might be fertilized with his blood. Since the kings were immortal gods, this sacrificial death was never declined…at least Potiphar had never heard of any king who refused his role in the ritual.

In a time of famine, when the priests decided that the kingdom had suffered enough, the high priest of Anubis would present himself to Pharaoh wearing the jackal mask of his god. In his arms he would carry the means of Pharaoh's death: a basket containing a cobra. Knowing that the time had come, the king would raise the lid from the basket and lift the cobra to his breast.

Death by cobra poison came swiftly. After the king's death, his internal organs were removed during the mummification process and his heart and lungs ceremonially buried in the soil, bringing breath and life to the earth. A new king, the heir, would confirm his right to succession by installing his predecessor in the tomb, thus insuring the dead king's place in the other world.

The kings of Egypt's eighteenth dynasty had died in various ways, but Potiphar could not name one who had sacrificed himself for the land. Did Amenhotep's new apprehension spring from some secret fear? Did he suppose the jackal-headed priest of Anubis to be lurking outside in a corridor?

"Do you anticipate a famine, my king?" Potiphar asked, his voice a subtle whisper in the room.

The king's head jerked toward Potiphar. "Surely, Potiphar, you know I fear nothing in this world or the next, and yet sometimes…I wonder. As God, I give everything to my people. I worship myself as God in living form, for I am the physical son of Re." Amenhotep pulled back his shoulders and lifted his granite jaw. At that moment, his dark, worried face seemed never to have known a smile. "And yet I am as mortal as other men. If I eat poison, I will die. Sometimes I do not feel like a god, and I am sobered by the possibility that I may not be." He threw Potiphar a look of half-startled wariness. "A life is a great treasure to risk on a lie, don't you think?"

For some shapeless reason Potiphar thought of Paneah. "My king, I cannot say. I am not a priest." He bowed, eager to leave the conversation. "If you will excuse me, sire, the royal baker and cupbearer await me. We will take great pains to stall your journey to the next world for as long as possible."

The hot wind of the sirocco blew sand into Abayomi's eyes, and his servants sighed in relief when Pharaoh's second son signaled for the company to halt. "We will pause from our hunt, for the sun is nearly overhead," the prince called, deepening his awkward voice to command the authority due a royal son. He stepped from his chariot and felt the heat of the desert sand through his sandals. "Lead the horses to shelter here, behind the Great Sphinx of Harmakhis, and prepare a resting place."

His servants scurried to do his bidding, removing the royal chariot to a place of shelter from the desert winds. Their dark bare feet skimmed over the blistering sand as they hastened to prepare a tent, but Abayomi placed his hands on his narrow hips and ignored them, choosing to study the Sphinx half buried in the sand. Khafra, a king long before his father, had modeled this monument after his own likeness in honor of the sun-god who ruled these vast deserts.

A smile twisted the corner of the prince's mouth. Where was the sun-god now, and did he care that the lion's body of his Great Sphinx lay buried beneath the desert? Only the wind-scarred head of Khafra was now visible, his chin resting on the sand like a creature resigned to inevitable suffocation.

"Prepare my tent here, before the Sphinx," the prince commanded the servants who fluttered nearby in anticipation of his wishes. "We will rest, then continue our hunt."

A canopy appeared as if from nowhere, four poles held its striped linen high above the earth. Another piece of linen, tightly woven to keep out irritating grains of sand, was spread on the ground, and on this the prince reclined.

The sun threw the shadow of his distinctive profile onto the ground. He knew he was handsome, and though his face still retained the softness of youth, his concentrated stare never failed to make a maiden blush or a servant grow pale. Taller than his mother, nearly as tall as his elder brother, he possessed strong limbs and a broad chest, set off by a fine linen kilt and the wide golden collar about his neck. One magnificent lock of black hair grew like an exclamation from his right temple, the seat of deep thought and wisdom.

The Great Sphinx sheltered him from the hot winds of the sirocco and his eyes closed in the heavy heat of the afternoon. Sleep, when it came, was welcome.

* * *

The Sphinx spoke to him. "Behold me, gaze on me, O my son Abayomi," the creature said, the wide eyes of stone unblinking and yet, seeing all. "For I, your father Harmakhis-Khopri-Tumu, grant you sovereignty over the Two Lands, in the South and the North, and you shall wear both the white and the red crowns of the throne of Sibu, the sovereign possessing the earth in its length and breadth."

The prince blinked and sat upright, but nothing else moved in the hot afternoon. Was this a dream? Or had he dared disturb the mighty sun-god with his irreverent thoughts?

"These are words of blessing, my son," the Sphinx continued, his voice a roar that reverberated through the desert. "You shall be called Tuthmosis, and the flashing eye of the lord of all shall cause to rain on you the possessions of Egypt. Vast tribute from all foreign countries, and a long life for many years as one chosen by the Sun, for my countenance is yours, my heart is yours, no other than you is mine."

"I am yours," the prince whispered, falling to his knees before the solid stone image. He lowered his head to the earth and felt the heat of the desert burn his forehead. "But I am only a second son. How can these things be?"

The massive stone head turned, the grating of stone on stone quivered the canopy poles. The prince slowly lifted his gaze. Beyond the Sphinx, sand dunes rippled and flowed like water toward the monument, and the mouth of the half-buried stone creature opened in an inhuman cry. "The first born of Egypt shall die," the monstrous voice shrieked. "You shall become King, my son Tuthmosis."

The prince moistened his lips as the horrible prophecy rang in his ears. "What would you have me do?"

As if by command, the sand stopped flowing, the wind

ceased. The Sphinx's mighty head returned to its resting place and the powerful mouth closed.

But still the voice reverberated in the prince's head. "Now I am covered by the sand of the mountain on which I rest, and have given you this prize that you may do for me what my heart desires. For I know you are my son, my defender. Draw nigh. I am with you, I am your well-beloved father. Release me from this mountain, and I shall give you what your heart desires."

"I will release you from the sand, I swear it," the prince answered, the scent of scorched linen filling his nostrils.

"Then this and more will I give to you, Tuthmosis, if you release me!" The mighty voice echoed through the desert stillness, growing louder and stronger until the boy's hands covered his ears and he screamed, too, his cry lost in the buried god's terrifying wail.

The prince jerked into wakefulness as an anxious servant touched his shoulder. Behind the servant, the sirocco blew past the Sphinx in a miserable, commanding howl. "May the gods grant you life, my prince," the servant said, bowing on the hot sand. "You have slept a long time. We feared you were not well."

"I am well," the prince answered, rising on his elbow. He moved slowly, half-afraid any sudden sound or action would tear the fabric of sanctity around the half-buried Sphinx. The fearsome sounds and images lingered in his brain, as vivid as the servant on the sand. His father would insist he had imagined the episode, for Amenhotep believed the gods spoke only to him. But the prince recalled the devastating power of the Sphinx's voice, and shivered despite the heat.

He stood and stepped from beneath the sheltering canopy. "Mark this well, all who hear," he called in his most authoritative tone. "If the gods will that I be King, on that day the sand of this mountain is to be cleared from the form of

Harmakhis-Khopri-Tumu, the sun-god, that he may reign in beauty over the Two Lands, in the South and the North. It shall be recorded that I have done this, in covenant between the god my father, and I."

The company bowed in honor of the royal proclamation. Abayomi nodded, satisfied, then climbed back into his chariot and led the procession back to Thebes, too shaken to continue the hunt.

Chapter Twenty-Four

The time of her travail caught Tuya by surprise. She barely had time to send for the priestess of Taweret, the patroness of childbirth, before her son dropped into the world.

As the grotesque priestess paraded throughout Tuya's chamber striking at invisible enemies with her ceremonial daggers, Tuya drew the mewling infant to her breast and tenderly wiped the birth fluids from his skin. How perfect he was, and how unique! He was the only thing in the world that had ever belonged to her, and she would never surrender him to anyone. She had been born a slave, but this child would forever be free.

"What will you call him?" one of her maids asked, her hands folded reverently. "As Pharaoh's grandson, he should have a fine name."

Tuya pressed her finger to the child's cheek and smiled as the boy turned his head, seeking a life-giving breast. She was about to answer when the door slammed open. Abayomi crossed the threshold, his eyes wide, his face stiff with fear. "I came as quickly as I could," he said, struggling to catch his breath.

"Would you like to see your son?" She smiled at the baby

in her arms. "He has just been born. I think he would like to meet his father."

Abayomi panted his way through the knot of maids and knelt at Tuya's side. He studied the baby for a long moment, then his worried face arranged itself into a grin. "He's beautiful, my wife," he said, giving her a warm smile. "What baby name will you give him?"

"I think—" she offered the baby to his father "—I shall call him Yosef."

Abayomi did not protest the strange-sounding name, but she knew he had a taste for the unusual. "Yosef," he murmured, taking the baby into his hands. "He is a fine son."

"He is," she murmured, running her hand over the baby's damp hair.

The prince looked at her with something fragile in his eyes, then returned the child to her arms. "I should go."

"Why?" she asked, startled. "You have a right to be here."

"But you have done *this*," he stammered, lifting his hands in a helpless gesture. "You have done a great thing! I want to get you something."

"Abayomi." She reached for the hand of the boy who was, in a way, as much her son as the infant in her arms. "You have given me a child, the greatest gift a man can give a woman. I ask for nothing more."

"I wish you would," he whispered, but she laughed off his suggestion and turned again to the baby, dimly aware that Abayomi watched as if she were some unparalleled work of art.

As a hot wind blew clouds of yellow dust down the alley between the walled cells, Yosef paused outside the structure where Pharaoh's newest prisoners had been incarcerated. His hands, calloused from hauling buckets to and from these cells, tingled with exhaustion after a long day in the blinding sun.

He lowered the buckets and wiped the sweat from his brow. He had hoped to return to his cell and go to sleep, but a riotous clamor had broken out beyond the prison walls adjacent to the streets of Thebes.

"What is the cause for this noise?" one of the new prisoners called. The two men in this cell, both servants from Pharaoh's palace, had been imprisoned nearly five months without an opportunity to stand before the king.

The one who had spoken finger-combed hair from his eyes to better glare at Yosef. "It is not a feast day, nor a festival, nor Pharaoh's birthday. Why does pandemonium rise from the streets?"

"Let me talk to him," another voice muttered. The second inmate pushed his way to the small opening in the iron door. He was a dusty man with an aging yellow face and deep half-moons under his eyes, but his smile seemed genuine. His gaze flickered over Yosef, then he bowed his head. "Do you know why Thebes celebrates?"

Yosef lifted the bolt on the door. "I do not know." The two prisoners stepped back as he moved inside to exchange a full bucket for their empty one.

The second man clapped his hands. "I may know the reason. It is time for the princess to deliver her child."

"Another royal brat," the other man groused, dropping onto the reed mat that served as his bed. "Another mouth to feed! I'm beginning to think I don't want to go back to Pharaoh's kitchen."

The second man wagged a scolding finger at his companion. "The lovely Tuya could not produce a brat if she were wed to Anubis."

Yosef's blood rose in a jet. "You know Tuya?"

"Know her?" The man laughed and leaned against the wall. "I've known her since she was a child. I was the butler for Donkor, and she a maid for Donkor's daughter. No one was more astounded than I to discover that she'd grown into a woman lovely enough for Pharaoh's son."

Yosef reached for the wall to steady himself. He had not dared to speak Tuya's name in five years, but her image rose before him, vivid and close, opening the door on hundreds of memories he'd tried to bury. The impulse to ask a thousand questions was hard to resist, for this man had talked to her, toiled with her, perhaps his work-worn hands had even gripped Tuya's slender fingers—

"Is she...well?"

The prisoner squinted at him, then nodded slowly. "Can it be that you have also known Tuya?"

Yosef nodded.

"Then let us talk."

"Please." Yosef overturned the empty bucket, then used it as a stool. "There is much I would like to know."

The prisoner lowered himself to his mat. "I am called Taharka," the man said, watching Yosef through eyes that had clouded with age. "I was summoned to work in Pharaoh's vineyard many months after Tuya left Donkor's house. Later she told me she had served in the house of the captain of Pharaoh's bodyguard."

"Potiphar." In a moment Taharka would mention his name, for surely Tuya had told her old friend about the love she shared with a Hebrew slave...

But Taharka only scratched at his arm. "Yes. And Potiphar later returned her to Pharaoh. The kitchen slaves are fond of saying that the young prince fell in love the moment he saw her. So she was married to Abayomi, and when I left the palace a royal child grew in her womb. Unless she met with misfortune, it is time for her baby to be born."

Yosef felt his smile twist. He could not picture Tuya with

another man or with a child in her arms. He had heard that Tuya married a boy-prince, but in the void of prison life he had forgotten that time did not stand still outside the stone walls. If Tuya's prince was mature enough to father children, she was married now to a man...

"I think we ought to discover," the dark-haired prisoner interrupted, "why the mention of our princess's name interests this slave."

Yosef turned, about to stammer out a truthful reply, but Taharka's eyes flashed a warning. Yosef looked away and shook his head. "Who has not heard of the lady's beauty?" he finished, shrugging. "Every man in Thebes has heard songs that praise her beauty. I never thought to speak—" his eyes met Taharka's "—with a man who had actually met her."

An understanding was reached and returned in that glance, and in that moment Yosef realized that Tuya's life at the palace was no more secure than it had been in Potiphar's house.

Terrorized by nightmares, three prisoners stirred in their sleep and awoke with clear and unsettling memories of the night they'd passed.

Yosef awoke slowly, burdened by the rueful acceptance of a terrible knowledge. The meaning of his dream was all too clear. He'd seen Tuya standing on the opposite bank of the Nile in the flood's ominous gray expanse. She wore an expression of incredible sadness on her pale face, but she carried a baby in her arms as a young boy clung to her skirt. Yosef watched as a wide crocodile rose from the engorged Nile and advanced toward her, its golden eyes focused on the babe in her arms. As Yosef called to her, the wavelets that had flecked the surface of the river flattened out, and a second crocodile crawled toward the unsuspecting Tuya.

She did not see, for her eyes were fastened on her child.

From the opposite bank, Yosef struggled to reach her, but his arms were held by iron bonds. He threw back his head and released a guttural cry, but his voice would not carry across the river.

Understanding hit him like a punch in the stomach, and Yosef awakened fully aware of what God wanted him to know. Tuya and her child were in danger. And if the boy clinging to her skirt was intended to represent her husband, his life would be also threatened.

But what could he do to warn her?

Seeking an answer, he climbed the rope from his pit and proceeded to go about his work. For the first time in years, the comments of the condemned prisoners did not register, so intent was he on recalling every detail of his dream. There had to be a way to reach Tuya. God would not have warned him unless he could do something to help. "Show me," he whispered, turning from the pits to the stone cells. "O God of understanding, make the way clear."

Abruptly, he remembered Taharka, Tuya's friend. If God would provide a way to release the cupbearer, Tuya could be warned. He quickened his steps down the path, eager to speak to Pharaoh's servant.

But Taharka was in no mood for conversation. A cloud of gloom lay over both of Pharaoh's servants, and Yosef dared not ask for a favor while the cupbearer and baker were in such foul moods. "Why are you upset?" he asked instead, tucking their empty food basket under his arm.

The butler scowled at his companion. "I didn't sleep well. The baker and I both had disturbing dreams that stole our rest."

"Why speak of it?" the baker groused, lying back on his mat. He shaded his eyes and frowned at Yosef. "And why do you care?"

"Interpretations belong to God." Yosef knelt beside Taharka's mat. "Tell me your dream."

Taharka's worried expression softened into one of fond reminiscence. "I dreamed I walked again in my vineyard. A vine sprouted in front of me, and three branches grew on the vine. It budded, its blossoms came forth, and its clusters produced ripe grapes, the finest I have ever seen. Pharaoh's cup appeared in my hand, so I took the grapes and squeezed them into Pharaoh's cup, then put the cup into Pharaoh's hand."

Yosef smiled. "God, the Almighty One, does not want you to be confused. This is the interpretation of your dream—the three branches are three days. Within three days Pharaoh will forgive you and restore you to your place, and you will once again put Pharaoh's cup into his hand as you used to do."

As a smile of relief spread across the old man's features, Yosef touched his arm. "Please, Taharka, keep me in mind when it goes well with you. Do me a kindness by mentioning me to Pharaoh, and get me out of this prison. You will not be circumventing justice, for I was kidnapped from the land of the Hebrews, and even here I have done nothing to deserve being put into a dungeon."

He did not dare mention Tuya, for he knew nothing of court life and did not know if even this man could be trusted. But Pharaoh could pardon any prisoner and if Yosef were free, he could keep a watchful eye on the situation at court. From a distance, he could search out danger that might threaten Tuya and her child…

"Fascinating," the baker remarked, his voice dry. "If I promise to speak to Pharaoh, will you give me a favorable interpretation, too?"

Though he was impatient to continue his conversation with Taharka, Yosef nodded to the other man. "Tell me of your dream."

The baker crossed his legs on his mat. "I saw three baskets of white bread on my head," he began. "In the top basket were all sorts of baked foods for Pharaoh, and birds were eating them out of the basket." He grinned. "In three days I'll be serving Pharaoh again, correct?"

Yosef lowered his head as he struggled for words. "The three baskets are three days," he whispered, a pang of regret striking his heart. "Within three days Pharaoh will lift you from this place and will hang you on a tree. The birds will eat your flesh from your bones."

The baker trembled as though a chill wind had blown over him. A full moment passed before he protested. "That can't be right," he said, smacking his fist into his palm. "How do I know you are telling the truth?"

Yosef froze as the silent voice spoke to his heart, then he met Taharka's steady gaze. "Pharaoh's eldest son will die before today's sun sets," he said, stunned by the awful revelation that had come to him. "You will know I speak truly when you hear of this thing."

At dinner that day, Prince Webensennu plucked a poisoned piece of fruit from Pharaoh's bowl and died within the hour. Potiphar and his guards surrounded the royal kitchens, where a junior baker confessed to the crime. Two days later, under torture, the condemned man exposed a year-old conspiracy that had been orchestrated by Pharaoh's chief baker and funded by a group of rebel Syrians. The poisoning of Pharaoh's taster many months before had been the first attempt to murder the divine king.

Satisfied with the answers he had received, Potiphar left his guards with the nearly dead traitor and stalked to the great hall where a somber king was attempting to observe his birthday. Potiphar did not bother to bow as he entered. Amenhotep sat on his throne, untouched bowls of rich food spread before him, his royal visage cloaked in grief. The queen and other family members ate with little enthusiasm, their eyes occasionally darting toward the place where Webensennu usually sat with his wives.

Pharaoh's brow lifted when Potiphar halted before him. "The murderers have been found," the captain announced, bowing his head. "Two bakers in your kitchens are guilty, urged to commit this crime by the chief baker now in my prison. They were paid in silver by the Syrian dignitaries who sat at meat with Pharaoh some months ago."

Pharaoh stood and held a quivering hand over the banqueting assembly. "Let the chief baker be removed from the prison and hanged on a tree outside the city walls. Let those who conspired with him be killed with the sword. And let all their bodies remain in place for the wild animals, for they do not deserve to enter immortality."

Potiphar bowed again. "It shall be done. But there still remains the matter of Taharka, your cupbearer." He looked up, reminding the grief-stricken king of unfinished business. "We could not tell whether the first attempt involved food or wine, and Taharka has awaited your judgment in prison."

Pharaoh took a deep breath and barreled his chest. "Let the cupbearer be restored to his former position and cleared of all suspicion." The king's eyes turned to meet those of his queen. "I have lost a son. Let no more innocent blood be shed."

When the seventy days of mourning for Prince Webensennu had passed, Pharaoh proclaimed that his fourteen-year-old second son, Abayomi, was henceforth to be known as Menkheprure, Beloved of Osiris, Tuthmosis, Crown Prince of Egypt. Tuya watched her husband's young shoulders brace for responsibility as his thoughts grew heavier during the months of mourning.

Though he had told her of his strange vision before the
Sphinx, she had not truly expected him to become Crown
Prince. But as soon as he was proclaimed heir, her husband,
the fourth to be named Tuthmosis, began to consider plans by
which the Great Sphinx might be evacuated from the sand that
had all but smothered it.

And Tuya, who had steadily and quietly prayed for her
friend Taharka's safety, thanked the Almighty God for the
cupbearer's release.

Tuya left her baby with a wet nurse and slipped from her
chamber to seek Taharka in the palace kitchens. Several
startled servants, unaccustomed to the sight of a royal lady in
the workrooms, dropped bowls and trays as they hurried to
prostrate themselves at her approach. "Do not trouble your-
selves," she said, glancing around. "Where is Taharka?"

One of the slaves pointed toward a back room, and Tuya
startled even the balding butler when she stepped through the
doorway. "By Seth's eyeballs, I didn't expect you to come,"
Taharka blustered, struggling to lower himself to his knees.

"Rise, Taharka, I came to congratulate you, not to accept
homage," Tuya said, injecting a teasing note into her voice.
"I was distressed when you were arrested. I have asked my
god to return you safely."

"Thanks to the gods, I am safe," the slave answered, wiping his hands on the stained apron over his kilt. "And thanks
to the divine pharaoh, of course. And to you, naturally. And
to Horus—"

"You need not pretend with me, old friend," Tuya whispered. She paused, wondering how she might ask the question
badgering her heart. "You were a long time in the prison."

"Six months." Taharka shrugged. "I'd do it again if Pharaoh
demanded it. I won't be having it said I'm disloyal or bitter
about it—"

"Be assured that I will say nothing of this conversation," Tuya said, wishing the cupbearer could forget that she was married to a royal prince. She wanted to ask a specific question, but Taharka knew nothing of her love for Yosef, and to tell him about it would be the worst kind of disloyalty to her husband. And Pharaoh could not abide disloyalty.

"Did you…meet many people in prison?" she asked, pretending to study a bowl of grapes.

"By the gods, no." Taharka leaned against a wall. "We were kept in a dark cell no bigger than this workroom. Much smaller, in fact. The baker, may the gods condemn his soul for all eternity, and I saw no one but the warden and his slave. The baker—and you may pass this on to whomever you like— behaved as a guilty man from the first day we were thrust together. He complained and uttered treasonous statements, he even called your son a brat, yes, that was his exact word—"

"Did you ever," she asked, unable to remain silent, "hear of a prisoner called Yosef?"

Taharka blinked. "We were kept alone, I tell you, that cursed baker and I. A most foul and disagreeable sort he was, a loathsome toad—"

The cupbearer knew nothing. "Thank you, Taharka," Tuya murmured, backing out of the room. "I wish you well."

The Nile rose and fell twice more, blessing the land with bounty.

Now the heir apparent, Prince Menkheprure left his wife and son at the palace and began his military training. His valiant efforts in battle earned him the title "Conqueror of Syria," and Tuya watched her dreaming husband become as fierce a warrior as his father. After his engagement in Syria, the courageous prince led a campaign in Nubia and proved himself worthy to assume his father's throne. Tuya saw little of him during those years, for when he was at home in Thebes, her husband spent hours being tutored by the high priests of Osiris for the role that would one day be his. A godling, it seemed, had much to learn.

As Tuya's husband equipped himself for the throne, the priests prepared the people for the eventuality of his ascension to power. They told the story of how Amon consulted with the other gods to see who should bear his divine child. Thoth suggested Queen Teo, one of Amenhotep's many wives, and Amon visited her in the physical form of Pharaoh so a divine child could be conceived. "Not once, but twice Amon visited a wife of Pharaoh," the priests explained to the people. "Pharaoh's second son is as divine as his first son was."

The afterbirth that had followed Menkheprure's body into the world was brought from its place of preservation. Wrapped as a mummy painted with a child's face, the deified placenta was known as the Khonsu. Just as Pharaoh's royal Khonsu was carried on a standard before the king on all state occasions, so Menkheprure's preserved placenta was paraded before the people whenever he appeared in the royal court. Soon just the appearance of the young prince's Khonsu elicited rapturous applause and cheering from curious crowds of well-wishers.

As Menkheprure progressed in his royal education, Tuya noticed that Pharaoh's smile widened in approval and relief. He had appeased the gods, he had led his kingdom, he had prepared his successor.

Shortly after celebrating his forty-fifth birthday, Amenhotep II retired to his chamber and surrendered to an illness that had sapped his strength for many months.

"My father's death is the beginning of his journey to resurrection," the crown prince proclaimed to the assembled court the next day. "The gods once lived on earth, begat children, and died, yet they still live and have needs. Like them, my father has passed from one state of life to another, and we will help him prepare for the needs of the other world."

The new king sought Tuya's eyes for an instant of reassurance. She gave him a smile of encouragement, then he cleared his throat and continued. "We will mourn for seventy days while the king's body is prepared for immortality."

During the seventy days of mourning, Tuya kept her three-year-old son by her side as much as possible. The stubby-legged toddler seemed to be the only person in the world she could love without risk, for just as Abayomi had become Prince Menkheprure, her prince had become Pharaoh, and Pharaoh belonged to his people. Now that her husband wore the red and white double crown, priests, counselors and diplomats would hold more power and influence over him than a wife. Tuthmosis IV would not need her approval, for a host of courtiers yearned to assure him of his strength, wisdom and authority.

And now that he was King, her husband no longer needed her as a wife. A harem of the kingdom's most beautiful women awaited his pleasure and attention.

Yet in those early days, Tuthmosis's devotion and adoration were reserved for the god who had spoken from the Sphinx. As the young pharaoh prepared for his coronation, he ordered slave crews to clear the sand from around the mammoth statue. Workmen labored in the blazing sun to repair the sacred figure, and between the monument's outstretched paws, Tuthmosis mounted a special stela engraved with the notice that he had restored the Sphinx in order to honor the god's prophecy. Tuthmosis believed that the Sphinx had brought about his kingship, and the impressionable young man was determined to honor the god who could work such a miracle.

As Tuthmosis attended to the Sphinx, the priests attended to the earthly remains of Amenhotep II. Tuya had beheld the face of death many times, but since her fellow slaves counted for nothing in the afterlife, their bodies were tossed into the Nile as food for the crocodiles. But Amenhotep had spent the latter part of his life preparing for paradise, and his divinity demanded that he be mummified with all ceremony and propriety.

Careful not to intrude, Tuya listened from a corner of the throne room as every morning the high priest of Osiris reported the progress of the dead king's funeral rites. First the king's viscera were removed and placed in canopic jars, then the priests split his body open with a flint. After seventy days of wrapping and encoffining, the royal cadaver, desiccated, resewn and reshaped, would be carried to the tomb to enact the entry of the king into the underworld. Tuthmosis would be required to preside over this elaborate ritual, for as the dead king had abdicated his earthly powers in favor of his son, the new king would establish the dead pharaoh as a god in the other world.

The Nile had just begun to recede when the seventy days drew to a close. Tuya clutched her tiny son's hand as she joined the funeral procession and left the Nile's east bank, the land of the living. Hundreds of mourners, all dressed in white, crossed the swollen river on ferryboats and walked deep into the western valleys where jagged cliffs rose like armed warriors. Here in the Valley of the Tombs, the eternal dwellings of the dead waited for yet another king.

An ox-drawn hearse, symbolizing the sun-god's blazing boat, led the procession with Amenhotep's mummified remains, and behind it followed a sledge bearing the four canopic jars containing the king's liver, lungs, stomach and intestines. Behind Pharaoh's body marched a host of slaves carrying the furniture and other equipment Amenhotep would require in the life to come.

A freshly painted portico had been erected before the tomb,

and at the left end of the shelter a pair of mummers performed a funeral dance. The special mortuary priests, the hemu-ka, slid the coffin from its sledge and stood it upright at the door of the tomb. One priest, his face hidden by the jackal mask of Anubis, supported the immense coffin while the chief mortuary priest symbolically restored speech to the dead king by touching the king's painted lips with an adze-shaped instrument. The ceremony was called wep-ro, "the Opening of the Mouth," and the priests believed the rite would give speech to the king in his new life.

Tuthmosis, looking young and frail in his heavy white head covering, stood with the other male mourners at the right of the portico. Tuya and the other women sat behind him, while Queen Merit-Amon wept and wailed at the side of the coffin.

The time had come for the dead to depart. The jackal-masked priest gently pulled the queen away from the coffin, then a score of attendants placed the gilded box inside the granite sarcophagus. Before the heavy lid was put in place, Amenhotep's wives walked by, each of them draping flowers over his painted coffin. When all the wives had passed, a score of shaven-headed priests heaved the lid into position, then lifted the sarcophagus onto rollers and proceeded to push this most intimate of the king's chambers through the tomb's tunnels.

Beneath the painted gazes of numerous gods and goddesses, the priests trudged to the somber rhythm of a funeral chant until they reached Amenhotep's burial chamber, an immense hall decorated with paintings that told the story of the king's life. The ceiling was supported by two rows of pillars decorated with life-sized images of the king in the presence of the gods. Beyond the last two pillars, steps led into a crypt where the great king's sarcophagus was laid on a granite slab.

When the sarcophagus and the canopic jars had been set

in their places, the priests and relatives filled the rooms of the tomb with supplies for the king's afterlife: furniture, baskets of food, pottery, glass, garlands of flowers, jewels, treasures, funerary statues of servants, slaves and wives. Several chambers already bulged with items Amenhotep had accumulated in his lifetime.

Tuya walked past a king's ransom in gold and riches as she carried her contribution for the king's eternal life: a small alabaster vase on which she had painted the likeness of her baby, Pharaoh's grandson. Wading through an assortment of earthly treasures, she crept to the innermost burial chamber and knelt before the remains of the man who had been her sovereign and father-in-law. After pressing her lips to the cold stone of the sarcophagus, she tenderly placed the vase within a wreath of lotus blossoms.

Queen Merit-Amon stood with wide eyes near the entrance to the burial chamber, and Tuya slipped her arm about the woman's waist as the priests installed magic amulets to guard against tomb robbers. As others lit the golden torches that would illuminate the chamber after they had gone, Tuya whispered in the queen's ear and coaxed her from the room. Carefully sweeping their footsteps from the sand as they backed out, the priests left the tomb, shutting and sealing the inner passageways one by one.

By the time Re's sun boat had sailed to the west, Egypt had a new king.

Chapter Twenty-Five

One aspect of her husband's coronation caught Tuya by surprise. Even before the dead pharaoh was entombed in his grave, rebellion stirred in the northern nomes. To ensure that the Mitanni Empire would enforce the peace and maintain Egyptian interests in the northernmost lands, the royal counselors unearthed an old treaty between Amenhotep and the king of the Mitanni tribe. Amenhotep had promised that one of the Mitanni king's daughters would marry the next king of Egypt, so a hasty union between Tuthmosis and Mutemwiya, a Mitanni princess, was arranged. Narmer, Amenhotep's faithful courtier, was dispatched to escort the bride to Thebes with a copy of the marriage contract. The agreement stipulated that the princess be designated as the Great Wife, Queen Mutemwiya. Since Tuthmosis had no royal sisters to vie for the title, the princess was readily accepted.

On her husband's coronation day, Tuya found herself standing with her son among various other members of the royal family as her husband and his new wife were crowned King and Queen of the Two Kingdoms. Tuya told herself the new marriage did not matter. The emotion she felt for her husband usually vacillated between affection and pity, and Mutemwiya would certainly struggle as she adapted to a new country, husband and king.

Tuya had never dreamed of wearing a crown. Even though she had borne the king's son, she had never thought she might actually reign over the land of her birth. No, Mutemwiya was a royal heiress, and the people would give her their allegiance. Tuya refused to allow anger or jealousy to prick her heart.

The foreign queen was lovely, Tuya had to admit. Older than Tuya and probably twice the age of Tuthmosis, the woman moved through the great hall with a subtle and sensuous bearing, her golden face marked by crimson lips and brilliant black eyes. Her hair, which she had not yet cut in order to adopt the Egyptian wig, spilled to her waist in a plume of black gold. Rumor had it that she had already buried one husband, and as she watched the coronation, Tuya thought the woman looked more like Pharaoh's mother than his bride.

Yet the eyes of every man in the room followed Mutemwiya as she moved toward her throne at Tuthmosis's side. She walked with the hard grace of one who has total control of herself, and her boldly confident eyes rebuffed every man who dared to look at her...except one. Narmer met the woman's flinty gaze head-on. Even as Mutemwiya stepped up to the dais and slipped her hand into Tuthmosis's, Tuya saw Narmer's bold eyes rake the new queen with a fiercely possessive look. What, she wondered, had transpired between these two on the journey from Mitanni?

As the high priest's voice droned in the stillness, filling the room with blessings of prosperity and promises of fealty, Tuya allowed her eyes to wander. Potiphar, watchful and paternal, stood at the head of the guard, his hooded eyes searching the gathering as though assassins waited behind every pillar. Beneath the Gold of Praise, the brown skin of his neck sagged with age and weariness. He was an old, tired man, ready to meet his gods—if he had any.

Sighing, Tuya returned her attention to the wedding canopy as the gathering cheered her husband and his new queen.

Tuthmosis sat bolt upright in bed and stared into the darkness, trying to see whatever it was that had slashed his sleep like a knife. Fear shook his body from toe to hair and twisted his face into an expression he was glad no one could see. He was alone, completely and totally alone with nameless terror, and he yearned for Tuya.

"Abasi!" He shouted for the eunuch who attended him. His grasping fingers found the silken cord hanging by his bed, and he yanked it sharply. "Bomani! Chike!"

His servant, his guard and his priest appeared in the doorway, their figures backlit by torches burning in the hallway. The servant and guard immediately prostrated themselves, but the old priest took his time.

"Rise, all of you," Tuthmosis said, his nerves at a full stretch. "Abasi, light the torches, then bring me the royal wife Tuya! Bomani—guard the door, and let no one in except Tuya. I fear for my life. Chike, high priest of Osiris—"

As light flooded the chamber, the aging priest inclined his bald head. "Yes, my king?"

"Say prayers for me. Offer sacrifices of blood, of fruit, of incense. Make sure the gods are pleased with my kingship."

The old man's face remained as inscrutable as stone, but he bowed. "It shall be done."

"Do it now." With white knuckles, Tuthmosis gripped the sheet that covered him. "Abasi, why do you wait? Fetch Tuya now!"

The eunuch sprinted out of the chamber as fast as his bare feet could carry him, and Bomani moved toward the door. The priest prepared to follow, but Tuthmosis did not want to be abandoned. "Wait—priest," he said, searching for words that would not reveal the terror that had frozen his heart. "Have any of the astrologers seen an ill omen in the skies?"

Chike lifted a brow. "None, my king."

"And the river—it flows according to schedule?"

"The goddess waters our land as always. You have won her favor, divine one."

"The cattle—I have not heard of any plagues on the cattle—"

"There are none, my king. All is well in the land."

The door opened and Tuya hurried into the room, clad only in a straight gown and a shawl. She had risen in such a hurry she forgot to don her wig, and despite his terror, the sight of her short, rumpled hair brought a smile to the king's face. None of the other wives would have come in such a disheveled state.

"O Pharaoh, live forever," Tuya whispered, falling to her knees.

"Chike, you may go," Tuthmosis commanded. When the aged priest had closed the door behind him, Tuthmosis crawled to the end of his bed and peered down at his wife. "I am frightened," he whispered, his voice strangely thin in his own ears. "I need you."

Her soft, understanding eyes met his. Without speaking, she rose and climbed into the royal bed.

"There, my king," she whispered, slipping her arms around him. "Tell me what has upset you."

"I don't know what it is," he murmured, allowing her to draw his head onto her shoulder. "For two nights now I have been awakened in the darkness. An evil premonition holds me in its grip and I cannot break free."

"Have you told anyone of this?"

He lifted his gaze to meet hers. "I do not want them to see my fear. And I don't know why I am afraid. I was not afraid to meet the Syrians, or to lead chariots into battle against the fierce Nubians. I am not afraid to die, yet this terror sends my blood sliding through my veins like needles. A god should not fear anything."

She lowered her forehead to his in silent understanding. Grateful, he reached for her and lightly pressed his lips to hers. The gulf that had once separated them had lessened, and even though Mutemwiya sat on the throne next to him, he still considered Tuya his favorite wife. She was the only one who understood him, the only one who never laughed at his dreams or scorned his fears. He loved her as he loved his gods, but though they demanded his attention, Tuya asked nothing of him. Sometimes he wished she would...

"Sleep, husband," she whispered, pulling him down to lie on perfumed sheets. "I will watch over you. If the terror comes again, wake and tell me of it, and together we shall decide what is to be done."

She wrapped her arms around him and kissed his cheek. Tuthmosis looked around the chamber to make sure the torches still burned, then he lowered his head to the softness of Tuya's body and murmured his thanks through the embracing folds of sleep.

Tuya stifled a yawn as her husband slept. She had promised to stay awake, but their son had kept her up late the previous night. The irresistible warmth of sleep bore down on her, and she struggled to keep her eyes open—

"Horus, help me!"

She startled as her husband sat up, his eyes like black holes in his pale face. "I know," he said, his voice resonating with fear and awe. "I have dreamed, Tuya, twice! In this light

I see clearly, for the demons of darkness have not stolen the visions away."

"You had a dream?"

"A vision as real as the dream when the Sphinx spoke to me." He brought his knees to his chest and wrapped his arms around them. "But the dreams are not clear. I see the visions, I recall every detail, but there is no voice to explain it. Since Horus has spoken to me before, why does he not speak now?"

"I don't know, husband." Tuya pressed her lips together. "Perhaps it is not Horus who speaks to you."

"Another god? But my priests speak for the others. Every day I hear a score of messages from all the local deities. Why would one of them come to me in a dream?"

"Perhaps…it is a god we do not know." She shifted until she faced him. "Long ago, husband, I knew a man who said an invisible god spoke to him in dreams. He called this god the Almighty One."

"An invisible god?" For a brief moment his face seemed to open. Tuya glimpsed bewilderment, a quick flicker of fear, then denial. "I am a god. I would know if an invisible god existed." He shook his head. "Tomorrow I will call the priests from every temple in Thebes and set the details of my dreams before them. One of them will know the meaning."

He shot her a questioning look, waiting for reassurance, so Tuya pressed her hand to his back. "I am sure you are right, my husband."

I hope you are.

The proclamation went out with the rising of the sun, and by midday a priest from each of Thebes's temples had appeared before Pharaoh and heard the details of the royal vision. The priests consulted their scrolls, the ancient Pyramid

Texts, the most gifted seers and the oracles, but no one could agree on the details of the interpretation.

"If a man dreams of a cow," one of the priests suggested in the throne room, "it means a happy day in his house."

"No," another priest countered, "it means nothing of the kind. The seven cows are seven children who will be born to Pharaoh." The second priest turned from his colleagues and nodded to the king. "It matters not what a man dreams, my king, because we can provide magic spells for the exorcism of bad dreams. If a man's face is smeared with pesen-bread together with a few fresh herbs moistened with beer and myrrh, all evil dreams that he has seen will be driven away."

"Dreams do matter," Tuthmosis declared, iron in his voice. He extended the crook and flail over the assembled crowd. "Dreams do matter, you foolish priests! Horus appeared to me in a dream and promised me this throne when I was a mere boy! The gods speak in dreams, and I would know which god speaks, and what he would have me know!"

"Pharaoh must decide which god speaks," the high priest of Osiris called, his voice ringing across the throne room. "Pharaoh has heard from every priest in Thebes, and each has his own interpretation. Which god, O Divine One, speaks to you?"

Tuthmosis slowly lifted his head, hearing the veiled threat in the words. *If you are our divine king, you should be able to tell us these things yourself.*

Abruptly, Pharaoh dismissed the lot of them.

Tuya uttered an indrawn gasp when she opened the door of her chamber and saw Tuthmosis standing in the hallway, but she smiled and gestured for him to enter. Never could she recall Amenhotep visiting the chamber of any of his wives; a king was supposed to command his wives to appear in *his* chambers. But Tuthmosis stepped inside as he always had, as comfortable with her as he would have been with a sister. In a way, she supposed, they had grown up together.

Pharaoh dropped to the floor, where their son was playing with a collection of small statues. "Shall I send for wine, my husband?"

He signaled his approval with a wave of his hand, and Tuya sent her maid in search of the king's cupbearer. After the maid left, Tuya sat beside her husband. Tuthmosis's handsome face was lined with exhaustion, his eyes puffy from sleeplessness. A worried crease divided his forehead, and his hands fluttered in his lap. Her son, oblivious to the king's anxiety, toddled over to his royal parent and tried to climb into Tuthmosis's lap.

"Not now, Yosef," Tuya gently scolded the child.

"Let him be," Tuthmosis answered, his large hands supporting the boy. "Perhaps the god who desires my attention can speak through the lips of a child."

A knock rapped on the door, and after a moment Taharka entered with his slave. "I have brought wine," he said, carefully pouring the red liquid into one of Pharaoh's golden goblets. The slave tasted the juice while Tuya and the king watched, then Taharka poured another cup and handed it to the king.

Tuya gave him the smile of an old friend. "Thank you, Taharka."

The cupbearer tried smiling at Pharaoh but seemed to sense that smiling was a bad idea. "I have heard of the commotion at court today," he whispered, more to Tuya than to the king who sat absorbed in his thoughts. "And now I find that I must confess one of my offenses."

"I'm sure your offenses are not grievous," Tuya said, trying to dismiss him. "Pharaoh has much on his mind."

"I know." Taharka stepped closer to the king, then handed the pitcher of wine to his servant and clasped his hands in an attitude of humility. "If it please you, mighty Pharaoh, hear me. Two years ago Pharaoh, your father, was furious with his servants, and put me in confinement in the house of the captain of the bodyguard, both me and the chief baker. We had a dream on the same night, the baker and I, each of us a different dream."

Tuthmosis gave the cupbearer a piercing glance. "Why do you speak of things in the past?"

Taharka shuffled his feet. "Because they might aid us in the present. A slave was with us in the prison, a servant of the captain of the bodyguard. We related our dreams to him, and he interpreted them for us. And it came to pass that everything happened according to his interpretation. Pharaoh restored me to my office, but hanged the baker."

Tuya's blood ran cold. "A slave? One who had served Potiphar, captain of the guard?"

"Do you know this slave?" Tuthmosis sat upright and leaned toward her. "You know someone who can interpret dreams?"

Though she sensed she walked the knife-edge of danger, she had to speak. "Last night, my husband, I told you of one who once told me that his unseen god often speaks in dreams. This is the man I spoke of. He is a Hebrew called Yosef."

"Not the same slave." Taharka shook his head. "My dreams were interpreted by Potiphar's steward, Paneah."

Tuya pressed her hand to her son's dark head. Would her eyes reveal her feelings? "Yosef and Paneah are one and the same."

"It matters not what he is called. Let him be brought at once." Tuthmosis clapped for his guards. "Send a messenger and escort to Potiphar's house, and have the captain of the guard bring this slave to me. He is to be brought safely, and at once."

The servants outside the door hastened to do their king's bidding.

Menkheprure, Pharaoh Tuthmosis IV

Then Pharaoh sent and called Yosef, and they brought him hastily out of the dungeon: and he shaved himself, and changed his raiment, and came in unto Pharaoh.

Genesis 41:14

Chapter Twenty-Six

"Potiphar! Pharaoh summons you!"

The sound of frantic shouting woke Potiphar from a deep sleep. He sat up in bed, fully awake, as servants pounded on his door. "I'm coming," he barked, thrusting his legs over the side of the bed. He snatched up his kilt and dressed while he cocked his ear for the noises stirring in the corridor beyond his chamber. Amid a few smothered laughs he heard the clink of weapons, so this was no trivial matter. "Master Potiphar!" his servant's voice came again. "Pharaoh's men await you."

"Have I not said I am coming? Take them to the courtyard. I will join them there." He might be nearly sixty, but he was still captain of the king's guards and capable of performing his duties. He stalked through his chamber, his hand reaching for the sword and dagger resting on a stand near the door.

The crowd of callers, whoever they were, had left the corridor. Potiphar swept forward, his eyes intent on the courtyard beyond, but a sudden movement in the dimly lit hall startled him.

"By all the gods, what's this?" a male voice slurred. Potiphar snapped a torch from its bracket in the wall and stepped toward the intruder. In the gleam of torchlight, he saw Sagira unconscious on the couch, her mouth open to the ceiling, her breath punctuated by drunken snoring. Her latest paramour knelt on the floor, blinking rapidly as he struggled to rise.

"This is the master of the house," Potiphar said, bridling his anger. "And you, sir, had best be gone when I return."

He turned with a quick snap of his shoulders and strode to the porch where a contingent of palace guards waited. "What is the trouble, Bomani?" Potiphar asked, recognizing Pharaoh's personal bodyguard. "For what reason would you leave the king unguarded?"

Bomani flushed to the roots of his dark hair. "Pharaoh sent me away. The king demands to see the slave imprisoned in your house."

"What slave?"

"The one called Paneah."

For a moment Potiphar's mind blocked the name. For six years he had shied away from tormenting thoughts of the Hebrew. Why should he be forced to think of the man now?

Surprised by the erratic rhythm of his heart, Potiphar stared at the bodyguard. "Why would Pharaoh want to see one of my prisoners?"

Bomani pressed his lips together as a silent reminder that it was not Potiphar's place to question Pharaoh. Potiphar nodded, acknowledging his blunder, and moved toward the barred gate that led to the prison.

Tuya. He fumbled with the keys at his belt. The girl had finally exerted her influence and acted to free the man she loved. But how did she do it without arousing the king's jealousy?

"If you must know," Bomani whispered, falling into step beside his captain, "Pharaoh has heard that this slave possesses the power of divination. Our king has been unable to sleep on account of strange and troubling dreams. I myself have seen him wearing the look of a man who wakes to find himself at the edge of a precipice."

Potiphar laughed as he fitted his key into the lock of the gate. "Dreams are but shadows of the mind, Bomani, surely our king knows this."

The guard lifted his chin as if Potiphar's answer had offended him. "Pharaoh is convinced that a god speaks to him. He believes this prisoner can divine the god's meaning."

Potiphar shook his head as the prison gate swung open. "Our king can have the slave," he said, stepping aside so Bomani could enter. "I surrendered Paneah long ago."

Khamat blinked in surprise when the captain of the guard appeared at his door in the dead of night. "Master," he said, falling to his knees in fear that a prisoner had escaped. His eyes darted to the sword in Potiphar's belt. "What brings you to me?"

"Do not fear, Khamat, we come only to relieve you of a prisoner." Potiphar gestured to the men behind him. "Pharaoh wants to see the slave Paneah."

Khamat widened his eyes. "Surely not tonight! Paneah stinks, he has fleas—"

"Clean him up," Potiphar said, moving into the lodge. "We will wait."

"Paneah won't want to be bothered tonight," Khamat said, wrapping his kilt about him. "He prays at night, sometimes for hours. He doesn't know I can hear him, but I've stood outside his cell and listened—"

"Since when does my chief jailer heed the wishes of his prisoners?" Potiphar snapped. "Bring him now. He can pray while we shave the filth from his body."

Khamat snatched a torch from one of the guards and hurried toward the prison pits.

* * *

Yosef usually finished his duties as the sun set, then lowered himself back into his pit where he enjoyed the bit of food in his bucket. After eating, he lay back on the sand and prayed as he watched night draw down like a black cowl. For the past four years Khamat had trusted him so completely that within the prison he was allowed to move about as he pleased. The knotted rope dangled always in Yosef's cell, and at night no one bothered to cover the opening of his pit.

Night after night, as Yosef watched the stars spin across his small circle of sky, he thought of God's promise that Avraham's children would some day be more numerous than the stars and as countless as the sand of the sea. Though Yosef could only see a small section of the night sky, he knew the heavens stretched well beyond the limit of his vision.

He had learned many things during six years of imprisonment. He had come to understand that humility was more precious to God than success, and that a man's reactions were often more important than his actions. He had questioned whether his old visions of the sun and stars and sheaves of wheat bowing down to him were inspired by God or implanted by the Evil One, and he had realized that his visions did not matter. When he had sought to fulfill them himself, the quest brought nothing but despair and disgrace. Better to be a happy, simple slave than dream of changing the world and stumble over pride.

Each night he ended his colloquy with a fervent request that God protect Tuya and her son from whatever dangers surrounded them. When he had dreamed of her two years before, the vision left him feeling frustrated and helpless. Why had God warned him of Tuya's peril when Yosef could do nothing for her but pray?

In that question he found his answer. And as he prayed, his

passion for her faded to a warm memory, replaced by a strong concern for her well-being.

He sighed and closed his eyes, surrendering to the exhaustion of a long day's work. He had nearly willed himself to sleep when noises from above brought him back to reality.

"Paneah! Rise at once!"

Yosef grimaced when he recognized Khamat's nasal whine. He was not eager to clean up after another drunken soldier who couldn't hold his beer.

He didn't open his eyes. "Can't it wait?" he called.

"Paneah! Pharaoh calls for you!"

That statement brought Yosef bolt upright. He lifted his gaze to the rim of the pit where Khamat stood with a torch. The jailer nudged the rope with his sandal. "Come up, my hairy one, and ready yourself for a bath and a shave. You look more like a monkey than a man, and if you wish to impress the royal eye, you'd best hurry."

"Pharaoh wishes to see me?" Yosef stood and grasped the rope, then looked up at Khamat again. "This is not a jest?"

Khamat glanced over his shoulder, then squatted and gestured for Yosef to hurry. "Master Potiphar waits in my lodge at this moment to escort you to the palace. So hurry, Paneah, before I land in the pit with you!"

Yosef braced his feet against the mud walls and began to climb.

Chapter Twenty-Seven

Tuthmosis paced for over an hour in Tuya's chamber, and nothing she could say or do would calm him. "Please, my husband," she said finally, gesturing to the child who slept with his head in her lap. "You will wake Yosef with that loud stomping. Sit, calm yourself and have another cup of wine. Bomani will return as soon as possible."

"I must know the meaning of the dream before I sleep," Pharaoh said, clenching his hands behind his back. "I cannot rest, Tuya, if the vision comes to me again. The dream's implications grew more frightening as priest after priest failed to explain it. When I think of it my blood roars in my ears like the howling of the Sphinx, and I cannot be calm."

Tuya leaned back in her chair. With every step, her husband's jaw became firmer, his muscles tighter, his heart more eager for a solution to the puzzle. He hungered for an answer, and if Yosef failed to provide it, Pharaoh would not be happy. With every moment that passed, the king became more certain of the slave's ability to provide an answer to his dilemma.

Silently, Tuya begged Yosef's unseen god to provide the interpretation.

Finally she heard the steady sound of approaching footsteps, then someone rapped on the door. Pharaoh stopped pacing as his eyes lit with expectation. Bomani pushed the door open without a word.

With the hesitancy of one whose eyes have been burned by the sun, Tuya turned toward the doorway. The guards' faces, even Potiphar's, blurred into irrelevance as Yosef stepped into the room, his wrists and ankles bound in shackles.

A thunderbolt jagged through her. Yosef had been attractive when she last saw him, but the man who stood before her now looked like a god.

The boy she had known as Yosef had vanished, replaced by a stranger in the prime of manhood. In the golden torchlight of her chamber, the prisoner's skin glowed over tightly defined muscles. He stood tall and impressive beside those who imagined themselves his guards, and rough black hair fell past his shoulders in a wild tangle. His face, cleanly shaved and sculpted with angular lines, shone with an aloof strength.

Tuya steeled herself as she gazed into his eyes. The dark orbs that had always made her heart beat faster now blazed brighter than the light from the torches on her walls.

She hid a thick swallow in her throat and turned away, wishing that Pharaoh had chosen to hold this interview in Queen Mutemwiya's chamber instead of this one. Only sorrow could come from this encounter. If Yosef failed Pharaoh, he would surely die, and her heart would never be able to erase the memory of him standing in her room. If he succeeded in this test, he would be rewarded. She would have to smile at him, offer her congratulations and pretend that her heart did not knock against her ribs with every breath.

Pharaoh did not even glance in her direction. He gazed in delight on his wild-haired visitor, and for a moment Tuya thought he would prostrate himself before the slave, so wide were the eyes he focused on the Hebrew. "Thanks be to Horus, you have arrived!"

Carefully maneuvering around the length of chain that bound his ankles, Yosef bowed and pressed his forehead to the floor. "May the king live forever," he said, his rich voice resonating throughout the room. "How may I serve you?"

Tuthmosis heard the voice through a daze of wonder. Surely the gods had fashioned and created this man! In all the temples of Egypt, there was not a priest like this, with tangled hair, a broad chest and skin as golden as ripe wheat! The priests who served the gods of Egypt were bald, flour-faced creatures who spoke in hoarse rasps and bedecked themselves with gold while proclaiming their poverty of spirit. Those weak-minded fools had been helpless before the complexity of his dream, but surely this man could unravel the enigma!

"Rise." Tuthmosis jerked his hand in Potiphar's direction. "Help him up, and remove those bonds." Stiffly, the captain of the guard knelt at the prisoner's feet and unfastened the shackles around the man's ankles.

Tuthmosis lifted his eyes to those of the stranger. "Your name is—?" he asked, his brows slanting the question.

The slave nodded in simple dignity. "I am called Paneah."

"'He lives,'" Tuthmosis interpreted. A fitting name for this one, and a good omen. But a king could not declare victory prematurely.

"Paneah—" he turned toward the chair at Tuya's side "—last night my sleep was broken by disturbing dreams. No one here can interpret them, but I have heard that you can explain any dream you are told." The prisoner's gaze remained fixed on him, and Tuthmosis hoped his excitement did not burn as bright in his eyes as it did in his heart.

"It is not in me to interpret dreams, mighty Pharaoh,"

Paneah said, inclining his head. "God will give Pharaoh a favorable answer."

Tuthmosis perched on the edge of his chair. After studying the prisoner another moment, he rested his chin on two fingers and recounted his nightmare: "My dream was this—I stood on the bank of the Nile, and behold, seven cows, fat and sleek, came up out of the water and grazed in the marsh grass. And then seven other cows came up after them, poor and ugly and gaunt, such as I have never seen for ugliness in all the land of Egypt. And the lean and ugly cows ate up the first seven fat cows. And yet when they had devoured them, I could not tell that they had eaten, for they were as ugly and gaunt as before."

A shudder shook him at the memory, and he paused to look away. "Then I awoke," he whispered, his eyes meeting Tuya's. "I remembered nothing but my fear, and my wife bid me sleep again. But I dreamed again, and saw seven ears of corn, full and good, come up on a single stalk. But then seven other ears, withered, thin and scorched by the east wind, sprouted up after them. And the thin ears swallowed the seven good ears. And I awoke, and remembered all, and told these things to the magicians, but no one could explain these things to me."

Every man in the room held his breath while Tuthmosis looked at the prisoner. Potiphar, the guards and even the servants leaned forward in anticipation of the slave's answer. What would it be?

Paneah bowed his head as if searching inside himself, then he lifted his chin and stared at Pharaoh with eyes that gave nothing away. "Pharaoh's dreams are one and the same," he said. "God has told Pharaoh what he is about to do."

Tuthmosis shook his head. "But which god speaks to me?"

"El Shaddai, the Almighty," Paneah answered, and the name rang a distant bell in Tuthmosis's memory. Tuya had spoken of this invisible god.

"The seven good cows are seven years," Paneah explained. "And the seven good ears are seven years. The dreams are one and the same. And the seven lean and ugly cows that came up after the others are seven years, and the seven thin ears scorched by the east wind are seven years of famine."

"Famine?" The fist of fear tightened in Tuthmosis's belly. If the people did not eat, the Divine Son must feed the earth...

"God has shown you what you must do," Paneah repeated. "Seven years of great abundance are coming in all the land of Egypt. After seven years famine will come, famine so severe that the abundance will be forgotten, and scarcity will ravage the land. Now as for the repeating of the dream to Pharaoh twice, it means the matter is determined by God, and he will soon bring it to pass."

"Famine," Tuthmosis repeated, his mind reeling. "Of what use are seven good years if famine will destroy us in the seven bad years that follow?"

"God is merciful," Paneah said. "Let Pharaoh look for a man discerning and wise, and set him over the land of Egypt. Let Pharaoh take action to appoint overseers in charge of the land, and let them exact a fifth of Egypt's produce in the seven years of abundance. Then let them store up the grain for food in the cities under Pharaoh's authority, and let them guard it. And let the food become a reserve for the seven years of famine, so the land of Egypt may not perish during the time of hunger."

Tuthmosis leaned on the arm of his chair. This Paneah had no ulterior motive, for he had not asked for an audience with the king. He had no contact with other nations who might wish to rape Egypt and rob it of its produce, for he had been a prisoner and cut off from the world. He had no reason to lie.

"El Shaddai revealed this to you?" Tuthmosis asked.

Paneah bowed. "He is the Almighty One, the god who

knows all things, the unseen god who cannot be represented by the work of men's hands."

"I will think on these things," Tuthmosis said, nodding. "You, Paneah, will sleep in the palace tonight as my guest. See to his comfort, Potiphar. You may all leave me now."

The knot of servants and guards at the door bowed and slipped from the room, taking Paneah with them. When they had gone, Tuthmosis turned to his silent wife and gestured to the space that still vibrated with the residue of the man's powerful presence. "Do you believe in him?"

"Yes," she whispered, her eyes watering as she stared across the empty room. "I do."

Tuthmosis left soon after Yosef had been led away. After placing her son in his bed, Tuya paced in her chamber. How could she sleep knowing that her old love breathed under the same roof? In Potiphar's house she could not sleep until she had gathered a good-night kiss from him, but those kisses belonged to another lifetime. Surely she was foolish to think of them now.

How strange that Yosef's appearance could put her husband's mind at ease and leave hers in turmoil. Tonight Tuthmosis would sleep like a child, his worries wiped away by Yosef's assurance, but she would watch and wait and pray—for what?

There were so many things she wanted to tell him. She wanted to confess her anger at the news that he had been arrested for attacking Sagira, and her falseness in believing him guilty. She wanted to explain the child in her arms, to define her love for the young man who was her king and her husband. She wanted to tell him she had prayed for his deliverance from death, and she had recognized El Shaddai's work in preserving Yosef in prison.

His eyes had not once caught hers during the interview with

Pharaoh. There had been a time when she and Yosef could read each other's thoughts—if she looked into his eyes now, would she understand all that had shaped him in the eight years since they parted? Would he understand her precarious position in the palace? Would he know she still dreamed of meeting him in Potiphar's garden?

Sighing in frustration, she paced the length of her chamber until a warm current of air brought the promise of dawn through the window.

Yosef found it hard to believe he was not dreaming when he awoke the next morning. The heady scent of lotus blossoms filled the room where he slept on a cushioned mattress. Gauzy curtains blew about his bed as a pair of slave girls tiptoed through the chamber. When he rose up on one elbow, one of the girls giggled and picked up her lute; within a moment the sweet sounds of music filled the room. The other girl, smiling behind a blush as bright as a desert flower, offered up a bowl of fruit.

Yosef smiled and waved the girl away, then sank back onto the bed. In prison he had not seen a woman, heard music or tasted the sweetness of fruit, yet all three had been offered to him in one moment. He closed his eyes, overwhelmed by the improbability of it all. What had God done? And why?

After a few moments, he sat up and looked around. A basin of water lay on the floor next to a pair of fine leather sandals. A linen kilt had been folded on a nearby chair, and he ran his hand over it, relishing its softness. Last night he had wanted to run his hand over the softness of Tuya's cheek, but he had forced himself to retain custody of his eyes. Interpreting Pharaoh's dream had been far easier than avoiding the magnetic pull of her beauty.

He rose and slipped into the new kilt. He sat in the chair and ate a few grapes, amazed at their juicy sweetness. One of the girls came forward and rested her hand on his shoulder in an attitude of suggestive submission.

"Dance," Yosef whispered hoarsely, understanding what she offered him. His skin burned beneath her touch. "Just dance. I must be ready when Pharaoh summons me."

And so, while one slave postured and the other played her lute, Yosef waited in silence and wondered what God was about to do.

A pair of servants—not guards, Yosef noticed—arrived to escort Yosef to Pharaoh's throne room. He paused at the threshold of the great double doors leading into Pharaoh's presence, his breath stolen by the opulence of the dazzling sight. He thought he had seen everything Egypt had to offer, but never had he imagined anything to rival the unabashed elegance and beauty of Pharaoh's royal chamber.

He walked on shining tiles arranged into the delicate designs of lotus blossoms. The walls of the grand hall glimmered with colorful pictures of the king and queen offering sacrifices to their gods. High windows far above Yosef's head let in light but not heat, and a gentle breeze swirled throughout the room, dispersing the sweet incense that burned to honor the god upon the throne. Hundreds of people, it seemed to Yosef, moved in orderly rows on the left and right sides of the chamber, but the center aisle had been left open for anyone who wished to approach Pharaoh, the reigning king and god of all Egypt.

At the end of the long aisle, on a golden throne, Pharaoh waited, his eyes lit with expectation. Next to him, on a similar throne, sat a lavishly decorated woman with eyes too hard for beauty. A gold tiara rested on her massive wig, and by her sandaled feet a monkey scampered on a leash. As Yosef approached, he could read the words engraved on the lady's

chair: "Follower of Horus, Guide of the Ruler, Favorite Lady."
If this woman was Pharaoh's favorite lady, why had he found
Tuthmosis in Tuya's chamber?

He could feel Tuya's presence shining from behind the
queen's throne, and knew without directly looking that she
stood with her small son by her side. He wanted to meet her
eyes and assure her he was well, but he did not dare acknowledge her before so many others. A richly dressed courtier
wearing the Gold of Praise stood at the queen's right hand, and
as their eyes met, Yosef was surprised at the strong emotion that
flickered over the man's face—hatred distilled to its essence.

Even here, there are enemies. No wonder Tuya is in danger.

Upon reaching the throne, Yosef bowed before Pharaoh,
who today wore his full regalia. His short linen garment was
girdled at the waist by an elaborate beadwork belt, supporting
a sporran of panther pelt. He wore the tall, helmetlike crown
on his noble head, and the artificial beard, another symbol of
his divine authority, extended from his chin, held in place by
two slender leather loops hanging from the king's ears.

Pharaoh stood, extending the crook and flail. "Rise, Paneah,
my much-beloved friend and servant," Tuthmosis said, his
voice like a warm embrace. "Last night you visited me and
gave me the interpretation of my dream. You were the light that
shone on the truth God sought to reveal, and through your voice
I saw the path that lies ahead for Egypt. Tell these assembled
here, Paneah, how you came to be my light in darkness."

Yosef cleared his throat. "I am not the light, mighty
Pharaoh. God is the one who reveals all."

"And which God is this light?" Pharaoh asked, spreading
his hands toward the scowling priests who had been unable
to solve his dilemma.

"The unseen god of my fathers," Yosef answered. "The
creator. The beginning of all that is, and all that shall ever be."

Pharaoh settled the crook and flail across his chest. "Take down my words, scribes, and hearken unto me, all who listen. Two nights ago I did not sleep, for I was troubled by the dream this god revealed to me. Last night I did not sleep, for I spent the night devising a plan to ensure Egypt's salvation. Seven years of abundance are coming to the Upper and Lower Kingdoms, then seven years of grievous famine. The god who declared this prophecy has also revealed how we are to prosper through it."

The room grew silent, as if the walls themselves had paused to listen to Pharaoh's words. Tuthmosis stood in the hush, then lifted his chin. "I have consulted with my counselors and the priests, and they have agreed with what I am about to do. Can we find another man like this, in whom is a divine spirit?" The king stretched his hand toward Yosef as he glanced around the assembled company. "Can we find a man better equipped to lead Egypt through the darkness than this man who has shone the light today?"

The crowd stirred, but no one dared offer another name. Pharaoh put aside the crook and flail, and a collective gasp broke the silence as the king descended from the dais and walked toward Yosef.

"Since God has informed you of the things that are to come," Pharaoh said, lifting his hand until it rested on Yosef's shoulder, "there is no one so discerning and wise as you. You shall be the One Over My House! To your orders shall all my people submit. Only by the throne will I be greater than you. I have set you today over all the land of Egypt, and to signify that you speak with my voice, I give you my ring."

When Pharaoh dropped his hand and fumbled with the scarab ring on his hand, Yosef caught a glimpse of the seventeen-year-old boy inside the king. The ring resisted, the boy-king frowned, then the scarab slid from Pharaoh's finger. With a sigh of relief, Tuthmosis held the golden band between his thumb and forefinger and presented it to Yosef.

"Thank you, my king." Yosef lowered himself to his knees. He wasn't sure what behavior was appropriate, but he took the ring and put it on his own finger while Tuthmosis smiled in approval. "You shall have garments of fine linen," Pharaoh went on. He clapped, and a group of slaves appeared from a room behind the throne, each carrying a box of garments.

"And then, there is this." Pharaoh lifted the gold chain from his neck. "My father bestowed the Gold of Praise only twice in his lifetime—once to Potiphar, captain of his guard, and once to Narmer, who has also served me well."

The courtier standing beside Queen Mutemwiya nodded in acknowledgment of the king's praise.

"But to you, Paneah, I give the Gold of Praise and every honor I can imagine. On this day you will ride throughout Thebes in the chariot behind me. When my warriors cry, 'Bow the Knee' in reference to me, every knee in Egypt shall bow in your honor as well." Tuthmosis slipped the Gold of Praise about Yosef's neck, then stepped back. "Though I am Pharaoh," he called, his voice echoing off the walls, "without your permission no one shall raise his hand or foot in all the land of Egypt."

No pharaoh had ever granted such authority. Every face in the room bore the stamp of astonishment.

"May Pharaoh live forever," Yosef replied, lowering his head to the floor. His mind swam with disconcerting thoughts, and he could think of no other reply. In less than a day he had traveled from a prison pit to a throne. How many men had covered so great a distance in so short a time?

"And there is this in conclusion," Pharaoh said, stepping back to the dais. "You have been called Paneah, 'he lives,' and today I decree that you shall henceforth be called Zaphenath-paneah, 'God speaks, he lives.' For today I have learned that the unknown god of whom I have heard much, truly lives and speaks through his servants. So that your seed may be forever established on the earth, Zaphenath-paneah, I give you Asenath, daughter of Potiphera, priest of On, to be your wife."

A murmur of pleased surprise rippled through the crowd, a pair of silver trumpets shrilled, and the double doors opened at the far end of the room. Yosef turned as four priests entered, each carrying a pole to support a wedding canopy. Under the canopy walked a slender maiden in a dark Egyptian wig. For some inexplicable reason, Yosef's eyes blurred with tears.

Pharaoh had passed a sleepless night in order to honor him. Yosef had not wanted a wife, but he could not insult the royal benevolence by refusing this tribute.

Whispering filled the air as Yosef walked toward his bride. Frankly jealous smiles and nodding faces wrapped around him as he took his place beneath the wedding canopy, as much a prisoner of fortune as Potiphar had been years before.

At the thought of Potiphar, Yosef turned to the girl at his side. He scanned her countenance with cautious appraisal, but on that lovely face he saw youth, freshness and a flicker of anxiety, but not a trace of Sagira's ambition.

Yosef turned to the priest and accepted the hand of his bride.

Chapter Twenty-Eight

The smile on Tuya's face chilled as Yosef's new wife nibbled on the traditional crust of bread he offered. Everything had been set in readiness for a wedding—the canopy, the flowers, the incense. Why had she not recognized the signs? She should have known what Tuthmosis would do. She should have prepared herself for this.

Of course Yosef should be married; what man did not want a wife and children? It would be unfair for her to expect Yosef to remain celibate while she enjoyed a husband, and unreasonable to think that Yosef's god would set him apart from other men. Though Yosef had been able to withstand the temptation Sagira flaunted, Tuya had heard his heart pound and felt the heat in his kiss. More than any other woman, she knew Yosef ought to be married. He had waited for love long enough.

But why couldn't she be the woman he loved? Why would the Almighty God not work another miracle? He freed Taharka from prison, he kept Yosef safe from Sagira, he lifted Yosef to the position of leadership and authority he deserved. She knew El Shaddai was powerful, she agreed with his purposes, so why couldn't he bring Yosef into her arms?

Perhaps the Almighty God concerned himself with matters of life and death, but not with matters of the heart. Yet Yosef had told her that his god loved his people with a jealous love. If this god felt human emotion, couldn't he see that her heart was breaking? If he loved her as he loved Yosef, why didn't he do something about her pain?

One of the priests lifted the traditional stone jar, another handed Yosef the sword. Yosef swung the blade in a clear arc, destroying the fragile pottery as surely as his marriage had shattered Tuya's heart.

The crowd roared in approval. Tuthmosis beamed, then stepped from the dais for the ceremonial chariot ride through the streets of Thebes. The crowd swept forward, emptying the great hall in an enthusiastic rush, but Tuya hung back, gripping her son's hand.

Yosef raised his chubby face to hers. "Mama sad?"

"No, dear, Mama is happy," she said, smiling through the tears that jeweled her lashes.

Pharaoh ordered his stonemasons to begin building a house for his new vizier, Zaphenath-paneah. From her chamber in the palace Tuya could hear the sounds of chisel and cudgel, ax and saw. The laborers worked from the rising of the sun till the setting of it, and as his house rose from a hilltop near the palace, Zaphenath-paneah conducted his affairs from Pharaoh's throne room.

Egypt had known viziers before, but never one with this much power. With Pharaoh's full authority, Zaphenath-paneah divided the kingdom into tracts of land and classified them according to their fertility. He specified three categories: lands that regularly received the Nile's fertile flood, lands that sometimes flooded, and lands that seldom or never did. For the next seven years, Zaphenath-paneah proclaimed, taxes would be calculated according to the flood state at various locations along the river, beginning at the isle of Elephantine near the first cataract. Based on this measurement, crop quotas would be assigned. Four-fifths of the land's expected bounty would belong to the people who worked it, but one-fifth would belong to Pharaoh, and must be surrendered for storage in Pharaoh's granaries.

Tuya wondered how well Asenath had come to know her husband, for almost immediately after his appointment Yosef set off on a tour of Egypt to determine if the present nomarchs would be capable of gathering the harvest from the coming years of plenty. A corps of scribes, accountants and engineers accompanied him on his travels, and Pharaoh received daily reports of his vizier busily collecting records of all the houses and estates in Egypt. While the scribes questioned the nomarchs about their past administration and the collection of taxes, engineers surveyed the land to determine where the huge, cone-shaped granaries should be built. In cities where the vizier found the nomarchs resentful, unscrupulous or inept, new officials were appointed to oversee the gathering of the earth's bounty.

Tuthmosis had been wise, Tuya realized, to appoint a vizier to handle the complicated details of taxation, for now the young king was free to concentrate on the work he loved. Already he had restored the ancient Sphinx to its former grandeur; now he concentrated on raising the fallen obelisk of Tuthmosis III at Karnak. Many ancient temples and monuments had fallen into disrepair, and Tuthmosis the dreamer was far happier restoring the glory of the past than working out the details of a complicated present.

Not only did Yosef have to contend with the coming famine, but to him also fell the traditional duties of a vizier. The viziers of Egypt's past had filled at least thirty major functions, including Manager of the King's Palace, Guardian of the Public Works, General of the King's Army, Commander of the King's Peacekeepers, Patron of the Royal Artisans, Dispenser of Justice and Keeper of the Law, Judge over the High Court of the Land, Overseer of the Royal Farms and Granaries, Hand to Distribute Food to Laborers and the King's Officials, and He Who Gathers in the King's Taxes.

Perhaps, Tuya thought as she listened to one of the reports Yosef sent to Tuthmosis, the Almighty God prevented her from marrying Yosef because Egypt's second in command had no time for a wife. But still her heart leapt with joy when she heard that Zaphenath-paneah had finally returned to Thebes. With difficulty she curbed her eagerness and waited two ten-day weeks before joining the others who assembled each morning at the palace in the hope of gaining an audience with the king's vizier.

"Dress me carefully," she told her handmaid, but she dared not speak the reason for her concern: *because this morning I have decided to face Yosef.*

Knowing Yosef's preference for simple things, from her wardrobe chest she selected a gown of cream-colored linen and a narrow band of gold for her throat. Modest leather slippers completed her outfit, and in her hand she carried a single lotus blossom, a symbol of their hours together in Potiphar's garden.

Leaving Yosef in the care of his nurse, Tuya slipped out of her chamber and down to the hall that had been designated as a temporary reception room for the vizier. A throng of dignitaries and nobles waited outside the chamber's closed doors, yet the crowd parted like the petals of a flower as she approached. No one dared question her presence, for anyone might approach the vizier and offer a word of advice or congratulation, but Tuya spied more than one lifted brow. Intuitively, she knew it would not be wise to speak with Yosef alone. The more witnesses to her audience with him, the safer they both would be.

Every morning the vizier went first to Pharaoh's chamber for an intimate council, so the esteemed Zaphenath-paneah had not yet arrived to face his visitors. Tuya waited, hoping Yosef would not leave her long with the men who cast furtive glances in her direction, and within a few moments she heard the steady tramping of an approaching entourage. Surrounded by a host of scribes and nobles, Yosef swept past her, but his eye caught hers and his lips mouthed her name: *Tuya!* She caught a glimpse of fondness in his gaze as his guards pulled him away, and her heart fluttered at the knowledge that he remembered.

For an hour, she waited. Those who had previous appointments came and went, then finally a servant dipped his knee before her. "Queen Tuya, the vizier bids me call for you," he said, motioning toward the reception chamber. Tuya rose and followed the servant.

Yosef sat on a gilded chair not unlike Pharaoh's throne. A thick carpet lay under his feet, the baton of state across his hands. The books of Egypt's laws, forty-two volumes containing all the wisdom of the world, stood open on stands behind his chair. An assortment of Pharaoh's officials and ministers clustered around the vizier, expressions of curiosity on their faces as Tuya approached.

She smiled at her husband's ministers, then turned to Yosef. On the night of his release from prison he had appeared as wild as an unbroken horse. Today he seemed no less powerful, but Zaphenath-paneah looked as Egyptian as any man born along the Nile. He wore a fine pleated kilt and a mantle of leopard skin, the traditional garb of a prince. A handsome wig covered his head, and his paint-lengthened eyes crinkled at the sight of her. "I am honored, Queen Tuya," he said, his voice reaching her as if from worlds away.

If not for the memories that came crowding back at the sound of his voice, she would have thought Yosef the Hebrew a figment of her imagination. She could see little of him in the king's vizier. Gone was the thick, unruly hair, the faltering accent, the boyish laugh. This stranger was an exquisite man, but he was not the youth she had known and loved.

He gave her a careful smile. "To what do I owe the honor of visiting with Pharaoh's wife?"

"One of Pharaoh's many wives," she said, searching for the meaning behind his greeting. Had he chosen those words as casually as his tone implied? Or was he trying to gently remind her that they were not the people they once had been?

"I come, my lord vizier, to welcome you to the palace." She bowed her head in a gesture of respect, grateful for the opportunity to lower her eyes as she forced out her next words: "And to congratulate you on your marriage."

"Thank you." He hesitated. "I hoped we would have a chance to speak, gracious lady."

"Truly?" She lifted her head. His eyes snapped with some urgent message he could not speak before the ministers who listened to every word. She tightened her hand around the flower she carried. Yosef wanted to speak freely—what would he say?

With a graceful economy of movement he stood and clapped his hands. "Clear the room of all who await business with the vizier," he ordered. "Queen Tuya should not have to speak before the common crowd."

"Let your servants remain, my lord," she whispered, catching his eye. Rash actions would arouse suspicion, and as much as Tuya wanted to speak with him alone, she knew she did not dare. Pharaoh's court was quicksand; she had seen how petty jealousies and ambitions could flare to injure the innocent. Amenhotep's court had been rife with strife, and Tuthmosis was young enough to be easily misled.

"Of course. My servants shall remain, but my scribes—" Yosef gave the three men who sat at his right hand a determined smile "—will wait in the anteroom. The words of Pharaoh's wife do not need to be recorded."

The grumbling men gathered their pens, parchments and books and left the room, casting curious glances over their shoulders as they exited. When everyone had gone but the two servants who lingered at the door, Yosef stepped from the dais. The stiff guise of the Egyptian vizier fell away, and the expression in his eyes brought heat to Tuya's cheeks. For a dizzying moment the room whirled around her.

"Steady," Yosef murmured in a low voice. "You must remember where you are."

"I'm all right." She pressed her hand to her throat and breathed deeply, aware that servants watched from the far side of the room. No doubt other faces were pressed to the narrow opening between the doors.

"I have wanted to thank you, Zaphenath-paneah." She strengthened her voice so the eavesdroppers could hear. "You have done my husband and the kingdom a great service."

"God has brought us to this place," Yosef answered. "But I am enjoying the work."

She turned her back to the spies at the door. "I have prayed to your god," she confessed in a whisper. "I prayed for Taharka's release. When I saw that your god could deliver him, I prayed for you, too."

Yosef laughed. "And I thought my prayers did all the work." He thrust his hands behind his back and regarded her with what looked like honest affection. "It is comforting to know I was in your thoughts."

A feeling of glorious happiness warmed her heart. "I nearly

gave up. But when I heard Potiphar had spared your life, I knew your god would preserve you. Even though I thought you guilty at first—"

"Speak no more of the past." Yosef lowered his voice. "I have prayed for you these many years, and I have begged God for an opportunity to speak to you."

His words stole her breath. Was he about to confess he still loved her? Would he suggest a rendezvous? For what purpose? If they were to meet, even as friends, questions would be asked. She stared at him, her mouth agape.

"I have dreamed again." His eyes darted toward the doors at the rear of the room; his voice became a thin whisper in the space between them. "The vision was another warning from God, Tuya. You and your son are in danger."

"Yosef?" she cried, momentarily forgetting everything else.

A corner of the vizier's mouth curled in a half smile. "Your son is called Yosef?"

"It is his baby name," she answered, feeling heat rise in her face. "Pharaoh does not know what it means. I thought that since I couldn't have you, at least I could love my Yosef—"

"You must take care, Tuya," he whispered, his voice dark with warning. "I don't know where the danger lies, but this evil would not hesitate to destroy Pharaoh as well."

Tuya gave him a rueful smile. "Like Tuthmosis, you are always dreaming. Is there danger in the court? Certainly, for even the suggestion of impropriety could spell exile for me and my son. But I am no threat to anyone. I hold no ambitions, I do not take much of Pharaoh's time. And Tuthmosis is a good king. He wants to do right and he has surrounded himself with wise counselors." She lifted a brow. "As you should know."

Yosef ignored the compliment. "Even so, you must be careful. When I first had the dream, prison walls hindered me from warning you. And now—" he grasped his hands "—I am hindered in other ways."

"I know," she cut him off. Again the conversation threatened to pick up the strings of time, and emotion choked off the words she wanted to say. She took a step toward him, hoping he could read her heart, but he lifted his hands in warning.

Tears stung her eyes. "Yosef—" she stared at the floor as she strained to push her embarrassment aside "—you need not fear me. I will not bait you as Sagira did. I will not touch you, I will not linger in the hall for a glimpse of you. I will not give anyone cause to say I am unfaithful to my husband."

She paused, struggling to gain control over her unsteady voice. Outside the room she could hear the murmur of voices, sudden laughter and shushing sounds as the waiting nobles remembered that a queen and the vizier held a conference nearby.

After a long moment, she met his eyes. "Perhaps the danger you dreamt of lies in Zaphenath-paneah. I am safe as long as I guard my heart…from you."

"And they say I am the one who is wise," he murmured, his eyes darkening with a shadow of the love she remembered.

Tuya felt her heart turn over the way it always had when he looked at her like that, and the memory made her smile. "Your god has surprised me yet again. I cannot fight against the Almighty."

"My god—" Yosef gave her a quick smile "—has our good in mind. We must trust him."

"Trust?" She could not keep a shade of bitterness from her laugh. "I don't know how. I know your god is powerful. I've seen him preserve life." She wanted to add, *but since he has kept us apart, my heart wonders if he is truly good!* She bit back those words and finished in a level voice: "You can trust in this, my Yosef—I have never loved another man the way I loved you."

Like the ripple of an underground spring, compassion stirred in his eyes. "Do not be sad, Tuya. God will not leave you alone. You must trust him to provide for your needs—"

"You keep using that word!" she hissed. "I want to trust, Yosef, throughout my entire life I've searched for one person who would remain with me no matter what. But there is no constancy in this world! I thought I could rely on you, but you wouldn't believe my warning about Sagira! And now, through a miracle, we face each other once again and my head tells me one thing while my heart screams something else. I know we cannot be together, but what am I to do with the unspent love in my heart?"

He locked his hands behind his back as his dark eyes moved away from hers. "Faith is the heart of the mind," he answered. "Despite the feelings of your heart and the reflections of your mind, trust God to work for your good."

"I see. I should trust El Shaddai to take care of me, so you will no longer be bothered by dreams." She jerked her chin upward. "So be it. Fret not for me or my son, Zaphenath-paneah. I will not be unfaithful to Pharaoh in thought or deed. I will not ask for the loyalty you wish to give your wife."

She nodded and pivoted on the ball of her foot, then stopped as a sudden thought whipped into her mind. "Priests for the ancient gods offer spells to destroy our enemies. Has the Almighty God a ritual to destroy this enemy love? Perhaps he will have mercy on me and rid my heart of this troublesome feeling."

"The Lord God does not engage in magic. But he often works in ways we cannot understand. My father, for instance, used to tell the story of my great-grandfather Avraham and his much-beloved son, Yitzhak." He spoke slowly, as if he dictated to scribes who were recording every word. "Yitzhak was the son of Avraham's old age, but El Shaddai commanded Avraham to offer the boy as a sacrifice."

Despite her own turmoil, Tuya felt a whisper of sympathy run through her. "Your god would command such a thing?"

"You asked if he would destroy love," Yosef said, sinking into his chair. He looked at her with a level gaze. "Judge for yourself. Avraham obeyed, placing his total trust in God. He risked everything he held dear, certain that God would not kill the one he loved. He was convinced God would raise the boy from the dead if necessary."

"Did the child die?"

Yosef tented his fingers. "Avraham climbed to the chosen mountain, gathered stones for an altar and embraced his son before binding the boy's hands and feet. He placed Yitzhak on the wood for a burnt offering and lifted his dagger to strike his son."

His voice softened as he gazed into private space. "But the angel of the Lord stopped Avraham's hand. A ram, caught in the thicket, was offered as the sacrifice instead of the boy."

Tuya frowned, unable to understand the point of the story. "If your god is all-mighty and all-knowing, why did he test this Avraham?"

"Avraham was not put to the test." Yosef looked up at her with an invitation in the depths of his eyes. "God was. Avraham tested the strength and goodness of El Shaddai. He learned that no one can live in doubt when he has prayed in faith."

Tuya considered the story. If any god asked her to sacrifice her son, she'd retreat, refuse, run away. Yosef was the only person in the world who belonged to her. She wouldn't surrender him even to the Almighty One.

As anxious as a child who has stumbled on something she doesn't understand, Tuya bid Yosef a hasty farewell and swept from the reception hall.

Two nights later, Pharaoh came to Tuya's chambers. He played for a few moments with Yosef, then motioned for the child's nurse to take the boy away. When they had gone, he sank onto the couch in the front room of Tuya's quarters and patted the empty space next to him. "So, my wife," he said, waiting for her to sit, "we have not spent much time together in the last few months. And it occurs to me that lately I have not told you how beautiful you are."

"Dear Pharaoh," she murmured, ducking his embrace as she bent to pick up one of Yosef's paddle dolls. "There has been no time. You spend more time with your new vizier than with me or your son—"

"He is a marvel, isn't he?"

"Our son? I have always thought so."

"I meant the vizier. He is so wise! For months the priests of Ptah in Memphis have badgered me about a territorial conflict, but Zaphenath-paneah heard their complaint and settled their dispute in an hour. The plan for storing the harvest is well-begun, and the Nile-readers from Elephantine have predicted the flood will be high this year. The land will be green this spring, and the abundance will be great—"

"Hush." Tuya sat, tucking one leg under her body, and leaned toward her husband, playfully pressing her finger over his lips. "I have already heard about the bountiful crop we will have. The entire palace is buzzing with talk of Zaphenath-paneah."

"He is a wonder."

"Would you choose anyone less than wonderful for your vizier? Now, let's talk about your temple or the work at

Karnak, anything but Zaphenath-paneah." She dropped her hands and folded them in her lap, aware that Tuthmosis's eyes had narrowed. "Is something wrong, my husband?"

He squinted at her as color flooded his face. "Did you know him when you lived in Potiphar's house?"

Fear spurred her heart to beat unevenly. He had merely asked a question, this was not an interrogation, and yet she felt her face stiffen. What had he heard? Someone must have told him of her visit to the vizier, of the whispered conversation, of the dismay on her face when she fled Yosef's presence. She must sort out her thoughts and impose order before she could answer, but she had no time for anything but simple honesty.

"Yes." She met his direct gaze. "I knew him."

"Did you love him?"

By all the gods, who had he talked to? Tuya closed her eyes, searching for a way to tell the truth without wounding the young man who was as vulnerable as he was powerful. He had been a child during the time she loved Yosef, and even though she carried the memory of that love in her heart, her passion did not burn with the intensity it once had...

She turned to lace her arms about Tuthmosis's neck. "Do you love me, husband?"

He drew back as if the question offended him. "You know I do."

"Do you love Queen Mutemwiya?"

He gave her an impenitent grin. "You shouldn't ask such things."

"I have known you forever, I can ask anything. So...do you love Queen Mut?"

His mouth tipped in a grudging smile. "A little."

Tuya traced his brow with her finger. "And the girls from the harem, do you love them?"

"Tuya, that is not a fair question. A king should not show partiality."

"Then I have my answer. You love all of us, my husband, but in different ways."

The king's smile flattened. "What has this to do with my vizier?"

She feathered her hands over his chest. "Yes, my husband, I knew Zaphenath-paneah when he served in Potiphar's house. I loved him. And then I entered the palace and married you. I love you in a different way, for you are my king, my husband, and the father of my son, who is dearer than life to me. And so, though I once loved Zaphenath-paneah, my love for you gives breath and purpose to my life."

She pressed her cheek to the flesh over his heart, hoping her words would assuage his doubts. He remained silent for a long moment, then she felt his lips brush her hair.

He rose from her bed early the next morning. "As soon as Zaphenath-paneah's trial is settled, we shall go down to Memphis and visit the temples," he said, stretching in the dim light of the room. "Would you like to come?"

"A trial?" Tuya echoed, trying to throw off lingering wisps of sleep. "What trial?"

Tuthmosis adjusted the striped linen headpiece he wore while within the palace. "The high priest has suggested that my vizier might be more respected if his name were cleared. Today we shall summon those who had him imprisoned. I shall render my judgment and the gods shall acquit the innocent and condemn the guilty."

"Those who had—" Tuya sat up, wide awake. "You will call Sagira and Potiphar as witnesses?"

"I will call Potiphar as the judge, and his wife as the accuser. Since the captain of my guard must report to my vizier, I am certain Potiphar will be relieved when Zaphenath-paneah is acquitted." He released a sympathetic chuckle. "Surely the captain feels awkward accepting orders from a man he sentenced to prison."

Tuthmosis strolled out of the room as if this day were like any other, but Tuya sprang out of bed and slipped into a morning dress, then clapped to summon her maids. High drama would visit Pharaoh's court today, and Tuya wanted to look her best. Like wasps shaken from their winter sleep, every noble in Thebes would swarm around the royal court.

The summons came before the Boat-of-Millions-of-Years had reached its zenith in the sky. Potiphar read the message with a quick glance, then let the scroll fall onto the dusty floor of his once-elegant villa.

So it had come to this. For two months he had dismissed the knowledge that his men snickered behind his back, but now the rumors would be publicly confirmed. Pharaoh's gallant Potiphar, who wore the Gold of Praise and commanded Tens of Thousands, had been duped by his wife. His temper had condemned an innocent man to a lifetime of imprisonment. Worst of all, since Pharaoh had declared that a divine spirit rested in the vizier, Potiphar had imprisoned a god.

"How was I to know?" Potiphar mumbled, looking around at the hall that had once been one of the loveliest rooms in Thebes. The furniture lay broken and soiled, the gardens and fields outside were withered and scorched. Few servants tended to the villa, for most had been sold to satisfy Sagira's gambling debts. The breath of blessing that arrived with Paneah departed with him, too.

At first Potiphar blamed his troubles on Sagira's drinking and the excesses of her lovers, but soon the truth would be whispered in every Theban home. "My neglect drove my wife to attempt the seduction of a god," he whispered, gripping the hilt of his sword until his knuckles whitened. "And now, Sagira, we will both pay for our crimes."

The message had summoned him to stand before Tuthmosis IV as he had stood before Amenhotep and Tuthmosis III. But instead of praise and honor, today he would hear condemnation from his king: "You, captain of the guard, Appointed One of Pharaoh, have grievously erred. You have stolen six years of an innocent man's life…"

The young king would not consider the injustice done to Sagira. Whatever her faults, she had married Pharaoh's choice, expecting a full measure of a husband's love and attention. She hadn't even received the full measure of a man.

Horses' hooves drummed against the dry earth of the courtyard and voices called him to the king's court. Potiphar straightened his posture and pulled his sword from its sheath. "Hail to thee, Zaphenath-paneah," he said, bringing the hilt of his sword to his scarred face. "God speaks, he lives! Live in peace, my son Paneah, for I cannot!"

With a defiant flourish, he swung the blade through the air, then he knelt, his knees cracking against the tile floor. Positioning the sharpened point of the blade in a space between his ribs, he saluted his king in a mocking whisper. "Farewell, Pharaoh, my only god."

Bracing the hilt of the sword against the floor, Potiphar thrust himself forward.

Chapter Twenty-Nine

News of Potiphar's suicide reached the court just ahead of Sagira. When one of the guards told her the news, she pulled her cloak about her shoulders and warily considered her prospects. Long ago she had dropped any values or dedications beyond her own pleasure, and Potiphar's death barely penetrated the veil of drunken bitterness that enclosed her.

Strolling into the throne room, she sensed that tide of public opinion had altered. An hour ago most of the nobles had considered her a foolish woman, hardly worthy of notice. But today the crowd in Pharaoh's great hall thirsted to right the wrong done to Zaphenath-paneah.

Potiphar, who might have borne more than his share of scorn and disgrace, had deserted her. She alone would face the society that now embraced her former slave. The painted faces that turned toward her seemed to whisper *outcast, she-devil*.

But she would not take Potiphar's cowardly way out. In the years since Paneah's rejection she had learned to distance herself from humiliation and pain. Nothing could hurt a cousin of Pharaoh. Royal blood would always flow in her veins.

The revenge-hungry crowd silenced as she walked forward, her mind thumbing through names and faces along the wall. She knew all these people, had drunk at their parties, danced for their entertainment. They had laughed with her, teased her, praised her for her jewelry, her fine clothes, her handsome servants.

She smiled with remembered pleasure. Paneah had liked her, too, despite his resolve to keep her at arms' length. He had been flattered by her interest, pleased at her attentiveness, honored by her desire to be with him. The memory of that final night shuddered through her mind like an unwelcome chill, but Sagira passed over it and let her mind run backward. She remembered Paneah's laugh, his awkward attempts to retreat from her embraces, his embarrassed fumbling with papers and pens whenever she happened to run her hand over his honey-colored skin. She had done everything for him because she loved him, and because of the prophecy about the child she had never borne...

She stopped before the golden throne. Pharaoh sat in front of her, looking very much like a teenager, and beside him sat the stern-faced foreign queen. Sagira gave her kingly cousin a brief smile and searched the royal family for Tuya. There! She stood behind a pair of guards, one arm across her chest, the other hanging limply, the pose of an insecure schoolgirl. But her features were still lovely, as handsomely sculpted as the statues of Isis around the temple.

A trumpet blared behind her and Sagira jumped, unused to the sound.

"O Pharaoh, live forever," someone called. Sagira hugged herself and trembled. Though she had not heard it in years, she knew that voice.

She turned. He stood there, dressed in the robe of a king, with a crown on his head and the Gold of Praise about his neck. Exultation filled Sagira's chest until she thought it would burst. Paneah, her Paneah, was more beautiful than ever, and today she would tell the world how badly he had wanted her!

Paneah spoke to Pharaoh, and the king replied, but Sagira hardly heard a word, so dazed was she by Paneah's presence. More magnificent than any mortal man, his very words made the pillars sway and shiver.

Without warning, the vision turned to her and spoke. She blinked and staggered on her feet. "What?" She gazed up at him from beneath the heavy fringe of her wig. "Did you speak, my beautiful one?"

The faces around her tumbled into laughter, but Sagira ignored them. Let them laugh. At last, finally, Paneah stood by her side.

He looked at her with a tinge of sadness in his eyes. "I will repeat the question. Do you still say that I, your slave, attacked you?"

Sagira flattened her smile. How long she had waited for this moment! "Of course you attacked me." She clenched her hands and leaned toward him. "You were in love with me. You wanted me to bear your son."

The laughter in the room ceased. Sagira stood in the silence, goading herself with bitterness. He had wanted her! He had kissed her! He had sought her arms for comfort; she had wiped his tears with her hands! She was not so foolish as to throw her pride at a slave, a man who could bring her nothing but heartache!

Paneah turned and said something to Pharaoh, who replied while Sagira played her smile on the assembled crowd. When the doors behind her opened with a sound like thunder, Sagira whirled to face another ghost from the past. "Ramla!"

The priestess walked forward, amused resentment evident in the slight curl of her upper lip. Tall and formidable, she saluted Pharaoh with a stiff bow.

"Tell us what you know about this situation," the vizier commanded, and then Ramla's voice, high-pitched and reedy, echoed in the hall. Her words poured over Sagira like water over a rock, an endless stream that had no meaning. Sagira heard the old prophecy, first spoken when the optimism of youth had colored their lives: *You will be remembered through all time... As long as men walk on the earth, they will speak of you. Your memory will be immortal... You will leave an imprint on the sands of time that cannot be erased.*

With a sudden gasp, Sagira returned to the present and heard Ramla's final comment: "She thought she would have a baby to replace the present line of pharaohs."

Treason!

"She wanted to conceive a child with a slave in order to punish her husband. And she was certain her child would rise to replace Amenhotep's son."

I shall die for this!

Pharaoh's face flushed. "I will hear no more," he said, his grip tightening around the crook and flail in his hands. "Sagira, wife of Potiphar, I find you guilty of treason, conspiracy and giving false witness against an innocent man."

The rage in him was a living thing; the assembly quaked before it.

With a visible effort, Pharaoh reined in his temper and addressed his vizier. "I have rendered judgment in your place," he said, his anger lingering like a dagger that must soon find its way into Sagira's breast. "But you are the Dispenser of Justice, Zaphenath-paneah. You shall decide this woman's fate."

"Pharaoh gives me complete freedom?"

"I do." The king's nose was pinched and white with resentful rage, but Sagira kept her eyes fixed on him, not daring to look at Paneah. Undoubtedly a deep-buried fire of anger had kept him alive in prison, and now those flames would consume her.

She closed her eyes, unwilling to bow her head. "I grant Lady Sagira freedom to return to her house," the vizier said, his voice soft. "Furthermore, I shall appoint a manager to oversee her affairs so Potiphar's estate may return to its full glory. From my own estate I grant her two handmaids who will care for her health and see that she does not harm herself."

Sagira stared at the king. Surely her mind had snapped. He had ordered her death, and her brain had mistranslated the sentence. Send her home? What a jest!

Yet Pharaoh seemed as surprised as she. "This is a most unusual judgment, Zaphenath-paneah. Are you certain this is what you wish?"

"For as long as the lady lives, she shall remain under my guardianship," the vizier answered. "I shall appoint honest and fair men to see that Lady Sagira will not want for anything. I believe she has suffered enough, my king."

The line of Pharaoh's mouth curved, then he nodded. "Thus shall it be," he said, his voice ringing through the judgment hall. "Let it be known throughout the kingdom that Zaphenath-paneah was unjustly accused and imprisoned, and the lady Sagira has this day been found guilty and shown mercy."

For the first time since hearing his ruling, Sagira looked at Paneah. If he had ordered her thrown to the crocodiles, she would have spat in his face, wrapped the rags of her dignity about her and marched down to the Nile. But how could she cope with kindness?

The double doors of the hall creaked and opened. After bowing to Pharaoh, the vizier turned and left the hall, his business complete. Sagira stared after him, realizing that the assembly waited for her response.

After a long moment, she lifted her chin and stepped toward the doors, walking in the wake of the looks of awe and respect directed at Zaphenath-paneah.

Chapter Thirty

As Yosef predicted, the kingdom prospered during the seven years of plenty. Zaphenath-paneah's overseers gathered the earth's bounty until the Egyptians had stored up grain as abundant as the sand of the sea.

Before the first year of famine arrived, two sons were born to Yosef and his wife, Asenath. Yosef named the first-born Manasseh, "making to forget." "For," he told his wife, "God has made me forget all my trouble and all my father's household." He named the second Ephraim, "fruitfulness," explaining, "God has made me fruitful in the land of my affliction."

During the years of plenty, Zaphenath-paneah redefined all that a vizier should be. So wide and broad were his duties that in years to come Egypt would find it necessary to have two viziers, one for the northern kingdom and another for the southern.

After taking private council with Pharaoh each morning, the Zaphenath-paneah stepped in full public view and reported to the king's chief treasurer that all was well within the kingdom. The vizier then unsealed the doors of the royal estate so the day's business could begin. Every person and item of property entering the palace doors was reported to the vizier, and it was said that Pharaoh could not cough without Zaphenath-paneah knowing about it.

The authorities in charge of each nome reported to the vizier on the first day of each season: inundation, emergence and drought. When the vizier was required to supervise disputes in local governments, he traveled up and down the Nile on Pharaoh's official barge. He also detailed the king's bodyguard, as well as the garrison of whatever city Pharaoh happened to visit. Army orders proceeded from the vizier, the forts of the south fell under his control, and the officials of Pharaoh's navy reported directly to him. Though the vizier was the official minister of war, whenever Pharaoh traveled with the army, Zaphenath-paneah remained at Thebes and conducted the administration of domestic affairs. No tree could be cut without his permission, no building begun without his approval.

Zaphenath-paneah's watchful eye regulated all things, and under Yosef's rule God blessed Egypt just as he had blessed Potiphar's house. In time, the Hebrew who had entered the land as a half-dead slave came to be regarded as the people's great protector.

When ambitious men sought positions in Zaphenath-paneah's service, they were carefully screened. After they passed a series of tests, the vizier's assistants were presented to Pharaoh and charged in a formal ceremony.

Tuya often joined the royal court for these rituals. She thought it important to honor her husband by understanding the affairs of the kingdom, and she yearned for opportunities to watch Yosef from a careful distance.

"Let not your heart be puffed up because of your knowledge," the vizier's voice rang out in a commissioning service one afternoon. "Be not confident because you are a learned man. Take counsel with the ignorant as well as with the wise. The full limits of skill cannot be attained, and no skilled man is equipped to his full advantage. Good speech is more hidden than the emerald, but may be found with maidservants at the most humble grindstone."

Tuya smiled. Only a man who had spent time in slavery could have gleaned that insight. "If you are a leader commanding the affairs of the multitude," the vizier further encouraged his assistants, "seek for yourself every beneficial deed, until your own affairs are completely without wrong. Justice is great, and its appropriateness is lasting. It has not been disturbed since the time of him who made it, whereas there is punishment for him who passes over its laws. Wrongdoing has never brought its undertaking into port. Fraud may gain riches, but the strength of justice is everlasting."

Tuya listened to Yosef's words about justice with a bemused smile. He had proved to be a firm disciplinarian with those who broke Pharaoh's laws, so why had he been so merciful to Sagira? That woman's folly had marred at least three lives, but she now lived in a restored and prosperous villa.

Perhaps Sagira paid for her crime in other ways. Tuya knew that Sagira had no friends among the nobility, for she had been cast from Pharaoh's favor. Court gossip reported that Potiphar's wife suffered from a wasting disease that would surely take her life unless the gods proved to be as merciful as Zaphenath-paneah.

A blaze of trumpet fanfare ended the ceremony; the flushed and happy civil servants bowed their knees to the vizier, then prostrated themselves before Pharaoh. Tuya sat silently in the cheering crowd, grateful for the anonymity of the assembly. In a gathering like this she could watch Yosef without worrying that her eyes revealed the love in her heart.

He had been Egypt's vizier for six years, and since their

first interview she had not spoken to him except in the most ceremonial of greetings when they chanced to pass in the palace hallways. With a lovely wife and two fine sons, Yosef had probably forgotten all about her.

But she still dreamed of Potiphar's garden.

Chapter Thirty-One

Narmer hurried through the halls, slinking through shadows until he reached the private corridor that led to Queen Mutemwiya's elegant chambers. After ducking through the doorway and the outer room, he insinuated himself between the heavy draperies on the queen's bed and waited until he heard footsteps approaching. "Thank you, ladies, but I shall not need you tonight," he heard her call, then Mutemwiya closed the door. "Narmer?"

"Here." He stepped out of the curtains and pressed his lips together as a sign of pique. "I thought you'd never come."

"That silly ceremony," she fussed, slipping the heavy wig from her head. She tossed it onto the floor, then took a seat on her couch, curling her legs beneath her. "Well," she purred, smiling in her unmirthful way, "come and tell me what you think of our grand vizier's new men."

"They are like the old ones," Narmer grumbled, sinking into the chair opposite her. "The same enthusiasm, the same impartial glances, the same glow of righteousness. What I would give for a single covetous soul!"

"There will be no bribing the vizier's assistants." Mutemwiya lifted a manicured finger and stroked her chin. "Do not attempt it, for they will tell Pharaoh what you have done and then where will you be, my ambitious love?"

Narmer grinned, accustomed to her sharp tongue. "In the underworld with you." He moved next to her, allowing her to drape her arm over his shoulders. "In any case, I will not bribe the vizier's fools. He has surrounded himself with souls who are faithful and true—even his wife cannot be swayed from his side. Believe me, I have tried to gain the lovely Asenath's attention—" he smiled at the anger in Mutemwiya's eyes "—and failed."

"She would not have an old goat like you," Mutemwiya snapped. "Why should she? The one they call the Pride of Egypt is hers."

"And the treasure of the kingdom is his. And Pharaoh, your young fool, is a puppet in the vizier's hands."

"As I am a puppet in yours." Mutemwiya looked up, her fascinating smile crinkling the corners of her eyes, and for a moment Narmer was distracted. Compared to his luxury-loving lioness, Egyptian maidens were hothouse flowers. Mutemwiya had been bred in the wild lands of the north country, and her temperament was as unpredictable as the weather in that changeable land. She moved with animal assurance and spoke with the confidence of a woman who knows the potency of her charm. Narmer had been in awe of her since the day he negotiated Pharaoh's marriage contract, and she had recognized his political talent, charisma and gift of persuasion. He owed her a great deal, for she had convinced Pharaoh that Narmer would be the natural choice to replace Potiphar as captain of the king's guard.

The strength of her gaze drew him now. Pleased at her open delight, he forgot what he had meant to say.

"The time is coming, my dear Narmer," she purred, leaning toward him, "when the people will tire of giving their abundance to Pharaoh. They will groan under the weight of this senseless hoarding."

"According to Zaphenath-paneah and his Almighty God, the Nile will not flood next year. Famine is coming."

She pulled away, yawning, and tapped her crimson lips with her hand. "I forgot."

He slipped from the couch and fell to his knees before her, his hands spanning her waist. "You don't believe him?"

"No." She rested her hands on his shoulders. "I have not heard the voice of this god, and neither have any of my priests. Only Zaphenath-paneah hears the unseen deity, and only Zaphenath-paneah profits from Egypt's abundance."

Her touch triggered primitive yearnings, but Narmer steeled himself to be patient. "There may be something in what you say," he said, catching her hand. "If the Nile floods next year, the people may well rise up and rebel against this vizier. But what if famine does come? How can we argue against one who has been proven right?"

"If famine comes—" she leaned closer to him "—your people will resent having to buy what they have put into the granaries. Grain will be precious. A loaf of bread will sell for a bag of silver, and the poor will starve. When they carry complaints instead of offerings to the temples, the priests will demand a sacrifice. The divine king will give his life to feed the earth, and since there is no royal heir, whomever I take as my husband will ascend to the throne."

"But what of Tuya's child? A son of Pharaoh lives."

Mutemwiya sniffed. "Tuya is a lesser wife, a former slave, and the life of her child is nothing. Trust me, Narmer, no one will stand in our way. If the land brings forth her abundance next year, you shall overthrow this vizier."

"And if famine comes, as the vizier has said it will—"

"Then we will wait until his food supply runs out." She

tucked her hand around his neck with easy familiarity. "Zaphe-nath-paneah has been busy running the palace and training as-sistants. Do you truly believe his granaries and storehouses contain enough to feed the entire kingdom of Egypt?"

He ran his hands over her arms. "It would be difficult to lead the people without the priests' approval."

"The priests will be eager to lead the people back to the ancient gods," Mutemwiya answered. "They have grown jealous of the vizier's Almighty God, for even Pharaoh has grown less fervent in his worship of Horus and Osiris. So we will begin to make generous offerings now, Narmer, and win the loyalty of the priests. If famine comes, in time the people will cry out against the harsh god who would smite the land of Egypt. We shall rise like the phoenix from the ashes of a burnt and starving kingdom."

Overcome by her clever logic, he pressed his lips to her palm in a fervent rush, and she lowered her forehead to his. "Yes, my Narmer, think of it! You and I as husband and wife, rulers of the Two Kingdoms and beyond. My Mitanni tribe will ally itself with us, and after that we shall rule the world."

Tuya felt a curious, tingling shock when her servant told her the king's vizier stood outside her door. "Zaphenath-paneah? The vizier wishes to see me?"

The frightened girl nodded.

"All right, give me a moment. Seat the vizier in the front room."

The girl padded away and Tuya hurried to her dressing table to check her makeup and wig. This wig was short, well above her shoulders, and fashionable among the ladies of Thebes. She hoped it made her look younger, for she was now thirty-four and the mother of a ten-year-old son. Under her wig, she had already sprouted more than a few gray hairs.

She adjusted her eyeliner and smudged the lines of kohl to disguise the crinkles at the corners of her eyes. After dropping the bronze mirror to her dressing table, she smoothed her dress and took a deep breath. Why should facing Yosef make her feel nervous? He was an old friend.

And he must bring news of some importance, or he would have sent a messenger instead of coming himself.

His back was to her when she entered the room, for he was watching Yosef play the lute. "Excellent, young prince," she heard him say. "I hope my sons show half as much talent."

Her son blushed and smiled when he saw her standing in the doorway. "Zaphenath-paneah likes my playing."

"So do I," Tuya answered. "Now go and show your nurse how skilled you are." As Yosef hurried away, Tuya turned to face her guest.

Yosef had aged more than she had. Contentment shone in his eyes, but stress and responsibility had etched lines in the forehead that had been smooth six years before.

"Tuya." The sound of joy in his voice brought a warm blush to her cheek.

"Zaphenath-paneah." She gave him a properly formal smile, aware that her servants moved about in the other rooms. "What brings our king's vizier to me?"

"Must we be so stilted with each other?" He gestured toward a couch. "You've never called me anything but Yosef."

She shrugged, not knowing what else to say. "All right. What brings you to me, Yosef?"

He smiled, and some of the starch went out of her knees. "I have come with something important to discuss, but thought I might at least ask about your health."

"My health is fine." Stepping to the couch, she perched on the edge while he sank beside her. She put her hands in her lap. "Why have you come?"

The air of convivial friendliness disappeared when he frowned. "This is not an easy request to make."

"Speak it."

He looked away for a moment, then stared at his hands. "Do you remember the story I once told you about Avraham?"

She stared at him. She recalled the story well, for every word he had uttered in her presence was precious. "The man who took his son to the mountain for a sacrifice."

"And God preserved them both."

"I remember."

"Tuya—" he pressed his hands together "—I have dreamed again of you and your son, and the danger is nearer than it was years ago. I believe you can save your son, but there is only one way."

"Save my son from what?"

"I am not sure."

"Well, you can't ask me to do something unless I know why." She lifted a brow. "And what, exactly, are you asking me to do?"

"Only one thing. Offer your son to Pharaoh, and let him be betrothed to Queen Mutemwiya. It must be done if he is to be declared the royal heir. You must do it now."

She sputtered in horror. "Yosef is Pharaoh's heir. None of the other wives have given birth to a son, so he is the heir, without question—"

"No." Yosef spoke in the firm voice of Justice and Egyptian Law. "If Pharaoh were to die today, Egypt would have no king until Queen Mutemwiya marries."

"But Yosef is Pharaoh's son."

"Pharaoh intends to declare the boy Crown Prince at some future time, but we dare not wait. Yosef must be named Crown Prince immediately. He must be recognized as the betrothed husband of the heiress. Thus he will be King on Pharaoh's death."

"My baby? Married to that queen?"

"Her ceremonial husband." Yosef closed his eyes as if he could not bear to bring her further pain. "Remember Avraham? He trusted God to spare the life of his child, yet he was willing to surrender that life."

Tuya stood and backed away. "I can't give my son to that witch, not now, not ever. Yosef won't understand. He'll think I care more for ambition than I do for him. And I don't care if he's King, I only want him safe—"

"If you do not do this thing," Yosef warned, "and Pharaoh dies, the queen who ascends will not allow Tuthmosis's son to live. He will have an accident, or a mysterious illness." He leaned forward, his eyes beseeching hers. "I will explain matters to Yosef. He will understand that you do this for his sake."

Tuya shook her head, unwilling to consider the possibility. Tuthmosis was not about to die! He was twenty-three, young and healthy, strong and sure…

Yosef stood and crossed the room in three long strides, then gripped her arms. She flinched, resenting his familiarity.

"Tuya, you must trust the Almighty. He has warned me and I have warned you. Do not be afraid."

"I can't do this," she cried, her voice breaking.

"You must."

The sound of hurried footsteps broke the silence. The vizier pulled away and slipped from the chamber as Tuya's maids entered from another doorway. "Mistress! What's wrong?"

She threw herself on the couch and sobbed, too broken for words.

For a week she spent her days debating Yosef's words and her nights praying by the small stone altar in her bedchamber. She had trusted the unseen god to aid Yosef and Taharka. She had seen his hand of blessing on both Potiphar's and

Pharaoh's houses. But she had never asked El Shaddai to help her.

It was one thing to support a god with offerings and petitions, another to place one's son in his hands. She had surrendered Yosef to Pharaoh, she had given her claim on his heart to Asenath, and all she had left was her son. And yet the vizier's god would have her place even her son in the hands of the woman who might be her enemy.

She paced until she was blind with fatigue, then fell onto her bed and slept. In slumber she drifted through clouds and temples and over mountaintops until she stood on a place of stone. A pile of timber had been gathered there, and a dagger lay in her hand. On the wood, curled up like a puppy, Yosef slept.

The hard fist of fear clutched at her stomach as sharp stones cut her bare feet. She knew where she was—Avraham's altar. But she could not offer what God asked of her.

A stentorian voice rumbled from a mass of clouds and echoed around the mountain:

I called for a famine on the land,
I broke the whole staff of bread.
I sent a man before Yisrael,
Yosef, who was sold as a slave.
They afflicted his feet with fetters,
He himself was laid in irons;
Until the time his word came to pass,
The word of the Lord refined him.
The king sent and released him,
The rulers of peoples, and set him free.
He made him lord of his house,
And ruler over all his possessions,
To imprison his princes at will,
That he might teach his elders wisdom.

Odd wind-borne sounds came to her, then the voice spoke again:

Tremble, and do not sin;
Meditate in your heart and be still.
Offer the sacrifices of righteousness,
And trust in the Lord.

Tuya stepped forward, clutching the dagger in her hand, and the form on the altar shifted. "I will trust Yosef to you," she cried, her voice mingling with the wind and the crack of the weathered wood on the altar. "I have no other choice." She lifted the blade and felt her heart break, then thrust it down into the blanket that had covered her son.

She felt no resistance. She pressed her hands to the scrap of wool and discovered that Yosef had vanished. Had he been spared...or carried to the other world?

Tuya spread her hands on the empty blanket and wept.

Tuya slipped into her best dress and wig, adorned herself in Pharaoh's favorite jewelry, and set out for the throne room. Tuthmosis had not come to see her in days. It would be difficult to offer her suggestion before a formal audience, and perhaps dangerous when she had no way to gauge the royal temperament. If the king was in a bad mood...

But El Shaddai would know these things, and her son's fate rested in his hands.

She found Pharaoh sitting on his throne, an assortment of maps and scrolls spread before him. Queen Mutemwiya sat beside him, a bored expression on her face. Beside her, the captain of the king's guard studied the open maps with a critical eye. Several military generals stood before Tuthmosis; perhaps they were planning a military expedition.

Tuya squared her shoulders as she approached the throne. Today she would go into battle, too.

Tuthmosis saw her coming and held out a hand in greeting. "My lovely Tuya," he said, giving her a disarming smile. "What brings you out of your bower?"

Tuya fell to her knees. "Only one thing, my husband and king. I have a boon to ask of you."

"What is it?" Honest pleasure shone from his eyes, and he leaned forward. "You shall have it, even if it requires that I sell half the equipment in my tomb."

"It is this." Mindful of Mutemwiya's cold glare, she lifted her gaze to meet his. "Take our son, husband, and declare him to be the crown prince and your heir. I surrender him to you this day."

Tuthmosis's eyes flickered in surprise. "You would surrender your son?"

"So there will be no doubt of his right to reign, I surrender him to be betrothed to Queen Mutemwiya," Tuya said, looking at the older woman. The queen's eyes were shrewd little chips of bright quartz in a dark face, impossible to read.

For a moment Pharaoh seemed speechless, then he lowered his voice. "In truth, I had thought to do this thing later," he said, his words for her ears alone. "I wanted our son to remain by your side for as long as possible."

"He is ten, and nearly grown," she answered, careful not to reveal Yosef's warning. "It is time he began his princely training. Take him, my husband, with my love…and my unfaltering trust."

Pharaoh gave her a frankly admiring smile and declared it would be done immediately. Tuya bowed in gratitude.

As she turned to leave, however, she caught a glimpse of Mutemwiya's face. The queen's sharp and surly features reminded Tuya of a watchful, hungry vulture.

* * *

The ceremony took place in the temple of Horus. Pharaoh and Queen Mutemwiya walked through the tall pillars of the temple with the young prince between them. As the child knelt before the altar, a temple priest proclaimed that the boy was the rightful heir of Pharaoh and the future husband of the Great Wife, Queen Mutemwiya.

"From this day forward," the priest intoned, "let him be called Amenhotep, the third of that name, in the tradition of the pharaohs of the Two Kingdoms."

From her place in the crowd, Sagira covered her lips with her hand and hiccupped, the sour taste of beer filling her mouth. Tuya's child, the crown prince? Impossible to believe. Tuya was nothing but a slave whom the gods had indifferently blessed with beauty, and that beauty alone had put her in Pharaoh's bed and begot her a child.

Sagira snickered. Pharaoh was doubly a fool. Not only had he embraced a slave, but he'd been foolish enough to marry an aging queen who could never give him a lawful son. "By the crust between Seth's toenails," Sagira snorted, not caring who heard, "that's no prince. There's more royal blood in my big toe than in that child."

Several people retreated as if she were dispensing poison, but Sagira only shrugged. "Can't bear the truth, can you?" she called, staggering. "I could tell you more, but you won't get a word out of me!"

Bystanders rippled away and pretended to ignore her, but one man stepped forward and bowed. "Lady Sagira, isn't it?" he asked, a smile on his darkly handsome face. "You may remember me. I helped arrange your marriage when your parents were alive. I am Narmer, the captain of the king's guard."

Sagira tipped her head back. The man did look familiar, and he was handsome, with a strong, dauntless air. "I am pleased to see you." She nodded with what she hoped was regal grace. "And because you've been so gracious, I'll forgive you for marrying me to Potiphar."

He laughed, then glanced up at the temple altar as if he did not approve of the ceremony. "Foolishness, isn't it?" he asked, lowering his voice. "I heard your comment. I was surprised to see that many people disagreed with you."

"They ought to agree, for I know about these things," she answered, arching a brow. "The one they call Queen Tuya was my slave, you know, both in Potiphar's house and in the house of my father. And my mother was Amenhotep's sister."

"Ah." Narmer bowed again. "I am more honored than ever, my lady. Mistress of a queen and Pharaoh's cousin! Now if you only knew our king's vizier—"

"Bah, I know him." She spat the words. "Of course, you know he attacked me."

"How could I have forgotten? My sympathies are with you, dear lady."

"They are?" She blinked at him, her heart warming.

"Yes." He gave her a suggestive smile. "And I would love to hear the entire story about this vizier and how he came to harm you."

Sagira felt her heart skip. It had been so long since a sober man noticed her. Fuddled by longing, she allowed Narmer to take her arm and lead her from the temple.

"Well," she said, feeling herself flow toward him as they walked, "Paneah was difficult from the beginning. In fact, Potiphar returned Tuya to Pharaoh's harem because she and the steward were lovers. Many's the night I found them in each other's arms…."

Tuthmosis allowed the priests and singers to finish their ceremonial hymns as they sent him off to bed, but when they had gone, he sat up and stared at the wall. His mind was too full for sleep, the day had been too eventful.

What wisdom had inspired Tuya to surrender their son? He had seen her grief-stricken face peering from behind a portal of the temple, and his heart swelled with such tender love for her that he nearly paused in his walk down the aisle. But she hadn't looked his way; she had eyes only for their son…

She had been right, as always. He should have begun to train his son months ago, for a prince had much to learn. If he hadn't been so caught up in his work with Zaphenath-paneah, he might have found time for the boy, but sometimes he still thought of himself as a prince. Twenty-three was not so young an age, yet he often felt like a schoolboy pretending to play at king.

He lay down and folded his arms beneath his head. He could send for one of the harem girls, but he wanted to talk to Tuya. But she would be upset, for tonight Yosef slept for the first time in his own chambers. Tuthmosis couldn't find the courage or the heart to face her red-rimmed eyes.

How he loved his first wife! He loved the loose wisps of hair that made half-moons on her slender neck and the sleepy-cat smile with which she greeted the morning. With every passing day she grew more precious and unique, and yet before her he often felt as awkward as an adolescent. She had mothered him, befriended him and borne him a son; now he yearned to make her love him.

None of the others loved him, and he didn't particularly care. They were his wives for political or pleasurable reasons, and they understood their roles. Spoiled and selfish, they had been born and bred to be pampered. Mutemwiya would never have surrendered a child to another wife. The harem girls would have demanded to be made queens themselves before they'd have given up a soul that had sprung from their womb.

But though the sacrifice had caused her pain, Tuya had

given her child into his care. She was always giving, never asking for anything, even when he begged her to name a gift he might find for her. He wanted to give her everything, yet all she had ever wanted was the son she surrendered today.

Filled with remembering, Tuthmosis stared at the ceiling. *You have given me a child, the greatest gift a man can give a woman,* she had told him on the day of Yosef's birth. *I ask for nothing more.*

And yet he yearned for her to ask for more, to ask for him. She liked him, she petted him, she showed him affection. But she never spoke to him in the adoring tone she used with their son, and she never looked at him in the dreamy way she watched Zaphenath-paneah from across the room.

Lonely in the darkness, the divine pharaoh of the Two Kingdoms curled into a ball, protecting the place in his heart only Tuya had reached.

Narmer was filling two golden goblets with wine when Mutemwiya finally entered. "To life," he said, lifting the cup as she stalked toward him. "To our success."

She frowned. "How can you drink to that when Tuthmosis has just set a roadblock before us?"

Narmer pressed a goblet into her hand. "Because when the time has come for our divine pharaoh to be sacrificed to satisfy his starving people, this child and the vizier can be removed in one swipe of the tongue."

She took the cup. "Explain."

He smiled. "I have had a most interesting conversation with Potiphar's drunken widow. It seems that Zaphenath-paneah and Pharaoh's favorite wife were lovers when they lived in Potiphar's house."

Mutemwiya's mouth curved with the faint beginnings of a smile.

"There is more," Narmer said, tapping the side of his goblet to hers. "I think we can convince all Egypt that the crown prince is not Pharaoh's son at all."

"How? Tuya is doggedly, boringly faithful. Anyone who knows her—"

"The people do not know her," Narmer replied, already tasting success. "And they will want to believe love found a way to unite our handsome vizier and our ravishing Tuya. And when the populace is convinced, the priests will never allow the son of slaves to assume the throne of a divine pharaoh."

Mutemwiya swirled the wine in her cup. "But I am betrothed to the boy. When Tuthmosis dies, the throne will be his."

"A ceremonial marriage that has never been consummated can easily be annulled," Narmer answered, shrugging. "And children are frail things, easy to be rid of."

A look of mad happiness gleamed in Mutemwiya's eyes. "My Narmer," she said, her smile as hard as marble. "Your war-zone ethics never cease to surprise me."

"Enjoy your princely husband while you can," he whispered, eyeing her over the rim of his cup. "For one day soon he will be nothing but the son of slaves."

Amenhotep III

So now it was not you that sent me hither, but God: and he hath made me a father to Pharaoh, and lord of all his house, and a ruler throughout all the land of Egypt.

Genesis 45:8

Chapter Thirty-Two

Pharaoh paused in his morning prayers and murmured a decidedly untraditional phrase under his breath: "And unto you, El Shaddai, I give praise, honor and obedience in gratitude for sending Zaphenath-paneah to Egypt."

Through the first seven years of Zaphenath-paneah's authority over the land of Egypt, the eternal cycle of inundation and irrigation, emergence and planting, drought and reaping had not varied. After the seventh year's harvest, the emerald grass grayed in the heat of the desert sun and withered. As the year ended, the astronomer-priests searched the skies for Sirius, the brightest of all stars, whose appearance just ahead of the rising sun would signal the coming flood. When at last Sirius rose through a hint of thinner darkness in the east, the priests sent the traditional messengers to Pharaoh. The new year had begun, and the Nile would flood within forty-eight hours.

On this new year's day the Nile-watchers at Elephantine checked and rechecked their measurements. The Nile rolled steadily northward, bright as a spill of magma, but the creeping floodwaters were barely above the level of the emergence. Hasty offerings were made at the temple of Hapi. Had the god fallen asleep? Had the limitless bounty of the river god's pitchers finally come to an end?

The glassy surface of the heaving river scarcely rose at all. Lands that had lain fallow during the arid days of summer received only a trace of moisture when the river dams were cut open. As the winter passed, the ground lay as hard as stone beneath the planters' feet, every sign of green burned away. Dust devils swept across dreary flats, and Egypt's fabled black earth blew as dry and barren as the gray deserts to the east and west. Unable to find hay, wealthy landowners released their grass-greedy cattle into the desert. The hunting of wild rabbits and waterfowl, once a sport, became a serious endeavor.

By the time of spring and the emergence, the river had thinned like a starving child, and only an occasional dew watered the thirsty earth. Summer arrived with desiccating winds that cloaked every exposed object in dust. The wind sucked the moisture from animals and men alike, drying skin until it cracked and bled, parching mouths and nostrils until every living creature gasped for breath.

While heat, drought and famine came at the world like a mortal enemy, the people of Thebes retreated behind the walls of their homes and gave thanks to Zaphenath-paneah's Almighty God, for news of the prophecy had reached even the lowest estate. As wind-blown sand scoured the fields, Zaphenath-paneah's assistants opened the granaries throughout Egypt. Even those who had ignored rumors of the coming famine were able to buy enough grain and corn to feed themselves and their families.

From the palace at Thebes, Pharaoh watched the sun burn the land to dust. Egypt had once been a land of severe contrasts: the verdure of the Nile Valley insinuated against the sterility of the desert, the dark gray waters of the inundation feeding the fertile green fields, the teeming life of the Nile abutting the desolate wasteland. Now the kingdom stretched before its king like a curling sheet of dingy parchment. Even though he knew the famine would last only seven years, it was often difficult to believe the land of Egypt would not be forever mottled and stained with death.

But the people would not starve. Tuthmosis shook his head, his mind whirling with grim thoughts of what might have been. If not for the unseen god who spoke to Zaphenath-paneah, the priests of Anubis would have come to his chamber with the cobra. How wise Zaphenath-paneah was! And how honorable, for he shed praise as easily as a duck sheds water. "It is God who works," Zaphenath-paneah protested whenever Pharaoh attempted to commend his vizier. "The Almighty has seen fit to save us for his pleasure."

As the first year of famine passed and the earth toughened beneath the sun's heat, Pharaoh urged his vizier to tutor eleven-year-old Amenhotep. In recent months Tuthmosis had realized the importance of the agriculture he had always taken for granted, and Zaphenath-paneah certainly understood more about cultivation and husbandry than Tuthmosis could ever hope to know.

"The vizier fills the room with light and wisdom," the king told Tuya one afternoon. "From him our son will receive straight talk and simple answers."

She nodded, her eyes brightening, but she said nothing. They sat together on a narrow couch beside his private garden as the sun boat rowed toward the west. Though Tuthmosis's head lay in her lap, she did not look at him.

Tuthmosis scratched his chin. Of late Tuya had often slumped into morose musings and neither his gifts nor his jokes lifted her sad countenance. Though she remained as beautiful and gentle as ever, some misfortune shadowed her. Tuthmosis often felt he held a wilting flower in his arms.

At first he thought the change in Tuya's mood related to the dismal landscape. She had always loved the gardens, so he assumed the withered aspect of the countryside accounted for her dampened spirits. But now, at the mention of Amenhotep's name, sunshine broke across her face until she reined in her emotions and pretended indifference.

He marveled that he had not linked cause and effect together. Was this melancholy only the result of a mother missing her beloved son?

"Tuya," he asked, grateful that they were sitting in the privacy of his quarters, "what occupies your mind?"

She managed a weak smile. "Nothing, my husband."

"Tuya." He slipped his hand around her neck as if he could pull her soul to him. "Talk to me. We are alone, and I speak now not as your king, but as your husband and friend. You have not been yourself in these past few months."

Tears jeweled her lashes as she smiled down at him. "I am sorry, Tuthmosis. I should work harder to please you."

"You have always pleased me," he said, feeling the chasm between them like an open wound. "Have I done something to drive you away? I know I've been busy with my work on the monuments and Zaphenath-paneah requires a great deal of my time—"

"You have done nothing," she said, resting her hands on his shoulders. Her eyes clouded with hazy sadness as she studied the acacia trees at the garden's edge. "I miss the lotus blossoms. Have you noticed that they have not grown up along the river's edge? I used to enjoy them when I was a girl, especially the fragrant blue ones."

"There are lotus blossoms in the water gardens. Walk there, and you can enjoy your fill of them."

"They're white. They're not the same," she whispered absently. "The blue ones bloom in the daytime, the white ones don't like the sun." She gave Tuthmosis an incomplete smile. "Do not fret about me, most honored husband. You are a good king and wise father. I have seen how you encourage Yosef—"

She bit her lip as if she'd said too much, and Tuthmosis blew out his cheeks. "By all the gods, Tuya, why didn't you say something sooner? Are you too proud to admit that you need to see your son?"

Her eyes widened. "Not proud, my lord. Afraid."

He sat up and stared at her. "Afraid of what?"

She shook her head, unable to speak in the face of his anger, and he took a deliberate breath to calm himself. He ought to be more gentle. Though she had never voluntarily spoken of her past, he knew she had been a slave, and no slave had an easy life.

"Speak freely," he said, softening his voice. "Has someone threatened you?"

She swallowed hard. "I didn't think it would be right for me to seek the prince. He is no longer my son. He is Mutemwiya's future husband and the kingdom's future pharaoh. The women of the harem are jealous. Your other wives would cause trouble if a former slave became overly familiar with the crown prince—"

"And yet even the lioness who drives her cub out of the den still watches for his safety." Tuthmosis ran his hand over the softness of her shoulder. "Our Amenhotep should thank the gods that you are his mother. Do not fret about Mutemwiya. She does not even think of him. When he is Pharaoh, he shall marry whomever else he pleases. But to ease your mind, tomorrow I shall ask Zaphenath-paneah to hold the prince's lessons in the garden where you may walk as freely as you please. Watch Amenhotep as often as you wish, talk to him, be with him."

Her eyes filled with a tenderness he'd never seen in them

before. "You are kind, husband." She lowered her cheek to his chest. "You are too good to me."

He slipped his fingers through the silkiness of her hair while a lace of confused, pleasant thoughts fuddled his mind. "I should have recognized the source of your sorrow long before this."

She sighed, the whisper of her breath warm on his skin.

"Tuya—" he squeezed her shoulder "—I am King. No one will hurt you, and no one will harm our son. This I swear to you on my own life."

She rested in the crook of his arm like a lion cub who nestles between its father's protective paws, and Tuthmosis relaxed in the satisfying victory. "You have missed our son," he said, grateful that the gathering darkness cloaked the schoolboy blush burning his face and neck. "Did you not think I would miss you? I did, you know."

When she lifted her head, Tuthmosis steeled himself for either laughter or sarcasm. Life had taught him to never reveal his true feelings to any of his wives lest they compare notes and torment him, but love urged him to risk opening his heart.

"How could you miss me?" she asked, a teasing note in her voice. "You sent for me often."

"And your mortal shell came to my bed." Tuthmosis relaxed at the tender touch of her arms about his neck. "But you, dear Tuya, remained far away."

"I'm here now." She tipped her head back, her eyes glowing with fire in the rising moon's light. Tuthmosis abandoned all reserve as he drew his arms about her and surrendered to the crush of feeling that drew them together.

As she dressed the next morning, Tuya realized that Tuthmosis would never know what a gift he had given her. Though her son lodged in his own chambers, the king had returned Yosef to her. She would be able to walk and talk with him in the garden, far away from the sniping eyes of the other wives. Best of all, Zaphenath-paneah would share in her happiness.

She knew she made a pretty picture as she dabbed her fingers in her makeup pot and colored her eyes and lips. Tuthmosis had been more understanding and sympathetic than she had ever dreamed he could be. In the years since he had learned of Yosef's El Shaddai, the king had been increasingly open to new ideas and less apt to adhere to the traditional, formal ways of living. The gods of Egypt had failed to predict or prevent the famine presently sweeping the world, and Tuthmosis knew only a greater god could have sent Zaphenath-paneah to lead them through the catastrophe of worldwide drought.

She spent the morning listening to the idle chatter of her maids, then she slipped into the gardens where she knew she'd find the crown prince and his tutor. The sky stretched pure blue from north to south, without even a suggestion of cloudiness. A living warmth emanated from the sun, and a delicious sense of anticipation spread through Tuya's limbs as she walked among the flowers and looked for her loved ones.

There. Ahead on the path, the prince walked with the vizier. Her son's head came to Yosef's shoulder, and with a tinge of pride Tuya noticed that Amenhotep's shoulders had begun to broaden. Already she could see Yosef's influence, for her son and his tutor moved down the path as if they were reflections of a single soul. Both walked with their heads held high, their hands clasped behind their backs, their shoulders squared.

Tuya called a greeting. "Oh, Zaphenath-paneah, live forever! And, Amenhotep, Crown Prince, may the gods grant you a hundred and ten years of prosperity!"

They turned, alike in their posture, and regarded her with pleased surprise. "Pharaoh said you might be joining us,"

Yosef said, warming her with his smile. "We are honored to walk with you, Queen Tuya."

Her son did not answer, and from the confusion in his eyes Tuya realized he did not know how to respond. She reached out and drew him to her side. "It's all right, my prince," she said, allowing herself to cling to him only for a moment. "Though you have a new name and a new position, I am still your mother and you may tell me anything you wish. I can keep a confidence as well as the vizier." She smiled. "And I am nearly as wise."

A chuckle escaped from Yosef, and the prince met Tuya's eyes with a smile that penetrated her heart. "It is good to see you, Royal Mother," Amenhotep said, his voice deeper than Tuya remembered it. "I have missed you."

"And I you." She draped her arm over the boy's shoulder and turned to Yosef. "Now, what were you discussing? Perhaps it would be helpful to have a woman's viewpoint."

"Indeed it might," Yosef answered, thrusting his hands behind his back again. And on they walked, discussing the plight of the farmers south of Thebes.

Not until Tuya returned to her chamber did she realize that during the time with Yosef she had not once thought of the garden at Potiphar's house.

Narmer leaned against the door to the queen's private chamber and regarded Mutemwiya with a sly smile.

"What?" she snapped. "Why do you stand there grinning like a fool? I told you not to come to me unless you had good news."

"Perhaps I do," he said, slinking toward her. He sat in a chair and crossed his legs, confident of his ability to please. "What sort of news do you want to hear?"

"I want to hear something I don't already know." Mutemwiya swung her legs from the bed and leaned toward him, her spine curving like a curious cat's. "Don't tell me the Nile has failed to flood a second time. Don't mention that the earth bakes beneath our feet and still there is food for all of Egypt. And don't remind me that Pharaoh is healthy, young and strong while you grow older every day—"

"You grow older, too, my dear Mut," Narmer answered, his eyes narrowing. "How many years have you waited for this rebellion? Forty? Forty-five? Or are you as ageless as the Sphinx our pharaoh honors?"

The queen crossed her arms. "Two years ago you told me it would be simple to destroy the vizier and the brat, yet the boy is almost of age! When Pharaoh dies, Amenhotep will not need me to be his regent. And if he suspects that you are less than devoted, he will be old enough to send you to the gallows."

Narmer lifted a brow. "That won't happen, for Egypt will starve soon—"

"Egypt will not starve! That cursed vizier has enough grain stored for ten years!"

"But he has not made provision for everything." Narmer uncrossed his legs and leaned forward, eager to share the plan he'd been formulating. "You are right, dear Mut, about the king's health and power. And I suspect you're right about the stored provisions, but none of Zaphenath-paneah's men will discuss the matter. Apparently he has warned them about attempted sabotage, and he does not trust even the captain of the king's guards."

"The vizier is a clever man. No wonder Pharaoh adores him."

Narmer shrugged. "The time has come, dear Mut, to take action of our own. We must send Tuthmosis into the underworld by the strength of our own hands."

She did not grow pale or scream at his suggestion, but studied him as if measuring his determination. "So…how can this be done?"

Narmer leaned forward. "I have thought on it for days. Tell me, dear Mut—what does your husband our pharaoh dearly love to do?"

Mutemwiya frowned. "Refurbish the ancient temples?"

Narmer resisted the temptation to roll his eyes. "He hunts. Don't you see? The other day while I was visiting his tomb, I studied the pictures painted on the walls. The artists have depicted him riding in his chariot and pulling back his golden bow. Before his chariot, the artists have drawn the many lions, tigers, antelopes and gazelles the king has slain—"

"What," the queen interrupted, "has this to do with us?"

"Don't you see? The king is young and powerful, but hunting is a dangerous sport."

Mutemwiya's eyes widened.

Narmer gave her a tight smile. "I shall take him hunting. I shall take Pharaoh to hunt the most vicious, most powerful animals on the earth. And he shall not come back alive."

Mutemwiya's hand clenched his arm like an eagle's talon. "Are you certain? He is a good hunter."

"Don't worry, my dear." Narmer leaned closer. "I can arrange it. Yet if the gods take my life instead of the king's, this conversation will perish with me. I assume all the risk...and when I return, I shall expect to be crowned with glory."

She eyed him with a calculating look, then promised him the world in a white-hot kiss.

For ten days Tuya did not see Tuthmosis, then she heard that Pharaoh was planning a hunting expedition in the lands south of the first cataract. He would be gone for some time, explained the slave who brought her the news, and so he was busy arranging matters with his vizier and giving gifts to all his wives and concubines.

She sighed at the news, then retreated to her chambers. For some reason the knowledge that he had visited the other women sparked jealousy in her heart, and she wondered that she could feel jealous after sixteen years of marriage to a man with a multitude of wives. But Tuthmosis had been more than kind, allowing her to visit with Amenhotep and Yosef in the garden. He could have forbidden her this favor, because Amenhotep was practically Mutemwiya's husband and legally no longer Tuya's son. By allowing her to continue her relationship with her child, he risked causing turmoil among the royal women.

Fortunately, Mutemwiya did not seem to care what Amenhotep did.

Tuya had everything she had ever dreamed of; still she wished Tuthmosis would send for her. He had always been able to make her laugh, and his companionship had been a great comfort. After missing him for many days, she felt as if a section of her body had been torn away. Surely this was not love—or was it? The emotion was not the same as what she had felt in Potiphar's garden with Yosef, yet sparks of unexpected happiness shot through her whenever she heard the steady tramp of the king's guard outside her door.

Two weeks later, Tuthmosis finally appeared at her chamber's threshold. The priests sang their hymns and symbolically put him to bed; their servants removed the double crown and the traditional elements of regalia. When everyone had gone and left Tuya alone with her husband, Pharaoh opened his arms and Tuya walked away.

"What's this?" Concern edged his voice. "Don't tell me you're angry because I'm going away."

"You've been away already," Tuya said, pretending to pout. "You've kept yourself from me as you said goodbye to all your other wives. Your servants told me what you were up to. You were so busy taking the others gifts—"

"I had to give them something," he said, tossing the ceremonial bedcovers away. He stood and approached her. Though she felt his breath on her neck, he did not touch her. "They are my wives, Tuya. I must honor them."

She opened her hand. "Fine, where's my gift? I suppose I can toss this gold necklace into the treasure box with the others."

"No." When a smile rippled through his voice, Tuya turned to discover that Tuthmosis had thrust his hands behind his back. "No gold necklace for you, bride of my youth. I married you because you were beautiful, you know. I keep you because you are honest."

His teasing smile brought a warm tingle to her heart. "Wives can be too honest, my husband. Now give me my present so I can wear it tomorrow as we watch you depart the palace. I don't want to be the only royal wife without whatever it is you are offering."

His eyes steadied upon her face. "I offer you my heart and soul."

She nodded. "I accept. Now give me my trinket so you can be on your way."

She stepped toward him, trying to reach whatever he had hidden behind his back, but he dodged her with athletic grace, grinning the entire time. Finally, breathless and smiling, she propped her hands on her hips. "Tuthmosis—" she struggled to keep laughter from her voice "—give me the cursed necklace!"

"I didn't bring you a necklace. I hope you won't mind being the only wife without one."

"What, then?"

"Put out your hand and close your eyes."

Tuya did so, reluctantly, and gasped when a feather-light

object brushed her palm. When she opened her eyes, she saw that her husband had given her a blue lotus blossom.

"Oh." She breathed in the heady scent. "Where did you find it?"

"I've had my most trusted men searching for blue lotus plants ever since you told me you loved them," he answered, his eyes fastened to her face. "We found some growing far south of here, and we will plant them in the pools of the garden where you walk every day. Zaphenath-paneah is to bring you a bowlful of blossoms every morning as long as we are apart. They are my gift to you, Tuya. Only you."

She ran her finger over the flower's delicate petals. "It's beautiful."

"Do you truly want a golden necklace?" Tuthmosis asked. "I could get one for you—"

"—with no trouble at all," Tuya finished, lifting her gaze to meet his. "And the gift would not mean nearly as much as this flower. I don't want gold, my husband. All I want is—" she extended her hand to him "—right here."

He opened his arms and she came into them, resting her head on his shoulder. Tuthmosis was more comforting than challenging, but he had invested more of himself in this gift than in a thousand chains of gold. In that moment she realized that Tuthmosis loved her with his life; she was his heart's companion. Though Mutemwiya wore the crown, though other wives were younger and more vivacious, she knew her husband best.

She lifted her head and looked at him. "Did you mean it when you offered me your heart and soul?"

"Yes." His hand brushed her hair. "And my love, Tuya, is yours if you will accept it. Now that I am a man, I know what love is, and I know I love you more than life itself. That is why I waited to come to you. I saved the best for last."

Why had her heart spent so much time yearning for the past? Yosef had been the love of her youth, the boy who taught her to lift her hopes above slavery, the man who taught her to dream. But love, genuine love, existed in the king who had given her a son, the heart that brought her lotus blossoms and called her friend.

His hand traveled up her back, and Tuya tilted her head to study his face. Had her infatuation for Yosef caused Tuthmosis much grief? She suspected he knew far more than he revealed, yet his was a trusting soul. Even knowing that she and Yosef shared a past, he was brave enough to trust Yosef as vizier, and loving enough to allow Tuya to spend time with Yosef and Amenhotep.

"Beloved husband—" she wrapped her arms about his slender waist "—I accept your love with gratitude and freely give mine in return. You are a good king and a wise man." She flushed as a wave of warmth swept through her. "God blessed me when he brought me to you. May he preserve you while we are apart."

"Love of my heart," Tuthmosis answered, his lips moving over her cheek with exquisite tenderness, "I'm half returned even before I go."

Chapter Thirty-Three

The sun sank toward a cloud-bank piled deep on the western horizon as the royal company reclined in the shadow of their tents and recounted the day's adventures. They had been away from Thebes a full month, and among their hunting trophies were scores of antelope, oryx and gazelles. On this day Pharaoh had shot and killed a lion with his golden bow, and already the men were composing songs to praise their divine king's skill and talent. "Even the lion knows his god Pharaoh," they sang, their voices rising in the wilderness. "He stands and awaits the golden arrow of his king."

But this hunt lacked the thrill of the chase, for the famine that had turned Egypt to dust had also wasted the African wilderness. Not a trace of green could be found. Even the wiry bushes in the gorges were as desiccated as the mummies of men dead a thousand years. The act of killing was a mercy, for the gazelle and the antelope had no grass to graze. The lion had been sleek and fat, but in time even the king of beasts would be unable to find prey. Only the vultures that fed on carrion would thrive during the famine.

Pharaoh sat by the fire, his eyes fixed on nothing, his thoughts a thousand miles away. Narmer pressed his lips together. The pensive look on the king's face could only mean that he had grown weary of the hunt and would want to return to Thebes. Tuthmosis loved hunting, but found little joy in pursuing skeletal animals with barely enough strength to outrun the chariots. He had enjoyed pursuing the lion, but as much as Pharaoh loved the chase, he also revered wild creatures. He would not want to take another of those magnificent beasts.

Time to present Pharaoh with the ultimate challenge. "They say," Narmer said, nodding casually to his king, "that south of us is a place of great trees with timber enough to build a house for every man in the world."

"I have heard of this place," Pharaoh said, looking up. A gleam of interest flickered in his eye. "But we have not left Thebes to hunt for timber."

"No, but another animal lurks in these forests," Narmer went on, fingering the Gold of Praise about his neck. "Elephants. Thousands of them. And on each bull's snout rests a king's ransom in ivory."

Pharaoh stared into the fire. "I have seen pictures of these elephants. They are slow, lazy creatures."

Narmer allowed his mouth to twist into an indulgent smile. "I have heard they are the greatest challenge a man can face. They say manhood is proved or lost when a hunter faces an elephant bull."

As Narmer had hoped he would, Pharaoh took up the challenge. "I had thought to return to Thebes tomorrow," he said, looking at the trusted warriors who awaited his instruction. "But we have strength enough for one more journey, don't we? We shall find this grove of great timber, and ride without fear into a herd of these creatures. And I shall bring home twin tusks of an elephant bull—one I shall offer to Zaphenath-paneah's Almighty God, and the other to Queen Tuya, mother of our crown prince."

"As you wish, my king," Narmer said.

Chapter Thirty-Four

Tuya sat up in the darkness and winced as if her flesh had been nipped. A dream, a horrible nightmare had disturbed the peace of her sleep, and her skin crawled with the memory of it.

She lay back down and turned onto her stomach, clinging to the soft darkness as hard as she could, but sleep would not return. Finally Tuya rose from the bed, wrapped herself in a light mantle, and crept out of the bedchamber. Moving to the front hall of her quarters, she pulled a cord and rang for her servant.

Within moments the maid stood in the room, her eyes heavy-lidded from sleep. "Quietly—" Tuya kept her voice low "—run to the vizier's house. Tell him Tuya summons him, and the matter is of great importance."

The girl nodded, then slipped out into the corridor. Tuya sat and rubbed her hands together, trying to banish worry from her mind. Yosef would know the meaning of this dream. And, being Yosef, he would know how to prevent the disaster it foretold.

At the sound of a quick step in the corridor, Mutemwiya darted into the shadows. She had grown lonely without

Narmer's company and sought to invite sleep by walking through the palace's torchlit halls. On a perverse whim, she had turned into the hall that led to Tuya's modest chambers.

She breathed a sigh of relief when she recognized Tuya's servant in the hall, then her curiosity roused. For what reason had Tuya summoned her handmaid in the darkest hour of the night? Had she taken ill? Or did she entertain a guest in Pharaoh's absence?

Scarcely daring to hope, Mutemwiya slipped from her hiding place and followed the slave girl. When the servant turned, a question in her eyes, Mutemwiya gave her a brilliant smile. "Do not fear," she said, her voice echoing in the empty hall. "Is Queen Tuya well?"

The girl's eyes narrowed. "Yes."

"Then she must have need of something. Is there something I can get for her from my rooms?"

"I think not." The girl twisted her hands. "I have an errand to run."

Mutemwiya lost her patience. "Speak, slave, and tell me what errand you are on." She gave the girl a brittle smile. "If you do not tell the truth, I will tell the guards I found you stealing from my room. You will spend the rest of your days in Pharaoh's prison—"

The maid lowered her voice to a whisper. "Lady Tuya has sent me for the vizier. That's all I know."

Stunned, Mutemwiya let the girl slip away. Why would the vizier be called at this hour? Was Tuya responding to some secret communication from the king? No, for if anyone brought word from the hunting party, she would have heard from Narmer. Why, then, would Queen Tuya want the vizier and send an inconspicuous handmaid for him under the cover of darkness? Mutemwiya slipped toward a hiding place among the pillars in the corridor. Like the cobra who sits motionless until the mama bird hops away from its nest, she would wait and see what this night brought to pass. Better yet, she would summon a royal scribe to witness this midnight liaison—no. A priest. One with power and authority, a man whose honor might easily be offended...

Quickening her step, Mutemwiya pressed through the halls and hurried toward the temple of Osiris.

Tuya wrapped her mantle closer as she hurried to answer the rap on the door. Yosef stood there with her slave, his wig askew, his face unpainted and strangely drawn in the dim light. He greeted her in a terse voice: "Is Amenhotep well?"

"Yes—I mean, no. I don't know." She dismissed the slave with a distracted wave and pulled Yosef inside. When the door had closed behind him, she turned toward the single candle in the room so he would not see the fear in her eyes. "Forgive me for pulling you from your family, but I have suffered much this night on account of a dream."

"I thought you did not believe in them."

"How can I not believe?" she answered, wiping a tear from her eyes. "I saw Pharaoh's dream come to pass. Your dreams, as grandiose as they were, have been fulfilled. And now I stand before you half-blind with terror that the events of my dream might come to pass..."

She heard him move to the chair; the wood creaked as he lowered his strong frame into it. "Tell me, Tuya," he urged. "God speaks through dreams. He is trying to speak to you."

Tuya wondered if her fragile soul could bear to relive the black vision, but she took a deep breath. "I am walking along the banks of the Nile," she said, not looking at Yosef. "Bundles of dry rushes are burning on the watch fires. It is dark, but the flames leap up and push the darkness back so I can see clearly."

"What do you see?"

Tuya shook her head. "I do not understand why, but Amen-hotep is a baby again, and in my arms. Pharaoh walks beside me, his hand holding the edge of my skirt."

She paused, feeling foolish. "I suppose it is quite silly. You must think me a coward."

"Never," Yosef answered. "Go on, please."

Tuya turned to face him. "There are crocodiles in the water, and they begin to advance toward me. One has his eyes fastened on the baby, and the other snaps his jaws toward Pharaoh."

She broke off and sat on the edge of a chair. "I'm sorry I summoned you, Yosef. It is probably nothing but a childish nightmare, brought on by the fact that Pharaoh is away. But something urged me to fetch you."

"Go on, Tuya," Yosef said, his eyes wide. "Please."

She pressed her lips together and struggled to maintain her composure. "The rest is too awful, I hesitate to speak it. The land grows dark, but the flames of the watch fires dance in the wind while streams of sparks whirl off into the darkness. I scream and try to shield Yosef as best I can, but while I am struggling to run from the first crocodile, the second lunges toward Pharaoh…and drags him into the Nile."

She shuddered at the memory. "That's when I awakened."

She sat silent, waiting for Yosef to assure her that the vision meant nothing. But he who had never been at a loss for words met her curious glance with astonished silence.

"I have had this same dream," he said, his voice trembling. "But not in many months. God has not spoken to me this time, Tuya, but to you."

"But what does it mean?"

His eyes veiled with sorrow. "You don't need me to tell you."

She sat motionless as the full meaning of his words sank into her mind, then she pressed her hands to her knees and bowed in despair. "Is there nothing we can do? You saw the coming famine and you urged Pharaoh to prepare for it! I see my beloved Tuthmosis dying, but if I can stop him—"

"The famine came." Yosef lowered his head into his hands. "And God was merciful, for we were prepared. What you have seen will come to pass, Tuya. In his mercy, God urges you to prepare for it."

He looked at her with weariness while Tuya floundered in a gulf of despair. "Why," she whispered, lifting tear-blurred eyes to his, "when I have just begun to love him as he ought to be loved?"

Yosef stood and rested his hand on her head. "Take heart in God's mercy," he said, genuine remorse in his voice. "Take courage in God's love. He has shown you what is to come and urges you to be ready."

"For what? Loneliness and suffering? I have already walked with those companions. I know them well enough to understand that the pain of losing someone never goes away."

"No, it doesn't. But you must be ready for your son's sake. In the dream, the baby remained in your arms. Amenhotep will need you when Pharaoh is gone."

"Oh, my dear baby," she whispered, staring past the lamp at the elongated shadows on the wall. "You will be a young and vulnerable pharaoh."

Mutemwiya waited until the vizier left Tuya's chamber and then turned wide eyes on Chike, the high priest of Osiris. "I thought to have you offer a blessing for Queen Tuya, who cannot sleep. But apparently our Tuya meets with our vizier this night."

Chike's aged eyes peered at the vizier's retreating form. "It is an odd time for a meeting."

"Isn't it," Mutemwiya murmured. "I am sorry I have disturbed you, Chike, but I only wanted to be of service to our dear sister. Forgive my mistake."

The old man bowed and shuffled off, grumbling under his breath.

"Hold this inconvenience entirely against me," Mutemwiya called, her voice echoing down the hall, "but do not forget this night."

For three weeks Pharaoh's party traveled down the course of the Nile. A broad savannah of grassland stretched before their chariots, blown by the hot wind and browned by the sizzling sun. The great trees Narmer had promised rose like a protective backdrop to the east and west.

One afternoon, just after the sun boat had reached its zenith, living gray mountains appeared on the horizon. "There!" Narmer lifted his arm and pointed. "See there, my king! Elephants!"

Like solid rocks in the plain, the great gray forms moved along the fringes of forest at a slow and steady pace. Thousands of them, large and small, strolled beside springing herds of antelope and gazelle with the haughtiness of a superior race.

"Let us stop and make camp." Pharaoh lifted his hand to signal the other charioteers. "We shall unload our supplies and ready our bows. Not a moment is to be wasted."

Narmer slapped his reins and turned his horse. From Nubian slaves he had heard bloodcurdling stories about the surprising might and power of the elephant. One man could never bring down a bull, the slaves said, not even ten men. But Pharaoh, trusting in his divinity, might be tempted to risk everything.

And his and Mutemwiya's hands would remain free of blood and blame.

"Give the horses drink," Narmer called to the warriors who were chattering like magpies. "Tighten and secure the traces. We ride in an hour."

Pharaoh dismounted and stood in a delighted trance as he studied the lumbering giants.

"May the gods be praised," Narmer called, "to have delivered such a goodly number of the elephants into our hands. I know Queen Tuya will be pleased to have an ivory carving for her chambers."

"Yes, yes indeed," Pharaoh murmured, his eyes alight. He gestured to his quiver-bearer. "Check my arrows and mark each with my motif. I will know which man's arrow kills one of these beasts."

"Which motif should I use, my king?" the servant asked.

Pharaoh's lips curved in a smile. "A lotus blossom."

After the provisions and tents had been dumped by the river's edge, Narmer, Pharaoh and a handful of the best hunters mounted their chariots. Pharaoh rode with only his chariot driver beside him, choosing to handle his own bow and arrow like a true sportsman. Narmer dismissed both his charioteer and his quiver-bearer with a single glance. "Get away, fools," he said, adjusting his leather gloves as he prepared to assume the reins. "I will not hunt. I ride only to guard Pharaoh."

The slaves backed away. Pharaoh's driver slapped his reins across his horses' backs and turned the royal chariot toward the herd of elephants. The giants moved slowly, feeding themselves from the foliage they had ripped from towering trees. Stout branches lay broken and scattered over the ground, evidence of the animals' great strength.

Narmer smothered a smile. An older king would have sent his men in to gather the trophy. But Tuthmosis possessed the stubborn courage of youth.

Pharaoh advanced to within a moment's ride of the animals and halted his chariot. The herd, unsettled by his approach, moved about, the females gathering the young into the midst of the herd, then turning outward to guard their offspring. The mammoth bull, however, grazed as if nothing had happened.

Not until Pharaoh's horse broke the silence with a nervous whinny did the bull lift his head and turn to face the divine ruler of the Two Kingdoms.

The creature's great, leathery ears spread and seemed to block out the sky. His tusks, broad yellow shafts, extended from his bewhiskered head, as solid as the pillars in Pharaoh's throne room.

Narmer called up to the king. "Imagine what the crown prince will say when he sees those tusks!"

Pharaoh gestured for his driver to wheel the chariot to the left. As the horses moved forward in a gentle trot, the old bull turned, keeping his eye on the intruder, and Narmer held tight to his reins. The other hunters dispersed to stalk other prey, leaving this bull to the divine king.

The chariot circled its quarry, leading the bull, then cut between the cows and the bull so the male was singled out from the herd. Pharaoh lifted his bow and notched a barbed arrow. He pulled and aimed, his muscles shining golden in the sun. As the elephant wheeled to turn again, Pharaoh let the arrow fly.

The missile lodged in the great bull's side and the beast let out a blood-chilling squeal. Narmer's horses shied at the sound and trembled in their traces, requiring all his strength to hold them steady. Pharaoh's team lurched forward. Quick as a gazelle, the bull snorted and charged with surprising speed. Narmer smiled when he saw Pharaoh's jaw. The chariot driver's face froze as the vehicle turned and raced away from the raging anger behind them.

Narmer tightened his hands on the reins as Pharaoh drew the mad beast nearer. As the king's chariot bounced over the uneven ground, Pharaoh lifted his bow and notched another arrow, but seemed to realize he was leading the bull toward Narmer. He yelled to the driver and the chariot swerved, drawing the bull to the east, but not before passing close enough for Narmer to see a look of deadly concentration on the king's face.

Pharaoh lifted his bow, took careful aim and told his driver to swerve again. The slave did so, this time to the north, and in the instant the bull's flank was exposed, the king released his arrow. The bronze-pointed barb went in behind the animal's shoulder and buried itself in the folds of gray skin.

The bull bellowed again in rage and pain, but he did not stop his charge or lessen his speed. As his leathery ears slapped against his shoulders, he pressed forward, bridging the gap between the king's chariot and those swordlike tusks.

"For the love of Osiris, run, you beast!" Narmer whispered.

Unfazed and undaunted, the king kept shouting directions to his driver. At each turn of the chariot, Tuthmosis managed to sink another arrow into the great bull's ribs. Arrows bristled from the beast's side; blood streamed from his flank like tears. With every trumpeting squeal, a red cloud spurted from the massive trunk, but still the creature reached for the king in an agony of fear and anger.

For a moment Narmer thought Pharaoh would escape. His chariot pulled away from the weakening beast, but the driver, frightened out of his wits by the bloody apparition off the chariot's footplate, veered too sharply at a turn. The chariot teetered on one wheel for a long moment, then fell on its side. Screaming in their traces, the horses dragged the splintered contraption out of the mad bull's reach, but the human cargo had spilled.

Goaded by pain and the frenzy of fear, the elephant vented his anger on the hapless driver, stomping the life out of him.

As Pharaoh rose to his knees, Narmer gripped the rim of his chariot. If he urged his horses forward, he could draw the rampaging monster away from his helpless king. But he had not come on this journey to save Tuthmosis.

Pharaoh broke into a sprint. Distracted by the flurry of movement, the bull turned and charged. Narmer watched in horror as one of the huge tusks gored the king as easily as a knife slices butter.

The elephant trumpeted in triumph, lifting Pharaoh from the ground. Narmer's fingers fluttered as his heart raced. He had hoped for such an accident, but he had never thought to witness it.

Despite the heat, cold air brushed across the back of his neck, and his scalp tingled beneath the heavy hair of his wig. *Oh, Mut, if you could see how the gods have answered our petitions...*

The bull shook Pharaoh the way a puppy shakes a rag toy. The body slid from the giant tusk and flew into a scrubby patch of brush as if it had been made of nothing but papyrus reeds. Narmer continued to watch as the bull shivered and staggered. A bright flood of blood rushed from his mouth, then the giant toppled onto its side.

Like a statue, Narmer remained frozen in place. The alarmed cries of the other hunters finally stirred him to action, and he slapped his reins and drove toward Pharaoh's broken body. A strange, cold excitement inside him threatened to explode into a fit of laughter, but he arranged his face in lines of dismay and despair. He was, after all, the captain of Pharaoh's guard, and responsible for his life. He must feel regret, grief and unrelenting guilt.

He did not look at the granite corpse of the elephant, but hurried to the grassy place where Pharaoh lay. Sweat and blood had soaked the royal chest and stained the linen kilt; a dark pool of life seeped into the ground beneath him.

Narmer knelt at the king's side and rested his hands on his knees, mindful of the others who watched from a respectful distance. "Poor Pharaoh," he murmured.

At the sound of his voice the king's eyes flew open. Narmer jerked backward, nearly losing his balance.

"Narmer," Tuthmosis said, a death rattle in his throat. The wounded king lifted a blood-streaked hand. "Carry word to the queen, Amenhotep now reigns. It is the will of the Almighty God."

"Yes, my king," Narmer replied, staring as the king's eyes rolled back into his head. Tuthmosis stiffened and shuddered, then released his last breath.

Narmer remained by the king's side until the others forced him to move away. Later he noted with satisfaction that not one drop of the king's blood had stained his hands.

Chapter Thirty-Five

Tuya paused to inhale the delicious scent of the blue lotus blossoms now growing in the pools of the palace garden. Yosef and Amenhotep, unaware that she lingered, kept walking, their hands lifting in emphasis as they debated the wisdom of the ancient laws.

Watching them, Tuya smiled. Yosef had appeared at her door each morning for over a month, offering her a bowl of blue lotus blossoms in the name of the king. As pleasant as the gift was, Tuya longed far more for the sight of Tuthmosis's royal barge on the Nile. Only when she had seen him safe again on his throne could she believe that her dream had been a meaningless premonition, a toothless lion stalking her in the dark.

A guard stepped into the path before Yosef and saluted. "I beg Zaphenath-paneah's and the prince's pardon," he said, bowing. "But a messenger has come from the river. He brings a message from Narmer and Pharaoh's hunting party."

A message from Narmer? Any message should have come from Pharaoh himself.

A wave of grayness passed over Tuya as Yosef nodded. "Bring the messenger to me at once. Bid him make haste."

Tuya put her hand to her throat and hurried toward the men. "Yosef," she called, her voice trembling.

He turned and cast her a warning glance, then placed his hand on Amenhotep's shoulder. "We should meet the messenger in the throne room." He offered a careful smile that said, *Remain calm. Remember your son.*

She lowered her hand. Despite the tight place of anxiety in her heart, she smiled and placed her hands on Amenhotep's shoulders. "Live, O Prince, and prosper forever," she murmured, lowering her forehead to rest on his. "Know that your father and I love you dearly."

She might have held him forever, but Yosef cleared his throat and led the prince toward the throne room.

Everything went silent within her as Tuya heard the forthright message: ten days before, while engaged in a brutal battle with an elephant, Pharaoh Tuthmosis IV died a glorious and victorious death. His body had been wrapped and was on its way home with the two tusks of the great elephant that had set him on his way to paradise.

The message had been witnessed and signed by Narmer, captain of the king's guard, who was traveling with Pharaoh's body.

A heavy silence fell over the throne room as Yosef finished reading the scroll, then Queen Mutemwiya broke into loud, hiccupping sobs. Her ladies helped her from the room while the priests hurried to make preparations and engage the professional mourners who would weep and wail for the departed king throughout the next seventy days.

Amenhotep stood by the vizier's side with wide eyes. In an oddly detached manner Tuya found herself thinking that twelve was too young to lose a father and king.

She looked at Yosef, waiting for soothing words. His hand,

which had been resting on the prince's shoulder, lifted, then Zaphenath-paneah, beloved of Pharaoh, dropped to his knees before the child. "O King, live forever," the vizier said, lifting his gaze to meet the wide brown eyes of the frightened boy. "Now you are no longer Prince, but Pharaoh in word and deed. Your people will look to you for leadership and courage."

The boy's chin quivered, and for a moment Tuya feared he would cry. But the steel of the royal bloodline asserted itself when the prince squared his shoulders. "Rise, Zaphenath-paneah," he said, his voice a childish treble in the room, "and help me prepare my father's tomb."

Yosef rose and nodded, then followed the new king from the room and into his private chamber.

A servant came for Tuya within the space of an hour. She dried her tears and washed her face, then hurried to the royal chamber that had been her husband's. The guards at the door stepped aside as she passed, and after her knock a servant admitted her to the royal presence.

Amenhotep lay on the bed, his eyes red and swollen. Yosef sat in a chair near him, his face strained with weariness, but he gave Tuya a helpless smile.

Pharaoh lifted his head. Tears had tangled his thick lashes and smeared the paint on his eyes. "Royal Mother," he whispered, his face locked with anxiety, "what am I to do?"

Tuya wanted to scream that she didn't know, but Yosef's words of warning washed over her. The dream that had warned her of Pharaoh's death urged her to protect and shelter this other love of her life, her child.

"My dear son," she whispered, rushing to him. She sat next to him and slipped her arm about his shoulders. "My boy. You shall be a great king. You have your father's most trusted advisor at your side, and Egypt awaits your command. The

Almighty God would not leave you unprepared at a time like this. You must trust me, my son, and you must trust God." Yosef's strong gaze pulled her eyes to meet his. "El Shaddai is great, my son, and you can trust him with the kingdom as your father did."

One of Yosef's eyebrows lifted in a silent question, but he said nothing as he motioned for a slave to fetch the priests who would put Pharaoh to bed.

The ceremonial barge of Tuthmosis IV appeared on the Nile three days later. Narmer had done his best to preserve the king's immortal body, emptying it of all organs but the heart, the organ of life and intelligence, and the kidneys, for they represented the sacred Nile. The body had been stuffed and sprinkled with salt, then wrapped in linen and hurried to the river. Fortunately, the low waters of the Nile ran swiftly northward in the hot winds. After taking the king's body aboard the barge at Elephantine, the royal party had made good time.

The royal party. Narmer liked the sound of those words, for Tuthmosis was no longer King. The court at Thebes did not yet know the full truth, but the men aboard the ship did not doubt that Narmer held the reins of power.

Tuya stood on a porch of the palace and lifted her gaze to the river. The priests, their bare heads gleaming in the bright light of the sun, lifted their arms in homage to their dead king, whose body was being lifted and carried toward the temple of Horus for mummification.

Tuya shivered as the dreadful ululations of mourning rose and fell like ghostly screams. For the first time she saw herself as a king's widow, a purposeless, useless object. Mutemwiya was Queen, Amenhotep officially her husband. Tuya had not felt so alone since the night she had been abandoned by Sagira.

The group of warriors who had accompanied the king walked at the side of the body, their swords lifted across their chests. Narmer walked at the fore, the Gold of Praise gleaming in the sunlight, his chin lifted as if in defiance of death. Solemnly he sang a song of mourning, his nasal voice cutting through the wails of the mourners on the riverbank:

Death is in my sight today
    as the odor of myrrh,
    as when sitting under sail on a breezy day.
Death is in my sight today
    as is the odor of lotus flowers,
    as is the presence of hearts heavy with grief.
Death is in my sight today
    as a well-trodden path,
    as when a man returns home to his house from war.
Death is in my sight today
    as a clearing of the sky,
    as a man discerning what he knew not.
Death is in my sight today
    as when a man longs to see his home again
    after he has spent many years in captivity.
Nay, but he who is Yonder in the Other World
    will be a living god,
    inflicting punishment for evil on him who does it.
Nay, but he who is Yonder
    will stand in the bark of the sun-god
    and will assign the choicest things therein to the temples.
Nay, but he who is Yonder
    will be a man of knowledge,
    not hindered from petitioning Ra when he speaks.
Nay, but my soul has set aside lamentation,

for when he is joined with the earth,
   I will alight after he goes to rest.
Then we shall make an abode together!

Tuya pressed her fingers to her lips, remembering Tuthmosis's energy and life, while from her porch, Mutemwiya
drew attention with much weeping and wailing. Amenhotep,
who stood by the queen's side with the double crown of
Egypt teetering on his head, looked to the vizier for comfort
and encouragement.

Tuya's eyes followed the white-wrapped bundle until it
passed into the outer courtyard of the temple, then she slipped
from the porch and walked to her chambers. She felt as
ancient as the pyramid of Khufu. Surely she had outlived her
usefulness, for she had outlived her love. In previous dynasties, the slaves and wives of great kings had been entombed
with the deceased pharaohs, but since that practice had been
ruled barbaric, stone representations of a king's slaves and
wives would be placed in the king's tomb to follow him into
the other world.

Would it not be better to follow Tuthmosis into death
than to spend a lifetime mourning him? She had wasted so
many years yearning for a love that was not meant to be...but
at least she had discovered her love for Tuthmosis before it
was too late.

She opened the door to her chamber and slipped off the
scarf she had used to shield her eyes from the sun. On a stand
in the middle of the room, a half-dozen blue lotus blossoms
floated in a silver bowl.

Yosef had not forgotten Pharaoh's last wish. He would
honor Tuthmosis, and his son, for as long as he lived.

Tuya pressed her face into the flowers and choked back a
sob as grief erupted anew.

* * *

The city mourned its lost king. Watch fires along the Nile dotted the darkness; huge tongues of flame leapt into the air, followed by boiling clouds of dust and debris. Keening wails from the mourning populace stretched across the city and filled the palace with a series of endless cries. The horrible sounds filled Tuya's ears and left her tossing on a bed of grief, unable to sleep.

In the darkest hour of the night, the doors of her chamber burst open. She sat up, half-afraid one of her dreams had materialized. "Who moves there?"

Two of Narmer's guards stalked into the room, spears in their hands and swords at their belts. A captain she did not recognize stepped into the dim rectangle of light cast from the lamp in the outer room. "Queen Tuya, you are summoned to appear in the throne room of the Two Kingdoms."

Anger overcame her fear. "Who summons me? Surely not Pharaoh."

"Narmer, captain of the king's guard, and Chike, high priest of Osiris, await you," the captain answered, his eyes glinting toward her. "You are to dress and come with me immediately."

"I will dress before no man but my husband," Tuya answered. "Leave my chamber and wait outside."

"I cannot."

"You will. There is no escape from this room, and no reason for you to guard me. I will be with you in a moment, so leave now, or by the life of Pharaoh I'll have you flogged!"

The captain grinned as if he would taunt her with a threat of his own, but then he turned and gestured for the two guards to follow. When they had gone, Tuya swung her legs out of the bed and dressed in a simple linen sheath. She was about to slip on her wig, then decided against it. They had roused her from her bed, and she was not about to dress to impress such ruffians.

She ran her fingers through her short hair, smoothed her skirt and opened the door. The two guards immediately stepped into position at her side.

With sudden understanding, she looked up at them. Tonight her dream would be fulfilled. The danger was real; the enemies waited in the throne room. They had taken Pharaoh, and they were about to threaten her son.

With the anger of a lioness, she glared at the captain. "Lead me to them."

Chapter Thirty-Six

Queen Mutemwiya sat in her gilded chair, the double crown of Egypt on her head. Amenhotep, who should have been on the throne with the regal beard of Pharaoh strapped to his chin, sat on a low stool before the queen. The throne itself stood empty, but Narmer paraded before it with the air of a conquering hero.

Tuya's blood boiled when she realized who had authored this unfolding plan of destruction. Narmer and the queen, no doubt. For Mutemwiya had not been pulled from her bed to witness an inquisition; that lady was fairly purring with expectation as Tuya walked into the throne room amid the buzzing of a curious crowd.

She felt Amenhotep's eyes on her, but she did not dare look at him lest her fear show in her face. "What is the meaning of this?" She pushed the words across the room. "Who has dared disturb the king's wife in her hour of grief?"

"Tuthmosis is King no longer," Narmer said, his eyes falling on her with a look that made her shiver. "And you were once a slave. Perhaps you shall be a slave again."

Tuya felt a heat in her chest and belly she recognized as rage. She wanted to scream, to stamp her feet and roar, but

Narmer was right—she had no power and no authority except
that which had been granted to her by Pharaoh. And Amenhotep
did not wear the crown at this moment—Mutemwiya did.

The double doors of the throne room opened again and
another bevy of guards approached. In the midst of them
walked Yosef, his hands bound together.

Tuya whirled to face Narmer. "What is the meaning of this?
What wrong has the vizier done?"

Narmer's mouth curved into a predatory smile. "You and
the vizier have been brought here to face a serious charge.
Queen Mutemwiya will serve as a witness. Chike will hear
the evidence and speak for the gods."

"What charge?" Yosef asked, his voice surprisingly calm.

Tuya swallowed a hysterical surge of angry laughter.
Someone had taken great pains to arrange this trial, for the
walls of the royal throne room were lined with somber-faced,
wide-eyed onlookers who should have been in bed.

Narmer held up a hand and turned to address the gathering.
Studying the crowd, Tuya saw that a host of people had been
assembled: nobles, warriors, priests and many of the hunters
who had accompanied Tuthmosis on the fateful trip. Barreling
his chest like a bantam rooster, Narmer preened before them.

"I was favored by the gods to reach the dying king before
he breathed his last," Narmer said, pausing to cast a look of
compassionate concern toward Mutemwiya. "Anyone in the
hunting party can support my words. They saw the king speak
to me. They saw me bow in grief at his words."

Queen Mutemwiya leaned forward, her hand pressed to her
heart. "What words did my beloved husband speak?"

"It grieves me, gentle Queen, to repeat our divine king's
last words before your ears. For he revealed a shameful thing,
a sorrow he has borne since his ascent to Egypt's throne."

The queen shot him a half-frightened look. "What sorrow?"

Narmer paused. "The divine Tuthmosis, on his way to the other world, told me that one of his wives was guilty of the worst kind of disloyalty. He said his greatest sorrow was that Queen Tuya had given her love to Zaphenath-paneah."

An audible gasp rose from the assembled crowd. Several of the nobles whispered among themselves. The priests raised their eyebrows and slanted questions at one another.

Tuya closed her eyes, recognizing the trap in which she would be caught.

The vizier stepped forward. "I do not believe you," he said, his voice ringing with authority.

"You dare question the dying words of a divine king?" Narmer asked.

"I dare question *you*," Yosef answered, his words quick and tempered with anger. "And any charge brought before this throne must have witnesses to prove it."

A murmur of voices, a palpable tenseness, washed through the room.

"Very well." Narmer's face settled into determined lines. "I have made investigation into this matter. With the aid of the gods, the pieces have fallen into place, and the picture shall be revealed this night, before this company. Before the sun-god takes his bark to ride across the sky, all you who hear shall know that the child you know as the crown prince—" he pointed at Amenhotep "—is the son of former slaves. Pharaoh, before he died, told me he would surrender his life rather than accept the child forced on him by Queen Tuya and his vizier. They thought to make their illegitimate son into a king of Egypt!"

Tuya felt the room spin as the buzzing grew louder. The claim was ridiculous, but over the years she had seen Narmer insinuate his way into honors and positions far above his rightful station. The dark gods had gifted him with intelligence and cunning.

Queen Mutemwiya rose from her throne, though her hands clung to the armrests as if she stood in danger of collapsing. "Prove this charge," she cried hoarsely. "Prove this, Narmer, and if you preserve the throne of Egypt from defilement, I will reward you. The people shall praise your name, and you will be honored above all men."

Narmer bowed as if he had already won his case. "O Queen, live forever. I shall do my best to serve you."

The litany of accusation began. Quaking beneath Narmer's fierce gaze, Tuya's servants testified that they had seen her walk in the garden every morning with the vizier and the prince. One girl admitted fetching Zaphenath-paneah to Queen Tuya's chambers in the dark of night. The prince's aged nurse told the crowd that Crown Prince's baby name had been "Yosef," the same name by which Queen Tuya addressed the vizier. Abu, the goatherd from Potiphar's house, told the gathering that everyone in Potiphar's household knew the steward and Tuya were deeply in love.

As the testimony against her droned on, Tuya felt her anger dissolve into despair. She had not yearned for Yosef in months, but what would that matter now? The witnesses were honest; the essence of the charge was true enough. She had been married to Pharaoh while her heart dreamed of another.

Guilt avalanched over her, burdening her with its weight. She would have collapsed before the company had Yosef not stepped forward. "These charges have nothing to do with the truth," he said, his elegant voice commanding attention and respect. "You have impugned the right of a prince to his throne. The child was fathered by Pharaoh. During the time of his conception and birth, I was a prisoner in the house of the captain of the guard."

A smirk crossed Narmer's face as he opened his hand to the crowd. "I invite Khamat to speak."

The assembly rippled as an aged man stepped forward. "Khamat was the chief jailer of Potiphar's prison at the time of our vizier's imprisonment," Narmer explained. "He will tell you how Tuya's son came to be born. Khamat, tell these nobles how you allowed the slave Paneah to come and go at will in your prison. Tell them how you left a rope dangling for him to climb in and out of his pit, how you trusted him completely and in all things."

The old man glared at Narmer, then he stepped forward and knelt at Yosef's feet.

Narmer frowned and gestured to guards who jerked Khamat upright. "Speak," Narmer growled, "and tell the truth. You allowed Paneah to come and go freely, didn't you?"

"Paneah was righteous and altogether honest," Khamat said, his voice like gravel. "He wanted to serve others in the jail. But he did not leave the prison."

"Do you know this for a fact?" Narmer said, scowling. "You kept a rope suspended in his cell. At any time he could have climbed forth. He knew the prison, he knew the house beyond, he knew how to sneak out in the dead of night and return before daybreak. He wormed his way into your confidence, old man, and convinced you that he was a humble servant, but look how he stands before you now!"

The old man glanced at Yosef's royal garments and the Gold of Praise, then he met Yosef's gaze. His eyes crinkled as he smiled. "I see a man whom the gods have elevated. I know him as a man in whom the spirit of God resides. He would not commit this evil you speak of."

Narmer gestured for the guards to carry Khamat away. "The gods will decide his guilt, not you."

Chike stepped forward. "If Zaphenath-paneah was confined in the prison, how are you to prove these things?"

The captain of the guard paused, then pressed his hands

together as if he pondered a weighty matter. "It is said, most high priest, that our kings are divine because the gods visit our queens and plant seed in their wombs," he said, conviction in his voice. "You will recall that our divine pharaoh recognized the spirit of a god in this one called Paneah. Khamat, foolish old man that he is, has just said the same thing."

Narmer waved his hands for emphasis. "How can we determine that his spirit did not visit Pharaoh's wife in her chamber? Look at the boy! He walks and talks like the vizier, he holds his head in the same angle as this foreigner who entered Egypt as a slave! If the act of disloyalty was not accomplished in the physical body, then it was accomplished in the spiritual, for the boy you see before you is the child of the vizier, and not of Pharaoh! It is recorded in the annals that on separate occasions, both the vizier and Queen Tuya came to Pharaoh and asked that the child be betrothed to Queen Mutemwiya in order to secure the succession. But our dying pharaoh decried this act! Restore justice, high priest and counselors, and keep the throne from this illegitimate who has no part in Egypt!"

Chike stepped aside to confer with several priests, but Tuya could see that they were not convinced that Narmer spoke the truth. Yosef himself was a powerful testimony to righteousness, for his visage and posture were regal, and the Egyptians were not eager to criticize those whom the gods had placed over them. But Narmer's words had cast strong doubt on Yosef's intentions and Amenhotep's pedigree.

"Noble Narmer, I have something to say regarding this matter," Mutemwiya said, standing again. She cleared her throat as if hesitant to speak, then cast her gaze to the ground. "My husband Tuthmosis loved me dearly, and confided in me one night as we lay together. He told me that the gods had told him he would father no children in this life, but his heirs would follow in the life to come. That is why my womb remained empty. As for this boy—"

She gestured toward Amenhotep and shrugged as if to say she did not know from where he had come. Tuya felt her cheeks burn as Amenhotep cringed. By all the gods, this was not right! Her son had done nothing wrong, nor had Yosef sinned. Pharaoh would rise from his grave if he knew what mischief his queen and captain were working on this night—

But if Mutemwiya could speak, so could she. "Can a mother not defend her child?" she called, her voice ringing through the room.

Narmer bowed in elegant hypocrisy. "You have said nothing. We thought you had nothing to say."

"I have much to say," Tuya replied, eyeing Mutemwiya with a stern gaze. "Amenhotep, my child, is Pharaoh's son. I loved Tuthmosis and was faithful to him from the day of our marriage."

"Do you deny that you loved Paneah?"

"I did love him, once," Tuya admitted, her voice softening at the memory. "As a young girl loves a young man. But that love faded in the light of adulthood, and in the light of my love for the king."

"And yet you are friends with Zaphenath-paneah."

"We are friends. He was a close advisor to Pharaoh, and is a tutor to the prince."

"Then tell us—" Narmer's brows lifted the question "—to this day, why does the vizier bring a bowl of lotus blossoms to your chamber? What sweet token of love is this?"

The question brought a hushed silence to the room, and Tuya felt the darkness of grief press down on her. "My husband's token," she said, her voice breaking. "He promised me blue lotus blossoms every morning we were apart. He said the vizier would bring them until he returned."

A stunned silence followed her declaration, but Narmer

broke the hush with a sharp laugh. "Has the king," he said, turning to Queen Mutemwiya, "ever brought you flowers?"

A scowl crossed Mutemwiya's face. "Why would a king bring flowers? The king presents his women with gold and jewels. Ask any one of Pharaoh's wives. This woman lies."

Narmer turned to Tuya with new fervor in his eyes. He had tasted victory, and knew the end was near. "Tell the truth, if you can. Is the prince a child of the divine pharaoh?"

"Yes."

"How, then, do you explain his resemblance to the vizier?"

"He looks nothing like Yosef. He is his father's—"

At the mention of the word *Yosef,* Narmer held up an interrupting hand. "You have used a Hebrew name, the same name you gave your son as a baby." He paced before the crowd, his hands thrust behind his back. "I believe, Queen Tuya, that you were unfaithful to Pharaoh. This child, called Amenhotep, was fathered by the Hebrew. While in Potiphar's house, you fell under the spell of the strange god that resides in this man, and together you plotted to usurp the authority of the gods of Egypt. You have conspired to take the throne from the rightful rulers."

"No!"

"Then why are there no statues of Horus or Hapi or Osiris in your chambers?" Narmer said, halting before the priests. "Why do you not offer gifts to the gods of Egypt? Tell us, lady, which god you worship."

The trap had been laid with cunning, and Tuya realized how completely she'd been snared. *Treason.* Yet unspoken, the word hung over her head like a mist, cutting off her breath. A moment ago she'd been about to hang for the crime of adultery, and now with one false word she would condemn herself, her friend and her son to the gallows.

Merciful God. Why have you allowed this to happen?

When Narmer's exultant face blurred before her eyes she

turned to Yosef. He stood like an oak between two guards, his steadfast confidence reducing them to stumps of manhood. *Have faith,* his eyes seemed to say. *You have trusted the unseen god for others. Now trust him for yourself.*

Tuya stared past his face into her own thoughts. All her life she had clung to those she could love: Sagira, Yosef, Amenhotep and Tuthmosis. One by one, her loved ones had vacated her life, leaving her shipwrecked by grief. Yet gently, persistently, the Almighty God had sheltered her, protected her…and brought her to a place where she had no one else to trust. Only him.

A memory opened before her. "Belief is a truth held in the mind, Tuya, but faith is a fire in the heart," Tuthmosis once told her, explaining why he believed Zaphenath-paneah's prediction of famine. "My heart burns to know the god who could speak to me in a dream."

In a breathless instant of release, faith freed her from fear. "I will tell you which god I serve." She turned to Narmer with a note of triumph in her voice. "I worship El Shaddai, the Almighty God, the creator of heaven and earth. I trust him alone with my life."

Narmer gasped. "You would cast aside the gods of Egypt?"

"I did not intend to cast them aside," she answered, "but I have found them helpless. The Almighty God is greater than all and wiser than all. Pharaoh realized this when he lifted Zaphenath-paneah to the position of vizier. God knew Pharaoh hungered after the true god. Therefore God has saved Egypt."

"Bah!" Narmer turned and gestured toward the priests. "Listen to this one, disloyal to her husband, her king and her kingdom! Look at this boy who would claim Egypt's throne! See how he favors the vizier, for he has the same beauty and clarity of features—"

"The beauty is his mother's," Yosef said, commanding attention with a nod of his head. "As God lives, I have fathered only two sons, Ephraim and Manasseh."

Narmer scowled at the vizier. "You are not capable of such restraint. There is yet another witness who will testify to your misdeeds. Another voice will prove my contentions and our pharaoh's dying words."

In a voice as cold as his eyes, Narmer turned toward the double doors of the throne room. "I call Sagira, widow of Potiphar, to speak to us!"

From the outer hall, Sagira heard the summons and ran her hands over her gown. The doors swung open to admit her, and she blinked, afraid she had forgotten some item of dress in her hurry to answer the midnight summons. Narmer's messenger had been most explicit—she must appear, she was important, she would be rewarded for her cooperation.

Her knees quivered as she stepped into the room, yet she held her head high. She had not been invited to the palace since Paneah's trial, and the magnificent room seemed broader and taller and more colorful than she remembered it. Her gaze drifted to the square of inlaid tiles where she had stood under a wedding canopy and received Potiphar as her husband. That memory belonged to another lifetime, to another girl, a younger girl.

The mood of the gathering was somber, the faces around her drawn and tense. In the open space before the throne, Tuya stood between a pair of royal guards like a lily between two watchdogs. Across from Tuya, Paneah stood surrounded by six of Pharaoh's bodyguards.

Drawn like a moth to a flame, Sagira stared at her former slave. She thought he nodded at her, and the friendliness in his smile puzzled her.

Between the prisoners, Narmer paced like a dog marking his boundaries. He said nothing as she approached, allowing her to make a suitably impressive entrance, and Sagira took advantage of the silence to run her gaze over the crowd. The gathering included half a dozen men and women wearing the shaved heads and the spotless robes of the priesthood, a few nobles, Paneah's stricken wife and her maids and a remnant of Pharaoh's guard. A dozen scribes sat in a corner, scribbling to record this event for posterity.

On her gilded chair, Queen Mutemwiya sat regal and composed, while the crown prince hunched on a stool at her feet, his pale face streaked with tears.

Sagira paused at the end of the aisle. To whom was she supposed to bow? Narmer must have sensed her discomfiture, for he launched into a long recitation of her history.

Sagira only half listened as her eyes drank in her surroundings. Everything in sight might have been hers if Ramla had spoken a true prophecy, but the priestess had lied. Sagira would die alone and forgotten, and she would die soon. The disease that had left her barren and bleeding was robbing her of life.

But she was still of royal blood, and by all rights, she should have been included among the family members seated behind the throne. This conviction sent her spirits soaring, and she smiled at the assembled crowd as Narmer finished his speech: "This gentle lady, the widow of Potiphar, can attest to Zaphenath-paneah's crime. She will prove his words false, for he has never been able to restrain himself when faced with a beautiful woman. He once attempted to force even her, his master's wife."

Like a many-eyed creature, the company turned to stare at her. She met their eyes with boldness, determined to face down the rumors that had circulated in Thebes for years. The gossips called her a drunkard, a harlot, a fool, but she was better these days. She was the daughter of a princess, a widow with authority, a woman not to be underestimated.

A pair of mirror-brilliant eyes in the crowd snagged Sagira's attention. Ramla! The priestess of Bastet stood behind Chike, her clawed hand hidden at her waist, her head inclined as if in mild interest. But from those dark eyes blazed ambition, hunger and zeal.

The priestess nodded, acknowledging Sagira's gaze, and flashed her brows in a silent signal: *Tell them, Sagira, what they want to know, and you will be rewarded. Narmer will allow you to assume your rightful place in the palace, and I will again be your priestess. Can you think we have not heard of your lonely and silent house? Tell them, Sagira. We are waiting.*

The intensity of those black eyes left Sagira feeling unsettled. She wrested her attention from Ramla and struggled to find her voice.

"Well?" Narmer stepped closer. "We are waiting for you to confirm the vizier's character."

"Pharaoh has already ruled on these accusations," Chike interrupted. "The divine pharaoh declared Zaphenath-paneah innocent of all charges."

"But Lady Sagira did not recant her charge," Narmer pointed out, his finger wagging like a scolding tutor's. "What if the vizier's magic was strong enough to dupe even a god?"

A murmur of wonder rippled through the crowd, and Narmer turned to Sagira again. "We are waiting, Lady."

"I will speak." She glanced around. Tuya stood straight and tall between her guards, surprisingly youthful without her heavy wig. How could they have been childhood friends? Though she had only lived thirty-three years, Sagira felt as though she had endured fifty.

Reluctantly, Sagira's gaze shifted toward Paneah. She expected to see revulsion, hatred, even resignation on his face, for hadn't she once destroyed him? Like the glorious Phoenix Paneah had arisen from the ashes, but now Narmer had offered a means with which she could crush him again. With a handful of words she could obliterate Paneah's unfairly favored life, snuff the intelligence from his exquisite eyes and send his soul to the other world. He had to know what she was thinking, that her soul yearned to find significance…for this she would be remembered as long as the Nile flowed.

She lifted her eyes to his. An odd mingling of compassion and curiosity stirred in his face, as though he didn't care what she might say, but felt pity for her need to say it. Pity! For her? She'd received no pity from the nobles of Thebes, from the women of Pharaoh's court or even from her servants. Only Paneah and Tuya had ever shown her the slightest bit of sincere compassion or concern. The two most caring people in her life had also been the most loved, the most hated and the most beautiful…

Her blood ran thick with guilt. In quiet serenity Paneah and Tuya stood beside her even now. Sagira had been surrounded by beauty throughout her life, but until this moment she had never realized that the beauty of Tuya and Paneah was not so much a physical manifestation as it was an inner one. The accused man standing beside her bore the fine wrinkles of his age with elegance. Gray hair sprouted from his temples, yet no man in the room was more striking. And though grief had left Tuya's face haggard and tense, her eyes shone with a peace Sagira had never known. Behind the throne, the ugliness of Ramla's ambition raised its horrid head, the same prideful zeal that had convinced Sagira to despise the only true friend she had ever known…

Abruptly, she turned to Chike. "I want the entire assembly to know the truth," she said, her voice ringing. "I tried to seduce my own slave, but he would not submit, nor would he be disloyal to his master. I believe Zaphenath-paneah to be incapable of disloyalty. He would not be unfaithful to Potiphar. He could not be unfaithful to Pharaoh. This inquest, this charade, is a naked attempt to steal the throne from Pharaoh's only son. If you must seek an adulteress, look to the woman who sits on the throne. She and this Narmer have been plotting to take the throne for years. Queen Mutemwiya plans to discredit the rightful prince, then marry Narmer and make him Pharaoh."

"She lies!" Mutemwiya rose from her chair with such force that it toppled from the dais and clattered to the floor.

"No." Sagira shook her head. "I have no reason to lie, and nothing to gain by falseness. Illness has shortened my days and only by blessing of the Almighty God will I live to see the land green again."

Narmer stuttered while Sagira prostrated herself on the floor before Amenhotep. After a moment of whispered consultation with his fellow priests, Chike stepped forward. "May Thoth, who judges the hearts of men, judge yours with mercy," he told Sagira as she huddled on the floor. "May the Almighty God bless you for what you have done here tonight. I speak for the gods of Egypt, who approve an honest heart, but never a deceitful one."

The priests murmured in agreement. One by one, they approached Amenhotep, who stood while they knelt before him. "This is an outrage," Narmer said, finally finding his tongue. He stamped his sandaled foot on the marble floor. "Pharaoh's dying words—"

The vizier held up his bound wrists to be unloosed. "Are known to the Almighty God, but not to us."

Sagira shivered in happiness when Zaphenath-paneah smiled at her.

Chapter Thirty-Seven

Two months later, as the sun continued to toast the Egyptian landscape, Pharaoh Tuthmosis IV was laid to rest in his extraordinary tomb. With the blessing of Queen Tuya, the high priest Chike appointed Zaphenath-paneah to act as Amenhotep's regent until he came to an age where he would be capable of ruling the kingdom. Thus the vizier inherited another title: "Father to Pharaoh." The fate of the two conspirators, Narmer and Mutemwiya, was left to Zaphenath-paneah, who decreed that the two should be exiled in the empire of the Mitannis, far from Egypt's borders.

The trade routes over which the Egyptian guards escorted the two evildoers had widened considerably in the last year, for men throughout the world heard that grain flowed like water in Egypt. Famine and drought had shrilled over the entire earth, and foreigners throughout civilization journeyed to trade in Egypt.

While the young pharaoh studied his lessons and prepared to lead his country, the treasure houses of Egypt filled as the princes of the world brought gold and jewels and silver in exchange for grain so they might live and not die. The people of Egypt blessed Zaphenath-paneah and their new king, for despite the famine, the hand of a protecting god had made provision for their lives.

Tuya still walked in the gardens with Yosef and her son, and often she stopped by the pool where the blue lotus flowers bloomed in abundance. After plucking a flowering stem, she would wrap the long tendrils around her bare arm and fondly remember the boy who had grown into a man and a truly great king.

"You miss him, don't you?" Yosef asked one afternoon as she savored the fragrance of a blossom. Amenhotep walked ahead of them, well beyond the range of their voices.

"I do." Tuya fingered the gentle petals of the flower. "I am sometimes sorry I did not appreciate him sooner. He was a noble king and a wise man. He hungered for God in a way few men do."

"I know." Yosef thrust his hands behind his back as they walked. "Amenhotep, you know, has a fine mind, sensitivity and courage. He could be the greatest king Egypt has ever known."

Tuya smiled. "We shall see."

They walked in companionable silence for a moment, then Yosef cleared his throat. "I don't want you to be lonely," he began, setting his jaw. "And at last the time is right. Will you marry me, Tuya? There is no reason why you should not."

Tuya laughed softly. "I can think of a good reason. Years ago, you told me about your father and his two wives."

"Lea and Rahel?"

She stopped on the path and turned to face him. "Your father loved one and was kind to the other. Yet because he did not love them both, you and your family have suffered greatly."

She lifted his precious hand and pressed it to her cheek. "Asenath is a lovely woman, and you have two fine sons. You will not be happy loving one wife and offering mere kindness to the other."

His hand curved around her cheek, then he nodded. A moment later, he was gone, following Amenhotep, but Tuya remained on the path, relishing the warmth on her face. "And I, having known love, could not live on kindness."

The hot wind blew the lotus plants on the water, and Tuya breathed in the sweet scent of them and smiled.

* * * * *

QUESTIONS FOR DISCUSSION

1. Are you familiar with the biblical story of Yosef, Potiphar and Pharaoh? How did this novel impact, increase or contradict your impression of the story in Genesis?

2. Could you identify with any of the characters in this novel? What character traits resonated with you?

3. In what ways were the people of ancient Egypt like people today? In what ways were they extremely different?

4. This is the first of three novels in a series. What do you think will happen to Yosef and Tuya in the books to come?

5. In most Sunday-school lessons, Yosef is portrayed as a hero, yet he had a fatal flaw. How does God use Yosef's weakness? How does God bring Yosef to an understanding of his weakness?

6. What are some things you find in historical fiction that you don't find in contemporary fiction? How does reading about people of the past enrich our lives in the present?

7. How did the love Tuthmosis felt for Tuya differ from the love Yosef felt for her? Which was the more mature love? How did her feelings for these two men change as time went by?

8. Was Sagira a victim of circumstance or a woman who suffered the results of her own choices? How were women more constrained in ancient Egypt than in modern times? How were they more liberated?

9. Do you believe that Yosef's slavery and imprisonment was part of God's perfect plan for his life? How did it change him? How did it work for good or ill?

10. What does the story of Yosef teach the modern reader about faith? How can you apply this lesson to your life?

*And now turn the page for a sneak preview
of BROTHERS, the second book in*
THE LEGACIES OF THE ANCIENT RIVER *trilogy
by* New York Times *bestselling author Angela Hunt.*

*Available February 2009 wherever books are sold,
including most bookstores, supermarkets,
drug stores and discount stores.*

Prologue

Thebes, Egypt

Zaphenath-paneah, Father to Pharaoh and acting ruler of all Egypt, caught his breath as Queen Tuya lifted his hand and pressed it to her cheek. The hot, dry wind of the famine's second year blew over the palace garden as the lovely woman struggled to frame an answer to his proposal of marriage.

"Asenath is a lovely woman, and you have two fine sons," she finally whispered, her eyes glinting with warmth. "You will not be happy loving one wife and offering kindness to the other."

A wave of relief flooded his soul. She was wise, his Tuya, but she had always been perceptive beyond her years. More than once in Potiphar's house she had guided him away from foolish mistakes, helping him remember that he was no longer Yosef, the pampered son of Yaakov, but Paneah, a slave to an Egyptian. And even though he now ruled all Egypt at the young pharaoh's side, Tuya's insight and love still sought the best for all.

Curving his hand around her cheek, he pressed his lips

together, not allowing himself to protest. The queen lowered her thick, black lashes and from the corner of his eye, Yosef saw a servant enter the garden. He dropped his hand and turned, composing his face into dignified lines as the dark-haired slave hurried past the reflecting pools where lotus blossoms bloomed in abundance.

The attendant fell at Yosef's feet. "Life, health and prosperity to you, most noble and excellent vizier!"

"Yes?"

The man lifted his head a few inches from the pathway. "The steward of your house begs your indulgence and your pardon for this interruption. He waits outside Pharaoh's gate to give you a message."

"A message?" Yosef asked, aware that Tuya had moved away. "What is of such importance that I must be interrupted when I am with the queen?"

"Ten men from Canaan wait at your house to buy food," the servant said, a note of apology in his voice. "Your steward says you would want to be told of them at once."

Yosef took a quick, sharp breath. "Ten Canaanites?"

"From Hebron, my lord."

A thrill of frightened anticipation touched Yosef's spine. "You were right to disturb me. Tell my steward I will join him in a moment."

As the servant leapt up and retreated, Yosef turned to say farewell to Tuya. But like the early part of his life, she had vanished amid the breathless beauty of a royal Egyptian garden.

Chapter One

"You two! Come away from there!"

Mandisa snapped her fingers at the two giggling slave girls who lingered in the doorway of the north loggia. With fewer manners than ignorant children, they had partially hidden themselves behind a pair of painted columns to gape at the dusty travelers milling about in the vestibule. At Mandisa's rebuke, the two young ones bowed their heads in shame.

Mandisa stepped forward to herd the girls away from the open doorway. "Ani will be far less gentle than I if he finds you away from the kitchen."

"But, my lady," the first girl said, a glint of wonder in her eyes, "they are so strange a group! So much hair covers their faces!"

"We were wondering—" the second slave lifted her fingers to her lips to suppress another giggle "—if they are as hairy all over. Look! Hair sprouts even from the throats of their garments!"

Despite her best intentions, Mandisa cast a quick glance through the doorway. She was accustomed to seeing foreign dignitaries in the vizier's vestibule, for since the advent of the famine, representatives from all the world's kingdoms had come to buy Egypt's grain. But the men who now stood in the house wore neither the richly patterned garments of the Assyrians nor the carefully pointed beards of the Mitannis. They were clothed in the common woven garments and animal skins of herdsmen. Compared to the shaven Egyptians, they were as hairy as apes, with hair to their shoulders and long, full beards.

What madness had possessed Tarik when he allowed this rabble through the gates of the vizier's villa?

She dismissed the question; the steward undoubtedly had his reasons. "Not everyone lives as the Egyptians do," she said, turning back to the ill-mannered slaves. She placed a firm hand on each girl's shoulder. "Now away with you, get back to your work in the kitchen. If the vizier has agreed to meet these men, he may want to feed them, and you may be sure that hairy men are hungry men. So hurry back to your grinding, lest Ani or Tarik finds you out here."

The two girls scurried away at the mention of the steward and the captain of the vizier's guard. Mandisa smiled, grateful that her words carried weight with someone in the house. Lately her son Adom had balked both at her requests and her suggestions, reminding her again how stubborn twelve-year-olds could be…

She folded her hands, ready to seek her mistress, but paused outside the vestibule, curiosity overcoming her finely tuned instincts. The men beyond were like thousands of others who had come to Egypt in this second year of famine, so why had this particular group of Canaanites been invited to meet Egypt's royal vizier?

The strangers did not appear wealthy or highborn. Theirs were the faces of sunburned herders; they gripped their staves with broad and calloused hands. Generous strands of gray ran through several of their heavy beards; only one or two possessed unlined faces. They stirred, their hands and eyes shifting as if at any moment they might have to reach for a knife or spear to defend themselves. With one look, anyone could see these unruly shepherds had run as wild as the wind since infancy.

Mandisa bit her lip. She had seen men like these before. Her father and brothers were herdsmen. Like dogs, they had marked their boundaries and charged any lion, bear or stranger who dared violate their territory. They, too, had habitually worn an uneasy look.

Memories came crowding back like unwelcome guests and Mandisa closed her eyes, refusing to entertain them. Whoever these men were, they had nothing to do with her past or present. They would probably not be allowed to waste more than five minutes of the vizier's valuable time.

A snatch of their conversation caught her ear and Mandisa tensed, recognizing the Canaanite tongue. The sound stirred up other memories of a time before Idogbe the Egyptian had carried her away from her clan. She reached for one of the pillars, steadying herself against the tide of strong emotions she could not stanch, then realized that the men in the room beyond had grown silent.

"This Egyptian prince has pretty slaves, I will not deny that." A sharp voice cut the silence as she opened her eyes. The man who had spoken stood apart from the others, his hands on his hips, a confident smile upon his face. An air of command exuded from him, and at the sound of his voice the entire group turned toward Mandisa.

She ducked behind the column, her cheeks burning. She had not meant to be seen! They must think her as ill-mannered as the two slave girls. And she was not a slave, but a free woman and the personal maid to Lady Asenath.

"Ah, you startled her," another man said, a thread of reproach in his voice. "You should not be so brash, Shim'on.

She will tell her master that we are brutes and then we shall never obtain what we have come for."

"We will, Levi, never fear," the commanding man answered. "We will get our grain and leave Egypt as soon as we can. But what is the harm in admiring a pretty face while we are here?"

Mandisa flew out of the hallway and flattened herself against the wall separating the vestibule from the north loggia. How foolish she had been, allowing these rough men to gawk at her. If they had not been ignorant foreigners, they would have known by her dress that she was no slave.

She shuddered in humiliation. The powerful one who had spoken had appraised her like a stockyard animal, then allowed his gaze to cling to her face as she burned in embarrassment.

By all that was holy, she hoped these herders were guilty of robbery or treason. She'd love to see them squirm before her master. Especially the bold one who had propelled her into such an undignified and hasty retreat.

Wrapping the rags of her fragile dignity about her, Mandisa peeled herself from the wall and went in search of her mistress.

* * * * *

AN INTERVIEW WITH ANGELA HUNT

Q: You must have done a lot of research to write this book.

A: Well, yes. In my library I have a couple of shelves reserved for the ancient Egyptians and Hebrews. Fortunately, scores of books have been written about both groups.

Q: I was surprised by the marriages of brothers and sisters. Did that really happen?

A: I know the arrangement of Egyptian royal marriages probably seems strange to modern readers, but the kings of Egypt's earliest dynasties married aristocratic women to augment their claims to the throne. Polygamy, therefore, was an accepted part of royal life. The more wives a king had, the stronger his position.

Unlike most of the world, where inheritances passed from father to son, Egyptian property descended from mother to daughter. A husband retained property and position as long as his wife lived. On her death, her daughter and her daughter's husband inherited the wife's property. Each pharaoh, therefore, safeguarded the throne for himself and his sons by marrying the family heiress no matter how close her relationship to him. The age of the heiress-bride did not matter—she might be an aged woman or an infant. The marriage was not necessarily consummated.

Q: Whenever I read historical novels, I always want to know—how much of this novel is fiction, and how much is fact?

A: Impossible to supply a percentage, but I can promise you two things. First, I took pains never to contradict the biblical account. Second, the pharaohs and queens mentioned in this book live in the annals of Egyptian history. Yosef, Potiphar and Potiphar's wife endure in the pages of holy Scripture. At one point, the two records must intersect.

Q: How certain are you that the king in this novel is the actual pharaoh Yosef served?

A: I wouldn't stake my life on it, but I'm fairly certain. During my research, I discovered some fascinating facts and some frustrating conditions. My chief problem arose when I tried to fix a time for Yosef and a time for Moses.

Using Exodus 12:40 as a guide ("Now the length of time the Israelite people lived in Egypt was 430 years. At the end of the 430 years, to the very day, all the Lord's divisions left Egypt"), if I put Yosef where I needed him to be, then added 430 years, my date for Moses was too late. If I put Moses where I needed him to be and subtracted 430 years, Yosef would have been in Egypt before the Hyksos brought horses to the region, but Scripture says that Pharaoh gave Yosef a chariot…and, I assume, a horse to pull it.

Then I discovered a tiny footnote: the Masoretic Text, the Samaritan Pentateuch and the Septuagint use the phrase *Egypt and Canaan* for *Egypt* in Exodus 12:40. So the Hebrews were actually living in Egypt only 215 years.

This view is bolstered by other Scriptures: In Galatians 3:16–17, Paul says that the Law came 430 years after God's covenant with Abraham (Avraham). So the clock didn't begin to tick when Jacob (Yaakov) took his family to Egypt, but when God made his covenant with Abraham. In Genesis 15:13, God told Abraham that his people would be strangers in a country not their own and would be enslaved and mistreated for 400 years. They did begin wandering at that point and did not enter "their own land" until Joshua led them into it.

Now it gets exciting—when I adjusted the time line, not only did the numbers work, but in Yosef's day I found a king who had mysterious dreams and in Moses's time I found a pharaoh who mysteriously lost a son.

Furthermore, Ruth 4:19–22 gives us a genealogy of the families of Israel: Hezron was the father of Ram, Ram the father of Amminadab, Amminadab the father of Nahshon, Nahshon the father of Salmon, Salmon the father of Boaz, etc. Notice that Hezron is in the list of people who went into Egypt with Jacob (Gen. 46:8–9).

Now look at Exodus 6:23: Aaron married Elisheba, daughter of Amminadab and sister of Nahshon, and she bore him Nadab and Abihu, Eleazar and Ithamar.

So Aaron—Moses's brother—married a woman whose grandfather came into Egypt with Jacob. The generations had to overlap, because we know Boaz and Jesse lived well into the time Israel was living in Canaan.

I love it when the puzzle pieces fit together.

Q: Can you give us any clues about what happens in the next two books?
A: I can tell you that the second book, *Brothers,* picks up exactly where *Dreamers* finishes…and *Journey* involves Yosef's children. But that's all I can say without giving too much away.

Q: Can't you even tell us if Yosef and Tuya ever get together?
A: You'll find out yourself if you read the next books in the series!

The author gratefully acknowledges help from the following sources:

Bianchi, Robert S. *Splendors of Ancient Egypt: From the Egyptian Museum Cairo.* London: Booth-Clibborn Editions, 1996.

Brier, Bob. *The Murder of Tutankhamen: A True Story.* New York: G. P. Putnam's Sons, 1998.

Budge, E. A. Wallis. *Egyptian Religion.* New York: Barnes & Noble, 1995.

—. *The Mummy: A History of the Extraordinary Practices of Ancient Egypt.* New York: Wings Books, 1989.

Bunson, Margaret. *The Encyclopedia of Ancient Egypt.* New York: Facts on File Publications, 1991.

Cahill, Thomas. *The Gifts of the Jews: How a Tribe of Desert Nomads Changed the Way Everyone Thinks and Feels.* New York: Doubleday, 1998.

Coleman, William. *Today's Handbook of Bible Times and Customs.* Minneapolis: Bethany House Publishers, 1984.

Comay, Joan. *Who's Who in the Old Testament.* Nashville: Abingdon Press, 1971.

Coogan, Michael D., ed. *The Oxford History of the Biblical World.* New York: Oxford University Press, 1998.

David, A. Rosalie and Rick Archbold. *Conversations with Mummies.* New York: HarperCollins, 2000.

Davis, J. D. *Illustrated Davis Dictionary of the Bible.* Nashville: Royal Publishers, 1973.

Fox, Everett. *The Five Books of Moses: Genesis, Exodus, Leviticus, Numbers, Deuteronomy: A New Translation with Introductions, Commentary and Notes.* New York: Schocken Books, 1995.

Grower, Ralph. *The New Manners and Customs of Bible Times*. Chicago: Moody Press, 1987.

Halley, Henry. *Halley's Bible Handbook*. Grand Rapids, MI: Zondervan Publishing House, 1927.

Hart, George. *Ancient Egypt*. New York: Alfred A. Knopf, 1990.

James, T. G. H. *Ancient Egypt: The Land and Its Legacy*. Austin: University of Texas Press, 1988.

Jenkins, Simon. *Nelson's 3-D Bible Mapbook: A Graphically Exciting New Way to Experience the Great Events and Places of the Bible*. Nashville: Thomas Nelson Publishers, 1995.

Kaiser, Walter C., Peter H. Davids, F. F. Bruce, and Manfred T. Brauch. *Hard Sayings of the Bible*. Downers Grove, IL: InterVarsity Press, 1996.

Kaster, Joseph. *The Wisdom of Ancient Egypt: Writings from the Time of the Pharaohs*. New York: Barnes & Noble, 1993.

Manniche, Lise. *An Ancient Egyptian Herbal*. Austin: University of Texas Press, 1989.

—. *Music and Musicians in Ancient Egypt*. London: British Museum Press, 1991.

Metzger, Bruce M., and Michael D. Coogan, eds. *The Oxford Companion to the Bible*. New York: Oxford University Press, 1993.

Montet, Pierre. *Everyday Life in Egypt in the Days of Rameses the Great*. Philadelphia: University of Pennsylvania Press, 1981.

Murray, Margaret Alice. *The Splendour That Was Egypt: A General Survey of Egyptian Culture and Civilization*. London: Sidgwick and Jackson, 1949.

Osman, Ahmed. *Stranger in the Valley of the Kings*. New York: HarperCollins, 1988.

Potok, Chaim. *Wanderings: Chaim Potok's History of the Jews*. New York: Alfred A. Knopf, 1978.

Pritchard, James, ed. *HarperCollins Concise Atlas of the Bible*. New York: HarperCollins, 1997.

Romer, John. *Valley of the Kings*. New York: HarperCollins, 1981.

Schaff, Philip. *Through Bible Lands: Notes on Travel in Egypt, the Desert, & Palestine*. New York: Arno Press, 1977.

Schulz, Regine, and Matthias Seidel, eds. *Egypt: The World of the Pharaohs*. Cologne: Konemann, 1998.

Smith, Wilbur. *River God*. New York: St. Martins Press, 1993.

Spencer, A. J. *Death in Ancient Egypt*. New York: Penguin Books, 1991.

Steindorff, George, and Keith C. Seele. *When Egypt Ruled the East*. Chicago: University of Chicago Press, 1957.

Stern, David H. *Complete Jewish Bible: An English Version of the Tanakh (Old Testament) and B'rit Hadashah (New Testament)*. Clarksville, MD: Jewish New Testament Publications, 1998.

Time-Life Books. *The Age of God-Kings*. Alexandria, VA: Time-Life Books, 1987.

—. *What Life Was Like on the Banks of the Nile*. Alexandria, VA: Time-Life Books, 1997.

Time-Life Books, and Dale M. Brown. *Egypt: Land of the Pharaohs*. Alexandria, VA: Time-Life Books, 1992.

Unstead, F. J., ed. *See Inside an Egyptian Town*. New York: Barnes & Noble, 1986.

Vercoutter, Jean. *The Search for Ancient Egypt*. New York: Harry N. Abrams, 1992.

Wilkinson, Richard H. *Reading Egyptian Art: A Hieroglyphic Guide to Ancient Egyptian Painting and Sculpture*. London: Thames and Hudson, 1992.

Willmington, Harold L. *Willmington's Bible Handbook*. Wheaton, IL: Tyndale House Publishers, 1997.

NEW YORK TIMES BESTSELLING AUTHOR
ANGELA HUNT

BORN WITHOUT A FACE . . .

Orphaned and severely deformed, from her earliest moments Sarah Sims has been kept hidden away in a secret CIA facility—until an unexpected discovery gives her an opportunity to make a life for herself at last.

Now Sarah has an ally, a long-lost aunt who has discovered her true identity. Aided by this brave psychologist, twenty-year-old Sarah must find the courage to confront the forces that have confined her for so long. And the strength to be reborn into a world she has never known.

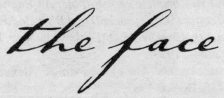

the face

"Hunt packs the maximum amount of drama into her story, and the pages turn quickly."
—*Publishers Weekly* on *The Elevator*

*Available the first week of November 2008
wherever books are sold!*

MIRA®

MAH2727

WHO WANTED HER TO SUFFER...AND WHY?

HANNAH ALEXANDER

After her husband is shot and she is hit by a speeding car, Willow Traynor flees to the Ozarks to find peace. But then, after arson destroys everything she has and almost kills her brother, she becomes certain that someone is targeting her. The support of new friends, especially Dr. Graham Vaughn and his sister, has rekindled her hope for a fresh start. But meanwhile her stalker is getting closer, bolder and more determined....

Fair Warning

Steeple Hill®

Available wherever paperbacks are sold!

REQUEST YOUR FREE BOOKS!

2 FREE INSPIRATIONAL NOVELS
PLUS 2
FREE
MYSTERY GIFTS

Love Inspired.
HISTORICAL
INSPIRATIONAL HISTORICAL ROMANCE

YES! Please send me 2 FREE Love Inspired® Historical novels and my 2 FREE mystery gifts (gifts are worth about $10). After receiving them, if I don't wish to receive any more books, I can return the shipping statement marked "cancel". If I don't cancel, I will receive 4 brand-new novels every other month and be billed just $4.24 per book in the U.S. or $4.74 per book in Canada, plus 25¢ shipping and handling per book and applicable taxes, if any*. That's a savings of over 20% off the cover price! I understand that accepting the 2 free books and gifts places me under no obligation to buy anything. I can always return a shipment and cancel at any time. Even if I never buy another book, the two free books and gifts are mine to keep forever.   102 IDN ERYA 302 IDN ERYM

Name	(PLEASE PRINT)	
Address		Apt. #
City	State/Prov.	Zip/Postal Code

Signature (if under 18, a parent or guardian must sign)

Mail to Steeple Hill Reader Service:
IN U.S.A.: P.O. Box 1867, Buffalo, NY 14240-1867
IN CANADA: P.O. Box 609, Fort Erie, Ontario L2A 5X3

Not valid to current subscribers of Love Inspired Historical books.

Want to try two free books from another series?
Call 1-800-873-8635 or visit www.morefreebooks.com

* Terms and prices subject to change without notice. N.Y. residents add applicable sales tax. Canadian residents will be charged applicable provincial taxes and GST. Offer not valid in Quebec. This offer is limited to one order per household. All orders subject to approval. Credit or debit balances in a customer's account(s) may be offset by any other outstanding balance owed by or to the customer. Please allow 4 to 6 weeks for delivery. Offer available while quantities last.

Your Privacy: Steeple Hill Books is committed to protecting your privacy. Our Privacy Policy is available online at www.SteepleHill.com or upon request from the Reader Service. From time to time we make our lists of customers available to reputable third parties who may have a product or service of interest to you. If you would prefer we not share your name and address, please check here. ☐

LIH08R